SPOTL
SHADOWS

Mila Lewis

ISBN-13: 9791097853419 (eBook)
ISBN-13: 9791097853402 (paperback)

Cover art: iStock.com/tomozina
Library of Congress Control Number: 2018675309
Printed in the United States of America

CONTENTS

DUET

There's an unwritten law of the universe that fame hunts those who flee from it—and even briefly crossing its path can rewrite an ordinary life in extraordinary ways. This cosmic joke was lost on Hana Rhee as she sipped bad wine in the city's most exclusive celebrity fishbowl, wondering how her Tuesday evening had gone so spectacularly wrong.

It was mid-January in Seoul—the holidays had passed, the glitter gone. The city had sobered up, buttoned its coat, and shuffled back to drab offices and subway commutes.

But not at Club Noir. Here, the beautiful and restless show business crowd danced like New Year's Eve was on a loop, leaving reality outside in the bitter cold.

Hana

Hana, on the other hand, had been dragged here against her will, her protests ignored with the cheerful ruthlessness that only best friends can wield. The bass from the speakers vibrated through the soles of her sensible leather pumps as she nursed a glass of too-cold Chablis—the only drink on the menu that hadn't been renamed "Stardust Fizz."

She scanned the club—lights flashing, bodies moving like a music video—while it looked like she could have wandered in straight from a tax seminar. She eyed her burgundy silk blouse and tried to blend into the wallpaper—which was impossible, because the wallpaper was mirrored and sent her awkwardness back at her in constant, unforgiving glares.

I could be home with a good book and a face mask, not here counting rhinestones per square foot.

How had Min-ji convinced her to come again? *Ah, yes. Emotional blackmail.*

"One drink," her friend had said, voice laced with false innocence. "It'll be fun! When was the last time you stayed out past 10 PM?"

One drink had turned into three. And now, Min-ji and her entourage of entertainment lawyers had vanished into the crowd to "network," leaving Hana alone with her wine and a low-grade existential crisis.

She was thirty-two, allergic to gossipy talk, and deeply suspicious of anyone who practiced smiling in the mirror. Her job as legal counsel for a charitable foundation didn't make her a fixture on the nightclub circuit. She checked her watch—eleven. Too early to leave without insulting someone. Too late to fake a work emergency. The perfect trap.

Her eyes landed on the small stage. The band was on break, their instruments resting like abandoned toys. The piano lid was still up, its black-and-white keys beckoning like a silent invitation.

Yoo-jin

Yoo-jin Lee slipped in through the side VIP entrance, switching on his bright, camera-ready smile as he cataloged the throng of people—career climbers with their laugh-and-touch, scouting agents scanning for the next breakout star, desperate former idols schmoozing their way back to relevance.

His eyes narrowed as neon strobes cut across the crowd—bare skin, glitter, the same hunger in a hundred different faces. This scene used to energize him. Now it only reminded him of how long he'd been orbiting this superficial world.

His jaded eye snagged on an anomaly—a power suit at the

bar, swirling her wine glass like it held answers to life's deepest disappointments. Everything about her looked wrong for this place, which somehow made her all the more intriguing.

Not a starlet. Not an influencer. No sequins. Her drink of choice wasn't neon. Her expression was somewhere between curious and unimpressed. She looked younger than she probably was—the way genuine people usually did when they weren't putting on a show.

He tracked her as she strode toward the stage. Tall, slim. The pencil skirt moved like a rebuke to the slouchy trends around her. Seating herself at the piano, she untied the silk bow at her neck—a small, absent gesture, like slipping off your mask when you thought no one was watching.

Before he knew it, Yoo-jin found himself drawn out of his cynical bubble.

Hana

"Mind if I play?" Hana asked the drummer, hunched over his beer, too cool to smile.

He gave her a once-over. Seeing no stylist, no entourage, no sheen of ambition, he shrugged. "Knock yourself out."

She sat, flexed her fingers, and settled them on the keys. Simple. Melodic. Background music, really. The kind of tune that she could disappear behind. Her shoulders dropped. Her spine relaxed.

At last, something that makes sense in this circus.

Yoo-jin

She could play. That was the first surprise.

The second was how she didn't try to impress anyone. No flourish. No affectation. Just the piano, played like it spoke to her and no one else.

He nodded reflexively at a producer's pitch about a revenge melodrama, while his attention kept drifting back to the piano.

A tipsy party girl called out, “Play something from Adele!”

He had expected her to demur. But she complied, transitioning into the opening bars of a popular ballad and then—this was the third surprise—she began to sing. Not with the flair of a performer working an audience, but with the careless ease of a girl alone in her car, half-lost in thought, humming through verses while stuck in traffic. Her voice was clear and unadorned, with no dramatic runs or overwrought emotion. Steady, strong, sincere—as if she weren’t trying to be heard, and that made everyone stop and listen.

Christ. She’s really good.

Hana

The first notes escaped her before she could second-guess herself. She kept it simple. No frills. No vocal gymnastics.

The drummer perked up. A brush tap. Followed by the guitarist. And soon, she wasn’t solo anymore. But she didn’t care. For once, the noise in her brain—emails, contract clauses, “Where do you see yourself in five years?”—faded into music.

Out of the corner of her eye, she saw the wonder boy himself. Standing a few feet away, his presence was as subtle as a billboard. Even she, who paid zero attention to celebrity culture, recognized Yoo-jin Lee. The face of a dozen luxury campaigns, star of some medical drama that had the entire country obsessed.

Of course, he’s even better looking in person. Because the universe has a twisted sense of humor.

He was watching her with unconcealed interest, head tilted like she was a puzzle he was trying to solve. *As if being famous gives him the right to stare.*

Yoo-jin

He saw the exact moment she spotted him—a flicker of recognition followed by a glint of dry amusement. But she didn’t blush or stumble over the lyrics. Just kept playing, as if he were just another ordinary face in the room.

No fan mode. No look-at-me grin. I'll be damned.

"Give us a song we can sing to!" someone yelled from the back of the room.

Her mouth quirked in a small smile—the first genuine expression he'd seen from her all evening—and launched into a Bruno Mars hit that got the crowd roaring with delight. Soon everyone was singing—off-key and half-drunk, tripping over the words but too far gone to care.

So Yoo-jin, half on instinct and half on impulse, joined the impromptu chorus as he approached the piano.

Hana

His voice rose above the din, confident, warm, and—*dammit*—right on pitch. A few people whooped. Others started filming. Hana kept her eyes on the keys, but when she looked up, bright lights blazed behind the golden boy, his height blocking the glare and casting her in shadow.

You've got to be kidding me.

There he was, towering over her. Korea's national heartthrob. Possibly a walking cologne ad. Casually singing next to her like it was Talent Night at the local karaoke bar.

And worse—he could really sing.

He slid onto the bench beside her without asking. She shifted—just enough to avoid contact—but their shoulders still brushed. He grinned, like this was a game and he was winning.

Alright, superstar. Let's see what you're made of.

She tossed in a jazzy variation on the melody. His eyebrow shot up, caught off guard but visibly amused. To his credit, he didn't miss a beat.

Yoo-jin

At first, he played to the crowd—a wink here, a knowing smile there. The usual tricks. But he paused at her unexpected curveball. She was baiting him.

Okay. Game on.

He dropped his act, leaned into the microphone, and just... sang. Her fingers adjusted, softening the accompaniment to let his voice through.

When she joined him in the second verse, their vocals weren't pitch-perfect—hers untrained but true, his polished yet somewhat vulnerable. Their clashing styles created a surprising chemistry, unfiltered and genuine.

As they hit the final note, a cheer went up from the crowd. Phones raised. The drummer gave a theatrical bow. And Yoo-jin? He turned to the girl beside him with an expression that almost betrayed how surprised he was.

"You play beautifully," he said, a little breathless.

"You sing well. For an actor."

He laughed—head back, eyes crinkled, no PR polish. He stayed seated, watching her rise from the bench.

Wait. Are you leaving? Don't you want—

Hana

No fangirl theatrics. No autograph. No selfie. *You're welcome.*

Hana stood, smoothing her skirt like it hadn't been a duet with Asia's "Sexiest Man Alive," third year running. Because really, when you thought about it, what was the big deal? His singing was tolerable, her piano playing was adequate, and now it was over. End of story.

Adiós, Don Juan. Don't flatter yourself—this isn't one of your sappy K-dramas.

She rejoined Min-ji, who looked like she might combust from excitement. "What," her friend hissed, grabbing her arm, "was *that*?"

"A duet?" Hana suggested mildly. *And no, I'm not going to squeal.*

As the night wound down—the music shifting to slower tempos, bartenders stacking glasses with the not-so-subtle energy of "please go home"—Hana picked up her briefcase. Min-ji linked her arm. "See? Wasn't so bad, was it?"

"It was a low bar." Hana slipped into her coat—the kind chosen for insulation, not aesthetic. "But it was... alright."

They pushed through the club's heavy doors into the winter night, the cold hitting her cheeks in the most honest moment of the evening.

Yoo-jin

Outside, Yoo-jin was leaning against the velvet rope with a coterie of actors and producers.

A figure cut from neon and myth, he stood like a movie poster come to life. Leather jacket, cashmere scarf. Eyes distant, lips curled in a cryptic smile. A cigarette—a habit he had quit and resumed numerous times—dangled from his fingertips, its ember glowing in the night like a tiny, winking star. It was a look that had graced countless magazine covers, one he wore without even trying. But his mind was still at the piano and the girl's fingers over the keys, the melody of their duet looping in his head.

The air shifted—and like a sudden breeze, she was there.

He straightened when he saw her stepping into the cold like she was walking out of another world. Briefcase in hand, a bright, happy laugh still lingering from whatever her friend was saying. No posing. No self-conscious backward glance.

He flicked away the cigarette and broke from the group. *Go ask her name.*

"Hey, Yoo-jin! Where are you going?" someone called out behind him, a little too curious, a little too loud.

He slowed mid-stride. She must have heard, because she paused and turned her head. A flicker. A half-smile. A shared awareness that they had almost—but not quite—escaped the script.

But her friend tugged her along, and she disappeared around the corner like a book closing too soon.

And... cut. End scene.

Gone. She was gone. He stood rooted to the sidewalk, the bitter night air slapping him back to reality. *You idiot. You couldn't even ask her name.*

* * *

Later, he sank into the backseat of his car, forehead pressed against the cool window as Seoul blurred past.

His manager, eyes gleaming, was scrolling through his phone and smelling opportunity. "You're trending. *#YoojinDuet* is at fifty thousand mentions. *#MysteryPianoGirl* is climbing too." He looked up, already strategizing. "We need to track her down. Plan a reunion. Fans go wild for this stuff."

Of course they do. Everything becomes content for the public.

Yoo-jin didn't answer right away. He studied his reflection in the glass—too clean, too symmetrical, too perfect. The sultry smile beaming from ads, peddling everything from luxury goods to coffee to insurance. After two decades of being polished and packaged, he sometimes forgot which version of himself came first—the man or the product.

"No," he said at last. "Leave it alone."

His manager's eyebrows shot up. "Why? This is gold."

"I said leave it alone. I don't want to ruin it."

The older man stared at him like he'd lost his mind—but Yoo-jin had already turned back to the window. It was better this way. In his world, happy endings were scripted for dramas, not stumbled into at nightclubs.

Let her have the night. Untouched. Undisturbed. Unknown.

He couldn't explain the protective instinct, but for those few minutes on that piano bench, she had made him feel normal—just a guy sitting next to a girl, singing a song. It was a moment free from expectations or consequences, one he wanted to keep pure. Nothing in his life ever was—but this might.

His phone buzzed with texts from friends, gossiping group chats: *Who's the mystery girl?*

He replied the same thing to everyone: *I don't know.*

As the night settled, one thought kept circling back.

But I damn wish I did.

PATHS CROSSED

Several weeks later, Hana wandered into a street market after a long business trip, weaving through the crowded stalls in search of lunch.

She stopped at a food stand and called out an order of anchovy noodle soup to the familiar vendor. "*Ajumma, myeolchi guksu, juseyo*."

"*Hana-ssi*! Back from your travels?" The woman ladled a clear, savory broth over thin wheat noodles, then clicked her tongue disapprovingly. "Too thin. Eat well today."

Hana laughed, pulling out her wallet. "I've been dreaming about your food even when I'm wide awake!"

She waited, foot tapping to an off-beat tune in her head and stomach growling in anticipation.

Looking around, she sensed eyes on her.

A few stands away, a man in a baseball cap lowered his face mask, and the pianist in her mind struck up Bruno Mars.

It was Yoo-jin Lee.

He had heard a bright laugh ring out, light and musical. He turned toward the sound and his breath caught.

There she was—the girl from the nightclub. Natural, unguarded, bantering with the vendor.

When she glanced up, he grinned at her and strolled over, dropping his incognito cover. "*Annyeonghaseyo*, piano girl," he greeted her with a playful half-bow. "Still making music?"

A smile tugged at her lips. "*Annyeonghaseyo*, Bruno Mars."

He laughed—a rich and unpolished laugh, not what she would have expected from a veteran actor.

"Yoo-jin Lee," he said, extending his hand as if they were meeting at a cocktail party and not in front of a noodle cart. "Since we were too busy showing off to exchange names properly."

"Hana Rhee. I know who you are. I have internet."

"Is that so? What are you getting?"

She nodded toward her bowl of *myeolchi guksu.*

"Mind if I crash?" he asked, eyeing her noodles with open hunger. "Just wrapped a commercial nearby. High-end organic food, but terrible catering."

Before she could say yes or no, he was already rattling off his order. The vendor did a double take.

"Aren't you that actor—?" she started.

"Only a poor, starving customer who's heard you make the best *myeolchi guksu* in Seoul."

The *ajumma* giggled like he just handed her a rose on national TV. She doubled his portion.

Hana sighed. *So much for a quiet, anonymous lunch.*

Minutes later, they sat under a blue tarp at a metal table that wobbled every time someone shifted. Rain clouds gathered overhead.

"So," he said, breaking apart his chopsticks, "was that night a one-off, or do you moonlight in secret at nightclubs?"

She took a bite of her noodles, slurping the broth. "It's my escape hatch—when the environment annoys me. What about you? You've got a pretty solid voice."

"I had vocal training for a musical role."

"Ah—" She racked her brain for the musical he referred to.

He laughed. "You have no idea, do you? I thought you said you had internet."

Between bites, Hana stole glances at him—before she caught herself and looked away. *Daylight's supposed to be unforgiving. But obviously not to him.*

A raindrop plinked against the tarp.

He pointed to her faded *Visit Myanmar* travel tote. "Myanmar? That's not a typical vacation spot."

"It was for work. My parents' charity organization. We support orphanages in Southeast Asia. I'm their legal counsel."

"That must be a tough job."

"It is, but—" She searched for the right words. "The kids have lost everything, yet they still laugh. Dream about futures they have no reason to believe in."

He studied her, impressed by the way she described her work—clear, unembellished, and without a hint of ego.

"And what does Yoo-jin Lee do when he's not hiding from the masses?"

"Animal shelters." His casual answer caught her by surprise. "I foster dogs between projects. Less impactful than orphanages, but I connect better with animals."

"Both matter. Kindness to children and animals—it's the baseline for being a decent human, isn't it?"

The rain intensified, drumming against the tarp. Hana finished her soup with a sigh. "Hate to cut this short, but I need to go to the office."

"On a Saturday? In this weather?"

"Catch up on emails. File expense reports. Live the dream."

He bought two *hotteoks* from a nearby stall, the paper bag still warm in his hands. "Dessert for the road." The golden pastries glistened, fresh from the griddle. They walked side by side past stands laden with exotic and colorful foods, breaking open the treats with care to avoid the molten filling inside. The sweet aroma of brown sugar and cinnamon escaped in a fragrant cloud.

A street guitarist strummed a soulful ballad under an awning. They slowed to listen. “He’s good,” Yoo-jin said, tossing bills into the guitar case. The musician recognized him and within seconds he was mobbed.

He swallowed a sigh. *Should've worn the bucket hat.* Instead, he smiled, signed whatever got shoved in his direction, crouched for selfies, complimented a little girl's sparkly hair clips. The whole routine.

Amid the noise and camera flashes, he glanced over at Hana. *Please don’t ghost me mid-photo op.*

She was standing a few stalls back, arms folded, casually observing the scene like she was narrating a wildlife documentary in her head. If she had a microphone, it would have gone like this: “*Here we see the celebrity in his natural habitat. Note the forced smile, the fan-circle choreography. Disturbing. Majestic.*”

When Yoo-jin lifted his head, he caught the wry smile curving at her lips. Fifteen minutes later, he began a slow retreat, bowing his thanks and waving goodbyes to fans. *Okay people, that's enough—everybody fuck off now.*

“Sorry about that,” he said, looking sheepish. “Hazard of the job. Thanks for sticking around.”

“You might want to upgrade your disguise.”

He laughed. “Do you have to go? I saw a decent coffee shop on the corner—”

“I have coffee at the office.” But seeing the hopeful look on his face, she said, “You can come if you’d like. Fair warning—I do have to work.”

A taxi pulled up, and as she gave the driver the address, Yoo-jin caught her eye.

“For the record,” he said, “I’m really glad I bumped into you today.”

The sincerity in his voice made her soften. “Yeah—me too.”

***

In the cramped backseat of the cab, Hana suddenly had no idea where to put her hands. His shoulder kept bumping hers every time the car turned. *He smells of cologne, sugar, and smoked squid—odd combo, but weirdly sexy.*

They were both staring straight ahead like strangers on a formal blind date.

The driver glanced in the rearview. "Aren't you Yoo-jin Lee? *Midnight in Busan*—my wife loves you. Watched it three times. She cried. I cried."

Yoo-jin smiled. "Thank you. It means a lot."

"Was the underwater kiss real? Looked real."

And they were off—locations, stunts, the co-star's skincare routine. Yoo-jin answered all of it with the calm of a man who had done this a hundred times and already knew he wasn't getting out of it.

Hana turned to the window, smirking. *This is his life? It's horrible.*

When they arrived at her office, she reached for her purse, but he beat her to it, sliding cash to the driver before stepping out. He offered her a hand.

She arched a brow, but accepted it with a glint of amusement. Once she was outside the car, he forced himself to let go.

***

The lobby was quiet, their footsteps echoing across marble floors. She swiped her keycard for the elevator and again at the office entrance.

"Welcome to my life." She flipped on the lights.

The open workspace had a hum of purpose. Photos lined the walls—children laughing, doctors working, ribbon-cuttings in far-flung places. A wooden plaque told the story of the Weston-Rhee Foundation, founded by Thomas Weston and Eun-ji Rhee twenty-five years ago.

She headed to the kitchenette. "Espresso, okay?"

He nodded, and pointed to a photo of a tall Caucasian man in wire glasses standing next to a striking Korean woman in a white smock. "Your parents?"

"Yes. My stepfather. He's a businessman. Mother's a doctor. They created the charity together. Their marriage didn't last, but their foundation did."

They sat on the small sofa, coffee cups balanced on a stack of folders. What should have been a quick break stretched over an hour.

He asked her how charities worked. She replied with clear and concise answers, honed from years of explaining complicated systems to well-meaning people with short attention spans.

He couldn't look away. *Her passion. Her conviction. God, I want to kiss her.*

Hana was perplexed at the way he was studying her—steady, thoughtful, a little intense. "Most people glaze over when I talk about compliance," she said, scanning his expression for signs of apathy. *Is he bored? Confused? Trying to remember my name?*

"My job is pretending to be what I'm not," he said, his tone was dry but his eyes serious. "You're the opposite. You do real work."

She blinked, surprised. *Flattering. Possibly manipulative. But it's working.*

"Speaking of work," she said, reaching for a folder, "I have to rewrite a speech for tonight's fundraiser. Been dodging it all week."

"What's the event?"

"Semi-annual gala. Fancy food, excessive champagne, massive ego stroking."

Her phone lit up with an incoming call. Hana put it on speaker. "*Annyeong*, Jin-ah."

"Morning, boss," her assistant's brisk voice clipped through. "Quick updates—the health minister confirmed. FYI —I hung your gown on your bedroom door. It's Elie Saab, since you complained the Valentino fit like punishment. This one's very romantic. Might even help you catch a husb—"

"Don't," Hana warned.

"—donor," Jin-ah finished, cackling. "Anyway, the coordinator needs to know if you're bringing a plus-one?"

Hana rolled her eyes. "Seriously? Same as always—"

"Could you take me?" Yoo-jin cut in, surprising even himself. "If you want company."

The sudden question caught her off-guard. *Wait. Did he just...?*

"Boss? Who was that?" Jin-ah's voice came through the speaker, confused.

"Um. A friend—I think." She eyed Yoo-jin, unsure whether to be annoyed or amused. "You'd be bored. Policy talk. Groveling speeches. Endless 10-course dinner." *Parading a vapid celebrity in front of the Seoul elite? The foundation board would have opinions about that.*

He shrugged. "It's for a worthy cause. I can help make rich people feel generous."

Her fingers tapped the armrest. The wise answer was no. Too risky. *A fundraising gala is not a date. It's a live-action press release with foie gras.*

But then she saw the way he was looking at her—eyes wide, a little pleading. Like a golden retriever that followed her home by accident and now hoped she wouldn't kick it out.

"Okay," she said at last. "Plus-one. Mr. Yoo-jin Lee—"

A gasp from the speaker. "*Yoo-jin Lee*? *The* Yoo-jin Lee? Boss—are you—"

"I'll see you at the venue, Jin-ah." Hana jabbed the screen

to hang up.

Turning to Yoo-jin, she said, "I hope you're sure about this." She rifled through a stack of papers and pulled out a creamy envelope. He accepted it with mock formality, as if she had invited him to Buckingham Palace.

After he left, she stared at her notes but saw none of the words.

Her phone chimed—Jin-ah: *You have so much explaining to do!*

Hana laughed under her breath, dropping her head in her hands. As if she had any idea what she'd just agreed to. A gala. A date. A flighty celebrity.

With any luck, he'll lose interest before dessert.

HER PLUS-ONE

Yoo-jin Lee arrived at the Grand Hyatt twenty minutes early. Despite countless red-carpet appearances, he was nervous tonight—a strange flutter unrelated to cameras or critics.

Relax. It's a fundraiser, not a Best Actor nomination.

He straightened his cufflinks and checked the time on his Patek Philippe watch. He had chosen the accessory with care, suspecting Hana Weston-Rhee would notice details.

Hana. Even her name had an elegant simplicity to it.

He had looked her up after leaving her office. Oxford. Harvard Law. Foundation director since she was twenty-six. The kind of credentials that made his own sound like a press kit.

She feeds and educates orphans. I've been fake-stabbed six times this year. But sure, we're both professionals.

Movement at the curb caught his eye. A black town car pulled up.

The woman who emerged looked nothing like the girl who had shared a street food lunch with him earlier that day. Hana Rhee stepped out in a gown that shimmered, her hair swept up to reveal the clean line of her neck.

He exhaled, adjusting his stance before she reached him.

Piano girl. Street foodie. Society diva. How many versions of her are there?

When she spotted him, her lips curved into a small smile —and for a second, the noise around him faded.

He came forward, holding out his arm with a slight bow. "Ms. Weston-Rhee."

"Mr. Lee." Her hand settled into the crook of his elbow. "Thank you for offering to be my escort tonight."

"My pleasure," he replied, amused at how she had reframed his impulsive offer to crash her party. "But I should thank you for saving me from another Fortnite losing streak. Vicious twelve-year-olds were calling me *noob*."

She bit back a grin. "Shall we?"

Whispers and glances followed them as they crossed the reception hall. *The country's elite is wondering what she's doing slumming it with the likes of me.*

She must have sensed his fleeting unease because her fingers tensed against his arm. "Having second thoughts about volunteering?" she murmured.

"Not even a little bit. Though I suspect I'm the most underprepared person in the room."

She gave him a reassuring smile. "You're doing fine."

He shadowed her like a well-behaved accessory as she glided through conversations with diplomats, politicians, and CEOs.

While Hana was occupied across the room, Yoo-jin found himself intercepted by a silver-haired man in a sharp suit.

"Kim Dae-jung," the man said with a nod. "Hyundai Capital."

Holy hell. "The" Kim Dae-jung. Not a man. An institution.

Yoo-jin bowed. "Lee Yoo-jin. It's an honor, sir."

"You're the actor," Kim said, appraising him openly. "That samurai assassin drama was surprisingly watchable."

Yoo-jin blinked. *One of Asia's richest men watches cable dramas?*

"Thank you, sir."

Kim sipped his drink. "Are you lending your image to the foundation's cause tonight?"

"I'm Ms. Weston-Rhee's guest," Yoo-jin replied. "I find her work compelling."

"They've been hounding me for a donation to their orphanage initiative," Kim said, voice flat. "I'm not sold on the execution."

Yoo-jin saw an opening. "If you mean the Myanmar project—I understand. But their model is community-led. They train the locals, not just drop money and leave."

Kim studied him. "You're familiar?"

"I understand they focus on longevity. Self-supporting systems requiring minimal oversight," Yoo-jin said, reciting Hana's explanations from earlier.

A pause. "You're not what I expected," Kim said.

"In what way, sir?"

"Less Hollywood... More substance."

With that, the older man drifted off.

Hana returned a moment later. "What did you say to Chairman Kim? I've been chasing him for eight months."

"Just shared what you told me about Myanmar."

She blinked. "He stayed longer than three minutes. I'm impressed."

"Actor," he said, deadpan. "We memorize fast."

Later, as waiters circulated with the first course, the host approached their table. Hana squeezed Yoo-jin's hand. "I'll be right back."

Under the soft spotlight, Hana stood with quiet confidence. She addressed the assembled guests in a clear voice, thanking them for their support before moving into the heart of her message.

"Last month in Laos," she said, "I met a young girl named

Suri who walked four kilometers each way to attend the school your generosity helped build. When I asked why she made this journey every day, she told me, 'Because when I learn, I am free.'"

Hana paused, genuine emotion in her eyes. "That freedom—to learn, to grow, to determine one's future—is what your contributions make possible. Not charity, but opportunity. Not handouts, but hands joined together."

Yoo-jin found himself moved. In his world, speeches were sound bites and photo ops. This was different—she believed every word.

***

Throughout dinner, Hana stole glances at her unexpected companion. He ate and drank without fuss, handling the multiple courses and wine pairings with the same ease he had shown eating street food under a plastic tarp. No hesitation over which fork to use, no affected mannerisms—only the quiet confidence of someone comfortable in any setting. She watched him navigate conversations with seasoned diplomats, showing genuine curiosity and asking well-timed questions that kept others talking.

Not just a pretty face. What am I going to do with him?

When he smiled, his lips quirked— *Enough. Eyes front, Rhee.*

The string quartet eased into slower melodies as the evening wound down. Across the room, Hana excused herself and made her way back, a hint of fatigue visible only in the slight loosening of her straight posture.

Yoo-jin stood and extended his hand. "One last dance?"

Surprise flickered over her face, followed by a warm smile. She placed her hand in his outstretched palm. "Just so you know—I've been in these heels for hours."

"I'll keep us upright," he promised, leading her to the

floor.

His hand settled at the small of her back as they swayed, maintaining respectable distance—close enough for conversation, far enough for propriety.

"It's not as exciting as celebrity galas, I imagine," she said after a moment. "No red carpet, no paparazzi."

"That's what makes it perfect," he replied. "No cameras in my face, no need to perform for publicity."

"You poor man," she teased, eyes sparkling. "All those people wanting your picture must be exhausting."

"Says the woman who's been working the room for three hours straight."

"That's different. I'm advancing a cause, not posing for Instagram."

"Ouch," he winced. "You think that's all I do?"

He twirled her in a smooth motion. "What do you say we go somewhere livelier after this?"

She arched her brow. *Say no. Be responsible. Think of the optics. Think of work on Monday.*

"I should really stay until the end."

"The end was ten minutes ago," he pointed out. "Now it's the epilogue."

She looked around the room and back at him. With a nod, she let him escort her from the dance floor. They stopped by their table to gather their belongings and headed out in perfect decorum.

Once they reached a side entrance, away from the main lobby, Yoo-jin's hand slipped down to grasp hers.

"Run," he whispered, a boyish grin flashing on his face.

Before she could protest, he pulled her through the door and down a service corridor, laughing as they burst through an exit into the crisp night air.

MOTHS TO FLAME

Ten minutes later, they were in his car. He had dismissed his driver, handing Hana into the passenger seat and sliding behind the wheel.

"Where to? I'm dying for a real drink!"

"Somewhere with worse lighting and better music," he winked. "And no cameras." He navigated through the maze of traffic until they reached Hongdae, where the nightlife was reaching its peak.

The club was tucked away on a side street, unmarked except for a small blue light. Inside, the atmosphere couldn't have been more different from the Grand Hyatt—pulsing music, bodies moving freely, a live band setting up on the stage.

"Know them?" Hana asked as he waved to the musicians.

"Old friends," he explained, loosening his collar. "They play here once a month. Best indie rock in Seoul."

They found a table near the bar, where Yoo-jin ordered drinks.

When the band played, they joined the crowd on the dance floor, their formal wear drawing curious glances. Song after song, they moved together, lost in a world where no one seemed to care who they were.

Hours blurred into cocktails and bass-heavy remixes. Yoo-jin's bow tie hung loose around his neck, and Hana's stockinged feet brushed against his ankle under the table.

In a pocket of relative quiet, she found herself observing his lips more than listening to him talk about a rock musical he had starred in.

"You haven't heard a word I've said." His eyes crinkled with amusement.

"I heard 'rock musical' and character development," she admitted, then laughed when his eyebrows rose. "Sorry—I was remembering that Tag Heuer ad where you were half submerged in a pool and wearing a wet t-shirt."

"The dive watch?" A surprised flicker crossed his face. "You saw that one?"

"Hard to miss when it was on every billboard and subway station in Seoul for weeks." She traced languid circles on his sleeve, a little tipsy from her third vodka soda. "Makes me wonder what else you're hiding beneath that dripping, sultry perfection." *Shit. Did I just say that out loud?*

His fingers brushed against hers as he reached for his drink. The contact wasn't accidental—she knew this by the way his movement slowed, giving her time to pull away. She didn't.

She met his gaze with a playful glint in her own. "The foundation board would be scandalized if they saw their legal counsel right now."

"Probably," he agreed. "Good thing they went to bed early."

When he leaned toward her, she surprised herself by meeting him halfway. The kiss was brief, almost ordinary in its simplicity. Yet when they separated, she felt oddly exposed, as if he had glimpsed something she usually kept guarded.

"That was—" he began.

"Unexpected?" she offered.

"I was going to say 'inevitable,'" he replied, his charm giving way to sincerity. "I've been wanting to do that since you explained corporate governance over coffee today."

"That was twelve hours ago," she said, laughing.

"Ten, to be precise." His hand found hers under the table, fingers interlacing with careful intention.

Later, they walked toward his car, his jacket draped over her shoulders.

"Your apartment is in Seongdong-gu, right?"

"Yes."

At the corner, they stopped. What happened next would complicate everything—her professional reputation, his public image. The sensible choice glowed in Hana's mind—a polite goodbye, separate cars, a casual text in the morning.

Yoo-jin paused, keys dangling. This wasn't in his management's script. Getting involved with a woman carried costs in the Korean entertainment industry.

Their eyes locked in the half-darkness, both seeing the same hesitation behind the other's gaze.

He should drive her home, say goodnight at her door. *Simple. Professional. Safe.*

She should thank him for a lovely evening and call her own taxi. *Clean. Uncomplicated. Wise.*

The moment stretched with possibility and consequence.

But then she reached up and straightened his crooked collar, letting her hands linger. "My apartment has a great view," she said. "But the mattress may be a little lumpy."

His smile transformed his face, as if caution had been set aside. "I've always had a thing about views," he said, eyes never leaving hers.

When he kissed her again, it carried the hush of decisions already made.

"Your fans will be heartbroken," she murmured in his ear, making him laugh against her neck.

"Of course, that's what you're thinking about right now," he said, opening the passenger door with a flourish. "Very practical."

***

The drive back to her apartment stretched through the night-glazed streets. Yoo-jin kept one hand on the wheel, the other finding Hana's across the console. The car's silence held their unspoken thoughts, punctuated only by the occasional flash of passing headlights.

She fumbled with the keypad at the door, not from nervousness but from the distraction of his breath warming her neck as he stood close behind. Inside, she turned to speak but saw that his eyes had already answered her unasked question.

They both moved at once, as if this hadn't been inevitable. She pushed his jacket from his shoulders while his fingers tangled in her hair. The hallway light caught her smile before she reached back to switch it off.

In the kitchen, they stopped. She leaned back against the counter, reaching for him. His hands found the delicate fabric of her Elie Saab gown and paused.

"Maybe we should—" he started.

"Not yet," she whispered, working his belt free. His keys or phone clattered to the floor; neither looked down.

"This dress probably costs—"

"Less than your watch."

Moments later, they stumbled toward her bedroom, bumping into walls, stopping to kiss, starting again. Against the doorframe, she pushed him back to look at him in the dim light. His shirttails hung loose, buttons half undone.

He caught her gaze and stopped. Her gown was somehow still intact. When he turned her around to find the zipper, his fingers were steady despite everything. The dress loosened and pooled at her feet, cool air running along her spine.

"You're beautiful," he said—simple words, but his voice caught on them.

They landed on her unmade bed, sheets cool against warm skin. Their movements found a rhythm, sort of —sometimes smooth, sometimes off-beat, but they kept adjusting. Once they both reached for the same thing and laughed when their hands collided. Another time, she moved and he misread it, leading to a brief, awkward tangle.

When it happened—that suspended moment when everything clicked—she was surprised. Not by the physical sensation, but the way she was fully *there*. No running mental commentary, no self-checking. Just him, eyes open and unguarded, holding her steady until she stilled.

They stumbled through the night in fragments—her snorting when he knocked over a lamp, him cursing when she elbowed his ribs. At one point, she almost rolled off the bed, saved by his arm shooting out to catch her, which turned into round two.

They whispered silly things, even shared a few coherent thoughts. By the second time, they had figured each other out a little more. The third was fast and messy and probably unnecessary, but they committed like good sports.

Afterward, they lay in comfortable proximity. One of her legs draped across his, his arm bent at an improbable angle beneath her pillow. She traced a faded scar on his shoulder while he told her about the stunt fail that caused it.

Neither mentioned tomorrow.

The conversation meandered, punctuated by yawns and long silences. At some point, they stopped talking altogether. His hand rested on her hip, warm and heavy. She fought sleep for a moment before giving up and letting herself drift off.

***

Awareness came in nudges, light peeking through her eyelids. Hana's pillow had a different feel—firmer, warmer, and appeared to be... human?

Her eyes flew open.

She fixed on the familiar Radiohead poster opposite her bed—Thom Yorke's melancholic stare, a relic from university days, anchored her surroundings.

Slowly, she turned her head to the left.

Yoo-jin Lee. In her bed. Not a hallucination, not even a vivid dream—but the actual celebrity, complete with long eyelashes that no man had any right to possess.

Last night. The gala. The club. And then... this—multiple times, if memory serves.

She was lying in the crook of his arm, and the warmth against her back wasn't only from her duvet but his entire body curved along hers like they had been designed as companion pieces. His breath tickled the back of her neck, warm and rhythmic. She shifted to extract herself without waking him.

His hand tightened around her waist. "Don't move," he murmured, voice morning-rough and muffled against her hair. "Five more minutes."

After a moment, curiosity won over embarrassment. She turned to face him, getting her first proper look at Yoo-jin Lee, The Morning After Edition.

It was... not what she expected.

His famous hair—the hair that had its own fanbase, if Min-ji was to be believed—stuck up in at least three different directions. A pillow crease marked his cheek. Morning stubble darkened his jaw, less "ruggedly handsome" and more "forgot to pack a razor." One eye was a bit more open than the other, giving him a comic lopsided expression.

And yet.

Those lips. Good lord, those lips. They were somehow even more ridiculous in daylight—full and beautiful, like someone had drawn them with excessive care while neglecting to make them look proportionate to actual human anatomy. They quirked up at one corner as he caught her staring.

"You're staring," he said, his mouth curving into a knowing smile.

"Doing my due diligence," she replied.

"And?"

"I think you'll do."

His eyes snapped open. Without warning, his fingers found her waist, targeting the spot he had discovered was ticklish hours earlier.

"Don't you dare—" She squealed, retaliating with a shove against his chest. "I was trying not to wake you."

"Terrible plan," he said, pulling her back as she attempted to escape. They tussled among the rumpled sheets.

"Not fair," she twisted beneath him when he used his weight advantage. "You're supposed to be tired after last night."

"Disappointed?" His eyebrow arched in challenge.

"Hardly." She hooked her leg around his, almost flipping them. He rolled with her momentum, drawing her back flush against his chest. Their laughter quieted. The banter slipped away.

"Sneaky," she murmured, settling into his hold.

"Strategic," he corrected in her ear, one hand splayed across her sternum while the other traced lower with deliberate patience.

She turned to face him. There was an intensity in his eyes that silenced everything else, gazing at her as if he had just stumbled onto something rare, unexpected.

Their kiss bore little resemblance to last night's spirited fumbles. Slower. Intentional. Her hands mapped the angles of his shoulders as he eased her back against the pillows. He hovered above her, steady on his forearms. "You okay?"

She nodded, tugging him back down.

His forehead dropped to hers as they began again, less a seduction than a conversation—push and yield, question and answer.

What followed had no pattern—fast then slow, gentle then not. Their bodies understood each other in ways they themselves had yet to—finding rhythm, anticipating, reacting. When he slowed, she whispered in his ear.

"Just—" he managed, the word strained. She arched against him and made him swear under his breath.

When she broke, her mind emptied like a room suddenly gone dark. No thoughts, no filter. Within seconds, he caught up with her, breath ragged, eyes open. No performance—just him, undone.

They stayed that way for a long moment, joined and sated. Sunlight crept across the sheets, catching the sheen of cooling sweat on their skin.

He brushed her damp hair back and kissed her forehead. "Good morning," he murmured.

She laughed—a breathless, incredulous laugh. "Good morning yourself."

***

Later, Hana headed for the shower, feeling Yoo-jin's eyes on her back. She resisted the urge to grab a robe to cover herself—it was a bit late for modesty.

Under the hot water, she tried to summon appropriate panic. A celebrity she'd known less than twenty-four hours. In her bed, her shower, and soon her kitchen. It all screamed poor judgment and future regret.

When she emerged from the bedroom in ancient jeans and a faded t-shirt, she found Yoo-jin at the stove. She stopped short, momentarily forgetting how to walk.

He stood at the counter in last night's dress pants hanging low on his hips, shirt unbuttoned, revealing the kind of torso that explained why people paid good money to see him take off his clothes on screen. Egg yolk streaked his forearm as he concentrated on cracking eggs one-handed.

Calm down. He's making breakfast, not doing a strip-tease.

She approached cautiously as if he might be a mirage that would vanish upon closer inspection. "I can't promise much," she said, reaching for coffee mugs to occupy her hands. "I haven't had time to shop this week."

"Already handled," he replied without looking up, nodding toward the ingredients he had excavated from her neglected refrigerator—bacon, half an onion, cheese, and a bell pepper that had seen better days. "Omelets. What you need is a lover who's also a chef."

Lover. The word should have sounded strange, too intimate for what they were. Instead, it slid into place.

He slipped an arm around her neck, pressing a kiss to her temple as if he'd done it every day for years. An easy gesture from someone who was as comfortable in his skin as he was in her kitchen.

"Do you like Cayenne pepper?" he asked, already scanning her spice rack. "It gives it a kick."

"I have no idea what's in there," she admitted. "Probably nothing from this decade."

He grinned, pulling out a dusty bottle. "Ah, 2019. A good year for exotic spices."

There they were—two near-strangers navigating the morning after—moving around her small space in what looked like a well-oiled routine. Him whisking eggs while she set out plates on the table. Her reaching over him for forks while he diced vegetables with knife skills from restaurant kitchens. His shirt brushing against her arm, reminding her that under different circumstances, they would still be in bed.

"What?" he asked, catching her staring.

"Nothing." She poured coffee into mugs. "Just wondering if this is what you do after all your one-night stands. Raid their refrigerators and make gourmet omelets."

His spatula stilled mid-flip. “Is that what this is?”

She hadn’t meant to bring it up while standing with coffee in hand and him half-dressed and frying eggs. But here they were.

“I don’t know,” she answered, aiming for nonchalance. “It doesn’t have to be anything. We’re both adults. It was fun.”

The words sounded off even as she said them, as if she were reading lines from someone else’s script. But pride made her commit to them. Better to appear coolly detached than eager for a connection that might go nowhere.

They studied each other for a moment in silence.

Behind their eyes, mirrored calculations unfolded—she weighed the risk to her professional reputation, while he considered the complications of dating outside his celebrity world.

“I want to see you again,” he said, more firmly than either of them expected. “I can’t explain it, but...” He paused, searching for words. “This doesn’t feel finished.”

He put down the spatula and turned toward her, the food forgotten. “Unless you’d rather keep it simple. One good night, and then goodbye.”

She took a slow sip of coffee. “I don’t generally do ‘simple.’ But I’m not sure I know how to do... whatever this might be.”

A smile tugged at his lips. “That makes two of us.”

***

Over breakfast, Hana poked her eggs with her fork. “These are quite good. I’m impressed.”

“Such high praise,” Yoo-jin deadpanned. “I’ll add it to my résumé.”

“Most people who look like you can’t cook at all.” She gestured toward his torso. “Abs like those often mean protein shakes and misery.”

“Speaking of which,” he said, “this butter is amazing.”

"Happy grass-fed cows."

"Until they're not."

"Way to ruin the mood." She picked at the crusts of her bread, removing it bit by bit.

Without comment, he took the toast from her hands and cut off the crusts with his knife, creating even edges. He buttered it before handing it back to her.

"This habit warrants deep psychoanalysis," he said, "but that's for another day."

When it was time for him to leave, he stuffed his tie into his jacket pocket. At the door, he hooked a finger into her belt loop to tug her closer.

"My place. In two hours. Jeans and sturdy boots."

"Why?" She slid her fingers under his shirt. "Are you dragging me on a torture hike?"

"If I wanted to torture you, I'd suggest stilettos." He kissed her hard, then pulled back. "Don't google the address."

"Now I definitely will."

"Lawyers," he muttered, stepping into the hallway. "Never met a surprise they didn't ruin."

***

The address led Hana to a gleaming Hannam-dong building. Yoo-jin was waiting in leather pants and a black T-shirt that somehow looked more expensive than her entire outfit.

"Perfect timing," he greeted her with a quick kiss. "Ready for an adventure?"

She followed him down to the building's garage, expecting to see a fleet of luxury cars. Instead, he paused in front of a shiny silver Ducati Diavel.

Of course, he rides a motorcycle. Of course, it looks like it belongs in Mission Impossible.

"You ride?" she asked, raising an eyebrow.

"One of the few useful skills I picked up for a role." He handed her a helmet. "It's incredibly safe—braking system, traction control. Not built for long journeys, but perfect for today."

He helped her with the strap, his fingers brushing her jaw. *Ah. One of those men who can make a seatbelt feel suggestive. Noted.*

"Hold on tight," he said as she climbed on behind him, smirking just enough to make it dangerous. The engine came to life with a low, elegant purr. Not a roar—more like a promise.

They wove through Seoul traffic, the city dissolving as the road opened up. Her arms wrapped around his waist, feeling the subtle shifts of his muscles as he steered into curves. *Okay, fine. This is hot.*

Suburbs blurred into countryside. Wind, motion, and a silence she appreciated.

Eventually, they turned down a narrow road that led to a modern building nestled among trees. A discreet sign read *New Hope Animal Sanctuary.*

"This is the surprise?" Hana asked, removing her helmet.

He took her hand casually, as if he hadn't driven her into the woods on a movie-grade motorcycle. "An operation I helped fund."

Inside, the vibe transformed. Yoo-jin changed, too—not into someone else, but into someone more real. He greeted the staff veterinarian, and crouched to scratch the dogs' ears and rub their bellies like it was second nature.

Okay, this is unexpected. Movie star by morning, part-time Saint Francis by afternoon?

When a young family entered, he stepped back from her, creating space. He knelt beside a hesitant girl and coaxed her toward an elderly dog. No fanfare. No posing for photos. Only quiet patience. The girl giggled as the dog licked her hand—Yoo-jin looked up and winked at Hana.

And now he's charming children. Is this a coordinated PR campaign or is he always like this?

Later, they stopped into a quieter wing. The lighting softened. The air settled heavier. "These are the ones that need more time," he said. "The ones most people overlook."

He greeted each animal by name. One dog, blind in one eye, leaned into his hand with total trust.

She peeked at his profile as he petted the dog's head.

"How many get adopted from here?"

"Not enough," he said.

As the afternoon softened into a mellow light, they made their way back to the parking lot.

Yoo-jin handed Hana her helmet and watched her clip it on without help this time. Twenty-six hours ago, she had side-eyed fishcakes at the food market like she wasn't sure whether to eat them or report a health violation. And twelve hours ago, she was in a couture gown orchestrating a high-society gala.

Now she was straddling his Ducati like it was her preferred mode of transport.

"Have you ridden before?" he asked, surprised.

"Yeah. My cousin had a bike. He's taken me riding since I was fourteen."

He turned to look at her. "Fourteen?"

"We told my mother I was at piano lessons." She grinned, unapologetic. "Which wasn't a complete lie. I had piano *after.*"

***

As they accelerated along the winding road away from the shelter, every curve brought them closer together. The physical intimacy of the motorcycle—her arms around his waist, her body pressed against his back—was charged with a new, unexpected sensation.

A yearning crept up on Yoo-jin with startling clarity: *I want her close to me.*

The strangeness of the idea almost made him miss a turn. He corrected quickly, and felt her grip tightening for a beat before relaxing again. She didn't ask questions. Didn't flinch. Just trusted him with the kind of ease that should have rattled them both.

But she wasn't from his celebrity world. She didn't know what came with being attached to someone like him. She didn't sign up for the headlines. *And still... she's here.*

For Hana, the wobble should have triggered her usual spiral—mental checklists, contingency plans, injury statistics. Instead, she found herself pressed against a man she barely knew, flying down a highway with no seatbelt, no plan, no backup. And she wasn't panicking. Her overactive brain, usually impossible to silence, went quiet. No warning lights. No hypotheticals. She only held on tighter.

As the Seoul skyline emerged ahead, gray and solemn and immutable, Yoo-jin's introspection sharpened: *I want to be her safe place.*

This odd wish carried surprising weight. Not just attraction or instinct, but deeper—a gut-level desire to be steady and solid for her in a way he'd never been for anyone. The irony wasn't lost on him: he barely understood what that meant, let alone how to do it. But he knew he wanted to try.

Behind him, Hana watched the city draw near—order, routine, the life she knew. *Land on your feet. Keep moving.* That was her rhythm. Instead, she felt oddly untethered, suspended somewhere between two versions of herself. *Is this how it happens? One decision after three vodka tonics, and suddenly you're not the same person you were yesterday?*

She should know better. But strangely, they fit—like mismatched puzzle pieces where one had trust issues and the other was emotionally evasive, yet somehow they still clicked. She didn't want to overthink it. Which, for her, was like not breathing.

When the Hannam-dong exit approached, he ignored it.

Took the longer way. Her arms stayed wrapped around him, her warmth against his back. Let the moment stretch.

His thoughts circled with more urgency now—the anxiety, the want, the pull.

The light ahead turned yellow. He could have made it, but slowed instead. Cars honked. He didn't care.

Because right now, he was not Yoo-jin Lee the actor. Not the product. Not the brand. Just a guy on a bike, holding on to a connection that didn't feel like a passing thing.

I want her close to me. I want to be her safe place.

He couldn't make any sense of either thought. But he didn't push them away—only held them close like convictions he couldn't bear to lose.

***

Silence enveloped them as Yoo-jin cut the engine in the parking garage.

Hana swung her leg over the motorcycle and dismounted, unfastening her helmet. She shook out her hair and stretched. She caught him watching, a smile tugging the corner of her mouth. "What?"

"You must be tired. Come on." He guided her toward the elevator, his hand hovering but never quite touching.

I spent an hour glued to his back, and now he's shy? Adorable.

They ascended in weighted silence, both of them stealing awkward glances in the mirrored walls.

"Penthouse? Really?" she asked as the numbers climbed.

"Twenty-third floor. There's no twenty-fourth. Sorry," he said, almost sheepish.

The elevator opened into a spacious foyer that gave way to an open living area. Floor-to-ceiling windows revealed a sweeping panorama with the Han River glowing on one side and a park swathed in shadow on the other.

Pretty impressive, he thought proudly. And a little

nervously. "Welcome to my lair," he said aloud—and winced.

She gave him a sideways glance, eyes dancing. "The girls you bring here must lose their minds."

"I never bring anyone here."

She arched a brow.

"And that's not even a line." He gestured down the hallway. "Bathroom's through there if you need."

When Hana emerged, she found him at the kitchen island, now dressed in soft linen pants and an open shirt that flirted between "relaxed" and "intentional." When he bent to grab an item from the fridge, she caught herself staring and looked away.

"Nice view," she said, nodding toward the windows.

He poured her a glass of San Pellegrino and another of Sancerre. She drained the water and wandered into the living room with the wine.

A baby grand piano sat in one corner, and a little further away, a guitar stand. "Piano. Guitar. But no drums? I'm disappointed," she called over her shoulder.

"The neighbors complained."

Near the far wall stood a vintage record player surrounded by stacks of vinyl. Shelves full of books—real ones, well-thumbed—lined the walls.

The room settled into a gentle hush, broken only by the sound of his knife against the chopping board. "Want some music?" *I'm crap at small talk.*

He wiped his hands and flipped through a stack of records. "What are you in the mood for? Chopin? Bob Marley? Dance Monkey?"

Hana pointed to Yiruma. Soon, the soft notes of *Kiss the Rain* curled through the room. She stood at the window, the city lights flickering before her. "Do you ever get lonely here?" *Because I sure as hell would.*

"I'm an introvert. I'm used to being around myself."

The garlic hit the butter in the pan with a satisfying sizzle, the aroma filling the space. Hana's stomach clenched with hunger pangs. *Cooks. Rides. Plays piano and guitar. Sings. Reads. Is he real or is this a Bachelor audition reel?*

She took a seat at the island and watched him hunched over the stove. Between stirs, he topped off their wine glasses. The risotto simmered, demanding his focus. "You need the patience of a saint to make that." *Though from what I saw last night, you're no saint.*

After dinner, they settled close to each other on the couch, but not quite touching—her legs tucked under her, his arm draped along the backrest.

"So," she said, "tell me everything you want me to know about yourself."

"You mean like a deposition?"

The conversation began light but drifted deeper.

Busan—middle-class home, teacher father, homemaker mother. A weirdly subdued household where people bottled up their feelings. *If you were upset, you journaled it.* It was like living in a mindfulness camp, minus the funny robes. Even now, he couldn't express emotions without a script. Shouting and slamming doors were taboo. Acting became therapy.

England—dogs and horses, boarding schools. A Korean mother full of drama, an English stepfather who elevated silence into an art form. Life was a constant high-pressure system—you never knew what storm would blow in. She learned early how to disappear into an emotional bunker.

Outside, night had claimed the city.

He twirled a strand of her hair around his finger. "This bunker of yours—can I visit? I'll bring wine. We can play house."

"You're fast."

"No, practical."

A beat passed. He placed a tentative hand on her leg. Not

seductive. Not suggestive. Hopeful. “Stay tonight.”

She didn’t move right away. She brought her arm over his on the backrest.

For a long moment, their eyes held a silent conversation:

Is this a part you’re playing?

No role—just me.

Can I believe that?

It's true. I really like you.

Hmm. I'm not sure if this is wise.

I don't know. But I still wish you'd stay.

A slow exhale. Then, breaking eye contact, she unfurled her legs from beneath her and stretched them across his lap. “Alright. But come midnight, no more fairy tales.”

His face broke into a wide smile. “Better get started then,” he said, pulling her into a hug.

SEPARATION ANXIETY

After their whirlwind weekend, Monday arrived with brutal inevitability.

Hana lay in bed and stared at the ceiling, replaying the night before—how they had explored each other—sometimes laughing, sometimes breathless—until they were both completely spent. When he drove her home, they had lingered in the backseat of his car, kissing like teenagers dodging curfew. No parting promises. No plans.

Now alone, she did the math: less than twenty-four hours from meet-cute at the market to full-frontal contact, and now at the thirty-six-hour mark, she was lying awake, wondering if he remembered her name.

You will not be that clingy, needy girlfriend.

Wait. Am I even his girlfriend? We only met the day before yesterday.

The term sounded too small and at the same time too presumptuous for whatever tornado had swept through her ordered life.

She rolled onto her side, pulling a pillow against her chest and breathing in the faint scent of him before forcing herself out of bed. A long week of work awaited, which was good—distraction to the rescue. *Keep perspective. But—*

An unwelcome thought hit her in the shower: perhaps she had merely been a weekend diversion for him. A-list celebrities were notorious for short attention spans. This sobering possibility made her straighten her spine. She would not be caught waiting by the phone. She lived a life that mattered before Yoo-jin Lee walked into it, and she would not become a lovestruck cliché now.

Thirty-seven hours and counting.

***

Yoo-jin woke to muscles that screamed when he stretched, each ache a pleasant reminder of the weekend. He reached for his phone—no message from Hana. *Eight AM—maybe she was still asleep?*

His thumb brushed over the screen before he put the device down. *Don't hover. Don't be that suffocating asshole.*

The apartment seemed empty this morning. Funny how one person could alter a space he'd lived in for years.

He wandered to the kitchen, brewing coffee on autopilot while reviewing his schedule. For the first time in a decade, his calendar held welcome gaps between commitments. *Midnight in Busan* had opened to packed theaters and critical acclaim. Now came the lull: business meetings, script readings, promotional appearances—the machinery of fame that operated nonstop.

At forty, Yoo-jin had perfected the art of being perpetually unattached. While his contemporaries got married, shuttled kids to weekend activities, and debated mortgage rates, his version of "long-term planning" was lining up enough projects to carry him through the awards seasons.

Success had narrowed his dating options. The public demanded their fantasy—the eternally single heartthrob onto whom millions could project their romantic daydreams. Management had made their expectations clear: discretion was non-negotiable and girlfriends were career suicide for leading man roles. *Because nothing says "romantic hero" like a man who can't actually woo anyone.*

His relationships never lasted long. The women who "understood" were in the same industry—the clashing schedules, tabloid gossip, and professional jealousy dressed up as encouragement. The ones outside it eventually realized they were dating a very good-looking ghost who only materialized between shoots.

Now, his life ran on a career path that demanded everything and repaid him with the privilege of staying in the game. He had come to accept his solitude, dabbled in a few hobbies, and generally enjoyed a quiet life with friends and an occasional canine.

Until Hana came along and flipped that complacency on its head. Hana, who stood with confidence in her own accomplished life, immune to his fame. She would not wait around for his attention or rearrange her schedule to accommodate his.

So he sat staring at his phone like a high schooler again, wondering why a woman he had known for less than forty-eight hours wasn't calling him.

Clearly, you get more pathetic with age.

***

The week dragged on, with a brain-fogged Wednesday bleeding into a sluggish Thursday. Hana couldn't pinpoint what she was waiting for, but it made time crawl. She slogged through her work, absentminded, checking off tasks like items on a grocery list.

She would catch herself mid-sentence speaking to an empty room. Coworkers noticed her wandering focus during meetings. Her foot tapped a ceaseless rhythm under the conference table, as if preparing to bolt at any moment.

Her phone remained quiet. Yoo-jin's silence now confirmed what she should have known all along: their weekend had only been another celebrity fling, intense and meaningless.

She forced her foot to stop its incessant tapping. *You will get over this. It's not like you're in a relationship with this man.*

That evening, as she nursed her third glass of wine, Hana catalogued her exes in her head. At thirty-two, her romantic history read like a tasting menu at an overpriced restaurant —varied, exotic, ultimately unsatisfying. She'd sampled every type: the tortured artist, the brilliant workaholic, the charming nomad. All fascinating in theory, exhausting in practice.

Her last long-term lover was Simon, who blew into her life like a category-five hurricane—a gorgeous war correspondent who challenged every word she said, turned arguments into foreplay, disappeared for months to cover conflicts in places she couldn't pronounce. Their reunions were worthy of romance novels, the kind with an inordinate amount of *ahem* detail. He made her feel alive, unbalanced, and constantly out of breath—and not always in a good way.

Until it became clear she spent more time waiting than living. Checking her phone turned into a nervous tic. The flutter in her stomach when it rang was pathetically Pavlovian. The night she found herself googling "how to tell if condoms have expired" because it had been *that* long, she knew they were over. When she ended it, he looked surprised, as if he had assumed she would always be there, like a book he could pick up where he had left off.

She swore then—no more waiting. No more being secondary to someone else's grand ambitions.

And yet here you are, waiting for a celebrity actor to call. Whatever happened to live and learn?

***

Yoo-jin sat through a script reading where he delivered his lines with detached emotion. For two hours, he managed not to think about Hana. But the moment they called a five-minute break, her image came rushing back. He checked his phone—

still nothing.

His thumb hovered over her contact. He told himself he'd wait until the weekend. He doubted she'd appreciate a full-grown man fidgeting in his seat like a schoolkid waiting for the recess bell.

Yet, he kept drafting and deleting messages. It was embarrassing, even to him. He placed his phone face down on the table, cursing under his breath.

For minutes he argued with himself over whether daily check-ins were clingy. He imagined Hana—cool, composed, allergic to sentimentality—would probably block any man who texted *"thinking of you"* before date three.

***

Friday arrived with the speed of molasses.

It was a light day for Yoo-jin—a commercial shoot for coffee or insurance—he couldn't remember which. The routine was always the same: hair and makeup, then hours of microscopic adjustments. *Stand here. Be more seductive. Less contemplative. And for god's sake don't look like you're actually thinking.*

Between takes, as he sat under hot lights holding a product he would never use, a decision crystallized. *Enough waiting. Enough guessing.*

The moment the director called the final wrap, Yoo-jin thanked the crew and slipped away. He drove to the upscale market in Gangnam, moving through imported goods aisles and selecting ingredients with care—fresh salmon, heavy cream, Swiss Gruyère, Valrhona chocolate from France.

He would make dinner for Hana—his own salmon quiche and the chocolate mousse that impressed even his most culinarily critical friends.

Whether she would eat it was another question. Whether she would even agree to see him was an even bigger one.

But Yoo-jin Lee hadn't built a career by waiting for certainty. Some roles required a leap of faith.

***

"*Hana-ssi,*" the grant coordinator repeated. "The due diligence report for Hoi An?"

Hana's eyes focused, though she couldn't recall the previous five minutes. "I'm sorry, which report?"

"The Vietnam children's center. Mr. Weston forwarded the compliance assessment on Tuesday."

"Ah, right." Hana reoriented herself. "If his committee vetted it, we're good."

She looked up at the wall clock: 3:10 PM. Fifty more minutes of this meeting to endure. She forced herself to concentrate as the discussion continued around her, but the words seemed to filter through glass.

The coldness in the pit of her stomach was unfamiliar and annoying. *Last weekend was a momentary lapse. Stay away from celebrities from now on.*

Yet somewhere beneath her practical self-talk, a rebellious voice piped up. *But this is only getting interesting.*

She weighed her options as the meeting dragged on. *Show light interest. Brace for inevitable disappointment. But at least give it a chance.*

At home, she changed into comfortable clothes and opened a bottle of wine. Into her second glass, she worked up the courage to type a casual message to Yoo-jin: *Hey there, what are you doing?*

His answer came instantly: *Missing you.*

Her heart skipped a beat. *Where are you?*

In front of your building. With a homemade dinner.

She dropped her phone. While fumbling to retrieve it, she knocked over her wine. She rushed to the window and saw him down on the street, leaning against his car. He looked up, spotted her, and waved.

It took her mere minutes to grab her keys, ride the elevator down nine floors, and hurry through the lobby. She paused at the curb only long enough for a break in traffic. *Slow down. Show dignity. It's not a good look to get run over in front of him.*

But when she reached the other side of the road, all pretense vanished.

She ran straight into his arms.

***

That night, Hana and Yoo-jin lounged on her couch in the semi-darkness, feeding each other remnants of quiche from a dinner interrupted at regular intervals by roaming hands and wandering lips. The past week's anxieties had evaporated, and tomorrow's responsibilities remained distant. Only the present moment counted.

The pattern established itself over the following weeks—periods of separation filled with work obligations, punctuated by firework reunions. They made noble declarations about maintaining independence, only to find themselves texting an hour later with less noble excuses to meet.

Hana's left brain cautioned, *This is reckless.* Her right brain countered, *But it feels so good.* Her left brain let out an exasperated sigh.

Meanwhile, Yoo-jin was busy losing an argument with himself. *Fuck me, what am I doing?* And just as quickly—*I don't know. I don't care.*

For now, the celebrity rules could wait. But soon, they'd have to toe the line.

INVISIBLE LINES

Those first weeks with Yoo-jin were spent learning a dance Hana never knew existed—maintaining perfect distance in public and collapsing it in private. Stolen glances, coded messages, constant awareness that they could never appear as a couple.

The thrill of secrecy made it irresistible.

Their Tuesday morning routine began with separate cars to Gwangjang Market. Yoo-jin would arrive first, face hidden behind a black mask and a baseball cap pulled low, while Hana followed fifteen minutes later wearing unremarkable clothes. They never walked together, never acknowledged each other, but their phones buzzed with playful exchanges.

That ajumma at the kimchi stall wants to set me up with her nephew. Should I get his number?

Three stalls away, Hana saw the subtle shake of Yoo-jin's shoulders as he laughed, fingers moving over his phone.

Only if he has a yacht and cooks better than me.

No one cooks better than you.

Correct answer. Your prize awaits at home.

At the fish stall, Yoo-jin came to an abrupt stop, and Hana—absorbed in her phone—walked right into him.

"Sorry," she murmured, loud enough for bystanders to hear.

He nodded with a neutral expression and continued his

transaction.

Later, in his kitchen overlooking the Han River, he nudged her. "Hey, stalker," he teased, bumping her hip. "You did that on purpose."

"What?" Hana arranged vegetables in the fridge, all innocence.

"Crashing into me."

"You stopped short."

"Right. And your hand happened to graze my ass?"

"Oh," she said, stepping closer, "but it felt so nice..."

His hands found her waist, hoisting her onto the counter.

"I'll show you what feels nice..." he murmured, burying his face in her neck.

***

The next morning Yoo-jin was in the makeup chair at Hanwha Studios for a motorcycle tire campaign. He hummed an old Turtles song, tapping his fingers against the armrest: ... *To think about the girl you love—And hold her tight—So happy together...*

"*Yoo-jin-ssi,* please," the makeup artist sighed, brandishing her lip liner. "I can't get a straight line if you're dancing in the chair."

"Sorry, *Soo-young-ssi.*" He grinned, then resumed singing once she stepped back.

Between takes, he wandered around the set offering lollipops to surprised crew members. "Have one—sugar makes everything better."

When the cameras rolled, he transformed—straddling the gleaming motorcycle in leather pants and designer shirt, metal chains glinting against his collarbone as he delivered smoldering looks that would sell tires to people who didn't even own vehicles.

"That's perfect, hold it..." the director called. "And... cut!"

Instantly, the brooding intensity vanished as Yoo-jin collapsed in a fit of laughter, running his hand through his carefully styled hair.

"Was that too much? It felt like I was mentally undressing the motorcycle."

The crew laughed, but his manager Ji-hoon, watching from the periphery, remained stone-faced. When they broke for lunch, he beckoned Yoo-jin to a corner.

"What's gotten into you?" the older man's analytical gaze dissected him.

"Just in a good mood." Yoo-jin unwrapped a cherry lollipop.

"In the fifteen years I've worked with you, I've never seen you bring candy to a set or sing during makeup. You're dating someone."

It wasn't a question.

Yoo-jin shrugged, casual. "I'm happy."

"You know the rules in our line of work." Ji-hoon lowered his voice. "The agency has been very clear about your image management. Your contract explicitly states—"

"That I'm not allowed to have a personal life?" Yoo-jin's smile hardened.

"That discretion is paramount. We've built your brand on accessibility—the attainable fantasy. Women need to believe they have a chance."

"I'm human, Ji-hoon. Not a fucking robot."

His manager's lips thinned. "Whatever you've got going on with this... individual—"

"This 'individual' has a name," Yoo-jin cut in. "It's Hana."

"I must discourage it in the strongest terms. The consequences to your career—"

Yoo-jin extended the lollipop bouquet. "Sugar makes everything better, Ji-hoon. Take one."

The older man glanced at the offering and back at Yoo-jin's unrepentant smile. "This isn't a joke."

"No," Yoo-jin agreed, voice light but eyes serious. "It's not."

***

A Friday night at Club Octave. Yoo-jin arrived with his usual crew. Hana showed up twenty minutes later with her lawyer friends, seating themselves across the room without even glancing in his direction.

When the DJ cued up a popular ballad, Yoo-jin let his best friend Sang-min drag him to the karaoke platform. Halfway through the first verse, he gestured toward Hana's table as if picking out random strangers. "I need a backup singer!" Hana's friends pushed her to the stage despite her mock squeals. The crowd cheered.

Their voices found each other on the chorus, their chemistry undeniable even with a careful foot of space between them—all explained away by the music. When the song ended, they bowed to opposite sides of the room and returned to their separate groups like actors exiting different sides of the stage, severing the moment cleanly as if it had never happened.

Three hours later, they collapsed on his sofa, still buzzing from their carefully orchestrated charade.

"That was exhausting," Hana said, kicking off her heels. "Remember that Hongdae club we went to the first time?"

He nuzzled her hair. "Mm-hmm?"

"You weren't worried about being seen kissing me."

"That's because you bewitched me. I wasn't thinking with my head."

"Can't we ever act like a couple at all?"

His expression dimmed. "It's complicated... But the short answer is no."

A shadow flickered over her eyes before she blinked it away. He caught it. "Do you really mind?" he asked, voice gentle.

"I'm just finding my footing. I've never been with a movie star before." She forced a smile. "The dating manual didn't cover this stuff."

"I know—I'm sorry." He pulled her closer. "It's no fun going out with a celebrity. That's why I've been as celibate as a monk."

"Bullshit." She gave him a playful shove, dissolving the tension. "No monk can do that thing you do so well..."

"Oh yeah?" His hand slid beneath her waistband, voice dropping. "What thing is that?"

***

One afternoon, Hana was reviewing the guest list for that evening's Donor Appreciation Cocktail.

"Mr. Yoo-jin Lee declines tonight's reception," her assistant Jin-ah read from her tablet. "But he sent white orchids—signed 'Leonardo DiCaprio.'"

Hana bit back a smile. "Jin-ah, I'd appreciate it if there was no gossip about Mr. Lee at the office."

"You wound me, boss." Jin-ah placed a hand over her heart in mock offense. "Have I ever betrayed your confidence?"

"No. And I'd like to keep it that way."

"Your secret boyfriend is safe with me." Jin-ah backed toward the door. "Oh, and Mr. Weston is waiting for you on Zoom. He's been there for two minutes already."

"What? Why didn't you—" Hana scrambled to smooth her hair before clicking the video icon.

Ian Weston appeared on screen—dark blond hair, piercing blue eyes, permanent scowl.

"How's my favorite cousin?" Hana greeted him with a bright smile.

"I'm your only cousin. What's with the ridiculous grin?"

She schooled her features into a serious expression.

"You haven't read the compliance documents," he continued. "It looks like your head is elsewhere. This work matters, Hana."

"I know," she said, more subdued.

He narrowed his eyes. "So I suspect you're either day-drinking or seeing someone—which is it?"

She blew into her cupped hand and sniffed theatrically. "Smells like mineral water to me."

Ian didn't laugh. "Who is he?"

"Nobody," Hana said, a little too fast.

His gaze sharpened. "Hana."

She shook her head, but a blush crept up her neck. "Why are you acting like a jealous boyfriend?"

"I don't want to see you hurt like last time. What was his name? That journalist who was always halfway across the world?"

"Simon," Hana muttered, her brightness dimming. "And yes, you were right about him."

"You deserve better. Someone who shows up."

"I just don't want to end up an old maid, alright?"

"You won't," he said. "You're too—" He paused. "You're not the type people forget."

She looked at him, brow creased in surprise, but he was already moving on. "Anyway. Read the documents properly this time. I won't always be around to clean up your mess." The screen blinked dark.

***

For a while, it was enough.

But one night, after changing plans yet again to avoid being recognized, Yoo-jin asked, "Does it bother you?"

Hana, curled against him on the sofa, considered the question. “Sometimes, I think about how nice it would be to hold your hand at the market. Or to post a selfie together when we visit the animal shelter.”

He waited, expression neutral.

“But then I remember that this—” she waved a hand over their tangled limbs under the throw blanket, his half-buttoned shirt, the faint smell of *bao* buns in the air, “—is the real us. The rest is dumb logistics.”

He pulled her close, relieved. “You’re too good for me, you know that?”

“I know,” she said. “But I’ll keep you for now.”

True, the dating manual didn’t mention the secrecy constraint—but Hana had already mastered that. What it also neglected to mention were the long absences. She’d learn that soon enough.

MILES APART

At breakfast, Yoo-jin's phone buzzed for the third time in five minutes. He frowned at the message.

"What?" Hana asked.

"Nothing—work stuff." He disappeared into the bathroom.

She turned her attention back to her emails. *Whatever. It's not like communication is important.*

Moments later, he re-emerged, hair still damp and cleanly shaved. He slipped a hand down her shirt front and nuzzled her neck. "Talk later?"

She turned her head to kiss him, accepting the non-explanation.

In the elevator, Yoo-jin reread the text from his manager: *Director Kang wants you for "Silent Witness." Congrats!*

Excitement and concern warred in his mind. This project would consume months, and he and Hana were still so new. But enthusiasm won out: *Awesome. Can't wait. Let's talk details.*

Mask and cap in place, he navigated the car out of her garage. *This is huge. Hana will be happy for me.*

He drummed his fingers on the steering wheel as if the rhythm might convince him it was true. *At least, let's hope so.*

***

By the end of April, they had fallen into a comfortable pattern.

Work kept them both busy. Hana had to deal with legal tangles and policy headaches. Yoo-jin juggled pre-production meetings and press obligations. Neither mentioned how little they ventured out anymore—their apartments had become their default world.

Yoo-jin dropped the bombshell one quiet evening over sea bream and overcooked asparagus. "I got the role," he said. "The one with Director Kang."

Hana set down her fork. "The political thriller guy?"

"Yeah. I play a diplomat caught in morally questionable dilemmas. Heavy stuff."

"Location?"

"Four weeks in Seoul." He took a slow sip of wine. "Then Prague, Vienna, Milan."

"How long?" she asked, bracing for the answer.

"Four months total."

She nodded. "Good for you," she said. "Big step up."

He reached for her hand. "I should've told you sooner."

"How much sooner?"

"Three weeks ago. I didn't want it hanging over our time together."

"Ah—so a surprise emotional ambush was the better option?" She bit her lip, regretting her sharp tone.

He winced. "When you put it that way..."

"Don't worry," she softened. "I'll survive. I've got that cross-border adoption nightmare to keep me busy. Lawyers in three time zones, constant emergencies. Like your movie but with less attractive people and worse lighting."

He laughed, pulling her into a hug. "We'll figure it out. Calls, texts, whatever."

Four months—an entire season. Long enough to fall in love, ruin it, and pretend it never happened. She smiled. Too wide.

Four months—I'll be lucky if she's still here when I come back.

He smiled back. Too fast.

***

May arrived and the first four weeks of filming passed in a blur of mismatched schedules and caffeine.

Yoo-jin would drag himself in past midnight, smelling of fake blood and stage makeup. Hana would glance up from her laptop and mutter, "You look like you lost a minor war."

They managed late-night meals—mostly takeout eaten on the floor, surrounded by scripts and legal briefs. Conversation was clipped but comforting: how many hours until call time, how many days until an adoption screening.

When they did see each other, it was quick: a kiss at the door, a shared yawn, a half-conscious cuddle that passed for a quickie.

"Romance," she said once, snuggling close to him, "is alive and well."

His lips brushed her cheek. "We're the ones on life support."

Still, they were together. That month was the easy part.

***

The real test began when he left for Europe in June.

During his first week abroad, they spoke daily—short video calls where he showed her glimpses of Prague between takes, messages exchanged over her lunch breaks. He appeared energized by the role, his eyes bright with that particular focus when he was deep in a character.

"I should've come with you," she teased one night. "Just to make sure you're fed."

"And by 'fed,' you mean hand-feeding me while sitting on my lap?"

Her breath caught at the way he said it, low and intimate. The look in his eyes made her notice the cold, empty bed around her.

By the second week, the time difference took its toll. Her mornings were his evenings. Her evenings were his early morning call times. *Sorry I missed your call. Eighteen-hour day. Talk tomorrow?*

Tomorrow became the next day, then the next. Day four: *How's it going?*

Three hours later: *Exhausted but good. This director is brilliant.*

Not *I miss you* or *Wish you were here*. Only a comment about work.

She stared at her phone, fingers hovering over the keyboard. She wanted to type: *I miss you so much it hurts.*

Instead, she wrote: *That's great. Can't wait to hear more when you have time.*

Dignified. Supportive. Unclingy. The gold standard of emotionally mature girlfriend texts.

***

June bled into July.

In Vienna, Yoo-jin sank into his chair during a lighting break. Fourteen hours down, three to go. The physically demanding scenes drained him. Hana had texted. Lately, her replies had been brief, but he assumed the adoption case was keeping her busy.

She understands, he told himself, tapping out a quick text. In the beginning, he would have put in more effort. But Hana wasn't the type to need constant reassurance. She had her own life, her own purpose. That's what made her different.

"Five minutes, Mr. Lee," the assistant director called, and Yoo-jin pocketed his phone, already sinking back into character.

Later that night, too tired to do more than shower before collapsing into bed, a fleeting worry crossed his mind. *Had*

Hana sounded distant?

But sleep claimed him before he could think more about it.

***

Three weeks in, Hana was thriving at work—a landmark case won, her legal team expanded, a packed calendar. Her weekends were filled with friends and social events.

And yet.

Their texts had taken on a different rhythm—short, functional, almost performative in their lightness:

Survived another 16-hour day. Send caffeine.

I'll overnight a gallon of espresso.

Make it two. And a clone to take my place.

I only accept the original. The clone would probably text back faster, though.

A long pause before his reply: *Ouch. But fair. I'll call tomorrow.*

'Tomorrow' came and went without a call. And the day after. And another.

***

"So, your boyfriend is now a pod person," Min-ji declared, pouring more soju into Hana's glass. Thursday night drinks with her friends had become sacred since Yoo-jin's departure.

"Method acting," Hana corrected. "There's a difference."

Sora smirked. "Right. He's not ignoring you. He's *becoming.*"

"Becoming an asshole?" Min-ji suggested.

"Becoming a diplomat with moral quandaries," Hana said. "Very complicated. Very deep."

"Very convenient," Sora muttered.

Hana's phone pinged. She glanced down to find another

contextless photo of Prague at twilight, beautiful and distant. No message.

"Oh look," she held up her screen. "A postcard from the emotional void."

Min-ji squinted at it. "It's like dating National Geographic."

"So what's your move?" Sora turned to Hana. "Send him one of those *We need to talk* texts that induces instant panic?"

Hana typed, deleted, and retyped several responses:

Nice picture. Did you forget I exist? (Delete)

I'm dating your cardboard cutout from your soju ad. It's less emotionally complex. (Delete)

Gorgeous. Hope filming is going well.

"Jesus Christ," Min-ji snatched the phone. "That's so bland it could be served at a hospital cafeteria."

"What do you want me to say?" Hana challenged. "'Hello, remember me'? No thanks."

"There's a vast ocean between doormat and iceberg," Sora said.

Hana reclaimed her device. "I'm not playing the whiny girlfriend. I have a foundation to run."

"And he has a movie to make," Min-ji said. "The question is whether you're both making the same relationship."

Hana waved her chopsticks at Min-ji. "That is exactly it. Normal couples fight about dishwasher loading techniques. We're working out if my boyfriend remembers I'm alive while he's play-acting."

"At least yours forgets you for a reason," Sora said. "Last month, mid-sex, mine said, 'We should file a motion to dismiss.'"

Min-ji choked on her drink. "Please tell me you kicked him out of bed."

"Worse. I agreed with his legal strategy."

They dissolved into laughter, but as the conversation shifted, Hana wondered which was harder—being the one who left or the one who stayed behind.

At least the one who left got to become someone else. The one who stayed became... more alone.

Her phone remained silent for the rest of the evening. She told herself it was fine. She was fine with dating a man whose career path demanded emotional disappearances.

It was a sound, reasonable life choice for an otherwise sane woman: to watch her celebrity boyfriend from afar, like any other fan—but she had yet to discover how uncomfortably close that fandom could get.

FANDOM'S GAZE

It began innocently enough.

Five weeks into Yoo-jin's absence, Hana missed him with an intensity that made her apartment feel like a mausoleum. Their morning call had been brief—him rushing to set, her pretending not to mind.

Restless, she opened her laptop and typed his name into the search bar: *Yoo-jin Lee.*

"Three million results?" she muttered. "That's... excessive."

She clicked the first link. A fan site with enough copyright violations to retain a law firm for a decade. Photos of Yoo-jin in various states of styled perfection dominated the page.

"'*Oppa's* Airport Fashion Evolution,'" she read aloud, scrolling through a timeline. "Fascinating. He went from expensive black clothes to... more expensive black clothes."

A forum thread titled "Yoo-jin Lee's Relationship History: THE DEFINITIVE TIMELINE" had over fifteen thousand comments. *Let's see what the internet thinks it knows about my boyfriend's love life. This should be amusing.*

It was, in fact, not amusing.

"'Sources close to the couple confirm they were secretly engaged.'" Her eyebrows climbed toward her hairline. The "couple" in question was Yoo-jin and an actress he had worked with three years ago. *What sources? The voices in your head?*

She scrolled further, finding a detailed analysis of body language between Yoo-jin and every female co-star from his last five projects. "'Note how his hand lingers at the small of her back. This is not a casual touch but indicates deep intimacy.'" *Or they were posing and he didn't want her to trip on her ridiculous dress.*

Two hours disappeared into a rabbit hole she hadn't known existed. Fan cafés, Instagram accounts dedicated to tracking his movements, YouTube channels analyzing his interviews frame by frame. She found a clip from two months ago, when they were already together.

The interviewer asked if he was dating. "I'm too busy right now," he had answered with an easy smile. "My work is my priority." *Wow. That was convincing. Acting award incoming.*

Of course, she wouldn't have expected him to announce their relationship on television. They had agreed to privacy. But hearing him flat out deny her existence without a hint of discomfort was... unsettling.

The comments beneath the video were worse: "He's too devoted to his craft for a girlfriend." "Any woman who dates him needs to understand he belongs to his fans first." "I've followed him for seven years. No one knows him like I do." *Except maybe the woman who's seen him naked? Just a thought.*

She was about to close her laptop when a new post appeared. "POSSIBLE GIRLFRIEND ALERT: High-end takeout being delivered to oppa's building regularly over the past two months. Same order each time (enough for two people)."

Hana's hand froze over the trackpad. "The deliveries always come at night after 9 PM. I tried to follow the delivery person last week but security stopped me before I could get in the elevator."

"What the actual..." Hana whispered.

"UPDATE: I offered the guy ₩100,000 for the name on the order, but he refused. Said something about "customer privacy" and "restraining orders." Whatever—I'll try again with the next one. Someone will talk." Attached was a blurry photo, taken from across the street, showing a delivery to Yoo-jin's building. The timestamp was from their last evening together, when they had ordered from his favorite sushi place.

Her skin crawled. This wasn't fans creating fantasy relationships. This was an individual actively attempting to invade their privacy, and maybe to expose her.

She shut her laptop with a snap, suddenly feeling vulnerable in her own apartment. Looking around, she half-expected to see a fan peering through her windows, stalking her movements for an internet forum.

Air. I need air. She texted Min-ji: *Free for shopping and drinks? Need to get out of my head.*

***

Downtown Cheongdam-dong buzzed with Saturday energy, sunlight bouncing off the glass facades of high-end boutiques where a simple white t-shirt required a small mortgage. Hana trailed behind Min-ji, who was power-browsing through racks with single-minded focus.

"That's the third time you've checked your phone in five minutes. Trouble in celebrity paradise?"

"He's running late for a video call."

"Again? Your boyfriend needs a better scheduling assistant." Min-ji held up a camel-colored blazer that cost roughly what Hana paid in monthly rent. "What about this?"

"For me or you?"

"You. You've got to up your game if you're dating 'Korea's Sexiest Man Alive.'"

"My clothes have to be compatible with subway commutes and sitting at a desk for fourteen hours."

Min-ji shrugged. "Speaking of your golden boy, have you told Jae-won yet?"

Hana pretended to examine a silk scarf. “No. And I’m not looking forward to it.”

“He’s going to lose his mind. Not because it’s Yoo-jin Lee, but because it’s Yoo-jin Lee—*his client.* I can’t wait to see his face.”

“That’s why you and Sora are there. Safety in numbers.”

“I still can’t believe you’re going out with him. When you first told me, I thought you were having a stroke.”

Hana grinned. “It took you long enough.”

“And you’ve managed to keep it secret from everyone but us. I’m impressed.” Min-ji examined a pair of earrings. “Though I’m still waiting for you to bring him to dinner. I need photographic evidence for posterity.”

“That’s why I don’t bring him anywhere.”

They left the boutique and stepped onto the crowded sidewalk. As they waited at the crosswalk, Hana’s eyes drifted up to a massive digital billboard across the street.

There was Yoo-jin in all his glory—the new campaign for Poseidon watches. Half-submerged in crystal blue water, dark hair slicked back, droplets clinging to his perfect shoulders. The watch gleamed on his wrist as he gazed into the camera with that smoldering intensity that made her knees weak even now.

Min-ji followed her gaze upward and smirked. “Must be weird seeing your boyfriend sixty feet tall and mostly naked in public.”

“I’m used to it,” Hana replied, though she wasn’t—not really.

“Fans mobbing him everywhere he goes, constant speculation about his love life, half of Korea thinking they’re dating him through their screens…” Min-ji shook her head. “I don’t know how you handle it.”

“Divide and survive.”

“Well, you can’t divide Jae-won’s reaction. He’ll have an

aneurysm." Min-ji grabbed her arm. "Come on, I want prime seating to see his face when you drop this bomb."

***

The Cobalt Room was quiet for a Saturday. Sora and Jae-won were already seated, scrolling through phones with mindless indifference.

Sora looked up first. "You're late. I just ordered martinis for everyone."

Min-ji slid into the booth with a mischievous smile. "Time to tell Jae-won your little secret. He's the only one left in the dark."

Jae-won gave her a pointed look. "What?"

"Hana's been dating someone," Sora said.

"Is that so?" Jae-won looked astonished. "Who is it? Do we know him?"

Hana took a deliberate sip of her martini. "Yoo-jin Lee."

Jae-won's face went slack. "Yoo-jin Lee," he repeated. "The actor. *My client.*"

"That's the one," Hana confirmed.

"When she told us, I almost choked on my *bibimbap,*" Sora laughed.

"Jesus," Jae-won muttered, looking like he was drafting liability waivers in his head. "How long?"

"Six months."

"Six months?" He stared at her, martini glass frozen halfway to his mouth, olive threatening to abandon ship. "And you didn't think to mention it to your friend who literally handles his contracts?" His expression cycled through shock, betrayal, and professional panic so fast it looked like he was going through a system reboot.

"I respect his privacy," Hana said. "And mine."

"Privacy doesn't exist when dating someone like Yoo-jin Lee," Jae-won said. "There are entire forums tracking his movements. Women who camp outside his building. Fan sites that speculate which side of the bed he sleeps on."

Hana stirred her martini. "I know. I... researched."

Sora reached for Hana's hand. "Hey... we're not judging. Okay, maybe a little. You know what you've signed up for, right?"

"Fan death squads?" Hana said dryly.

"You joke, but remember what happened to Karina from *aespa*?" Min-ji countered. "When news leaked that she was going out with Lee Jae-wook, fans sent protest trucks to SM Entertainment with electronic billboards saying 'Is the love given to you by your fans not enough?' They harassed her until they broke up, and she had to publicly apologize—for dating."

"And Chen from EXO," Jae-won added. "When he got married, fans demanded he leave the group. They held actual candlelight vigils like someone had died."

"For what?" Hana asked. "The death of their fantasy?"

"Precisely," Sora said. "A thirty-two-year-old man wanted a family, and they acted like he'd committed treason."

"Or take Goo Hara," Min-ji's voice dropped. "Her ex-boyfriend threatened to release their sex videos. After years of harassment from the public, she—"

A somber silence fell over the table.

"And remember Yoon Ji-eun?" he continued.

"Who?" Hana asked.

"Exactly," he said. "She was a rising indie songwriter. Won the KBS New Artist Award three years ago, composed for some top groups. She and Yoo-jin were photographed next to each other at an industry dinner with twenty other people."

"What happened?" A chill crept up Hana's spine.

"Rumors started. His more obsessive fans—*saesangs*, they call themselves—dug into her past, found old social media posts they deemed 'disrespectful.' They tracked her movements, harassed her online. Within a week, she lost two major contracts. Brands dropped her. Her agency reconsidered their relationship."

"Did he help her?" Hana asked.

"His management advised against it," Jae-won replied. "Engaging only validates the connection."

"Jesus," Sora breathed.

"That's the industry," Min-ji shrugged. "It's like dating royalty, except the kingdom's full of unhinged teenagers with too much time and adults who think they own his soul because they watched all his movies and dramas ten times."

"These celebrities sneak around like they're in a spy movie," Sora said. "Even that's not enough sometimes."

"For the record," Jae-won added, "most of his fans are decent humans. They run charity projects in his name and send gifts to orphanages on his birthday. The majority would love to see him happy."

"The majority doesn't matter when the minority is willing to slash your tires and send you dead animals," Min-ji muttered.

"Has that happened?" Hana asked, alarmed.

"Not with Yoo-jin's fan base specifically," Jae-won clarified, shooting Min-ji a stern look.

"Which is why," Sora said, "we think you might be happier with someone... normal. Someone whose job description doesn't include being the object of mass worship."

"Like Hyun-woo from tax litigation," Jae-won suggested. "Stable. Dependable. Hasn't had death threats since the Samsung audit."

"I didn't plan this," Hana sighed. "It... just happened."

"We're only worried," Sora squeezed her hand. "The power imbalance alone—"

"There is no power imbalance," Hana cut in. "I have my own career. I'm not some starry-eyed fangirl."

"True," Min-ji conceded. "You're probably the only

woman in Seoul who had to google him after meeting him."

"I knew who he was," Hana protested. "Vaguely."

"Vaguely," Jae-won repeated. "The man's face is on the Lotte World Tower."

"Is it really?" Hana blinked.

"No, but the fact that you believed it proves my point," Jae-won said. "If you're determined to do this, at least let me help with security protocols, media strategies—"

"I don't need a media strategy to date someone."

"In this case, you absolutely do," Sora insisted. "But whatever happens, we've got your back. And we know people who can make bodies disappear if those psycho fans come for you."

"That's comforting... and disturbing," Hana said.

Min-ji raised her glass. "To Hana dating above her station."

"To inevitable heartbreak and excellent rebound stories," Sora added.

Hana clinked her glass against theirs, laughing despite herself.

"So," Min-ji leaned in, eyes gleaming, "does he really have an eight-pack, or are those abs computer-generated?"

MISSING MOMENTS

Milan

"Again! From the top!"

Yoo-jin dragged himself from the murky lake water for the twentieth time, clothes plastered to his skin. Eight hours of jumping into the same damn spot.

"I need more authenticity," the director shouted.

You pretentious asshole. What does "more authentic drowning" even mean?

"Problem with take nineteen?" he asked, knees almost buckling from fatigue.

The director gestured emphatically. "Your face when you break the surface—I want more desperation, more primal fear."

The crew looked as haggard as he did, moving equipment with the slowness of people pushing past exhaustion. 11:45 PM.

"Action!"

Yoo-jin flung himself backward into the dark water, letting it consume him. He thrashed beneath the surface, lungs burning before clawing his way up in a frenzy of desperate movement.

"Cut! Perfect! That's the one."

Twenty takes to get one usable shot. This fucking guy.

In his trailer, he peeled off the soaked clothes, pulled on a robe, and collapsed into a chair. The skin on his face was raw, his eyes bloodshot. Almost reflexively, he opened Instagram, thumb scrolling until he stopped, finger hovering over the screen.

Hana's face filled the display, surrounded by friends in what looked like a private room at an upscale restaurant. Candles flickered on a cake before her. The caption was understated: *Great night, great company.*

But the comments told a different story:

Happy birthday, Hana!

Wish I could've been there!

Hope you had the best night!

Another year wiser and more beautiful.

"No. No, no," he thought, his blood running cold.

He checked the date of the post. Four days ago.

Her birthday. He had completely missed her birthday. Not only did he not call on the day, but he didn't even realize he'd forgotten.

You worthless shit. Just like with Ji-yeon. His ex-girlfriend's birthday ten years ago, rescheduled four times for shoots until she walked out. "I just can't compete with your career." He'd sworn never to repeat that mistake.

Despite the late hour in Milan, it would be early morning in Seoul. Before he could overthink it, he hit the call button.

Seoul

Hana stirred at the insistent buzzing of her phone. 7:08 AM.

When she saw his name, her first thought was something bad had happened. Yoo-jin didn't make spontaneous calls these days.

"Hello? Is everything all right?" Her voice was thick with sleep.

"Baby, I'm sorry. I'm so sorry," his words tumbled out in a rush. "I deserve to die."

She blinked, pushing herself up against the headboard. She understood. He had seen the Instagram post—four days after her birthday.

A wave of disappointment washed over her, followed by guilt. She'd wondered if he would notice at all. The day had passed with no call, no message, only rationalization that he was busy. *What did you expect? That he'd stop production to call you? Get over yourself.*

Now, hearing the genuine distress in his voice, she softened. "Don't be dramatic. If you die, I'll have to go back to dating apps, and we both know how that ends," she replied with forced lightness.

"Hana... I don't deserve you being nice about this."

"I'm not," she said, shifting under her sheets. "I'm practical. Do you know how exhausting it would be to train a new man to find the right spots?"

A surprised laugh escaped him, tension breaking. "I can't believe I forgot. There's no excuse."

"You're right, there isn't," she agreed, an edge in her voice. "But right now, I'm lying in bed half-naked, and that seems more interesting to discuss than your failings as a boyfriend."

It was deliberate, this pivot to sexy banter, this distraction from his guilt. Not because she wasn't hurt, but because she was hurting for both of them. For what their relationship was becoming under the strain of distance.

By the time they disconnected, the sharp edge of disappointment had dulled—but not disappeared. *Get used to it. If you want this man, you'll have to adjust expectations.*

Back in Milan

Yoo-jin hung up, staring at the ceiling of his trailer. The call had ended better than he deserved, but the knot in his stomach remained.

He searched for a Seoul florist and ordered their largest arrangement of peonies. Card: *Consider this down payment on proper groveling when I get back. The next fifty birthdays will be celebrated with embarrassing extravagance.*

He hit send, then second-guessed himself. Too presumptuous to assume they'd have fifty years together when he couldn't even remember one birthday?

That night, between wardrobe fittings and script revisions, he typed another message: *One more month of filming. Not asking you to wait, only letting you know I'm counting the days.*

Her response came as he was climbing into bed: *I'll be here.*

Not a promise of forever, but an acknowledgment of present commitment. That would have to be enough for now.

Two Weeks Later

"Positions, everyone!"

Today's scene: Yoo-jin's character confronting the woman he loved after discovering her involvement in a deadly conspiracy. The actress Choi Min-ah took her mark.

"Remember," the director said, "this is more than anger or betrayal. There's still love here—complicated, perhaps impossible, but there."

Yoo-jin nodded, but his mind was already drifting to his call with Hana. Now, on set, Yoo-jin let that moment fill him—her unexpected grace, his guilt, the absurdity and tenderness of someone who knew all his blind spots and forgave him anyway.

"Action!"

Yoo-jin moved across the ornate hotel suite with measured steps, stopping at the window where Min-ah stood with her back to him.

"Were you ever going to tell me?" His voice carried an

intensity that hadn't been there in rehearsals.

Min-ah turned, her expression faltering at this different approach. "Would you have believed me if I had?"

"I would have believed anything you said." *I believed Hana when she said she forgave me.*

As the scene progressed, Yoo-jin reached for emotions drawn from real experiences. When he pulled Min-ah to him, he wasn't seeing her face. He was remembering Hana the night before he left—how she'd clung to him. "Don't you dare forget me," she'd whispered. His lips trembled as he kissed his co-star.

"Cut!" the director called, his voice thick with emotion. "That was... top-notch."

Min-ah stepped back, fanning herself. "Wow," she murmured, giving Yoo-jin an appraising look. "Whatever you're channeling today, keep it coming."

***

The pattern only deepened as filming went on. For tenderness, Yoo-jin summoned the memory of Hana's drowsy morning smiles. For fury, he bled out the helplessness of missing her across continents and time zones. After an intense scene, Min-ah hurried to catch up as Yoo-jin walked to his trailer. "That was something else," she said. "The way you looked at me... it was so real."

It was real. Just not for you. "That's the job, right? Making the audience believe."

The photographer captured it all: his hand on Min-ah's back, fingers tucking hair behind her ear—gestures so familiar with Hana he didn't realize he was doing them with another woman.

"You two have amazing energy together," the documentarian commented one day.

"It's all him. He makes it easy."

Yoo-jin, distracted, didn't notice how Min-ah's smile

sharpened when the camera turned away, or the way her eyes tracked him with intent.

***

"The dailies look incredible," His manager Ji-hoon told him over dinner. "The studio execs are calling it your breakthrough performance."

Yoo-jin only shrugged, checking his watch for his scheduled call with Hana.

"There's something else," the older man added, his tone shifting. "The promotional team noticed the chemistry between you and Min-ah. They want to leverage it for marketing."

"Meaning what, exactly?"

"Nothing explicit. Just... allowing speculation about a romance to build interest."

"That's not happening." Yoo-jin's voice cut like steel.

"It would be temporary," Ji-hoon pressed. "Only through the launch period."

"The work speaks for itself. I won't disrespect what I have with Hana for publicity."

Ji-hoon nodded. "I'll convey your position. But be prepared—if the attraction on screen is as powerful as everyone's saying, the gossip will happen regardless."

***

After the filming wrapped, Min-ah scrolled through the photographs the documentarian had shared in private. Dozens of images of Yoo-jin looking at her with apparent longing, his hands on her waist, shoulder, arm. Without context, they told a specific story.

She selected several suggestive ones and sent them to her publicist with a brief message: *Save these. We'll use them when the film releases.*

She poured herself a glass of wine and studied the photos again. She recognized the difference between acting and reality —and knew whatever Yoo-jin was channeling in their scenes had nothing to do with her.

The emotion was real. The target was someone else.

But the public wouldn't know that. Only that her name would be linked with his in the press, her own star rising alongside his performance.

"Thanks for the career boost, Yoo-jin." She raised her glass to the images on her screen. "And sorry about your girlfriend."

HONEYMOON REPRIEVE

September arrived at last.

Three months had passed like an eternity. Yoo-jin stepped through Incheon's VIP gate, enveloped by four suited men creating a barrier between him and the crowd. Despite his agency's attempts at discretion, photographers and well-wishers had tracked his arrival.

"Oppa! Oppa!" His fans chanted.

"Hana! Hana!" His brain furiously countered.

His legs wanted to break into a sprint. Every muscle urged him to push past security, to move faster toward the door where he knew she was waiting. Instead, he maintained the unhurried pace expected of a celebrity, smiling and bowing with a camera-ready expression that revealed nothing of the countdown clock in his head.

Walk, don't run. Smile, don't search. Twenty more steps to the exit. Nineteen. Eighteen.

The escorts took a different route to avoid the densest part of the crowd. Yoo-jin followed, his smile in place, while his knuckles whitened on the handle of his carry-on.

Outside, a black Escalade with heavy tinted windows idled at the curb, engine running. After a final farewell gesture to the persistent throng, he slipped into the vehicle's cool interior, his movements casual despite the flutter behind his ribs.

***

Inside the car, Hana checked her reflection for the fourth time in five minutes. Her nails tapped an impatient rhythm against her phone. Through the glass, she could see the main entrance where Yoo-jin would emerge.

When his security appeared, she scooted to the opposite side of the backseat, attempting to look relaxed instead of counting down the seconds. To her annoyance, her heart leapt as she caught a glimpse of him in the midst of the crowd. *Act normal. Don't lunge at him like some desperate Harlequin heroine.*

The car door opened at last.

Yoo-jin slid in beside her, filling the small space. He looked exhausted, a bit thinner, and so familiar that Hana had to curl her fingers into her palm to keep from reaching for him.

"Hi," he said, voice rough with emotion. His eyes said everything he couldn't.

"Welcome back," she said with a grin, a maelstrom of feelings in those two words.

The driver pulled into traffic. In the front passenger seat, his manager focused on his phone, giving them the illusion of privacy.

Under the cover of the center console, Yoo-jin's pinky finger found Hana's. That small touch—a ridiculous, teenage gesture—sent electricity up her arm. Three months. She wouldn't last three minutes.

They kept an appropriate distance during the ride through Seoul. She pointed out construction along the Han River while he commented on the weather in Milan. Anyone watching would have seen nothing but old acquaintances catching up.

But Yoo-jin's smile—the real one, not the one he used for cameras—made Hana check her watch.

When the elevator door of his penthouse closed, Hana

tossed her purse onto the entryway table. It missed, hitting the floor with a thud.

"Hi," he said, now shy despite the racy text messages they had been exchanging over the last twenty-four hours.

"Three months away and that's what you open with?" She gave him a dry look, but couldn't maintain the façade. "Hi yourself."

They collided somewhere between the foyer and the living room—her elbow catching him in the jaw as she whipped off her sweater, his watch tangling in her hair.

"Sorry," he said, not sounding sorry at all as he kissed her neck. "Coordination suffers after twelve hours on a plane."

"And yet your hair looks perfect. I hate you a little."

"No, you don't," he murmured against her ear.

Her impatient fingers found the buttons of his shirt, fumbling until she gave up and yanked. A button pinged off the lamp and rolled somewhere under the couch.

She stepped back to examine him. "You've lost weight."

He ran his hands up her arms. "You've been lifting."

"Boxing, actually. Min-ji's idea. She said I was getting cranky."

His laugh was interrupted when she pulled him toward the bedroom, both of them stumbling over his discarded jacket.

"This is going well..." He steadied himself on the doorframe.

She was already working at his belt. "Shut up. We can be graceful next time."

They hit the bed with more enthusiasm than elegance.

He drew back, eyes traveling over her face, suddenly serious. "Some days in Milan, I wasn't sure if I'd made you up."

She caressed his face. "I'm here. I'm real. And I'm getting impatient."

Their kiss had an edge of desperation, as if afraid the other might disappear again.

When he moved inside her, they stilled, playfulness gone. She blinked at the sudden emotion. “Don't you dare stop now,” she said, voice catching. They found their rhythm somewhere between familiar and new, as if picking up a conversation interrupted mid-sentence months ago.

Later, wrapped in bedsheets, Yoo-jin traced patterns on Hana's bare shoulder.

“I thought about this every day. Sometimes it was the only thing that got me through those endless filming days.”

She propped herself up on one elbow, studying his face—thinner than when he had left, more lines of fatigue around his eyes. “Was it worth it?”

“Professionally? Yes. The film will be good. But personally—it was a struggle.” He pulled her closer. “What about you?”

“I won't lie. It was... hard.”

“Poor baby,” he whispered, stroking her cheek. “I'm sorry.”

She brushed hair from his forehead. “Plus, I had to explain to my assistant why I couldn't date her dentist brother.”

He laughed. “A dentist? Should I be worried?”

“Absolutely. Perfect teeth and a steady income—I'm doomed.”

“I've missed your sass,” he said, pulling her close.

Her fingers traced the outline of his lips. “I know. That's why you came back.”

***

Late October.

Yoo-jin had been back fifty-eight days. Not that Hana was counting—except she was. Counted them like rosary beads: one for each lazy morning in bed, every meeting she bolted from early, each smug text he sent with a shirtless selfie and a smoothie in hand. His physical recovery required hydration, protein, and enough sex to qualify as cardio. *I should be ashamed how fast I rearranged my life for him. But I'm not.*

He slept for hours those first few weeks, knocked out cold on her sofa like a man who had run a marathon with no finish line. She would cover him with a blanket, set a bowl of blueberries on the coffee table, and go back to her emails—all the while pretending she wasn't mildly obsessed. *How is this man real?*

He would sometimes open his eyes to catch a glimpse of her next to him. *How is she still here? After that vanishing act. And yet—the blueberries.*

When he wasn't asleep, he was a chaos machine. Tossing protein powder across her kitchen like it was confetti, doing pull-ups on her balcony, complaining his body forgot how to ride a motorcycle after returning from a solo spin and grumbling, "My ass hurts."

"You're soft now," she teased.

He scowled. "I'm healing."

"Same thing."

All that time away and she's still vicious. Thank god. He got her back that night—twice.

They developed a rhythm: quiet breakfasts, late-night walks, running through parks like fugitives with him trailing her by thirty feet, hoodie up. They never arrived together at social events. But across a crowded room, he would raise his glass to her, the softest smirk tugging at his mouth. Their own little secret. She would return a discreet signal from the other side. *This is ridiculous. We're grown adults playing spy games at cocktail parties.*

Sometimes it was too perfect. Like a fairytale waiting for someone to slam the book shut.

He knew it too. She would catch it in his eyes when he held her like she might vanish. But she didn't. Instead, she stuffed her freezer with mangoes, put protein powder on auto-delivery. *Nesting. That's what birds do before the storm comes.*

They made music together. Her on the piano, him humming nonsense lyrics.

They fought at times. About dumb things. His diet, her meetings, his innovative recipes. "I'm a creative," he sniffed over burned scallops. "You're stifling me." But then he would sidle up to her as she chopped vegetables and wrap his arms around her waist, bury his face in her neck, and whisper something filthy to make her drop the knife.

She loved him. God help her, she did. For those few weeks, it was enough. The rest of the world could fall away.

But niggling thoughts intruded. *The musical tour is coming up. Then the film launch. More absences. More secrecy.*

For now, they were in their bubble. But bubbles, as they both knew from childhood, didn't last.

ADORATION'S PRICE

Over breakfast one day in November, Yoo-jin took a deep breath before speaking. "I need to tell you something."

Hana looked up from her coffee, alert to his tone.

"I have to leave again. In three days." The statement hung between them, heavy.

"For how long?"

"Six weeks. It's for a rock musical. A four-country tour." He reached for her hand. "I committed to it last year, long before we met."

"*Midnight Reverie?*" she asked, surprising him with her knowledge.

"You know it?"

"I saw clips on YouTube while you were in Europe."

Midnight Reverie had been an unexpected hit five years ago, cementing his crossover appeal. Playing Milo, a composer who lost his hearing and descended into madness, Yoo-jin had turned a potentially gimmicky character into a transcendent role. The critics had been skeptical until opening night, when his performance silenced every doubt. Two years of sold-out shows followed.

"It's the fifth-anniversary revival," he explained. "I couldn't say no. *Milo* changed everything for me."

"Six weeks—that's not too long," she repeated, fiddling with her coffee cup. *Liar. It is too long. We just got back our rhythm, and now—*

"The Tokyo run is two weeks. You could come for a weekend and see the show."

She nodded, attempting a weak smile. "Sure—why not?" *Don't complain. Don't explain. What else is new?*

That night, as they lay together in the darkness, Hana voiced the thought in her head since his announcement. "This is your life, isn't it? Coming and going. Long absences, brief reunions."

Yoo-jin was quiet for a long moment. "Yes. At least for now. There are times when projects cluster, momentum builds. Opportunities can't be passed up."

"And other times?"

"Quieter periods. Time to breathe."

Hana thought about Simon, who'd made similar promises: *One final story in Tibet, and I'll be back for a while.* That "while" had been three days before he was gone again.

"I mean it," Yoo-jin said. "I've come to a point where I can choose what matters."

Simon never reached that point. His work had always been his priority. Now, looking at Yoo-jin's earnest expression, Hana recalled that familiar dread.

What she didn't yet realize was that Simon's unpredictable schedule would seem simple compared to sharing Yoo-jin with millions of strangers who worshipped him.

***

Two weeks into Yoo-jin's tour, Hana traveled to Tokyo with Min-ji and Sora. Their itinerary had been equal parts sightseeing and self-indulgence—laughter over ramen, getting lost in Harajuku, Sora dragging them through an entire underground mall for socks with cartoon dogs. But tonight wasn't about tourist thrills.

It was the night of Yoo-jin's show.

"I still can't believe we're seeing your boyfriend on stage," Min-ji said as they threaded through the crowd around Shibuya Crossing. "And not just seeing—witnessing the man, the myth, the walking fever dream."

Hana gave her a sidelong glance. "He's not a myth. He leaves towels on the floor."

The street hummed with anticipation. Fans streamed in clusters, LED signs blinking his name. Yoo-jin's face stared out from every surface—eyes smudged with kohl, bleeding charisma.

Outside the venue, excitement had curdled to frenzy. Not so much a queue as a living organism—people jostling, clutching photocards, sobbing into plushies. Hana's stomach did a slow turn. *So this is what devotion looks like.*

"Is it too late to pretend I'm a tourist who got lost?" she muttered, eyeing a group doing a fan chant with frightening fervor.

Inside, the energy doubled down. The theater wasn't cavernous, but appeared to have no ceiling. Lights gleamed in concentric rings overhead, and the velvet seats were deep enough to swallow her. The air was a battleground of scents—vanilla, strawberry, florals—all layered over sweat and overheated bodies, erupting like a panic attack in a cosmetics aisle.

"He sobbed in Osaka." The girl behind Hana clutched her chest. "I watched that clip a hundred times. My soul left my body." Someone else whispered, "I brought my letter. Sprayed it with my blood-type perfume. He'll know it's me."

Hana pressed her palms to her knees. *This is totally normal. Only ten thousand people waiting to fall in love with your boyfriend.*

The lights dimmed, and the crowd exhaled as one. What came next struck like a thunderclap. People screamed—not cheered, screeched. Spotlights exploded, smoke curled, and he appeared.

Not Yoo-jin. *Milo.*

He strode through the haze, face tortured and magnetic. The transformation was immediate, terrifying. His voice cut through the chaos—low, rough, beautiful. He sang like the world was ending and he meant to go out with a confession. When he moved across the stage, it was a merging of choreography and instinct.

The audience was feral. Women clutched their chests, reached out to him, mouthed the lyrics with trembling lips. One woman had tears streaming down her cheeks. Hana tried to ground herself—checked for Sora, who was leaning forward grinning like a kid at a magic show, and Min-ji, who whispered "*Holy hell*" under her breath.

But their energy wasn't hers. *People are losing their minds over a guy singing. This isn't fandom, it's hysteria.*

The show surged onward—sharp scene changes, shadow play, crescendos that made her jump. Then midway through the second act, the storm quieted.

A spotlight dropped, pressing Yoo-jin in the center like a pin through silk.

The stage went dark around him. No set, no distractions. Only him, a microphone, and silence so thick it pressed against her ribs.

He was dressed in black from head to toe. His jacket shimmered with sequins, catching light and scattering it like mirror shards. Sweat darkened the collar of his shirt, and his artfully tousled hair clung to his temples.

The first notes of *Midnight Confession* broke through. A whisper, fragile, broken. When he looked up, his eyes found her like a radar. His expression shifted—barely—but it struck her like a jolt. The world shrank. Ten thousand people disappeared. His voice lifted, deeper now, warmer, threaded with a private message meant only for her. *Is he—? No. He can't be—*

But she knew that look. The slight narrowing of his eyes. The way he anchored his weight on one leg. The tension in his grip on the mic. The half-reach of his hand. Not choreographed. Not rehearsed. He locked eyes with her. His voice climbed, trembled, steadied.

"When midnight finds us both awake—

And darkness gives us room to break—

I'll tell you everything I've held inside—

No more lies, no more pride—"

Around her, women were crying. Others swayed. A few clasped hands like they were praying. *They all think it's for them. Exactly like I think it's for me.*

When the final note faded, he bowed his head, eyes closed.

For a heartbeat, silence—before the theater detonated.

Not applause but eruption. People launched to their feet, stomping, screaming. Glowsticks slashed the air. A young woman sobbed, mouthing "Marry me, marry me." Fans chanted his name like a battle cry.

It wasn't a curtain call, but a fevered chaos of a street protest—only with pink headbands and rhinestones. Their love for him wasn't polite or restrained—it was ferocious. Every cheer and every outstretched hand were pulling him toward them.

They were worshiping *her* man.

A hot panic shot through her ribcage. She shrank down in her seat, pulse screaming in her ears. Her fingernails dug into the armrest. *This isn't applause. This is a stampede.*

She darted a look at Sora and Min-ji—both cheering, laughing, caught up in the moment like kids on a thrill ride. They didn't feel the significance of it. But Hana did.

And all she could think was: *How do you hold onto someone*

the whole world wants to claim?

***

"Come on," Min-ji tugged her arm. "VIP passes, remember? Let's go backstage."

Hana's brain was still buzzing from the performance as they approached the stage door. They turned the corner, and the sight rooted her in place.

The narrow corridor leading to the dressing rooms was a human sardine can—jam-packed with women crying, shouting, clutching photos and gifts like sacrificial offerings. The air smelled of cheap perfume and sweat.

Two security guards stood at the entrance, faces strained like they were holding up a dam with their bare hands. "Step back! Authorized guests only!" one shouted as if into a hurricane.

Min-ji pulled out their VIP passes, assessing the chaos. "This doesn't look promising."

The crowd was a swaying mob, closing in. A woman caught sight of their passes, eyes narrowing with suspicion. "Where did you get those?"

Sora shoved her way through, waving her pass like a flag of defiance. The crowd shifted like an angry tide. The energy went from curious to hostile in an instant. "*Ya*, you bitch!" someone spat, eyes fixed on Hana, "Who do you think you are?"

A tall, heavyset woman at the back spoke up, her voice cutting through the din like a blade. "Hey princess—you think you're special?" An icy sneer. "Watch yourself, or someone'll teach you what happens to girls like you."

Hana's stomach twisted. *What the hell did that mean?*

She lifted her eyes to the woman's and found nothing warm. No fan worship. Only cold, unfeeling possessiveness. *Holy shit, does she have his name tattooed on her chest or what?*

"Let's go," Hana said, voice tight. "This isn't worth it."

Min-ji gave her a confused look, but Hana was already backing away, weaving through the press of bodies toward the exit. Behind her, the murmurs rose into a low, menacing hum that made her skin crawl.

***

"Oh, cheer up! We should've expected this!" Sora and Min-ji were happily downing beer and savoring sushi. The restaurant was quiet and exclusive, a welcome refuge after the backstage chaos. Hana stayed silent.

"Okay, spill," Min-ji said, waving her chopsticks at her. "You just saw your man deliver the performance of a lifetime, and you're sitting there like you just got your tax bill."

Hana exhaled, rolling her glass between her hands. "It's nothing."

Sora gave her a skeptical look. "That's a lie."

Hana sighed. "Fine. It's... watching him up there, seeing how he owns the stage, how much people worship him—it's kind of insane, right?"

Min-ji smirked. "Oh, completely. Did you see those women in the front? Tears. Full-on religious experience. I was expecting someone to throw a wedding veil at his feet."

"That's a level of devotion I cannot compete with."

Sora snorted. "Who's competing? They're in love with a *concept*. You're dating the actual human man."

"Yeah, but the concept is very well-packaged."

Min-ji cackled. "Hey, if I can have his face on a kitchen magnet, I wouldn't complain."

Sora leaned in. "Okay, but seriously. Why are you weird about this? You knew he was famous."

"I know that." Hana twisted her napkin. "I didn't realize how much people claim him. I made the mistake of reading fan comments—"

Min-ji raised a brow. "We talked about this, didn't we?"

"Yes. And based on the way they discuss his last rumored girlfriend, I should preemptively flee the country."

Sora's expression turned thoughtful. "And does Yoo-jin know you feel this way?"

Hana shrugged. "Not really. I mean—what do I say? 'Hey, babe, I love what you do, but your fans terrify me?'"

"As a matter of fact—yes. Exactly that."

***

When Hana returned to her hotel, several messages from Yoo-jin were waiting:

Saw you in the audience. Meant everything to have you there.

Was hoping to see you after, but I heard about the mob outside.

Call me when you get back?

She fidgeted before typing: *Just got in. Call in 10?*

Her phone rang within five minutes. "Impatient much?" she teased.

"I was giving you a head start," he shot back, his voice still humming with post-performance adrenaline. "What did you think?"

"You were amazing. I'm so proud of you."

"Really?" The eagerness in his tone made her smile. Despite thousands of adoring fans, her opinion counted for him.

"Really. The way you strutted across the stage, connected with the audience... It was something else."

"During *Midnight Confession*—it was like all the stars aligned. Performing with you watching... it was perfect."

"Funny, I thought you were singing to that girl sobbing in the second row."

Yoo-jin groaned. "Don't remind me. I was terrified she'd

throw something at me."

"Like her dignity?"

"Like her bra," he deadpanned. "Which, by the way, happened once. Full launch from the balcony."

She snorted. "Iconic."

"Hana, focus. I'm being *romantic* here."

"Right, right." She bit back a laugh. "Stars aligning, perfect moment, deep artistic fulfillment. Got it."

He huffed. "You're impossible."

"You love it."

A pause on his end. Then, softer: "I do."

Her teasing faded, warmth unfurling under her skin. "Get some rest, rock star. I'll talk to you tomorrow."

"Hana, wait—" He cleared his throat. "I—I love you."

Her heart stuttered for a beat. *Love.* He'd actually said it, making everything real and pitching her into uncharted territory.

She wet her lips, buying herself a second she didn't have. "I—um... me too."

She hung up, staring at her phone. *Am I really ready for this?*

***

That night, Hana was wide awake in bed and reviewing every red flag from the evening. *Could I really be a part of his world—when another part of it wants to claw my face off if it knows I'm dating him?*

She had not expected the fan hostility, as if she had wandered into their private fantasy uninvited. No words had been exchanged, but the message was clear: *You don't belong here. He's ours.*

Not Yoo-jin the man. *Yoo-jin the K-drama star and public property*. Trimmed, polished, and available in the way they demanded. She tried to rationalize it. *It's a fringe. A small, unhinged subset. Most of his fans are normal, kind. Just a little overexcited.*

She rolled onto her side, mind still prickling with unease. Not quite fear, but a sharp awareness of what it meant to be with Yoo-jin. *This is what dating a celebrity entails. The fine print I didn't read. And I call myself a lawyer.*

She wouldn't run away. But she wouldn't pretend it didn't rattle her either. She sighed into the darkness—it would be a problem for another day.

SOLO SPOTLIGHT

It was mid-December when Yoo-jin completed his tour to rave reviews. He'd sung and emoted across Asia, leaving behind weeping fans and a glittering press. His final performance went viral before he even changed out of his costume.

It was the kind of career high people spent years chasing. He rode it like a seasoned surfer—graceful, effortless, and a tad smug.

Offers rolled in—Cannes directors, Netflix thrillers, variety shows. Photo shoots, luxury brand campaigns, private screenings. Baseball games with friends, midweek golf, rooftop industry mixers.

He always texted Hana. *Thinking of you* or *Wish you were here.* But he never asked her to come. And she never invited herself.

He still came over, still reached for her in bed. Still kissed her shoulder and called her *"baby."* But his schedule was full in that bright, self-satisfied way when life was going exceedingly well, and you didn't stop to ask why it felt so good.

Hana beamed at every accolade, storing each glowing review with the secret pride of a mother watching her prodigy. In the meantime, her foundation's calendar also filled up—a pediatric care drive, an orphanage reform initiative, a closed-door session with a visiting ambassador. She hosted donor brunches and receptions. Sent him invitations, like always.

He declined, like always. Sent flowers, as if they could attend in his place.

She put them in the hallway. To anyone observing, she was radiant, poised. No one commented when she switched her phone to silent around 8 PM. In case he texted—or didn't.

***

They maintained the illusion that nothing had changed in the weeks following Yoo-jin's return.

Christmas came and went. Hana had turned down the Westons in Surrey, that close-knit tribe and their strange holiday rituals—*joke gifts, charades, pudding that might explode.*

And what had he done? Taken endless calls. Smiled through congratulations. Forgotten her. *Who needs a family that notices when you go quiet—when you've got a boyfriend who replies "lol" three hours later?*

They stole nights at his apartment or hers—never consecutive, never establishing a pattern anyone could track. The careful maintenance of his public image as Korea's most eligible bachelor hung over them like an unspoken contract. *Clause one: Do not be photographed looking even remotely acquainted.*

He was always rushing somewhere—rehearsals, interviews, meetings—arriving late and leaving early. She never complained. And he never asked if she was okay. They both smiled, touched, laughed like before. But beneath the surface, their dynamic had shifted—quiet, invisible, like a fault line forming. *A few tiny cracks. Nothing to worry about. Smile, nod, and kick a rug over them.*

"Min-ji's having a small dinner party on Saturday," Hana mentioned one evening as they washed dishes side by side. "Nothing fancy. Six people at her apartment."

Yoo-jin's hands stilled under the running water. "Six is

still six witnesses."

"They're lawyers, not paparazzi," she said, keeping her tone casual. "And her place is in a secure building."

"Even so." He handed her a dripping plate. "It might get awkward."

She nodded, accepting both the plate and the deflection. "True. But thought I'd mention it."

He brushed a kiss against her temple. "Thanks for understanding."

"Of course." She dried the plate, putting away the disappointment with the dish towel.

She didn't tell him about the legal aid fundraiser the following week at the Singaporean Embassy. Or her colleague's wedding where she danced alone while the older matrons assessed her marriageability. Just as she didn't comment when he canceled their dinner plans because fans were tracking his movements more than usual that day. *He's not yours in public. But at least he's consistent.*

This was the arrangement. This was what she signed up for. *But it's still crap.*

***

Hana was half-asleep when the door clicked open. 2:03 AM. The scent of beer, cologne, and bad decisions drifted in before Yoo-jin did. He kicked off his shoes and stumbled through her apartment like he'd lived there for years.

He slipped under the covers and wrapped himself around her—arm across her waist, leg thrown over her hip, face buried in her neck. "Hey," he murmured, voice thick with sleep and something mildly fermented. "How was your day?"

She smiled in the dark. "Pretty good. Making progress on the Laos-Minnesota caseload—"

His breathing evened out mid-sentence. Her gaze wandered up to the ceiling—a little amused, a little annoyed, and somewhat tender. This was becoming a pattern. She settled into his hold and fell asleep sometime around dawn.

In the morning, he was awake before her. Hair flattened on one side, sitting at her kitchen counter like a kid caught sneaking in past curfew. He looked sheepish when she handed him his coffee. "I dreamt you were mad at me."

"I was." She sipped her tea. "In my dream, I replaced you with a very attentive bank clerk named Yeon-seok who listens when I talk."

He winced. "Ouch. Brutal."

"He wore glasses. Brought me snacks. And showed up to my friend's art opening." The last part slipped out before she could catch it.

A shadow flicked across his face—recognition, guilt. "Was that yesterday?"

"Wednesday." She kept her tone neutral, factual. "It's fine. It was boring." *It wasn't boring. Ji-young sold three pieces. I wanted you to meet her.*

"I'm sorry." He reached for her hand. "Things have been crazy with the film promotion ramping up."

"I know. I'm not keeping score." *Liar. You are keeping score. But what else can you do when you're sitting home all alone?*

In bed, he curled against her, lips brushing her neck. She turned toward him, answered his kiss, let his weight settle over her. A nuzzle, a tickle, a small laugh. The act was pure muscle memory, the old intensity giving way to stray thoughts—contracts, appointments, dry cleaning. It was pleasant enough, like following a foolproof recipe you'd memorized but stopped tasting. And like most of their recent conversations, over before it got too deep.

Afterward, she stretched out beside him, staring at the wall again. He faced her, eyes soft. "I'm sorry about Wednesday. The event ran late and—"

"It's fine," she cut him off with a small smile. "It's no big deal."

He kissed her shoulder. "I'll make it up to you."

She nodded. *Let him believe it.*

When they said goodbye at the door, she stopped herself from asking when she would see him next.

Instead, she showered, dressed, and headed to the office as she did every day when he was filming in Europe. The routine was familiar. Only now the distance between them was measured in all the words they didn't say.

***

At the beginning of February, the promotional machine devoured Yoo-jin whole. Weeks of non-stop brand endorsements took him to five cities across Korea, then Tokyo, Bangkok, and Singapore in rapid succession. Red-eye flights and hotel rooms blurring together, photographers shouting his name, fans pressing against barricades. His face on billboards, his smile seductive, his presence everywhere except where Hana most wanted him to be.

From afar, she followed his activities through text exchanges and calls that always ended with his eyes closing mid-sentence from exhaustion.

She'd spent three months arranging this Cambodia orphanage visit. It was her passion project—a sanctuary for displaced children. She'd convinced five donors to attend and agreed with his manager on an optimal time slot for him to attend. No cameras, no publicity risks. Yoo-jin had promised to be there.

Now, alone in a Phnom Penh hotel room and packing for her return flight to Seoul, Hana folded each item with deliberate care, as if imposing order on her chaotic thoughts.

Her phone rang. Yoo-jin. She stared at his name for several rings before answering.

"How was the site visit?" he asked, voice rough with

fatigue.

"Productive. We got funding for the next three years."

"That's amazing. I knew you'd nail it."

You could have seen it yourself if you'd been here. "Thanks. How's it going in Busan?"

"Exhausting. Endless parade of reporters asking the same questions." A heavy sigh. "My face hurts from smiling for a thousand photos today."

"That's the job." The words came out flatter than she intended.

"Yeah." A pause. "I miss you."

Her hands stilled. *Do you really? Or do you miss someone waiting for you and expecting nothing?*

"I miss you too," she said at last, because it was true despite everything.

A weighty silence.

"I'm sorry about Cambodia," he said. "The Tokyo schedule changed at the last minute and the brand threatened to pull the entire campaign if I didn't stay."

"There'll be other visits." She zipped her suitcase closed with finality.

He sounded distressed. "I knew how important this was for you."

Sudden tears pricked her eyes. *Important enough to accommodate your constraints. To find ways to protect your image. To create an opportunity for us to do something meaningful together.*

"Don't worry about it," she said in her neutral lawyer voice. Not angry. Accepting. Like she expected nothing more.

"I'll make it up to you," he said, the old refrain sounding hollow even to him. "I'll be back in Seoul in a few days. Can I see you?"

A pause. "I have meetings on Thursday morning."

"Wednesday night, then. I'll come straight from the airport."

"If you're not too tired." She didn't refuse, but she didn't reach for him like before.

"I'm never too tired for you." He attempted the playful tone that used to make her laugh.

She didn't laugh. "We'll see. Safe travels tomorrow."

***

Three days later, Yoo-jin arrived at Hana's door, suitcase in hand. Eighteen hours of travel sat heavy in his bones like the unease in his gut. Hana answered wearing an oversized t-shirt and reading glasses, hair pulled into a messy knot. He registered the coolness in her eyes at once. *So this is how it is.*

"You came," she said, stepping aside to let him in. Not *I missed you* or *I'm glad you're here*—only an acknowledgment of his presence, like noting the arrival of expected rain.

His guilt retracted like a defensive reflex. He straightened his shoulders. "Of course, I did. I told you I would."

Their kiss was brief, perfunctory. No lingering, no heat—a greeting between people who knew the motions but had forgotten the melody. He dropped his bag by the door with forced casualness. He could sense himself retreating behind a polite indifference, a self-protective barrier against her quiet hurt.

She had prepared dinner and kept it warm for him despite the late hour. They sat at her small dining table—him filling the silence with anecdotes from his promotional tour, her nodding at appropriate intervals.

"And how about you?" he asked. "Tell me about Cambodia."

"It was good." She pushed rice around her bowl. "Hot. Overwhelming. Productive."

"I want to hear everything."

She looked at him as if gauging his sincerity. "Do you really?"

Her question stung with its quiet challenge. "Yes. Everything."

She told him about children following her through the village, donors increasing pledges, a seven-year-old presenting her with a handmade bracelet. Hana twisted the colorful threads around her wrist. "She's being adopted by a family in Copenhagen after three years in the system."

"That's amazing."

"It is." Her smile faded. "She saw your photo on my phone. Asked if you were my husband."

His chopsticks stilled. "What did you tell her?"

Silence. Hana's expression shut down again. "I just explained you were working."

Kids could say the darndest things. "I brought you something." He reached for his bag, eager to change the subject, and handed her a wooden box with intricate carvings from Bangkok.

She thanked him with a polite smile. "It's beautiful," she said, setting it aside without opening it.

They finished dinner in silence. He helped her clear the dishes, their movements a careful choreography of avoiding accidental touches.

In the bedroom, the lights stayed off. They undressed without a word.

He leaned in to kiss her. She averted her face—his lips landed on her cheek. They lay down side by side. He hovered above her, eyes fixed on the pillow. She set her hand on his chest. He moved it away gently, pressing it flat to the mattress. The rest unfolded in silence. Steady. Mechanical. When it was over, she let out a quiet breath, her eyes already open in the dark. Relief, not release.

They lay next to each other, not touching, staring at the

ceiling as if waiting for the other to speak.

"My schedule eases up next month," he said into the darkness. "We could take a weekend somewhere."

"That would be nice." Her voice revealed nothing.

"I mean it, Hana."

"I know you do." She turned away from him, curling into herself. "Goodnight, Yoo-jin."

He studied the curve of her back. He reached out a hand, fingers hovering above her shoulder, but withdrew without making contact.

"Goodnight," he whispered to the space between them.

THE CHALLENGER

Hana placed her phone on her desk, fighting a familiar disappointment. Yoo-jin's text was brief: *Can't make dinner tonight. Brand wants additional shots. Rain check?*

She understood his commitments—the relentless pace of his industry, the lucrative prospects he had to seize. *Three rain checks in two weeks.*

"Boss?" Her assistant Jin-ah knocked on the open office door. "The board members are in the conference room. They're ready for you."

"Thank you, Jin-ah." Hana stood and gathered her notes.

The meeting proceeded at a brisk pace until they reached the final agenda item: donor recognition for the upcoming gala.

"We've received a sizable contribution," the financial director announced, sliding a document across the table. "Five million dollars from Seraphine Holdings. Specifically earmarked for our Cambodian initiatives."

Murmurs rippled through the room. Seraphine Holdings didn't often involve themselves in international aid work, focusing instead on their luxury brand empire and emerging tech investments.

"Their CEO requested a meeting to discuss potential partnership opportunities," Jin-ah added. "His office called this morning."

Hana narrowed her eyes. "Seo Ji-hwan himself? Not a representative?"

"Correct."

***

Seo Ji-hwan was forty-one, Cambridge-educated, Harvard MBA, and heir to what *Forbes* once dubbed "Korea's most sophisticated conglomerate."

What the company's quarterly briefings didn't include—though it loomed large over every board meeting and family gathering—was that Ji-hwan was the only son and sole male descendant of a dynasty built on generational prestige, hand-stitched leather, and patented microchips. Producing an heir wasn't a mere personal milestone—it was a fiduciary duty.

Professionally, he had outperformed expectation by taking a third-generation boutique family concern with legacy quirks and transforming it into a profitable multinational. Strategic partnerships, ethical sourcing, digital pivots, and a green initiative that even passed international scrutiny. His father had called him "methodical." His grandfather, "dangerously modern."

He had approached dating with the same precision he brought to high-stakes mergers. Yet Cinderella continued to elude him, while the stepsisters showed up in more imaginative disguises. The socialites confused legacy with labels. The executives tried to fold him into five-year plans. His mother had moved past subtle hints and now left dossiers at his breakfast table with notes like, *"Strong jawline. Doesn't flinch at foie gras."*

Until the Weston-Rhee Foundation annual report landed on his desk.

He had glanced at it out of habit—another glossy appeal for donor funds—and almost flipped past it. But the name caught his eye. Hana Weston-Rhee, 33, dual British-

Korean citizenship. Oxford-educated. Executive Director. Sharp résumé. He took a second look. A striking photograph accompanied her profile.

It had been years since he had heard the name. But the face sparked a recollection.

It was a weekend at the Westons' home in England, where he and a few Cambridge friends had gathered for shooting and politics. What struck him most was his host's teenage stepdaughter. She had, without a license, commandeered the family's battered Land Rover and shadowed the hunting party through the estate grounds, almost mowing down a hedge and the son of an ambassador.

He had found it hilarious. The other guests had not. *She was such a pretty girl. Long-limbed, fresh-faced. But oh-so underaged.*

He had looked, perhaps a little too intently, and been quickly warned off. Her cousin had cornered him with the subtlety of a rugby tackle and made his position clear: *Look elsewhere.*

Ji-hwan, of course, had goaded the cousin—purely on principle—but hadn't given the girl much thought afterward. Until now.

But there was one complication: the rumors connecting her to the actor Lee Yoo-jin. Nothing was confirmed, but his investigators had noted patterns suggesting a relationship. However, the TV star was often absent with constant travel and public appearances that excluded her. *A relationship showing strain. Perfect timing.*

"Mr. Seo, Ms. Weston will see you now," the assistant announced, interrupting his thoughts.

Ji-hwan stood and straightened his tie.

***

Hana rose as Seo Ji-hwan entered her office, her expectations of a stuffy executive evaporating. He was younger than she had expected, tall and lean, with a full head of dark hair and a half-smirk tugging at his lips. The Savile Row suit and Windsor knot depicted a man steeped in power, not dazzled by it. *This is a plot twist. Where's my balding bean-counter?*

His eyes caught her attention—warm brown, with smile lines that suggested time spent outside a boardroom. Sharp mind, certainly. But also a spark of mischief, like he wanted to make an inappropriate comment just to see if she would laugh. When he smiled, she instinctively straightened up and smoothed her hair. *What do you know—this meeting just got more interesting.*

"Ms. Weston-Rhee," he said, extending his hand. "Thank you for making time to see me."

"Mr. Seo," she replied with a firm handshake. "Your generous donation warranted immediate attention. Please, have a seat."

He settled into the chair across from her. "I've been following your foundation's work for some time. I was thoroughly impressed by your Children's Village project in Cambodia."

"That's very kind. Most corporate donors prefer local initiatives with more visibility."

"I'm not most corporate donors." A half smile touched his lips. "I had suggested sponsoring a Formula One team to our PR department. They sent back a 15-page report on orphanage sustainability metrics."

His comment made her laugh. "I imagine that was quite a read. Though I must admit, children learning to walk do move slower than race cars."

"In all seriousness, I like your approach—integrating education, healthcare, and legal support. Most organizations tackle only one aspect."

Over the next hour, his questions revealed genuine

interest and knowledge in humanitarian work. "You're well-versed in this field," she observed.

"Don't look so shocked," he said, mock-offended. "Many of us read more than just quarterly business reports."

"My apologies. I'm used to donors who can't locate Cambodia on a map."

"Second peninsula from the right, under Vietnam, correct?" He maintained a straight face for all of three seconds before breaking into a smile. "I'm joking. I've been there several times. Seraphine has manufacturing interests in Phnom Penh."

Charming and self-aware. Unusual combination. "Well, we're grateful for your support," she said, rising from her chair.

He remained seated. "Actually, I had hoped to discuss a more substantial partnership. The British Embassy is hosting a reception next week for organizations working with child welfare. Ambassador Hamilton specifically mentioned your foundation's work."

Hana blinked, surprised. "Alistair? He knows my stepfather well. I wonder why he didn't reach out to me."

"It's a rather small gathering. However, as one of your major supporters, I could ensure you get recognition. These diplomatic connections often lead to generous funding."

She folded her arms, wary of his interest yet intrigued by the opportunity.

"If you're interested, my assistant will contact yours with the details."

"That would be lovely. Thank you."

"Brilliant. And I promise no embarrassing stories about teenage joyrides." He gave her a conspiratorial wink. "At least not until the second glass of champagne."

Hana paused. "I'm sorry?"

"I'm pretty sure it was 2010. Your family estate in Surrey?

A hunting weekend. You, very much unlicensed, behind the wheel of a Land Rover. And a certain diplomat's son who ended up in a hedge with whisky down his trousers and a severely bruised ego."

Her jaw dropped. "You were there? You saw that?"

"Indeed. Most entertaining part of the weekend, if I'm honest." He smiled at her mortified expression. "Don't worry. Your secret's safe with me. Unless, of course, it becomes useful as leverage."

Despite her embarrassment, Hana laughed. "Blackmail already? We've only met."

"I like establishing clear terms early in any relationship." He stood and buttoned his suit jacket. "Business or otherwise."

There was a teasing inflection in the way he said "otherwise" that made her aware of how long it had been since anyone had flirted so openly with her.

She reined in a smile. "I look forward to the embassy reception."

"Brilliant. Until next week, then."

After he left, Hana sank into her chair with a strange, unsettled feeling. Seo Ji-hwan's demeanor had struck her as both familiar and foreign, like hearing a melody she knew by heart but played in a different key—and somehow reminding her of home.

A text notification chimed—Yoo-jin. *Schedule cleared for Saturday night. Dinner at my place?*

She read the message with the usual mix of hope and skepticism. *Sure, until something more important comes along.*

***

The gathering at the British Embassy was reminiscent of Hana's Oxford days—same accents, tailored suits, passive-aggressive jabs couched in polite laughter. Only with better champagne.

She navigated through the assembly like muscle memory, smiling in the right places, offering the right number of nods. Honed since her youth at her parents' side, the diplomatic code was second nature: *"We should discuss this further"* meant *"never in a million years,"* while *"an interesting perspective"* was universal for *"what complete nonsense."*

The ambassador pounced when he saw her. "My dear girl! Weston's brilliant daughter!" He had dragged her from one important guest to another like a prized show pony. "Hana runs the Weston-Rhee Foundation. Absolutely marvelous work in Cambodia—you must hear about it."

By her third glass of champagne, she'd secured support from three donors and a Geneva speaking slot. But it was Seo Ji-hwan who really surprised her.

She had expected smooth charm, maybe a bit of arrogant polish. What she hadn't anticipated was an intuitive political radar, fluent in both Korean intricacies and Western subtleties. He moved among the assembled guests with uncanny precision, knowing which egos needed stroking, which officials wanted substance, and which guests were there for the free alcohol. When conversation lagged, he would slide in with diplomatic sleight of hand: *"The Ambassador would like to introduce Ms. Weston to the German delegation,"* or better yet, *"Shall we let the Minister attend to his other guests?"* Translation: *"You're boring her to death."*

Hana watched him with dry amusement. *Who knew billionaires could be socially useful? And fine—he's also quite good-looking. That doesn't hurt.*

"That went rather well," Ji-hwan remarked as they stood on the embassy's terrace, stealing a breath of fresh air.

"Thanks to your strategic rescues. You're like a diplomatic GPS—recalculating routes every time I'm about to crash into a windbag."

His voice softened. "Supporting meaningful work makes it worthwhile. Your mother and stepfather would be proud."

It was the kind of thing people said. But he didn't say it with formality. No Hallmark packaging, no velvet glove—only a quiet, matter-of-fact statement. And that made it land.

Before she could reply, the ambassador returned. "Hana, Ji-hwan—I hope you're enjoying yourselves."

"Immensely. We were just discussing Ms. Weston's upcoming presentation at the Blue House social welfare forum."

Hana's eyes narrowed. "I'm sorry—my what?"

"You haven't received the invitation?" the ambassador blinked. "Strange. The First Lady asked for you specifically. Seraphine Holdings is one of the event's main patrons."

"Indeed," Ji-hwan said, unbothered. "I hoped it would be a pleasant surprise. There's a state dinner as part of the program. Good visibility for your organization."

"How thoughtful," she managed, swallowing her suspicion with another sip of champagne.

After the ambassador moved on, she turned to Ji-hwan, eyebrows arched. "A state dinner at the Blue House. That's not a casual invitation."

"No, it's an opportunity. Ministers from four ASEAN nations will be in attendance. They're key allies for your Cambodia expansion."

Hana searched his face for tells, but he only offered a cryptic smile. *He's playing some kind of long game.*

She thought of Yoo-jin, who would have hated this type of event—the soft lies wrapped in charm, the tactical compliments disguised as curiosity. He couldn't stand performance unless it was scripted. The real-life theater of diplomacy was not his world. But the truth was that they could never be in a room like this together. Not in public.

But here was Seo Ji-hwan, gliding through the same sphere with her like a charming, unexpected wingman.

As they rejoined the reception, Hana's phone vibrated.

Yoo-jin, canceling their Saturday plans—again. A delay with last-minute reshoots. Her disappointment had become so habitual it no longer registered.

"Everything alright?" Ji-hwan asked, noting her expression as she slipped the device back into her clutch.

"Fine. Just work."

He didn't press. "Shall we visit the Japanese delegation? Their foundation just expanded their grants program."

"Lead the way," she agreed, pushing thoughts of Yoo-jin aside. "Though I should warn you, my Japanese is limited to ordering sushi and apologizing."

"Perfect," he grinned. "I can insult people, but can't apologize. We'll make a brilliant team."

***

When they arrived at Hana's building, Ji-hwan walked around to open her car door, offering his hand as she stepped out.

"Thank you for a lovely evening."

"The pleasure was all mine." He held her hand for a moment before lifting it to his lips in a gesture both old-England and deliberate. "Until next time."

The move caught her off guard—he could see the brief widening of her eyes—but she didn't pull away. When he released her hand and stepped back, the twinkle in his eye acknowledged the theatrical nature of it.

"Very Edwardian," she said, amused.

"I was going for 'cheeky,' but 'Edwardian' has a nice ring. Goodnight, Ms. Weston."

Ji-hwan watched Hana go inside. He smiled to himself, replaying the evening. She was exactly what he'd been looking for. But she was also striking in ways he hadn't imagined—quick-witted, funny, and direct. *This might be more entertaining than I thought.*

The invitation to the Blue House state dinner, secured

weeks ago, had landed as he had hoped. The donation to her foundation, the well-timed embassy reception, the offhand reference to her stepfather—all pieces that had fallen into place.

He dialed his assistant. "Schedule a lunch with Ms. Weston tomorrow. And send flowers to her office in the morning—peonies. I think she said they were her favorite."

She had not, of course—he was only guessing.

***

The next day, Hana admired a magnificent arrangement of peonies sitting on her desk with a card: *Enjoyed our conversation last night. Looking forward to lunch.—SJH*

Her assistant Jin-ah stood at the door. "How did Mr. Seo know you liked peonies?"

"No idea," Hana said, puzzled. *The same flowers Yoo-jin sent after forgetting my birthday.*

"Then he did his homework. Or made a lucky guess."

She reached for her phone to text Yoo-jin about the Blue House event—but stopped herself. *What would I say? "A handsome billionaire wants to take me to a presidential gala. Thoughts?"*

Their recent exchanges had been brief calls and texts and rescheduled plans. *When did "we" become a glitch in the timeline instead of the main plan?*

She turned to her computer and pulled up information about the Blue House social welfare forum. The attendance list included power players whose support could fund her efforts in Southeast Asia. Going with the Seraphine CEO made professional sense. She sighed. *Certainly better than waiting around for Yoo-jin.*

She typed a message to Ji-hwan: *Lunch sounds lovely. How did you know I love peonies?*

***

Two weeks later, Hana glanced at the empty seat beside her at a foundation event. She'd invited Yoo-jin, knowing it was a long shot. He was taping a variety show and preparing for an upcoming cameo role in Japan.

His response had been careful but distant: *You know how my schedule is. I'm booked solid.*

She had accepted it, even though it stung. But now, as cameras flashed at the high-profile guests in attendance, she couldn't ignore the nagging suspicion that it wasn't about his timetable. Later that evening, she received a message: *Hope the event went well.*

Her reply was polite, measured: *It did. The education fund got large pledges.*

No follow-up from him. No apology, no regret. Only silence. *So this is how it works: I adjusted, he vanished, and we both pretend it wasn't personal.*

***

At a promotional event, Yoo-jin paced, nervous and conflicted about turning down Hana yet again. He had not told her everything—his management had discouraged his presence at any non-entertainment events with her.

"It complicates your persona," his manager had said. "You're an actor, not a businessman or a philanthropist. If you're seen with someone outside the industry too often, people start speculating. Are you changing careers? Getting married? It's a distraction."

"But if she's an actress, it's good publicity?"

"You know how it works. Fans buy into a fantasy, not just a performance. We manage that image so nothing undermines it."

Yoo-jin complied out of habit. But of late, each deflection appeared like a quiet betrayal. That night, he tried phoning Hana, but the call went to voicemail. He sent a text: *Missed you.*

Hope your day went well.

The response came hours later: *Sorry I missed your call. Tied up with meetings. Hope you had a good day.*

Polite. Distant. And just like that, a cold fear hit him: *what if she's already moving on?*

DIVIDED ATTENTION

The Blue House gleamed against the night sky as Seo Ji-hwan's Mercedes-Maybach joined the line of cars depositing guests at the entrance. Hana adjusted the midnight blue Carolina Herrera gown she had chosen for its understatement.

"Ready?" Ji-hwan asked, looking everbiy bit the polished chaebol heir in his bespoke tuxedo.

"Let's do it."

As they stepped out, camera flashes popped—nothing like the celebrity red carpet frenzy, but enough to make Hana conscious of making a public appearance with Seo Ji-hwan. They smiled and nodded at photographers as she placed her hand in the crook of his arm. *Was there ever a time when Yoo-jin and I were seen anywhere together? Oh, right—once. Back in the Middle Ages before we were a couple.*

"Not hiding?" she teased, thinking of Yoo-jin, who would never risk being photographed with her.

"Why? We make a gorgeous pair." His delivery was so matter-of-fact it almost made her falter mid-stride.

The First Lady greeted them warmly, praising the foundation's work with enough details to show she had been briefed. The event was its own kind of theater—cabinet ministers rehearsing party lines, CEOs mentally comparing net worths, and politicians smiling like campaign posters.

There were glances and whispers when they entered—the Seraphine CEO and the Weston-Rhee Foundation director making an unlikely but photogenic pair.

At the reception line, they fell into an easy rhythm, finishing each other's sentences so neatly it made one foreign diplomat blink. Hana handled the policy experts with diplomatic finesse while Ji-hwan kept the lighter touch, translating bureaucratic jargon into actual conversation. Protocol had seated them apart, though it hardly mattered. When the agriculture minister launched into an account of rural development that grew more fictional with each glass of wine, their eyes found each other across the table. Ji-hwan's barely perceptible eyebrow lift met Hana's napkin-muffled snort. To everyone else, they were model guests—attentive, engaged, appropriately reverent. To each other, they were partners in crime, sharing the evening like a well-timed joke.

When the dancing began, he led her to the floor.

"You dance well," she said. "Not what I expected."

He tilted his head, amused. "What *did* you expect?"

"Something stiffer. More... straitlaced."

He inched closer, enough to make her pulse stall. "I don't do straitlaced."

She arched a brow. "And this?"

"This is pleasure," he said, letting his hand settle at her waist.

"Is that so?"

"You tell me." He spun her gently before drawing her back in. "You're the one with the law degree and the devastating poker face."

"This is your show—you orchestrated this entire evening." Her eyes met his directly. "Don't think I haven't noticed."

"I find a good partner makes everything easier to endure."

Hana held his gaze, letting a beat pass. "So do I."

As they turned again, she smiled at their reflection—her in midnight blue, him in black and white, moving together like they'd been doing it for years.

***

On the drive home, they tore into the evening like theater critics after opening night—gossiping, mocking, deciphering.

"Did you see the Commerce Secretary's face when the Japanese envoy brought up trade?"

"—Like he wanted to stab him in the eyes with his chopsticks," Hana cut in, laughing. "Murder vibes."

"Meanwhile the German press secretary…"

"Oh my god, he thought they cared about Oktoberfest—

"—and spilled his team's entire comm strategy!" he laughed, slapping his thigh.

"The French attaché though—one bite of fermented beans and—" Hana choked on her laughter.

"—she looked like karma caught up with her!"

"Exactly! Then she knocked back two shots of soju like it was antidote." Hana caught her breath and wiped her eyes. "We're absolutely going to hell."

"First class all the way. With diplomatic immunity."

She gave him a sidelong glance. "You're not as dull as your résumé."

"Careful. Flattery might get you a second date."

They laughed again, and Hana caught herself. *Wait—am I actually having fun?*

Ji-hwan felt a pleasant warmth fill his chest. At first, Hana Weston-Rhee seemed a strategic choice to become Mrs. Seo Ji-hwan on paper. He hadn't expected much more. But now he wanted to hear her laugh again, to listen to what she had to say, to spend more time with her.

"Do you still ride?" he asked.

She gave him a questioning look and shook her head. "Only when I'm home in Surrey. Why?"

"If you're interested, there's a beautiful trail not far from the city. We could go riding."

She blinked. *There it is. Making his move. Decline—sort out your feelings about Yoo-jin first.* Instead, she heard herself say, "That sounds lovely."

At her building, Ji-hwan walked her to the entrance.

"Thank you for tonight. It was really nice—" She paused, chewing her lip. "I meant—it was nice to attend an event and not have to... hide."

He cocked his head, surprised. "Hide? You're Hana Weston. Why should you have to hide?"

The simple statement landed hard. *Why do I need this man to remind me I'm a Weston? Oh right—because living in Yoo-jin's shadow had made me forget.*

He took her hand and brushed his lips across her knuckles, his eyes warm. "Good night, Hana. Sleep well."

In her bedroom moments later, Hana caught her reflection—cheeks flushed, eyes bright, expression lighter than it had been in months.

You have a boyfriend and you're flirting with another man, a voice in her head accused.

I have a boyfriend who fits me into his schedule when convenient.

Her mobile buzzed—Yoo-jin. *How was your night?*

While she debated on how to respond, another message appeared: *Screening went well. Exhausted. Talk tomorrow?*

Not waiting for her answer. Already postponing her.

A brief internal struggle went through her mind before she set the phone down. *You're a Weston. Have some pride.*

***

Yoo-jin's variety show *Sail & Savor* had become the season's most-watched episode. Five celebrities on a yacht, cooking and eating fresh catch. On screen, he was all charm—sea breeze in his hair, showing viewers how to prepare fish.

"Only sea salt and lemon," he said, sliding the fillets onto a grill. "Let the flavor speak for itself." *God, that's such a line,* he thought as he watched the playback later. *But sure, poetic fish guy. Why not?*

For a while, even Yoo-jin forgot he was performing. The ocean, the food, the laughter. Easy. Until someone behind him laughed, a bright, high-pitched sound that for a split second sounded *exactly* like Hana.

His hand froze mid-cut. The knife hovered, the sizzle of the food fading into the background. An ache filled his chest.

He blinked. Of course, the laugh belonged to somebody else. He finished the cut—too forcefully—but kept the smile on his face. *Perfect lines. Perfect lighting. Perfect fantasy.*

What no one saw was the version that came after—the one who dropped into the back seat of the car, silent. Who pulled out his phone to check for a message that hadn't come. Who sat in his hotel room, full from filming but somehow still starving.

He scrolled through the fan buzz. *Husband material. Marry me, Chef Yoo-jin.* He tossed the device on the nightstand and lay back on the bed, arm over his eyes. *Yeah. And still, the only person I want to feed is the one who'd ask me why I'm using a microplane like a poser.*

***

The stables were tucked in the hills an hour outside Seoul, flanked by a scatter of pine trees and the faint smell of damp earth. Hana came out of the changing room to find Ji-hwan already mounted atop a bay gelding with the smug ease of someone who had once competed for school colors and never quite let it go.

"You're late," he said, reins in one hand, the other resting lazily on his thigh. "I thought you'd chickened out."

She raised an eyebrow, adjusting her gloves. "You invited me. If anyone should be nervous, it's the one with something to prove."

He grinned and gave her a slow once-over—not inappropriate, but thorough. "In that case, let me start over. You look devastating, and I am terrified."

A groom led out her horse, a tall chestnut mare with a no-nonsense gait. She mounted, settling into the stirrups. They started off at a trot, the path winding along low hills and pastures.

"You haven't lost your seat," he commented after a brief canter.

"Neither have you. Though I assume your saddle's had more time in climate control than mine."

"Please. The only thing I pamper more than my horses is my ego." His lips quirked in a small smile—half-innocent, half roguish.

The trail opened up into a wide, grassy clearing. Ji-hwan arched an eyebrow at Hana, a slight twitch. A dare.

She didn't need more than that. She kicked her mare forward into a gallop, heart pounding like she was sixteen again and skipping class. Behind her, hooves thundered as he gave chase.

"You *cheat*!" he shouted, gleeful.

She laughed a throaty laugh, open and reckless. *God, I remember this. Marmite under me. Ian daring me to take the next fence. The smell of crushed grass and horse sweat.*

For an hour, they tore through tree-shadowed trails and sunlit clearings, all muscle and speed to the sound of wind and the drum of hooves. When the horses tired, they dismounted near a shallow stream. Hana leaned against a tree while the animals drank, stretching muscles she'd forgotten existed. The sun warmed her face as she watched a hawk circle overhead.

"What?" she asked, catching his gaze.

"Just wondering what put that look on your face."

"What look?"

"Like you just remembered something you've been missing."

Yes, remembering my old life—before I shrank myself down to fit around Yoo-jin. "Probably the endorphins from riding. It's been too long."

As they mounted to continue their ride, Ji-hwan's phone buzzed. He glanced at it, frowning, and silenced it without responding.

"Problem?" she asked.

"Nothing that can't wait. Some crises tend to resolve themselves."

"Must be nice to be the one deciding what constitutes a crisis."

"It is," he admitted without pretense. "Just a matter of prioritization. And right now, I'm prioritizing you."

Hana's hands stilled on the reins.

They rode off side by side. "We have time for an early dinner if you're hungry. There's a place near here that serves the best *bibimbap* outside of Jeonju."

The casual invitation brought Yoo-jin to mind, but she pushed the thought away. "I could eat," she heard herself say instead.

Later, as he opened the car door for her, their hands brushed. A small, intentional touch, but lingering long enough for her to notice. *Easy, Hana. It's only dinner.*

***

Ji-hwan guided his Aston Martin along the winding country roads, keeping Hana's profile in his peripheral vision. The day had begun as a reconnaissance mission to assess their compatibility. But somewhere between watching her mount the chestnut mare and hearing her laugh mid-gallop, the operation had gone rogue.

"This was…" Hana paused, searching for the right word, "…exactly what I needed. Thank you."

He glanced over—her cheeks were still flushed from the wind and sun, her guard more relaxed than he had previously seen. "You seem different today. More yourself, perhaps."

"And how would you know what 'myself' is?" she teased. "We barely know each other."

"I'm a good observer."

The comment seemed to make her uneasy. She looked away.

Too close, too fast. Retreat. He gestured toward the dashboard. "Music?"

"Yes, please."

"Preferences?" He swiped through options on the touchscreen.

"Surprise me. No Wagner, though."

"No Wagner?" His eyebrows shot up in mock horror. "Granny swears the Ring Cycle cured everything from melancholy to indigestion."

"I'll take my chances."

A mischievous smile tugged at his mouth as his finger drifted over the screen before tapping decisively. The unmistakable tolling of AC/DC's "Hell's Bells" filled the car.

She burst out laughing. "This is what you listen to in your fancy British car?"

"The car might be British," he said, "but I spent my rebellious years at Harvard Business School."

"Rebellious," she echoed. "What—alternating econ lectures with headbanging in your dorm?"

Instead of answering, he turned up the volume and sang along as the beat kicked in. What he hadn't expected was her reaction—the slight widening of her eyes and a bemused smile before she gave in and joined him. They sang their way through a procession of heavy metal rock anthems, windows cracked despite the chill. *God, she's lovely.*

By the time they reached her neighborhood, his voice was hoarse and his face hurt from smiling. He pulled into a parking space and cut the engine.

"So," he said.

"So," she echoed.

"This is the part that gets awkward?"

She laughed, dissolving the sudden tension. He gestured to a small square at the corner. "A moment before you go?"

They strolled toward the shade of a maple tree, and Hana let out a happy, satisfied sigh. "I had a wonderful time today. I'd forgotten how much I love riding."

"The horses were adequate company, then?" *Fishing for compliments. Standards are slipping fast.*

"The horses were excellent. The human element wasn't terrible either."

"Such high praise. I'll have to work harder next time." *Planning ahead already. So much for strategic detachment.*

He reached for her hand and brushed his lips across her knuckles. When she didn't pull away, he brought it to his chest, placing it gently over his sternum.

Her eyes, reflecting the streetlights, held a look he couldn't quite decode. It was as if she were opening the door just a crack, wondering if she would let him in.

She stepped closer and rose onto her toes.

He waited half a beat—his inner voice drowned in a sudden rush of want. He bent to meet her halfway. The kiss was gentle but lingering, his fingers caressing the line of her jaw. The strategic thinker, the dynasty-builder—silenced by a simple, honest kiss.

They stayed there for a moment before she drew back. "I

should tell you—I'm in a relationship."

"I know," he replied. *Of course. That actor who keeps her stashed away like his personal guilty pleasure. He has no idea what she's really worth.*

"You knew," she repeated. It wasn't a question.

"Part of my due diligence." He didn't deflect or appear ashamed. "I like to know what I'm walking into."

"And yet here you are." She didn't act offended. If anything, she seemed to appreciate the directness.

"Here I am." His thumb traced small circles on the back of her hand, which still rested on his chest. "I find you compelling, Hana. More than I anticipated."

"That's not a very romantic declaration."

He laughed. "Would you prefer a boombox held outside your window?"

She smiled, shaking her head.

His expression grew serious. "I won't push. Whatever this is—" he gestured between them, "—it happens at your pace. But I'd like to pursue it." *More than just pursue. I want to win this. Not only for the dynasty. For me.*

"Why?"

"Because I think we could build something nice together." A smile tugged at his mouth. "As partners, as spouses—and maybe even raising children who value both Metallica and solid investment strategies."

The absurdity of the statement startled a laugh from her. "You're getting ahead of yourself."

"That's because I already know what I want." He released her hand but didn't step back.

She didn't blink. Didn't act embarrassed. Simply let the quiet settle before pressing a kiss to his cheek. "Thank you for today."

"My pleasure."

After she disappeared inside, Ji-hwan returned to his car, where he sat without starting the engine. This had begun as a calculated move. The Weston heiress. Perfect breeding. Excellent connections. A strategic match for Seraphine's global ambitions.

But now? Now, he was sitting there, grinning like a fool and planning their next date like a besotted teenager.

***

The first few days after returning to Seoul, Yoo-jin called Hana hourly. By day four, she replied: *Swamped with work. Board meetings. Will call when things settle down.*

No emoji. No warmth. Only cool detachment. It stung more than silence. *Is this it? Is she done?*

He stopped calling, telling himself he was being respectful, but in truth he was afraid. The photos from the Blue House state banquet had hit him like a gut punch. Hana, radiant in a couture gown, posing beside the Seraphine CEO. An ugly feeling twisted inside him. *She never asked to be tucked away. I just never offered anything else.*

He began drafting messages. *I'm sorry. I miss you. Are you with him now?* But sent none.

Instead, he rehearsed scenarios like lines in a script: a public gesture, a soft launch, something to show Hana she mattered. Would she believe him then?

When he gathered enough courage to call, she sounded busy. "I saw a picture. You and someone named Seo Ji-hwan?"

"It was the Blue House state banquet," she said. "He's a major donor."

"I have to be out of town again in a few days. Can I see you before?"

"I'll call you," she deflected.

He sat on the couch, phone still in hand, screen lit with the photo of her beside another man. *She kept waiting for me to show up. I didn't—and now she's with someone else.*

He dropped his head into his hands, breath shaky, eyes stinging. *Apologies? Too late. Promises? Too easy. Career, image—the ultimate trap.*

***

The outing with Seo Ji-hwan had stirred forgotten sensations in Hana—being seen and thriving in the company of someone present and caring. The opposite of whatever she was experiencing with Yoo-jin.

It had been thirty-seven days since they had last been together. Thirty-seven days of perfunctory text messages and abbreviated phone calls that sounded more like status updates than conversations.

Landing in Dubai. Hotel nice. Miss you.

In Singapore. Brand event tomorrow. How are you?

It was like reading weather reports from distant cities. Factual. Impersonal. Devoid of any real connection. Soon, she responded in kind.

Foundation meeting went well.

At embassy function. Minister pledged support.

Hana read his latest message, sent three hours ago: *Kuala Lumpur press junket running long. Call you tomorrow?*

She didn't reply. What was the point? "Tomorrow" was a moving target he lobbed from wherever he was that day. Another city, another excuse. If he made it back to Seoul, she'd probably find out through the internet before she heard from him.

Her apartment had become a weird museum of their relationship—Yoo-jin's toothbrush still in the holder, his sweatshirt draped over her reading chair, the half-used cologne bottle on her dresser. Little exhibits of a man who had stopped sharing her daily life.

She woke up in the middle of the night, finding the bed

too wide. His pillow was cold and smelled of cotton. Not surprising. Thirty-seven nights were more than enough time to erase a scent.

She shut her eyes and waited for sleep to return. It did not.

***

The following days were quiet at the foundation. Initiatives wrapped, events scheduled, numbers clean. The lull should have been a relief.

Instead, it made everything louder—in particular the silence between Hana and Yoo-jin.

Bored, she opened his Instagram. Photos loaded: a group of friends around a campfire, with Yoo-jin snuggling an English Setter. The timestamp was last weekend, when he'd delayed his return to Seoul due to a "scheduling conflict."

She stared at the screen, jaw clenched. *No, he hadn't lied. Camping was technically a schedule.*

A pang of hurt gripped her chest. Not heartbreak exactly —but smaller, meaner. Like getting stood up and realizing you were never even on the calendar. She slammed her laptop shut.

Her assistant jumped. "Everything okay?"

"Peachy," she said, forcing a smile that stretched her skin too tight. *Too busy to be near me but enough time for camping. Even that mutt got more love than me.*

"Mr. Seo's office called. He asked if you're free for dinner tomorrow."

Ji-hwan. The name landed like a lifeline tossed into murky water. "Confirm it. I'm available."

She grabbed her gym bag and headed out. "I'll be at Phoenix for the next two hours," she told Jin-ah. "Text only if the building catches fire."

***

At the gym, the burn of kickboxing dulled Hana's frustration.

Her strikes came fast and clean, body falling into rhythm. Punch. Kick. Breathe. The bag swayed under the force of the pounding.

She focused on Yoo-jin's missed calls. His ghost messages. His bullshit smiles. *Just tell him you're pissed. Tell him he's an asshole.*

Yet underneath, her own silence gnawed at her. It had seemed noble at first, like some grand attempt at self-control, but now she had to admit it was cowardly. *As if confrontation ever worked for Mother and Thomas. Now they're divorced and living in different time zones.*

She stopped mid-strike, arms falling to her sides. *Or maybe I'm just beyond caring this much.*

She launched forward again to shake the thought loose. Another punch, then another. The final blow made her stumble. She steadied, bracing against the bag, breath shaky.

Tears came all of a sudden—hot, angry, unwelcome. She pressed her forehead to the bag, furious at everything—Yoo-jin, herself, the mess they were pretending wasn't a mess. *How did I become this pathetic? This waiting room girlfriend. This polite silence.*

She stayed there, head down, until her sobs quieted. She wiped her face, squared her shoulders, and hit the bag again. Hard.

Over the steady thud of her fists on leather, Hana didn't hear the gym door creak open—or notice the figure in the corner watching her.

FAMILY TIES

"Your stance is all wrong. You're going to dislocate something if you keep that up."

The familiar voice with a British accent cut through Hana's concentration like a well-aimed knife. She froze mid-punch, turning toward the spot where a tall man leaned against the wall, arms crossed, amusement tugging at his lips.

"Ian?"

"In the flesh, darling cousin."

Ian Weston was a lean 6'2" of casual elegance. Pale oxford shirt, tailored trousers, artfully disheveled blond hair. His piercing blue eyes—the unmistakable Weston hallmark—gleamed with playfulness.

Hana let out a sound between a laugh and a sob, dropping her pose and sprinting across the mat. She launched herself at him, legs wrapping around his waist as his arms came up to catch her with easy affection. He spun her once, twice, their laughter mingling.

When he set her down, she grabbed his face with both her hands and planted a kiss squarely on his mouth, the kind of close-lipped but lingering kiss that would raise eyebrows among strangers but had been their greeting since childhood.

"What are you doing here?" she demanded, gripping his shoulders as if to check his solidity. "Shouldn't you be in

London terrorizing multinational corporations?"

"Mergers and acquisitions, if you please," he corrected her with mock severity. "And I can do that from anywhere, thank you very much." He glanced around the gym with exaggerated distaste. "Though I prefer places with less perspiration."

Hana laughed, the sound brighter than anything she had managed in weeks. Her tension dropped.

Ian stepped back, inspecting her at arm's length. "Now then, what's this about? You're giving that bag a proper thrashing, and it's not your usual workout routine. I know how you handle stress."

Hana's smile dimmed. "It's nothing."

"Ah, the Weston specialty—'nothing' invariably means 'everything I'd rather not discuss.'" He tapped her nose, a gesture from when she was small. "But we'll leave that for now. I'm absolutely famished and we're going out for a proper meal. Cousin or not, I refuse to be seen in public with someone who looks like she's been dragged through a hedge backwards." His tone was light, but his eyes caught the shadows beneath her smooth exterior.

"Alright." She turned toward the women's locker room and paused. "Ian?"

"Hmm?"

"I'm so glad you're here."

His face softened, charm giving way to tenderness. "Me too, Banana."

The childhood nickname—from when her toddler self couldn't say 'Hana'—settled around her like a warm blanket. As she left, Ian's smile stayed on his face but his eyes were distant. There was something else there now, heavier. Want. Possibly regret. A growing certainty he could no longer play the part she had cast him in.

He dragged a hand through his hair and faced away before she could look back.

***

Twenty minutes later, they were seated at a corner table in a trendy restaurant. He signaled for wine without consulting the list—a presumption Hana would accept only from Ian.

"Right then, my news first, as promised."

She sat up straight with mock deference. "I'm all ears."

"I've taken a sabbatical from my law firm to expand my role with the foundation."

Hana's eyebrows shot up. "Seriously? Beyond the grant compliance committee?"

"Indeed. The board approved my proposal to take Weston-Rhee international." His casual tone didn't mask the significance of the decision. "I'm in Seoul for the foreseeable future—staying at that ridiculously overpriced hotel downtown until I find a suitable flat."

"Why you?" she asked, curiosity piqued. "I mean, why did they choose you for this role?"

"Because I'm family. And nepotism is a family tradition."

"But what about London? Your place in town?"

Ian's expression turned wry. "It's becoming rather... limiting. And the foundation needs someone to navigate international regulations. That's where I excel."

The wine arrived, pausing their conversation. Ian raised his glass. "To new adventures."

They clinked. "How long have you been in town?"

"Three days. I would have rung sooner, but I've been in back-to-back meetings with the board." He looked at her with a gleam in his eyes. "I went to surprise you at your office, but they told me you were taking out your frustrations at the gym."

"It's... focus," she protested.

He smirked. "Focused on someone's face on that punching bag, I'd wager. Anyone I know?"

She sighed, knowing Ian's tenacity. "It's complicated."

"Isn't it always?" He inched forward, all traces of flippancy vanishing. "Come on, Banana—this is me. You needn't manage my reaction."

She twisted her napkin. "I've been seeing someone."

"Have you indeed? And this is the first I'm hearing of it?"

"We've kept it private."

Understanding dawned. "Somebody high-profile, then?"

"An actor. One of the most recognizable faces in the country."

Ian sipped his wine, assessing. "Image constraints?"

"It's been difficult," she exhaled, relieved to unburden her mind. "His career demands discretion."

"And you've been accommodating that demand." He cut straight to the point. "At what cost?"

"That's what I'm trying to figure out."

"Hence the punching bag."

They fell silent as their first course arrived.

After the server left, Hana took a bite of her tuna tartare. "He's been away constantly. Concerts, promotional tours... we've barely seen each other. When we're together, it's —" she paused, searching for words. "It's incredible. But those moments are becoming rather rare."

"Classic. I dated a semi-famous musician once. Three canceled dates later, my pride admitted defeat."

"It's not only his schedule. It's the way we have to keep everything separate. We're two different people in public."

Ian tapped his fingers against his glass. When he spoke, his tone was lighter, but his aim precise. "So, rather than sharing your resentment with him, you pummel a punching bag."

"I do not—" She stopped. "Right, so I tend to avoid conflict."

"*Tend?* Darling, it's your signature move." Ian's playful expression didn't hide the steel beneath. "Your trouble is retreating when things get difficult. Unlike your parents, who turned the house into a war zone, you learned confrontation leads to destruction."

Hana flinched. "That's not—"

"It is," he interrupted. "But sometimes, Banana, the things worth having require a bit of mess."

The words settled between them, heavy and undeniable. She looked down at her plate. It was so obvious now that he voiced it.

He reached across the table, covering her hand with his. "Don't fret. Your stepcousin is here to provide distraction, alcohol, and a shoulder to cry on—though I hope that won't be necessary, as tears are murder on cashmere."

***

After lunch, Ian walked Hana back to her office under the late April afternoon sunshine. She slipped her arm through his, her steps light, a lilt in her voice as she chatted. Her face tilted up to his with the same easy affection he had always known.

At the entrance, she planted a parting kiss on his cheek and disappeared inside.

He lingered on the sidewalk, watching the glass doors close. He took a cigarette from his silver case and lit it. The first drag steadied his thoughts.

Seoul buzzed around him, impatient and bright. But his mind had already pulled him elsewhere.

Surrey, England, thirty years earlier

The Weston garden was in full bloom—white roses, clipped hedges, enough champagne to drown half the county. Eleven-year-old Ian, sweating under a too-stiff collar, squirmed through the wedding with restless impatience. His uncle Thomas, normally too buried in work to even make it to Christmas dinner, was now at the altar marrying a Korean doctor with a three-year-old daughter.

"Ian! Come meet your new cousin!"

His mother's voice snapped him out of his thoughts. The bride stood elegant in cream silk—part *hanbok,* part Givenchy. And next to her—or rather behind her—was a tiny girl, half-hidden in the folds of fabric, watching everything with wide, wondering eyes.

"This is Hana," his mother said. "Hana, darling, this is Ian."

The child said nothing. Her mother added, "She's not very talkative. Only makes baby sounds, I'm afraid." She didn't offer any justification, only the facts.

Ian crouched, holding out his hand and leveling his gaze with the girl's. "Hello Hana," he said. "Want to find some cake?"

She blinked at him. Then, slowly, she stepped out from behind her mother and put her hand in his.

That was it.

Later, they sat on garden chairs, watching the adults mingle. She said nothing—only kept her eyes on him, curious and quiet. He offered her a fruit jelly. She eyed the sweet like it might explode.

"Try it," he said. "It's good."

When she still didn't move, he bit half and held up the rest. After a beat, she leaned in, mouth open, and let him place it on her tongue. Her eyes widened and she smiled.

He heard his mother say to the bride, "Ian's always been so serious. Having a little cousin will be good for him."

No one knew then how right she would be.

The in-between years

Memories blurred into each other.

Hana at five, racing across the lawn the moment he stepped out of the car, home for the school holidays, flinging herself into his arms like she had been holding her breath until he returned.

At eight, teaching her to fish, both of them ankle-deep in cold water and mosquito bites.

At ten, riding her pony beside his horse, refusing to fall behind despite her feet barely reaching the stirrups.

At sixteen, he taught her to drive. He was twenty-four. She gripped the steering wheel like it might buck, eyes dead ahead, knuckles white.

"Relax. You're scaring the car."

She cracked a smile. A flicker. But it remained with him longer than it should have.

Always there. Other people came and went—classmates, girlfriends, friends of convenience. But Hana stayed. Steady. Loyal.

The turning point

It wasn't a single moment that changed everything. It crept up on him, slow and quiet, until one day it was irreversible.

Perhaps it started that weekend he picked Hana up from boarding school. She was seventeen, almost off to university, and no more that little girl who used to launch herself at him like a cannonball.

They drove to his London flat. His parents were in Singapore, hers scattered across time zones, and their Surrey house would have been all staff and silence. He made dinner while she perched on the counter, legs swinging, chatting about college plans and classes.

"Oxford," she'd said, eyes bright. "Then America. Harvard Law."

"Following in my illustrious footsteps?"

"Hardly. I want to make a difference in the world, not shuffle paper for multinationals."

"Ouch. You wound me, cousin."

She hopped off and leaned over his shoulder, sampling the sauce. As he stirred, she sliced a wedge of Gouda from the cheese board, took a bite, and held out the other half to him. He opened his mouth and took it from her fingers like they had always done. Half a strawberry, a biscuit split in two, toast with too much jam. Their version of affection had always been edible.

He began observing her, noticing the line of her jaw, the way she tucked her hair behind her ear. Her laugh wasn't a girl's anymore; it had depth, warmth, a rhythm that vibrated in his chest.

By the time he drove her back to school, Ian was not himself.

He tried to shake loose the hold, convinced it was nostalgia or a hormonal glitch.

And to really round out the denial, he recalled the most obvious fact: she was his cousin.

Stepcousin, a rebellious part of his brain muttered.

Still unacceptable, his better judgment snapped back. *You're twenty-five. She's seventeen. You're not in a French film.*

He spent the next few months in self-loathing. He worked like a fiend, avoided family gatherings, and told himself he would get over it.

But on many nights, he would lie awake for hours. Until he admitted at last that he would never get over Hana.

And there was nothing appropriate about it.

The decision

When Hana left for Harvard, Ian decided to bury his feelings. For years, he kept his distance. Toasted her graduation, sent champagne for her promotions, watched from across the ocean as she built a life in New York.

He played the role of cousin with discipline, listening

with patience when she called about flighty men, offering advice while swallowing his jealousy like bitter medicine.

He dated sharp, elegant, accomplished women who admired his intellect and dry humor. But they all noted his withdrawal when things edged too close to real intimacy.

He built his professional reputation with quiet ruthlessness. By his mid-thirties, he was one of the most respected M&A specialists in London, known for staying three steps ahead of everyone else and never losing his temper.

But always, there was Hana.

The late-night calls. Long weekends in Surrey. Holiday dinners where they would end up together, trading stories over whisky or tea. That old affection never wavered—her head on his shoulder, her laughter at his driest jokes, the way she still nudged food onto his plate.

And every time, he would tell himself: *This is enough.*

Until it wasn't.

When she announced her move to Seoul at twenty-six, he smiled, outwardly supportive. But he suffered as if a vital organ had been scooped out of his chest.

Ian had joined the Weston-Rhee board early in his legal career, taking a seat on the grant compliance committee, where his meticulous eye and preference for structure found a natural home. Now, with the foundation expanding its operations, he saw his opening.

He only needed to be near Hana. Become essential to her again. And this time, he would not let go.

***

Ian stubbed out his cigarette, the last curl of smoke trailing behind him like memory. He straightened his cuff and stepped forward.

Thirty years since she first reached for his hand in a garden of roses. Fifteen since the shift he never spoke of. Seven since he stopped pretending time would dull its edge.

From London, he had tracked Seo Ji-hwan's appearance in Hana's life. The heir played his part well—tailored suits, strategic philanthropy, family expectations masquerading as affection. The same man who'd once goaded him when he'd warned him off a teenage Hana.

Ian hadn't forgotten. He would clear Seo from the board—that had always been the plan.

What he hadn't accounted for was the actor. Flashbulbs, fandoms, flimsy illusions. He was a disruption, certainly, but not a threat.

He allowed himself the barest smile as he walked.

Fame was fleeting. Power, even in Seoul, moved in cycles. But he had never cared for momentum. His strength was in staying still. Quiet, present, unshakable.

Let the others come and go. He would remain until the end.

PUBLICITY GAMES

Yoo-jin sat motionless in the screening room as a trailer for *Silent Witness* played for the fifth time. Rain-drenched alleys, loaded silences, that meme-worthy kiss. Choi Min-ah's character looked up at his with a trembling chin and glistening eyes. The tagline flashed across the screen: *Love or Betrayal: Which Will Win?*

He sighed as the clip looped again. *Apparently, betrayal. Every fucking time.*

"The online engagement's insane," a manager said, vibrating with glee. "That kiss scene's getting more replays than the World Cup final."

"The fans are already shipping you two. The studio loves it."

"Keep playing up the dating rumors—junkets, interviews, award shows. Lean into the chemistry."

Chemistry. What a word. I have more chemistry with my goddamn toaster. Yoo-jin stared at the screen, eyes blank. "I'm an actor," he said. "That should be enough."

Polite chuckles rippled across the room. "It is," a producer grinned. "That's why the audience believes it. But this is marketing. People want the fantasy to follow them home."

Of course, they do. And I get to live in the mess after the fantasy's done screwing me over.

His phone buzzed. A message from his co-star Min-ah: *Let's keep the spark going tomorrow.* Below it, her latest Instagram post with a behind-the-scenes selfie. Their faces close, her cheek basically on his. The caption read: *Method acting, or something more?* Two million likes and counting.

He flipped the mobile face down. *Christ. Not her overactive imagination too.*

The actress was playing her part to perfection—flirting in interviews, posting enough to stir the pot. Each coy smile saw her popularity climb with his.

Yoo-jin shifted in his seat, suddenly claustrophobic in the air-conditioned room. Somewhere in Seoul, he suspected Hana was seeing the same content. The scandalous headlines. The misleading comments. And what would she think? That he was enjoying it? That he chose this circus over her? *What a fucking mess.*

He hadn't touched her in over a month. Kept putting off calls, missing every chance to see her. She had gone quiet, and now she was drifting—he was certain of it. *She probably thinks I'm an asshole. She's not wrong.*

He rubbed his chin, regret and guilt crashing down on him. He stood abruptly, chair scraping. Ignored the assistant calling his name. Strode out of the building and into the parking lot, jaw clenched so tight it hurt.

He wanted to punch a wall. Scream. Break the glass of his own damn car. He was halfway to kicking a trash can when he heard it.

"Oppa?"

A breathy voice beyond the barrier. Then another. A few fans, clutching phones, holding up cards and gifts, their faces lit up like Christmas.

He froze. This was it. The fan adoration. The price of fame.

He smoothed his face. Walked toward them with a smile. Grinned like he wasn't dying inside. *Because the show would always go on. And I'm stuck in it.*

***

The *Silent Witness* premiere buzzed with energy.

The moment they stepped onto the red carpet, Yoo-jin schooled his features to mask his foul mood. He offered his arm to his co-star, who clung to it with an excessive display of possessiveness. *Jesus, woman. Have some self-respect.*

As they walked, he maintained a calculated distance—close enough for PR, far enough to keep his sanity. His co-star, however, kept eliminating that buffer, leaning into him with each photo op, her hip brushing against his.

"Look this way!" a photographer called. "Closer together!"

His jaw tightened as the actress' hand glided up his arm to rest on his shoulder, her body angling toward his. She laughed at something he hadn't said, her fingers trailing across his chest as she turned to wave at fans. He tamped down his irritation. *Three more hours of this shit.*

The press conference was more orchestrated. Questions about the film gave way to personal inquiries. "What was it like doing those intense scenes?" asked a reporter from Entertainment Weekly.

"*Oppa* made it easy," Min-ah answered before he could speak. "When you have that kind of connection, the emotions... just flow." She placed her hand over his, a move picked up by the front-row photographers. Under the table, he moved his knee away from hers.

"The chemistry between you two was palpable," another journalist called out. "Was that all in the script, or was it improvised?"

Yoo-jin leaned toward the microphone. "The script was excellent—"

"But some things... happen naturally when the cameras roll," Min-ah interrupted, her grin playful as she turned to him.

"Don't they, *oppa*?"

A reporter with wide-rimmed glasses, her face sharp and owl-like, raised her hand. Her rapacious energy and knowing smile made the room stir before she even spoke. "*Yoo-jin-ssi*," she said, "You must be a man in love. That haunted look on your face these past weeks—it speaks louder than words. Tell us, what does that feel like?"

The room went still.

Yoo-jin drew a sharp breath, narrowing his eyes. He had answered thousands of questions in his career, most of them pointless, some of them cruel—but this one slid under his skin with vicious precision.

Beside him, Min-ah shifted. He glanced at her and caught it—the faintest curl of her mouth, not quite a smile. A sneer, small but unmistakable, as if she were savoring the moment like a predator watching its prey bleed.

He turned back to the journalist, letting the silence hang for a second too long, and curved his lips into an easy smile, smooth as glass.

"You tell me, Ms. Oh," he said, tone light, almost playful. "Weren't you married for twenty years before your divorce?"

A ripple of laughter broke across the room, quick and biting. When they stepped away from the stage, Yoo-jin put distance between him and Min-ah. In the privacy of the greenroom, he lit into the actress. "You need to back off," he said, voice stern. "The studio wanted subtle hints about our characters' connection, not you announcing we're sleeping together."

Min-ah shrugged, checking her lipstick in a mirror. "Too late. We're already trending."

***

In a café across town, Hana sat with Ian, stirring her latte. The cup sleeve featured Yoo-jin's face inches from his co-star's. She turned it so their almost-kiss faced away.

She scrolled through her phone, past yet another article analyzing their "electric chemistry." A social media thread dissected every interaction: Yoo-jin's hand on the vulture's back, her fingers lingering on his arm, their "secret smile" during the press conference. *He can't sit next to me at a restaurant, but he'll play besotted lover to a D-list actress who uses his fame like a ladder.*

Ian observed her from the corner of his eye. "You're quiet today. Everything okay?"

She set the device face down on the table. "Fine—just fine." *Just watching my relationship disintegrate in front of my eyes and on every screen in the city.*

"That's their marketing strategy, isn't it? Making everyone think they're dating."

"It's publicity," she said.

"Still," he pressed, "seeing your boyfriend flirting with another woman has got to mess with your head."

A bus passed outside the window, its entire side a billboard for *Silent Witness*—Yoo-jin's face looming eight feet tall, his co-star's delicate hand splayed over his chest.

"There's really nothing—" A sudden thought surfaced with such clarity that it stopped her mid-sentence. *Maybe there's nothing to be jealous of because there's nothing left.*

"Hana? You alright?"

"Fine." *Just fine. We're over and I'm not doing a damn thing about it.*

***

The bistro was tucked away on a quiet street, its warm lights spilling onto the sidewalk like a beacon in the early evening darkness. *Le Petit Jardin* had become "their place" over the past few weeks. It was small and intimate but public enough to be noticed.

Ji-hwan was already at their usual corner table when Hana arrived. He stood as she approached and kissed her cheek, as if they were meeting in Mayfair instead of Gangnam. Their now-default European-style greeting no longer made the waiters blink.

"You're early," she said as he helped her out of her coat.

"I wanted to steal more of your evening."

The server came with menus, but he waved them away. "We'll have the seafood platter to share, and the William Fèvre Grand Cru Chablis."

"My favorite wine," she said, surprised.

"I know." It was an unspoken challenge and a quiet confession.

Hana leaned back, studying him across the table. "You know a lot about me."

"I pay attention." The words were simple—the look wasn't.

Her eyes dipped to the tablecloth before fixing on him again. "You know who he is, don't you?"

"Yes, I do." He didn't blink. "And I also know you're struggling when you bite the corner of your lip like that."

Embarrassed, she looked away. "I thought you were supposed to entertain me," she said in a lighter tone.

"I'm failing miserably." He topped off her wine. "Introspection before the main course is very rude. I'll save the existential discussion for dessert."

Their seafood platter arrived—oysters, scallops, and prawns arranged like jewels on ice. The conversation softened, circling around music, travel, and absurd hypotheticals involving time machines and outlawed cheeses.

After the waiter cleared their plates, Hana leaned forward. "Tell me what you're thinking."

His lips quirked. "About what? The economic implications of cryptocurrency? Whether aliens built the pyramids?"

"You know what."

Instead of answering, he reached across the table and took her hand, his touch confident but light, his thumb brushing over her knuckles in lazy circles.

"I think this media circus is wearing you down. And I don't like seeing you become collateral damage for someone else's ambition."

"Really? And what would you do about it?"

"If you want," he said, voice low, "I could dismantle his career brick by brick and force him to take a job at the post office."

She laughed—but stopped herself when she saw his expression. It was half teasing, half serious. "You're not joking, are you?"

"All you have to do is say the word." He squeezed her hand before letting go. "But enough about that. The chocolate soufflé here is exceptional."

After they ordered dessert, Hana returned the favor. "Why aren't you married? You're successful, intelligent... and far from hideous."

"High praise." His smile faded, replaced by a quiet warmth in his eyes. "The answer's simple. I want a woman I like. Who I hope also likes me."

"That's it?"

"Were you expecting an elaborate psychological profile?"

"Why only *like*? Not *love*?"

"*Like* is harder. Love can be dramatic. Messy. Obsessive. But *like*... that's knowing the worst bits and still wanting to stay."

Their soufflés arrived, steam curling off their perfect dome. He waited until the server disappeared before leaning close again. "It doesn't have to be complicated, *Hana-ya*."

That simple, affectionate form of her name—casual to

others, intimate to her—landed like a feather on skin. Weeks had passed since anyone had spoken to her with such tenderness. *Everything is complex with Yoo-jin. It's exhausting.*

Ji-hwan didn't press. "Eat your soufflé before it collapses."

She broke the crust. *He's right. It shouldn't have to be difficult.*

When she glanced up, he was observing her with that easy smile on his face, as if he'd just let her in on a secret. Unlike Yoo-jin, there was no guessing with Ji-hwan. His intentions had always been clear.

All she had to do was lean closer.

***

It was past midnight when Yoo-jin stepped into his penthouse. Sharp modern glow revealed clean lines and curated stillness. Quiet. Expensive. Empty.

He kicked off his shoes and loosened his tie as he walked to the couch. His shoulders ached from a day of standing too long, smiling too hard, and repeating the same answers in different ways.

His phone buzzed. He ignored it. It buzzed again.

His manager: *Great job today with Min-ah. The internet's on fire. #YoojinMinahCouple is trending. Let's keep the momentum until release.*

He let his head fall back against the cushion, eyes shut. *Perfect. Now I'm a fucking algorithm.*

The actress had laughed too loudly at every joke. Touched his arm more than necessary. He hadn't corrected her—the cameras had been rolling. But when the director praised their "natural chemistry," he had almost blurted out something reckless.

He scrolled to Hana's last message, four days ago: *Hope the screening went well.* No emoji, no warmth. *When did we start sounding like acquaintances?*

He typed: *I hope you're doing okay. I know the promotional stuff with Min-ah looks intense, but it's for the cameras—you know that, right?*

Too defensive? Too late?

The worst part wasn't the silence. It was not knowing if she was choosing it. If she was letting go of him, one unanswered text at a time.

He looked around his spotless apartment. The last time Hana was here, her coat was thrown over that chair. Her coffee mug left by the sink. Her laughter echoed off these walls. Now it was only him and his perfect lighting and his pathetic life.

He bent forward, clasping his head in his hands. Tired in the kind of way that sleep didn't fix. He didn't want applause. He didn't want trending hashtags. He only wanted to come home and find her here.

And right now, that didn't feel like something he could ask for.

Still, he swore he'd do better, fight harder for Hana. What he didn't know—he wasn't the only one lining up to play.

CROSSED SIGNALS

Hana's arms tightened around Ian as he accelerated the BMW motorcycle through a gap in traffic. The bike had been his first purchase in Seoul. Though he called it "practical transportation," it was pure indulgence. Worth every ₩on for moments like this—Hana's closeness to him, her complete trust in him.

On this mild May morning, the market was crowded with people on lunch break, the air thick with the aroma of frying dumplings and grilled meats. After he parked, Hana led him to her favorite food stall. The elderly proprietress looked up as they approached, her face creasing into a smile at the sight of Hana.

"*Aigoo,* my best customer! Who is this handsome man?" she asked in Korean, eyeing Ian with open appraisal.

"My cousin," Hana explained, settling onto a stool. "From England."

Cousin. The word hit Ian with its familiar sting. *The box I'd spent fifteen years trying to redefine.*

The woman nodded her approval. "Good-looking family. The usual for you?"

He noted the tension draining from Hana's shoulders as she set out napkins and utensils for them. He opened her soda can, a habit from childhood.

"Try this one," she said after taking a bite of dumpling

and holding the other half to his lips. "The kimchi filling is incredible."

He took it straight from her chopsticks, chewing with appreciation. "Not bad," he said, pointing to another. "Now this one. What's in it?"

Their conversation flowed through topics both meaningful and trivial—his impressions of Seoul, her social life, shared memories from summers in Surrey. Until he rounded on a subject he had been saving.

"Seo Ji-hwan," he said. "Interesting character."

The name was still bitter on his tongue. Seventeen years hadn't dulled the memory of the chaebol heir at their family estate, his eyes following sixteen-year-old Hana across the lawn during that shooting weekend. The naked assessment in the other man's gaze had triggered a visceral reaction in him. Their confrontation—Ian backing Seo against the library wall, warning him to keep his distance—remained crystal clear. As did Seo's sneer and his quiet promise: *For now.*

She looked up from her plate, surprised. "You know about Ji-hwan?"

"I'm on the board—I know everything. All your invitations and events." He poked at a pickled radish but changed his mind. "He's circling you. I'm sure you've noticed."

Her face became more guarded. "He's nice, plus his company could be a powerful partner for the foundation."

Ian suppressed a smirk. *Of course, she'd start with the pros. Rationality as armor, analysis as avoidance.* "That photo of you two at the Blue House. Striking. You make quite a power couple." He had studied that picture for an hour when it appeared in the press. The way the billionaire had positioned himself beside Hana—angled toward her, hand hovering near her back without touching—claiming without appearing to claim.

"We're not a couple," she protested.

"Of course not," he agreed, allowing enough skepticism into his tone.

She flushed, barely noticeable, but he caught it.

Two gala invitations in three weeks. A series of "business" lunches that lasted far longer than necessary. Seo was executing a textbook campaign of steady escalation. Not too fast to frighten, not too slow to lose momentum.

"It was an official function. That's the only reason he invited me—networking for the foundation."

"I'm sure he did," Ian murmured, taking a deliberate sip of his soda. "Ji-hwan was always strategically brilliant."

The bait worked. Her eyes widened. "You know him?"

He considered how much to reveal. The full history would sound petty, obsessive. "Cambridge," he said. "Different years, same social circles. Formidable intellect, ruthless ambition. He's a billionaire now, while I remain a humble millionaire. Some of us clearly applied our education better than others."

"You never talked about him before."

"Why would I? Until now, he was just another successful businessman I had gone to school with." He noted the subtle shift in her posture. "But now he's orbiting my favorite cousin. That changes the math."

"He never mentioned knowing you. Do you think he made the connection between you and the foundation?"

"Of course, he did. But I'm also not surprised he omitted me from his narrative."

Hana fidgeted in her seat. "We've only been on a few dates. That doesn't mean he's interested—"

"Don't be naïve. Seo Ji-hwan isn't looking for a simple trophy wife. He's looking for substance." For all their mutual dislike, he understood the Seraphine CEO. He'd want Hana's mind, her integrity, her fire—everything Ian wanted for himself.

"And you, my darling, are just that," he continued,

measuring each word. "I've seen aristocratic ladies throw themselves at Ji-hwan. His family is filthy rich. But he's smart. He wants more than a fancy name—someone who shines, who does work that matters, whom people respect."

"If that's true and Ji-hwan is interested in me—is that a bad thing?"

"That depends on what you want. A hollow partnership that looks good, or a loving one that respects your integrity?" The words came too close to revealing too much. He forced himself to stay casual—the concerned cousin, not the man who'd loved her all her life.

"I think Ji-hwan is sincere, and I like him."

Ian managed not to roll his eyes.

"But it's a long shot. It's not like he'll propose tomorrow. Besides—"

He cut her off. "Hana—you deserve better. Not as a convenient lover for a celebrity or a status symbol for a tycoon." He leaned in and brushed a crumb from her lip. "You deserve to be loved for who you are." *By me. Before the chaebol. Before the actor. Before the titles and the gowns and the cautious way you choose your words now.*

"*Loved for who I am*—that sounds awfully corny."

"When you get to my age, 'corny' is what people call wisdom." He rubbed her elbow. "Come on, finish up and let's go unleash my machine on the open road."

Ian helped her back into her leather vest, fastening it with deft fingers. "Sweet?" he asked, unwrapping a piece of candy and biting into it before popping the other half into Hana's mouth. Then he checked her helmet straps and they took off into traffic, her arms wrapped securely around him. *Right next to me. Right where you belong.*

Neither saw the cameras across the street or the figure observing their interaction with quiet devastation.

***

The cosmetics campaign was another commercial obligation for *Silent Witness*. Yoo-jin moved on autopilot, every smile hollowed out and rehearsed. *Same shit, different day. This fucking nightmare.*

Min-ah, ever the professional, mirrored him. Their scripted chemistry was now a marketing blueprint. The Myeongdong storefront had transformed into a pop-up studio. "Five minutes—then we'll roll the formal segment," the brand rep said, leading them to the backdrop. Yoo-jin gave a stiff nod, eyes glazed.

The throaty purr of a sleek motorcycle across the street made people look up. A tall man in all black leather dismounted, tugged off his helmet, and raked a hand through his dark blond hair. He turned and helped down his passenger. She tipped her head back as she took off her headgear, hair tumbling loose around her shoulders.

Hana.

Yoo-jin's vision tunneled. *No. No, no—*

The couple walked toward a food stall, talking, smiling. The man's hand brushed her back as she relaxed against him.

Yoo-jin's breath stuttered. His hands clenched. His jaw locked. *Get your goddamn hands off my girl.*

The man opened her soda can. She fed him food from her chopsticks. Their heads leaned close as they spoke. He wiped a smudge from her lip. Yoo-jin's heart punched upward into his throat. *I should go over there. Ask her what the fuck this is. Ask him if he wants to lose a few teeth.*

But he didn't move—couldn't move. Because here, in public, he wasn't her boyfriend.

As they prepared to leave, the man tugged Hana's leather jacket closed, fingers lingering a beat too long at her chest. Then he bit off a piece of candy and slipped the rest between her lips with the familiarity of a lover.

Yoo-jin jammed his shaking hands into his pockets. *Has*

she been lying to me all this time? Or have I abandoned her for so long she's found someone else?

The thought made him nauseous. The crowd buzzed in the small space, phones raised, oblivious to the implosion taking place beneath his skin.

"*Yoo-jin-ssi?* We're ready."

His eyes stayed locked on where Hana had stood. The motorcycle was gone, but the smell of exhaust lingered, foul and clinging.

"Oppa," Min-ah said, laying a careful hand on his back, her smile trained on the cameras. "They're waiting."

He glanced down at her as if only remembering she existed. In a daze, he slid his arm around her shoulders to steady himself. *I can't scream. I can't cry. I need—*

Without thinking, he pressed a kiss on top of her head. It wasn't out of affection but desperation, a soothing gesture to anchor him.

The crowd erupted in delighted gasps. Phones flashed. The press director whooped behind the camera. "That was perfect. Natural and sweet—exactly what we wanted."

Yoo-jin didn't hear any of it.

***

Weeks passed and Hana remained elusive.

Yoo-jin sank into his couch and swirled a glass of Chablis —the one she liked. He had learned her preferences the way he studied scripts: methodically, obsessively. The exact temperature for her white wine. The damn rooibos tea she needed when she was stressed. All catalogued in his head, like lines from a role he used to play to perfection. *And now? I'm here drinking alone like a fucking loser.*

He opened Hana's messages. Their last thread was a graveyard of short, neutral replies. The emotionless language of two people pretending they weren't hurt. *Call her. Speak up, for fuck's sake.*

He started typing, but the wine disrupted his coordination, forcing him to stop and start again. *You're probably asleep. Or busy. Or done. I don't know. I miss you. I hate it. Say something. Anything. But don't shut me out.*

He hit "Send." Waited. Ten minutes. No reply. Fifteen. Still nothing. He stood and paced the room.

Before he could overthink, he pressed the call button, holding his breath as the phone rang—once, twice, three times when the line connected.

"Hello?" Hana's voice was cautious, as if unsure whether to accept the call.

"Hi. I hope I'm not calling too late."

"No, it's fine." A pause. "How are you?"

The polite inquiry landed hard. "I'm okay. Busy." A lie to avoid admitting he was alone and missing her. "How about you?"

"Good—I'm good."

A silence filled with unasked questions. No bantering, laughing, and sharing stories like before. At last, he dropped the pretense. "I miss you."

A beat passed on Hana's end. "Work's been intense."

"I understand." He took a deep breath. "Can I see you? Maybe tomorrow? Or the day after? Whenever works for you. I'm clearing my schedule."

"I'll have to see," she said, noncommittal.

"What are you doing right now?"

"Nothing special—zoning out in front of the TV."

A cautious pause. "Alone?"

"No, with—someone."

Someone. The casual reference made his stomach heave. The blond guy was probably in her living room, sprawled out on her couch.

Who's the fucking someone? He wanted to explode, to demand answers. Every cold text hit him like a slap, proof he had been played. He was the judge, the jury, the idiot on trial.

But the words jammed behind his clenched teeth. Jealousy burned in his throat—hot, metallic—but he couldn't voice it. He wouldn't confront Hana unless he could be calm.

"I should go," she said after an awkward silence. "It's getting late."

"Right. Goodnight, then."

"Goodnight, Yoo-jin."

The sound of his full name—stiff, formal—made his heart sink. The call cut off, leaving nothing but his lonely reflection on the screen.

He took another sip of Chablis, now sharp and bitter on his tongue. He'd let the work pull him away, let the secrecy choke what was left. Him always gone, her always hidden.

And in that silence, she was drifting toward someone else.

THE REAL PERFORMANCE

Saturday night found Hana still at her desk at the office. Budget projections for the Cambodia project needed adjusting, and each moment was time not spent thinking of Yoo-jin.

Her mobile vibrated with a text from Ji-hwan: *Downstairs. No rush. The play doesn't start for an hour.*

Ten minutes later, she emerged from the building to find not Ji-hwan's usual Aston Martin but an understated black Audi SUV waiting at the curb. She slid inside and saw him scrolling on his phone.

He looked up with a smile and leaned forward to kiss her cheek. "Working on a Saturday?" he asked by way of greeting. "I'm beginning to think workaholism is contagious in Seoul."

"Says the man checking emails in a chauffeured car on his way to the theater."

"Touché." He grinned and pocketed the device.

As they pulled into traffic, he settled back against the leather seat. "I thought a play would be better than the movies. No opening commercials."

"But no popcorn," she pointed out.

"A small sacrifice. Besides, *The Crucible* is supposedly excellent—though I'm not sure witch trials qualify as entertainment for a Saturday night."

"It's a metaphor for political persecution and mass

hysteria," she said. "Miller wrote it during the McCarthy era."

"See? This is why I bring you to these things. I get culture and education in one sitting."

By the time they reached the National Theater, Hana was feeling lighter than she had in weeks. The grand lobby bustled with well-dressed patrons, voices echoing off marble floors and high ceilings. Ji-hwan kept a hand on her waist as they wove through the crowd, the gesture both protective and casually possessive.

"I got us center orchestra. Better than those pretentious VIP boxes where you can't see half the stage and have to sit up straight because everyone's watching the watchers."

"The horror," she teased. "How would you survive?"

He laughed, drawing glances from nearby theater-goers. He leaned closer to whisper, "If I fall asleep, elbow me before I start snoring."

"If you fall asleep during Miller, I'm leaving you here."

***

"You need to get out," Sang-min said, eyeing Yoo-jin slumped on the couch, thumb scrolling over the same old photos of Hana. "This wallowing is pathetic."

"I'm not in the mood for crowds."

But Yoo-jin had to admit his friend was right—his penthouse had become a prison of memories. He crossed the crowded theater lobby with his head down, cap pulled low, shoulders hunched as he trailed Sang-min to their seats. *What a life. Hiding like a damn criminal just to see a play.*

Then he heard it—a laugh cutting through the ambient noise like a knife slashing his chest. Light, musical, unmistakable. His head snapped up, eyes scanning the space until they landed on her.

Hana was standing several rows ahead, animated and bright beside a tall, well-dressed man. The sight of the

Seraphine CEO hit him like a truck. *You've got to be kidding me—the chaebol heir? What happened to the blond guy? Is he a different day of the week?*

"What's wrong?" Sang-min asked, noticing his friend's sudden stiffness.

"Nothing." Yoo-jin dropped into his seat, keeping his gaze locked on Hana. *Everything. My whole goddamn life is wrong.*

Their seats offered him a clear view of the couple in front. He observed their easy rhythm, settling in as if they belonged in each other's space.

"Isn't that Seo Ji-hwan?" Sang-min breathed, following his friend's death stare. "The Seraphine Holdings guy?"

Yoo-jin's jaw clenched so tight he thought his teeth might crack.

"And... isn't that your Hana with him?"

The possessive *your Hana* mocked him like an ill-timed joke. *Was she ever mine? I kept her hidden away while this corporate prick gets to parade her in public.*

The stage blurred. The real performance was playing rows ahead—the whispered jokes, her laughter tucked into her sleeve, his shoulder too near hers. *I want to climb over these seats and rip his smug face off.*

When the house lights came up, he could see the billionaire helping Hana into her coat.

"That was surprisingly good," he said, voice carrying far enough for Yoo-jin to catch. "Though I still think witch hunts are a downer for a date."

Yoo-jin couldn't help rolling his eyes. *A date—a public goddamn date. Something I never had the balls to give her.*

"You laughed during the serious part," she scolded him, warm with affection.

"Sorry—was that the heavy stuff?" he grinned, taking her hand. "Come on, I'm starving. Let's get some dinner."

The tender look that passed between them was like a

knife plunged into Yoo-jin's heart. "Can we wait a bit?" he managed, voice strained.

Sang-min acquiesced without questions. They stayed seated as the theater emptied, with Yoo-jin tracking the couple until they disappeared from view. *This is the price. This is what my stupid career costs.*

The cool night air slapped his face as they exited, but the fog in his mind remained. He had only taken about ten steps when he heard it—

"Yoo-jin oppa!" A young woman cried out, followed by excited whispers spreading like wildfire.

Great. Right on fucking cue. Bodies closed in around him, phones raised, voices overlapping. He shifted to autopilot—smile, bow, sign. The performance he could do in his sleep.

Through the chaos, he noticed a stillness at the edge of the crowd. Hana stood watching him—her expression cycling through surprise and confusion. For a suspended moment, they locked eyes across the sea of fans.

Yoo-jin tried to fray a path to reach her. But before he could break through the wall of people, the tycoon appeared at her side. He placed a light hand on her shoulder, steering her toward a luxury SUV idling at the curb just beyond the pedestrian space. His gaze flicked to Yoo-jin to acknowledge him with a brief, polite nod. He turned to help Hana inside and slid in beside her. The car merged into traffic and vanished from sight.

Yoo-jin stood rooted to the sidewalk. *She's gone. With a man who isn't concealing her like a blemish on his image.*

***

Inside the car, silence settled like fine dust, delicate and impossible to ignore.

Ji-hwan tracked Hana from the corner of his eye, her profile lit by passing streetlights. For a moment, he considered pretending not to have seen the actor mobbed by fans, or the charged glance between him and Hana. But willful blindness wasn't his style, and she deserved better than feigned ignorance.

"So," he said, tone conversational but cautious, "that was Lee Yoo-jin."

Hana fixed her gaze on the road ahead. "Yes."

"I read the reviews. Critically acclaimed movie. In particular the lead actors' chemistry together."

She didn't flinch. "Choi Min-ah is a talented actress."

Silence stretched again. He could leave it there, change the subject, and move to safer territory. But the unspoken tension would remain with them for the rest of the evening.

"Hana, we don't have to pretend."

She turned to face him. "Pretend what?"

"That seeing Lee doesn't affect you."

A small, rueful smile touched her lips. "You're very observant, aren't you?"

"One of my many toxic traits, I'm afraid." He paused, weighing his next words. "I won't ask you to explain—that's your business. But I want you to know—I didn't pick the theater tonight to ambush you. I had no idea he'd be there."

"But you know more than you're letting on."

"I know his film's promotion has been... extensive. And it's taking a toll on you."

"That's diplomatic phrasing. What else?"

Ji-hwan considered his options. Full disclosure risked overplaying his hand. But evasion would undermine her trust in him.

"Celebrities often have publicity relationships that aren't real. While real ones suffer." He shifted in his seat. "Would you rather skip dinner? I can take you home."

"No," she said, with surprising firmness. "I'm tired of

changing plans because of him."

He nodded. "There's a new place in Cheongdam-dong—excellent wine list. And I promise, not a single celebrity in sight. The maître d' is practically on my payroll."

She bit back a smile. "You're silly."

"Only occasionally. And always for a good cause."

"Which is?"

"Making you laugh instead of watching you hurting."

The honesty caught her off guard. For a moment, Hana's armor slipped, revealing the hurt beneath. "I haven't been very good company, have I?" she murmured.

"You've been as you need to be," he said. "I don't care for performative cheerfulness, Hana. I'm interested in you—whatever state you happen to be in."

She pondered his comment, as if discovering a new facet of him—or herself. "Thank you, for that—and for the way you're handling... all of this."

The car pulled up to the restaurant, but neither moved.

"Shall we?" he asked, gesturing toward the entrance.

She let the mood settle before leaning in and pressing a soft kiss to his lips. "Now we can." Her smile was free of the earlier shadow.

Outside the car, Ji-hwan found himself adjusting Hana's coat, pulling it closer around her shoulders. As they walked inside, he draped his arm around her—a gesture that could have been presumptuous, but instead felt natural, inevitable.

TRIPLE CROWN GAMBIT

The presidential campaign gala that June had transformed the National Museum into a glittering shrine to influence. Politicians mingled with CEOs and celebrities, all gathered under the noble banner of childhood education—which also doubled as excellent public relations.

Hana, in a sleeveless metallic Erdem gown, entered alongside Ian, her arm linked with his. He was in sharp black tie, nodding to acquaintances as they crossed the reception hall.

"Remind me why we're subjecting ourselves to this again?" he murmured close to her ear.

"Because the First Lady personally invited the foundation, and turning her down would be career suicide," she replied. "Plus—our fathers would disown us if we snubbed the president's wife."

"Fair point. Though I suspect he'd understand if I claimed a sudden bout of diplomatic food poisoning."

As they reached the ballroom, Seo Ji-hwan materialized before them, devastating in a bespoke tuxedo. His eyes warmed when they settled on Hana. "Ms. Weston-Rhee," he greeted her with a light kiss on her cheek. "A pleasure, as always."

The familiar gesture wasn't lost on Ian, who squared his shoulders.

"Mr. Seo," she acknowledged the greeting. "I didn't know Seraphine Holdings had an interest in early childhood education."

"We have interests wherever the First Lady directs us," he smirked, before turning to Ian. "Weston."

"Seo." Ian offered a firm, brief handshake. "Cambridge feels a lifetime ago."

"Indeed. Always hosting those agonizing wine and cheese nights."

"Someone had to teach you scholarship boys the difference between Bordeaux and Beaujolais," Ian returned with velvet steel.

Hana's eyes flicked from one man to the other, catching their decades-old rivalry hidden beneath cordial tones.

"I understand Seraphine's expansion continues," Ian said. "Still with the family firm, then?"

Ji-hwan's smile didn't falter. "Some of us build on legacies rather than inheriting them."

"And some of us work for a living because we weren't handed a multi-billion-dollar playground," Ian replied.

"How's the legal world these days? Still managing other people's crises to avoid your own?"

Hana opened her mouth to intervene—but froze. Both men followed her gaze and turned.

Yoo-jin was cutting through the crowd toward them. No handlers, no press—only the raw magnetism of a man needing to speak his mind. The tuxedo was midnight blue, the expression unyielding. Nearly two months had passed since he'd been this close to Hana.

"Hello, Hana." He said her name like a declaration.

"Yoo-jin—" Color drained from her face. "I didn't know you'd be here."

"Last-minute campaign request. Celebrity endorsement duty." He turned to the others with a cool nod, extending his hand. "Yoo-jin Lee. We have mutual friends."

"How do you do? Ian Weston."

Yoo-jin gave him a cold smile of recognition. *The blond guy —finally putting a name to the face I've been wanting to punch.*

"Seo Ji-hwan, Seraphine Holdings. It's a pleasure."

Their handshake was firm, almost challenging. *The chaebol heir—looking even more smug up close.* "The luxury group—I believe I wore one of your labels in Venice."

"We appreciate the visibility," Ji-hwan replied, tone smooth. "Always good sales when celebrities showcase our designs on the red carpet."

Yoo-jin's smile stayed fixed, but there was no warmth in his eyes. "I'm sorry to intrude. I only wanted to say hello. Hana always seems to be... everywhere lately."

"You're not intruding at all," Ian said with exaggerated politeness. "We're all interlopers here, aren't we? Some more than others, perhaps, but you're in good company."

Ji-hwan leveled a skeptical stare. "Speak for yourself, Weston. Some of us were actually invited."

"Thanks to deep pockets, no doubt," Ian said.

"As opposed to inherited privilege?" Ji-hwan returned.

Yoo-jin followed this exchange, assessing his opponents. "I'm afraid I'm the real outsider. Only an actor among serious people."

"Don't sell yourself short," Ji-hwan said. "Entertainment is Korea's most visible export. Though maybe not its most substantial."

"Substantial—like luxury handbags?" Yoo-jin asked, all innocence.

"Or high-profile mergers?" Ji-hwan quipped, glancing at Ian.

Ian laughed—dry, sharp. "Actors and lawyers create value. Better than living off your father's work."

"Says the man riding his family name through London legal circles," Ji-hwan returned pleasantly. "How's the family shipping business, Weston? Still bleeding market shares to the Chinese?"

"Gentlemen, please—" Hana attempted to interject. But they weren't listening, locked in a closed circuit of posturing and testosterone.

Yoo-jin kept his eyes on Ji-hwan and Ian but aimed his words at her. "I wasn't aware foundation directors needed such a... vigilant male entourage."

Ji-hwan didn't miss a beat. "When one partner is consistently absent, alternatives tend to step in."

"At least he's not searching for a trophy wife," Ian added drily. "Ivy League pedigree, faultless lineage. Very twenty-first century of you, Seo."

"Spoken like a man whose relationship with his cousin raises more eyebrows than the British monarchy's genetic tree," Ji-hwan returned silkily. "Glass houses, Weston."

Ian's smile thinned. "Hard to mistake vulgarity for wit. Even when dressed in Savile Row."

Yoo-jin's voice dropped a shade. "And pursuing someone who's already attached—that's a moral gray area, isn't it?"

Ji-hwan turned to him, eyes glinting. "I thought certain romances were like Schrödinger's cat—real and not real, depending on who's watching."

"Indeed," Ian agreed. "Though some might say sacrificing personal life for career ambition shows questionable values."

A few feet away, two socialites followed the scene with amusement.

"Would you look at that—three eligible men circling one woman," one commented behind her champagne glass.

"Tragic, really," the other replied. "Honestly, with the nation's birthrate in freefall, it seems like a criminal misuse of manpower."

Near the bar, a junior aide whispered to a colleague. "Ten thousand ₩on says the actor throws the first punch."

"Twenty says it's the Brit," his friend countered. "They're deceptively scrappy. All that repressed emotion beneath the tailored suits."

Hana forced a smile at nothing. Her gaze kept flicking toward Yoo-jin like a moth battering itself against the light. Her face was pale, her pulse hammering in her throat.

Yoo-jin's voice was sharp at the edges but fraying underneath. He volleyed jabs, words hitting their mark, yet his eyes betrayed the fight. They clung to Hana—hungry, unblinking, like a drowning man searching for shore.

Ji-hwan's mouth tightened, finally noticing Hana's distress. He decided to de-escalate when she spoke.

"Enough!" Her voice carried a fierceness that silenced all three men. "I've had it."

They turned—her outburst snapped them back to reality.

"Hana, please—" Yoo-jin started, his face softening.

"I need a drink," she cut him off, her composure hinging on a thread.

"I'll come with you," Ian offered.

"Allow me," Ji-hwan countered.

Hana looked between them, fury and hurt in her eyes. "No. Stay and carry on with your fascinating spectacle. Let's not deprive the other guests of good entertainment."

Before any of them could respond, she spun around and stalked away, her gown shimmering under the lights as she disappeared into the crowd.

For a moment, all three men stood in stunned silence. They separated with curt nods, but not one of them moved to join Hana.

***

Across the room, Hana's hand shook as she accepted a flute

of champagne from a passing waiter. From her new vantage point, she could see the group dispersing like planets forced from their orbits. She emptied the glass in a single swallow before slipping through the side exit and into a waiting taxi.

From different corners of the ballroom, the men witnessed her departure with identical expressions of dismay.

Yoo-jin maintained his camera-ready smile as he chatted with a film producer, but his eyes tracked Hana's shiny gown until it disappeared from view.

Two months of silence had stretched between them like an eternity. And now, when fate had granted him this chance, he squandered it. The raw hurt he glimpsed in her eyes pierced him to his core. *This is the part where I chase after her, catch her in the rain, tell her I can't live without her.*

Except this wasn't a movie. And she wasn't running toward him in slow motion. She had turned away, back straight, dignity intact, while he stood frozen, watching the only woman who counted for him disappear once again. *I'm losing her. And all I can do is smile like a moronic Ken doll for people who don't give a damn.*

Ian sipped his whisky as he conversed with a British diplomat, but his attention was fixed on the terrace doors where Hana had vanished. *Well, bloody hell. That was unforgivably rude of me.*

He'd arrived under the pretext of 'family business,' when Hana was the only business at heart. Instead, he'd acted like a prat in front of Seoul's elite. *Father would be appalled.* Growing up English had instilled principles—one didn't make scenes, especially over women, and never in public. Yet there he'd been, dropping to schoolyard insults with all the refinement of a football hooligan.

But the worst part wasn't the breach of decorum. It was the pain on Hana's face. He hadn't meant to wound her. Quite the opposite. *And now she thinks I'm another entitled arse treating her like chattel to be claimed.*

He took another sip of whisky, allowing its burn to punish him. He would have to make amends, but not now. Tonight, he had thoroughly blown his chances.

Ji-hwan paused with a martini halfway to his lips, watching Hana's departure. Outwardly, he showed nothing—but inside, disappointment drummed a slow, steady beat. *Well, that was a masterclass in how to sabotage weeks of strategy in under five minutes. Good job, Ji-hwanie. Really nailed that one.*

He almost raised a glass to his performance—petty, reactive, clumsy. A jealous schoolboy lashing out because the actor got there first and the Brit pulled the family card. *Granny would be so proud. "That's my grandson, getting into pissing contests at state functions. The Seo dynasty is well and secure."*

The worst part was how transparent he had been. Subtlety and discretion, his strong suits, had taken the night off along with his common sense. And for what? A few barbed comments? A half-baked territorial display?

He had handed Hana every reason to pull away. Still, that wasn't what gnawed at him. It was the moment he saw her falter in public—eyes glassy, lip trembling. Fighting tears she didn't want anyone to see. Her distress had struck him like a punch to the solar plexus.

He took a slow sip of his drink, not tasting it.

She had looked at Yoo-jin Lee like a woman watching her heart break. That was more than history—that was unfinished business, the kind that still hummed under her skin. The kind he would be a fool to underestimate.

But the game wasn't over. It was changing.

***

The next day, Hana arrived at the foundation offices to find a frantic Jin-ah rearranging furniture in the reception area. "Good morning?"

"Boss! You're here." Jin-ah straightened, looking flustered.

"I was trying to make room."

"For what, exactly?"

The assistant gestured toward Hana's office. "Maybe you should see for yourself."

The hallway had transformed into a floral wonderland—or nightmare, depending on one's perspective. Three massive displays of peonies dominated the space, each competing for visual dominance.

"Dear god," Hana muttered, approaching the first arrangement. She plucked the small card nestled among the blooms. *Forgive my behavior last night. I'm a better man than that display suggested. Please give me another chance.—YJ*

The second bouquet, larger than the first, came with a handwritten note in elegant script: *Still schoolboys at heart. My sincere apologies for the rudeness. Dinner this weekend to make amends?—Ian*

The third—peonies in a deeper shade of pink arranged like art work—was the most beautiful. *Three grown men behaving like idiots. I have no excuse except that the others started it. Can we talk? - SJH*

A small laugh escaped her. "This is ridiculous."

"I rather think it's sweet," Jin-ah said, admiring the flowers. "Three handsome, successful men vying for your attention? Some women would consider it a dream scenario."

"It's like a funeral parlor in here. Break these up and distribute them around the office. The staff might as well enjoy them." Hana retreated to her desk to type a brief text to Ji-hwan: *Lunch?*

His response came immediately: *Our usual place?*

***

Ji-hwan was already seated at *Le Petit Jardin* when Hana arrived, rising from his chair with the instinctive courtesy that was second nature to him. He leaned down and brushed a cautious kiss on her cheek. "I feel like I've been summoned to the headmistress' office," he said, tone light but eyes serious.

She took her seat. "You sent flowers."

"I did."

"Any particular reason?"

He adjusted his cuffs. "Let's order first. It's hard to grovel on an empty stomach."

"What looks good?" she asked, opening the leather-bound card. "I don't see humble pie on the menu."

They ordered—duck confit for Ji-hwan and sea bass for Hana—and fell into a silence that stretched past comfortable.

"So," he said, swirling his wine, "about last night."

"Yes. That was quite a show."

"In my defense, I was provoked."

"Were you? I must have missed that part when you three were comparing the sizes of your... achievements."

He had the grace to look chagrined. "That's fair."

"Is it always like this? Three grown men forgetting a woman exists while competing for her attention?"

"Not always," he replied thoughtfully. "Sometimes there are four or five men."

She bit back a smile. "You're impossible."

"I'm self-aware, which is different." His features softened. "And genuinely sorry. It was rude."

They ate in silence for a few moments, the awkwardness easing as they fell into their usual rhythm.

"How's the sea bass?" he asked.

"Excellent. Your duck?"

"Perfect—though my taste buds may be off from last night's foot in my mouth."

Their desserts arrived—his a dark chocolate torte laced with raspberry *coulis,* hers a delicate *tarte tatin*. Hana took a bite and made a face.

"Not what you expected?" Ji-hwan asked.

"It's fine. Just a bit... predictable." She eyed his plate with obvious interest. "That, however, looks properly decadent."

"Try it." He cut off a piece and held out the fork to her.

She leaned forward to accept the offer, closing her eyes as she tasted it. "Oh, that's lovely. The raspberry cuts through the chocolate perfectly."

"I thought so too." His fork was loaded again before she'd even swallowed.

"Are you trying to seduce me with dessert?" she asked, but accepted the second forkful anyway.

"Is it working?"

She nodded, mock serious. "Possibly."

They shared his dessert while hers sat abandoned. The silence between them felt weighted, expectant.

"I've been thinking about us," he said at last, voice quieter. "About what we could be together."

She looked up, caught off guard. He reached across the table, covering her hand with his.

"I know I'm not the obvious choice. I'm probably too old for you, definitely too set in my ways, and I have strong opinions about wine pairings."

A small smile tugged at her lips despite the sudden shift.

"But I care for you, Hana. Deeply." His thumb traced gentle circles across her skin.

"You deserve someone who isn't afraid to be seen with you. Someone who can say your name without checking over his shoulder."

His eyes held hers, steady and certain. "I want to build something real with you—a partnership, a home, maybe a family. Something we don't have to hide."

He chuckled. "I know the timing's terrible. Wine, chocolate, candlelight—every cliché in the book."

Her breath caught as his humor faded.

"But I love you, Hana. And I'd very much like you to marry me."

She went still. Her lips curved into a small smile—part surprise, part tenderness—he couldn't quite tell.

"Cliché or not, it's effective. You're rather good at this."

"I meant every word."

"I know." She lifted his hand, pressing a soft kiss to his knuckles. Resting her chin on their joined fingers, she drew a slow breath. "You would make an amazing husband. Steady. Generous. Brilliant. Always in my corner."

He watched her face, noting the shift in her features, the gentle sadness creeping into her eyes. *Don't say it. Please don't say 'but.'*

"But..." She paused, and he felt his heart sink. "You see me as someone who belongs in your world. And perhaps I do. Maybe we'd even be happy."

She placed his hand back on the table without releasing it. "But there's someone I can't seem to walk away from. Even when he makes it impossible. With him... it's not about sense —it's like gravity."

Ji-hwan's expression remained composed, though a coldness settled in his stomach. *He's not even here. And still.*

Her voice dropped. "If I married you, I would always know there's something unfinished. It wouldn't be fair to either of us."

He exhaled slowly, nodding once. "No, it wouldn't."

"I'm sorry." Her fingers tightened around his.

Without a word, he kissed the back of her hand, lingering for a moment. "I suspected as much. But I had to ask."

"You've always been a kindness when I needed it," she said softly.

"Well, at least I managed that." His mouth quirked in a rueful smile. "My ego is taking this rather personally. Even though I knew it was an uphill battle."

Despite everything, she laughed—a soft, grateful sound. Silence settled between them, affectionate but tinged with regret.

"Friends?" she asked.

"Of course." His tone was light, carefully measured. He raised his glass with theatrical solemnity. "To the one that got away."

She smiled and lifted hers. "To terrible timing." They clinked glasses, and he returned her smile—warm enough to be genuine, controlled enough to mask the ache in his chest.

But as he sipped the wine, one thought simmered at the back of his mind: *This was never a game to me. And I wasn't supposed to fall this hard.*

***

Later, at her office, Ji-hwan walked Hana to the entrance. He leaned down and kissed her cheek. "Until next time, Hana."

She gave his arm a gentle squeeze. "Goodbye, Ji-hwan."

For a few moments, she stood watching him return to his car—his posture straight, movements unhurried. He didn't look back.

But as she walked inside and the door shut behind her, a dull weight caught in her chest. A delayed pang, deep and slow. She rested against the wall for a beat.

Somewhere deep down, she had begun to miss him. Not in the way that unraveled you, but in the quiet way that stayed.

POISONED KISS

Bass vibrated in Hana's bones as she tried to catch Jin-ah's words over the pulsating music. The trendy club had been Ian's choice for their team to celebrate a funding win.

Hana hadn't wanted to come. *Nightclubs and I are never a good mix. Always something life-altering.* But she didn't want to be a killjoy.

Ian draped his arm over the back of her chair, now his default posture. Around them, colleagues shed their reserve, professionals by day now laughing and swaying on the dance floor.

All of a sudden, the crowd parted like the Red Sea. God had a twisted sense of humor.

Hana looked up to see Yoo-jin entering with his entourage—his sharp-eyed manager Ji-hoon, studio executives in expensive suits, and Min-ah, that human barnacle clinging to his arm, her sequined dress catching every light. *He brings his little arm candy here. I can't believe my eyes.*

Hana's smile froze. Across the room, Yoo-jin's expression transformed from indifference to shock as their eyes locked. The club faded to background noise. Questions, explanations, and apologies passed between them, resolving nothing but acknowledging everything.

Jealousy coiled in her stomach. *Is there anything worse*

than seeing another woman wrapped around your boyfriend like shrink wrap? Ex-boyfriend. Whatever the hell he is now.

She resumed talking, refusing to acknowledge the emotional gut punch. *Don't look. Don't give him the satisfaction. Keep it together.*

"You okay?" Ian's question cut through her thoughts.

"Fine." She took a large gulp of her vodka tonic. "Thought I recognized someone."

He followed her gaze, his eyes registering Yoo-jin Lee. "Ah. I see."

She changed the subject, forcing a high-pitched laugh. "Do you remember when I got drunk and passed out at that Soho club after graduation?"

He played along. "Hard to forget. I had to carry you out over my shoulder like a sack of potatoes. You were half-conscious and swearing like a sailor."

She laughed while tracking Yoo-jin from the corner of her eye, now seated in the VIP section with the sparkle vulture hovering at his side. *She's practically in his lap. Has she zero self-respect? Or is this in their work contract?*

All night, she could feel his eyes on her. But she didn't give him the satisfaction of looking back. She smiled brighter. Clinked glasses harder. Let Ian tug her onto the dance floor. *Two can play at this.*

Hana was mid-story about her bar exam when Ian's face changed. Excited whispers rippled through nearby tables. "Oh my god, look! They're definitely together! Someone get a picture!"

What fresh hell is this? She turned toward the VIP section. There, spotlit by revolving beams, the fame-leech had her arms wrapped around Yoo-jin's neck, lips locked with his in a passionate kiss. Phones rose like periscopes despite the club's privacy policy.

In public? With me watching? She saw Yoo-jin's hands

gripping the actress' shoulders—to pull her closer or push her away? Hana couldn't tell, her vision blurring with white, hot rage. The spectacle humiliated her, even if no one else knew why.

"Celebrities." Ian's dismissive snort cut through her shock. "Always performing."

"I'm not sure they're performing." She scraped back her chair. "I need air." *Get out before you fall apart. Or worse, get arrested for assaulting that woman with her own stiletto.*

Ian stood. "I'll come—"

"No—stay." Her voice cracked like shattered glass. "I'll just be a minute. Order another round." *Don't follow me. Don't watch me break.*

Whatever was going on with Yoo-jin—media hype, fake infatuation—she could no longer pretend it didn't affect her. Seeing it on screen was one thing. Watching it live was something else. She had just enough time to reach a corner of the parking lot before she vomited. *I hate him. I hate her. I hate myself.*

Within moments, Ian appeared beside her. He held her coat and purse in one hand, and with the other wiped her lips with his handkerchief. "Let's bail," he said, draping the jacket over her shoulders. "They're wasted in there—won't even notice."

***

Inside the club, Yoo-jin managed at last to disentangle himself from his co-star. He searched for Hana's table, his heart sinking when he saw only her colleagues. She had disappeared.

"You should be thrilled," the actress whispered, her breath hot with expensive champagne. "Those photos will be everywhere by morning."

He said nothing, aware of watching eyes. His career obligations now weighed him down like chains. He went to the restroom, where he splashed cold water on his face and stared at his reflection with mounting disgust. *Fuck this. Fuck it all.*

***

Later, alone in his penthouse, Yoo-jin got up the courage to call Hana. It was two AM, an ungodly hour, but he was desperate.

She answered on the third ring, her voice thick with tears.

"Hana... baby— I'm so sorry," he said without preamble. "What you saw... it wasn't what it looked like."

A long pause on Hana's end. "I don't know what anything looks like anymore."

"Min-ah was drunk. She's been... impossible. The studio loves the speculation, but there's nothing real. You have to believe me."

"I want to." The simple honesty was more devastating than any accusation.

"Can I see you in the morning? Face to face, not like this."

She sniffed. "Yes. There's... someone I want you to meet properly."

The suggestion sent ice through his veins, but he agreed. "I'll be there first thing," he promised. "Get some sleep."

"You too. Goodnight."

***

Yoo-jin arrived at Hana's apartment just after eight, running on fumes after a sleepless night. His fingers shook as he punched in the door code. The fact that it still worked was a relief.

The hallway was quiet except for the low hum of the coffee maker and the gentle sizzle of something cooking. He expected to find Hana, perhaps still angry but at least willing to hear him out.

Instead, he stopped cold in the entryway. *What the actual fuck?*

The tall blond guy was standing by the stove, shirtless, wearing only a pair of loose pajama pants. He moved around the kitchen with unsettling familiarity, cutting the crust off the toast while monitoring eggs in a frying pan. He turned as Yoo-jin entered, knife still in hand, his expression shifting from surprise to guarded.

"Mr. Lee—an unexpected pleasure. Though I don't recall hearing the doorbell."

Yoo-jin's mouth went dry. The early hour, the bare skin, the man's smug confidence painted an undeniable picture. This was not his paranoia—it was brutal reality standing in front of him, cooking eggs.

"I know the code," Yoo-jin said through gritted teeth. "Why the hell are *you* here?" His eyes swept the apartment, searching for Hana. The bathroom door was closed, the shower running. The pieces clicked into place.

"As you can see, it's morning—and breakfast doesn't make itself."

Yoo-jin gestured toward the kitchen. "This is *my* job—*I'm* the one who cooks for her."

Ian's eyebrow rose a fraction. "Times change, don't they?" He set down the knife and picked up the spatula to poke the eggs. "Though I must say, this looks inappropriate. Entering a woman's flat unannounced... I believe they call that stalking."

Yoo-jin crossed the room in three quick strides and grabbed Ian. "I'm not a stalker—I'm her fucking boyfriend!"

Ian looked pointedly at Yoo-jin's hand on his arm, then jerked it away from his grasp. "Is that so? Tell me—is that drunk actress still hanging all over you? The tabloids had plenty to say about your kiss last night."

The words struck him like a sucker punch, reducing Yoo-jin to that single, humiliating moment—the very reason he was here to beg Hana's forgiveness.

"That wasn't—" Yoo-jin started, then changed direction,

shoving Ian back against the counter. "You know damn well it wasn't what it looked like."

"Do I?" Ian straightened to his full height, a deliberate reminder that he had two inches on Yoo-jin. He reached for his shirt draped over a kitchen chair and slipped it on. "All I know is that I've been picking up the pieces of a woman who deserves far better."

"You have no idea what Hana and I have."

"Had," Ian corrected. "Past tense—wouldn't you agree?"

Yoo-jin slammed a fist on the countertop, rattling dishes. "I didn't come here to talk to you!"

"And yet, here we are." Ian's eyes almost gleamed with enjoyment. "Rather like at the campaign reception, when you had to insert yourself into our group."

Recognition flickered. Yoo-jin hadn't made the connection a week ago, too tangled in his own emotions to catch his rival's surname—the same as Hana's. "Weston," he said at last, the name slotting into place. "You're the cousin."

"Stepcousin," Ian corrected, amused at Yoo-jin's confusion. "Though the distinction hardly matters anymore, does it?"

Yoo-jin's hand closed on Ian's shirt, yanking him forward. "What the hell does that mean?"

"I wouldn't do that if I were you," Ian advised, still composed despite being manhandled. "Causing a scene in her home wouldn't improve her opinion of you. She's already seen enough of your... antics."

Yoo-jin released him with a disgusted shove, taking a step back but still thrumming with tension. "I came to talk to Hana," he bit out. "To explain—"

"Explain what?" Ian interrupted, smoothing his shirt with exaggerated care. "The actress draped over you like a second skin? Or your two-month disappearing act? I'm curious to know."

"Our relationship is none of your business," Yoo-jin's hands balled into fists at his sides.

"On the contrary. When someone I love gets hurt, it becomes very much my business."

In a fit of rage, Yoo-jin grabbed a mug from the counter and hurled it against the wall, where it shattered with a satisfying crash. "She doesn't need your fucking protection from me!"

"The proof suggests otherwise," Ian remarked, glancing at the broken ceramic. "If she walked in right now and saw this." He gestured to the mess and Yoo-jin's fury like an attorney presenting evidence. "Would that help your cause?"

The implication hung heavy. Yoo-jin's eyes darted back to the closed bathroom door. A flicker of doubt crossed his face. "You're playing me. You want me to think you and Hana are—"

"Are what?" Ian's smile thinned. "Lovers? I never said that. Interesting that would be your assumption."

The coffee maker finished its cycle with a final hiss of steam, punctuating the charged silence.

Ian turned back to the stove, tending to the eggs. "She never said you two were still together," he dropped casually, as if he were discussing the weather and not driving a knife into Yoo-jin's heart. "Quite the opposite, in fact."

Yoo-jin blinked, dragging a slow hand over his face.

"Tell her—" he began, swallowing hard. What was there to say? A beat passed. "Never mind—don't fucking tell her anything."

Without another word, he spun on his heels and stalked out, the door clicking shut with quiet finality.

In the elevator, the gravity of it all crashed down on him. Weeks of building courage to face her, of rehearsing explanations and apologies, all for nothing. He slammed his fist against the wall, a raw, cracked sound escaping his throat. Tears spilled down his face, hot and humiliating. But he no longer cared about his meticulous image.

He only knew he had lost Hana.

***

Back in the apartment, Ian swept up the broken mug with a small smile. The actor had believed he and Hana were a couple, which explained his wrecked state of mind. And he wouldn't be rushing to correct the assumption.

The bathroom door opened, releasing a cloud of steam. "Was someone at the door?" she called out, towel wrapped around her hair. "I thought I heard voices. And did something break?"

"Knocked over a mug. It was only the delivery man with a wrong address," he lied. He loaded her plate and pushed it toward her. "Eat up."

She accepted the food but remained distracted, checking her calls every few minutes. Ian recognized the signs—emotional retreat, mechanical eating, the slight furrow in her brow whenever she was expecting something. Or someone.

"You look like you lost your favorite toy." He rose to clear their plates. "Want to talk about it?"

"There's nothing to say."

He didn't press. Instead, he asked, "How about a ride? Perfect weather."

Hana sighed, tucking away her mobile, unaware the visit she awaited had already come and gone.

***

An hour later, they were on his motorcycle, winding through scenic roads outside Seoul.

At one picturesque stop, Ian snapped a picture of Hana with wind in her hair, a subdued smile, and his bike in the background. The kind of casual, carefree image that seemed like a feat after the tension from recent days. She posted it to her private Instagram with a simple caption: *Finding peace on the open road.*

By lunchtime, at a roadside restaurant with weathered wooden tables and panoramic views, he addressed the elephant that had been trailing them for hours. "So," he said, swirling noodles around his chopsticks, "are we going to talk about your boyfriend?"

She choked on her water. "What?"

"The actor from last night. Your boyfriend—or ex-boyfriend? It wasn't clear from his reaction."

She set down her glass with exaggerated care. "His reaction to what?"

"To finding me in your flat this morning." His delivery was matter-of-fact, as if he were reading a news bulletin and not dropping a bomb in the middle of lunch. "He didn't seem especially pleased."

Hana's stomach dropped. "He came by? This morning?"

He nodded, taking a casual sip of tea. "Used his keycode to get in. Not sure if that's appropriate for an ex, but who am I to judge?"

"He's not an ex—" she started, but stopped herself. "What happened?"

"We had a brief chat," he replied with deliberate understatement. "He was under the impression you and I were together. I... don't know why."

His words stopped her cold. "Why did you let him think we were..." she couldn't finish the sentence.

"I didn't say anything of the sort," he countered, all innocence. "He drew his own conclusions."

Hana's fingers pressed against her temples. "Oh my god."

"I may also have mentioned the drunk actress who was all over him," he added as an afterthought. "That seemed to hit a nerve."

"You had no right—" she began, heat rising in her voice.

"To protect you? From someone who hides you away like a dirty secret while flaunting another woman in public? Who couldn't be bothered to talk to you for two months?"

They stared each other down across the table.

"Things got a bit heated," he continued. "He may have broken one of your mugs."

"He— what?"

"Threw it against the wall. Quite a temper, your actor."

She swallowed hard, trying to picture Yoo-jin losing control. This was not the restrained man she knew. But then— how well did she know him anymore? "What else happened?"

"Not much to tell. He left real quick. Looked like he was kicked in the guts, if I'm honest."

"You didn't tell me any of this," she said, bitter accusation in her voice. "You lied to me this morning."

He had the grace to look contrite. "I was sparing you immediate distress. You've been through enough."

"That wasn't your decision to make."

"Perhaps not." He reached across the table, his hand stopping short of touching hers. "But I've seen you check your phone a hundred times, waiting for a call or text. How you change channels when his commercials come on. The way you shut down whenever you hear his name."

Hana's throat tightened. Had she been that transparent?

"You're a Weston. You deserve better," he said.

She looked away. "You still should have told me."

"You're right. I should have. I'm sorry." He feigned mild regret as he signaled for the check. "Let's hit a few more spots while the light's still good."

***

Alone in her kitchen after Ian dropped her off, Hana picked up the small garbage can where he had put the broken mug fragments. Physical evidence of Yoo-jin's presence, of his pain and anger. It tempered her own jealousy from the previous night.

She sat and stared at her phone for a long moment before typing a message: *Can we talk?*

The text showed delivered but not read. She waited another hour and sent another: *It's not what you think.*

Still no response. She walked to her bedroom. On the nightstand was the small wooden box he had brought back from Bangkok months ago—a reminder of how much had changed since then.

She closed her eyes, exhausted by it all.

***

Miles away, Yoo-jin's laptop pinged with an Instagram notification. He had downed his third shot of soju to numb the scene from Hana's kitchen that had been looping in his head like some sadistic director's cut.

The image on his screen sealed the devastation: Hana with wind-tousled hair and that half-smile he once thought belonged only to him, seated on the black BMW motorcycle he had seen parked in her building's garage. *Of course it's that asshole's bike. Of course she'd ride with him.*

The caption was a masterpiece of subtle cruelty. *Peace? Is that what he gives you?*

Not a week since their run-in at the campaign reception, and she was now living her best Instagram life with the cousin. He shut the laptop and paced the penthouse, each echo of his footsteps swallowed by silence. The space, once their haven, was now dark and cold like a mausoleum.

He was pouring another shot of soju when his phone gave a soft chime. It powered on—barely charged—and the screen lit up with a message from hours ago. *Can we talk?*

His fingers stilled, torn between laughing and hurling the device against the wall. *Now she wants to talk? After this morning? After her damn motorcycle ride?*

Then another text: *It's not what you think.*

He tipped his head back and let the soju burn his throat. *No? Did I not see a half-naked man at your place? Tell me—what am I missing?*

The tabloids always called him the heartbreaker, the charmer, the one who would never stay. And yet here he was: nursing heartbreak, spiraling, abandoned.

He switched the phone off. *No, baby, I don't want to talk. I don't want to hear you tell me we're over.*

***

Later that week, the actress Choi Min-ah appeared on *Celebrity Spotlight*, the nation's most-watched talk show. When the host brought up Yoo-jin, she gave a smug little giggle she reserved for the cameras.

"What I *can* tell you," she said with cloying sweetness, "is that neither of us is dating anyone else." She leaned in, winking: "Interpret that however you wish."

Hana gaped, heart pounding like a war drum. *You manipulative bitch.*

She wanted to hurl her coffee mug at the screen, into the woman's cocky face. *And he lets her speak for both of them like she has the right.*

She slammed the cup down. Liquid sloshed over the rim. She grabbed a pen and stabbed it into a notepad, over and over, until the tip broke and the pages tore. Her knuckles went white. She bit down on them before she screamed out something reckless.

No message. No apology. Not one denial. Behind the actress, photos of Yoo-jin and his co-star cycled in an endless loop—intimate moments at galas, shared smiles, trending hashtags that linked their names like destiny.

Five days. Five days of nothing, and this is his answer.

LONDON CALLING

The plane touched down at London's Heathrow Airport. Hana blinked awake and straightened, feeling the knots in her shoulders loosening. *Not in Seoul anymore.*

Ian reached over and patted her hand. "Welcome home."

It was mid-June and a light rain hit the car windows as they drove to Hampstead. She gazed out at the familiar streets, the gray sky a comfort after Seoul's bright harshness.

The Weston townhouse was unchanged with its ivy-covered brick, the old creak in the third step, the grandfather clock still running five minutes fast. Her bedroom remained as she had left it: university pennants, competition photos, the antique writing desk.

And the silence. The security of home. The relief was immediate and physical.

***

Days settled into a healing rhythm. Mornings with her stepfather over coffee and newspapers. Ian appearing mid-morning bearing gifts like a courtier: books, theater tickets, pastries.

Hana moved through London like a woman trying on old clothes and finding they still fit. The Tate Modern, pausing at the Rothko like always. Kew Gardens, getting delightfully lost. Fortnum & Mason, dropping £80 on oolong.

She turned off Instagram notifications. Then Twitter. Then email.

Lunches with old friends filled her afternoons: women with sharp tongues and warmer hearts. Long, gossipy teas on Belgravia terraces smelling of roses and quiet privilege. No one asked her for selfies or to explain her life—they had seen her grow up at their dinner tables, on their family vacations, at the Queen's Cup.

Evenings belonged to Ian. Restaurants with crisp linens and waiters who knew them by name. Cocktails with actual conversation. The easy shorthand of shared years. They never spoke of Seoul. Never of Yoo-jin.

On their fifth night out, he said, almost to himself, "You're smiling more."

Hana swirled her Negroni. "I needed this."

***

Weekends in Surrey were like slipping into well-worn silk. An easygoing, relaxed version of herself she hadn't realized she missed.

Mornings were spent in the stables brushing Marmite, her sulky Cleveland Bay. The head groom, Albie, still called her "Miss Hanapops" like when she was five years old. He used to settle her in the saddle in front of him and take her on slow laps around the paddock, telling her about every horse by name and temperament. Now he only handed her the reins and said, "Don't let him toss you."

She galloped across the fields, the wind slicing through her sweater, breathing in that intoxicating smell of English countryside. *Manure and moss and woodsmoke. Better than any spa.*

After her ride, she would lounge at the kitchen table, sipping tea and savoring a jam-slathered scone while the cook filleted sole for lunch, often glancing in her direction with a conspiratorial smile. *Good thing Mother isn't here or we'd both be busted.*

The library still smelled like dry paper and old leather. She wandered its rows at dusk, fingers trailing spines she had memorized. *There you are, darlings. Waugh, Wilde, Woolf. Still judging me.*

Zadig and Voltaire, the family's chocolate Labradors, trotted in behind her, sniffing and snuffling at her heels. She knelt to scratch their ears, one warm head under each hand. *No, pups. It's not treat time yet.* They ambled off to their usual spots on either side of Thomas's desk with quiet sighs. Some things didn't change.

Ian took a photo of her on horseback, and later coaxed her into a selfie with him and Thomas on the veranda. She laughed, cheek pressed to her stepfather's shoulder, the sunset soft in the background. She posted both photos to Instagram.

As they walked the edge of the property one afternoon, he glanced at her. "Do you miss it? Seoul, I mean."

She looked around, remembering the endless urban buzz, the late-night takeout runs, the hush of Yoo-jin's penthouse when the world was shut out. "No," she said. "Not the city itself."

***

Night was different.

In her childhood bedroom, sleep wouldn't come. Hana listened to rain against the windows, counting minutes. She turned onto her side, pulling the duvet tighter. What was Yoo-jin doing now? Did he care that she had left without telling him? *Why would he? Five days of silence. Then fourteen more.*

She looked at the clock: 3:24 AM. In Seoul, it would be 11:24 AM. He might be on set. Or having coffee and reading scripts with the second-rate actress. Moving forward and forgetting her.

She flipped the pillow to find the cooler side. During

daylight, London gave her everything she needed—freedom, peace of mind.

But night stripped away pretense. In the dim quiet, her body remembered his arm across her waist, his breath in her hair, his hand finding hers in sleep.

***

In Seoul, Yoo-jin was wide awake at 3:47 AM, his phone's blue glow illuminating his unshaven face. Cups littered his table alongside takeout containers he couldn't remember ordering. Naps were snatched in irregular, nightmare-filled bursts.

His phone chimed with a notification: *hanawrhee posted for the first time in a while.* His heart hammered against his ribs, his hands fumbling to open the app.

The first image flooded him with relief, followed by anxiety. Hana on horseback, sunlight in her hair, the green English countryside stretching behind her. Her smile was bright like he hadn't seen in months. She looked... unburdened. *She's happy. Without you. Let that sink in.*

He swiped to the next photo and felt the air leaving his lungs. A selfie with Hana between two men—the older one he recognized from photos as her stepfather, Thomas Weston, and the younger was that half-naked he-man, Ian Weston. The captions: *#surrey #homesweethome*

Home. She's gone home.

This wasn't a break. It was a return to a life that preceded him. A family where she belonged, where she could smile in a picture without a second thought. *She's where she belongs. You're where you belong—alone in your expensive cage.*

"I should have called her," he whispered to no one. "On that first day." *Brilliant insight. But too damn late now.*

***

In Surrey, Ian's gaze followed Hana as she crossed the golf

course's dining terrace toward Charlotte Henderson's table. Two weeks in England had begun to erase the tightness around her eyes. The English air had restored color to her cheeks.

He sipped his tea, enjoying the view of the lush countryside and Hana laughing with her old schoolmate. In their world, people like the Hendersons always considered Hana as a Weston, never as his uncle's Korean stepdaughter. Here, she belonged without question or explanation.

Her mobile on the tablecloth lit up, vibrating against the white linen. Ian glanced at the screen: *Yoo-jin Lee.*

His hand froze midway to his cup. The timing wasn't coincidental. Hana had posted on Instagram looking happy, and now the great Yoo-jin Lee remembered she existed?

The vibration continued like a countdown. She would turn around any second.

His finger tapped "Decline." The screen went dark. He swiped to clear the missed call notification. *You had your chance, movie star. You don't get to ruin this now.*

The phone stayed silent for the remainder of lunch, as if the actor had understood the message. Ian allowed himself a private smile. *Let's see if I can make this trip stretch one more week.*

***

In Seoul, Yoo-jin's heart sank as his call went to voice mail.

In their year and a half together, he had never really dug into Hana's background, being too wrapped up in his own machinery of fame. And she had made it easy for him. Her legal counsel job. The modest apartment. The street food and the sensible shoes. *A grounded, average girl. Lucky me.*

Now, with nothing but time and regret, he began his research.

Hana Weston-Rhee, daughter of a British businessman. But not any businessman. *Thomas Keller Weston*, shipping and banking magnate. *Billionaire with a capital B.*

The house in Surrey? Not a cozy cottage. A sprawling estate with stables, grounds, staff. A place where you didn't simply host garden parties—you hosted *the international elite.*

Their social life? The Royal Enclosure at Ascot. Charity polo matches. State dinners. Gala balls.

Hana never flaunted it. But the clues were there from the beginning. She had never been impressed by his fame. He had offered to escort her to that fundraising dinner, thinking he was doing her a favor. She had worn couture like she was born in it, and floated through that ballroom like it was her living room. *And I thought I was the one out of her league.*

He opened Instagram again and typed *Ian Weston* before he could stop himself. Unlike Hana, the cousin posted like it was a brand campaign. Polished images. Crisp captions. A curated stream of wealth and privilege.

Two days ago: Hana on horseback at a Weston charity event. £2M raised for the cancer research. *Me? I blow kisses to fans at charity basketball games.* Three days ago: Royal Ballet. Hana laughing with David Beckham like old friends. Last week: Society gala. Hana flanked by the Westons like royalty. *#happybirthdaycatherine—as in Catherine, Princess of Wales. Casual.*

Every photo told the same story. Hana as a Weston. Hana as part of something older, deeper, more powerful than he had ever imagined.

The Seraphine heir had known it all along. At the Blue House reception, he hadn't treated Hana like a peculiar guest. He had treated her like a peer. They shared the same language, the same class, the same altitude.

Not Yoo-jin. He had taken someone extraordinary and kept her boxed into the corners of his life. Concealed her like a defect that marred the brand. *When did you ever give her the dignity of being seen?*

Not once. No premieres. No red carpets. No public events. Every outing came with planning, precautions, back entrances. Weekends and evenings holed up at home. She never complained. She had shrunk herself to fit into *his* world, so he wouldn't have to stretch. *What a gift. Truly.*

Yoo-jin dragged a hand down his face. Regret gnawed at him, like a man watching a grand prize lottery slip through careless fingers. *Do you get it now? She loved you more than you ever loved her. How does that feel, superstar?*

***

It first dawned on Hana when Ian took her hand to cross Piccadilly Circus. Not a grab, not a tug—a natural clasp, his fingers finding hers without searching. The gesture was unremarkable until she found he didn't let go once they reached the other side. *Strange. But not unpleasant.*

The awareness grew stronger over the following days. The way their friends treated them as a unit during dinner parties at Ian's townhouse. The way they moved around each other in the kitchen, passing wine glasses and finishing each other's sentences. Their shared eye-rolls at inside jokes no one else understood. *When did his smile start to linger that way?*

***

Breakfast with her stepfather Thomas had been their ritual since childhood. Just them, silverware clinking, newspaper rustling, Earl Grey steaming.

Hana buttered her toast with the crusts removed, a quiet household custom no one ever thought to question. She hadn't realized bread had crusts until she was seven or eight, watching the cook slice them off with care as if they were an insult to aesthetics.

The companionable silence wrapped them like a worn, comfortable sweater.

"It's lovely having you home," Thomas said. "Just like old

times. Peaceful."

She smirked. "Peaceful because Mother is in America terrorizing some poor aid workers."

"Precisely." His eyes crinkled. "Though I do miss her chaos, oddly enough." Her mother was exhausting and exhilarating in equal measure. Thomas had loved that about her, until he couldn't anymore.

"I'm glad you and Ian are close," he continued, turning the pages. "Always have been. You can rely on him, you know. Stay close to Ian."

Something in his tone made her look up. *Wait. Does he think—?*

The thought clicked into place like a key in a lock. All the casual touches, the lingering glances, the way Ian's hand rested on her back during society events. *This is no longer cousinship.*

More alarming: her own comfort with it. The ease with which she had slipped into a couple's rhythm with him. The warmth under her skin when he laughed. The giddiness of waking up knowing he would be part of her day.

"Daddy—" she began, but stopped. *What would I say? That there's somebody else? Someone who disappeared for days, weeks? Someone I still—*

"Just thinking out loud, darling," Thomas said, misreading her hesitation. "You seem happy here. Lighter." He gave her hand a little squeeze and a smile before returning to his newspaper.

Hana's appetite was gone. She couldn't explain the Yoo-jin predicament when she didn't understand it herself. But one thing was certain: it wasn't over between them. Not by a mile. And if Ian was developing feelings for her, and she was responding to them, she needed clarity sooner rather than later. *I have to go back. I need to face him. See if there's anything left to save.*

***

Back in Seoul three days later, Ian tugged at his cuffs, betraying only the edge of his mood. He observed Hana moving through her office, slotting herself back into a routine London had disturbed, as though nothing had changed. When she announced her wish to return, he had kept a supportive smile while his mind raged. *Going to London was one step forward. Returning to Seoul was two steps back.*

"Did Mrs. Park reschedule the donor meeting?" she asked, not looking up from her laptop.

"Tuesday at 3 PM. I've already confirmed."

"Thank you." Her tone was distracted, professional, the same one she used with other staff. Their natural closeness and easy rhythm in London had evaporated the moment they landed in Seoul.

He leaned against her desk, forcing a relaxed posture. "Are you sure about this? The office was fine with you working remotely."

She sorted papers into neat stacks, her movements calm and precise. "The foundation needs me here. And running away doesn't solve anything."

Running away. Not how I would characterize our time together. Ian studied her profile, noting a new tension in her shoulders.

No more beating around the bush. "Have you decided what to do about him?" His voice was neutral as he straightened a paperweight on her desk.

Hana's hands stilled over a document. "He's been texting and calling. I haven't responded."

"Any particular reason?"

"I needed space. An emotional response wouldn't have helped either of us."

He noted her careful words. Not rejection but postponement. Not anger but calculation. She had simply waited.

"And now?" he prompted, moving closer and handing her a folder. "Will you take him back if that's what he's asking?"

"I don't know," Hana admitted after a moment. "I need to understand what happened to us."

Us. Still an 'us' in her mind. She was still invested enough to want understanding rather than closure. Ian pinched the bridge of his nose, shifting course. "If you do consider reconciliation," he said with genuine concern, "you must demand better treatment. That relationship was becoming toxic."

Her head snapped up. "Toxic?" She looked surprised. "It was complicated, but not toxic."

"From the outside, it sure appeared that way. The secrecy, the absences, the public humiliation with his co-star—none of that was healthy for you."

She seemed to mull over his words, weighing them against her own experience. For an instant, he saw doubt flicker across her face.

"We had problems," she conceded, "but our bond was real."

Ian kept his expression sympathetic, but his fingers drummed an irritated rhythm on the desk. *Still defending him.* "Whatever you decide," he said, retreating for the moment. "I'm here to support you."

His reassuring words came out hollow—but she was only half listening anyway, already leaning away from him.

BACK IN STEP

The car slowed outside Hana's apartment building. Through the passenger window, she saw Yoo-jin standing beneath the streetlight, hands in pockets. His hair was longer than she remembered, tousled by the warm July breeze. Even from this distance, the hollows below his eyes were visible.

Her phone sat in her lap with his message still open: *I know you're back. Can I see you? Please let me see you.*

Ian's hand found her arm. His eyes flicked toward Yoo-jin, resigned. "Call tomorrow. Check in."

She watched Yoo-jin shift his weight, his eyes trained on the car but not quite meeting hers through the tinted window. His nervous, uncertain posture tugged at her. "It's okay," she said, leaning over to place a quick kiss on his cheek. "I'll be fine."

***

As she stepped out, the evening air warm against her skin, Hana felt caught between two forces—Ian's protective gaze from behind, Yoo-jin's emotional pull ahead. Their eyes met across the sidewalk as Ian pulled away, leaving them alone in the pool of streetlight.

"Thank you," Yoo-jin said when she approached. The words seemed to cost him something.

She fiddled with her bag strap. “We should go up.”

The elevator ride was silent. In the polished doors, their distorted reflections showed curved shoulders and vulnerable postures. The weeks apart had changed them both.

Inside the apartment, she set down her purse and turned to him. “Water?” she asked, moving toward the kitchen.

“Please.”

She filled two glasses, the action steadying her hands. When she returned, he was standing by the window, silhouetted against city lights.

“Your hair’s longer,” she said, handing him his glass.

His fingers brushed hers as he took it. “Your apartment’s the same.”

“Did you expect it to change?”

“I don’t know what I expected.”

They stood in awkward silence, drinking water neither of them wanted.

“London looked good on you.”

“It was... clarifying.”

“And your... cousin?”

She shook her head. “That’s not why I came back.”

His mask slipped, like a tension breaking. He moved to the couch and sank down, dropping his head into his hands. “I don’t know where to start. Except that I’m sorry. I’m so sorry.”

His voice broke on the final words, and the wall inside Hana crumbled. She put her glass aside and went to him. Her fingers found his hair, drawing his head against her middle. His shoulders trembled with sobs as his arms circled her.

“I should have called that first night,” he mumbled. “I should have tried harder.”

“We both stopped trying,” she admitted, stroking the nape of his neck. She slid onto his lap. His hands settled at her waist—familiar territory yet somehow new.

She kissed him first, covering his lips with the certainty of muscle memory. No hesitation, no preamble. He gripped the back of her head, almost too tight. "I missed you so much," he said against her mouth. "Every day."

There was no conversation. They had always been better at touching than talking. Without a word, they headed to the bedroom, holding hands. His fingers fumbled with her buttons. Hers tugged at his shirt. Plain, simple need. They undressed each other with tenderness, cataloguing changes. Weight lost around his middle. A new freckle on her shoulder that his thumb found at once.

On the bed, skin to skin, their bodies remembered what their minds had forgotten: that they fit, that they belonged.

He buried his face in her hair, breathing hard, like he'd been holding his breath for months. She caught the salt of his skin on her tongue, savoring it like a memory.

"I'll make mistakes again," he said, forehead pressed to hers.

"So will I. Different ones, hopefully."

They moved together on instinct. Her nails cut into his back, sharp and claiming. His grip on her hip was bruising, anchoring her to him. His eyes never left hers—no hiding, no performance.

When it hit, she bit down on his shoulder to keep from crying out. He felt the wetness on her cheek and thumbed it away, almost rough.

"I didn't know how to get back to you," he said, voice raw.

"You're here now."

In the calm that followed, they knew they still had ground to cover. Explanations. Boundaries. Trust. But they had found their starting point again.

She ran a finger down his sternum, watching goosebumps dot his skin. Later, they would talk. Right now was for remembering.

***

City lights filtered through the blinds, revealing their entwined forms—sweat cooling, bodies satisfied. Their minds were now clear.

Yoo-jin's hand circled Hana's wrist, his thumb and forefinger meeting with room to spare. "You've lost weight," he said, voice tight. His palm slid to her ribs, feeling each one through her skin.

She traced the new hollows beneath his cheekbones. "So have you."

He sat up. "Come on. I'm making us pancakes."

In the kitchen, she poured wine into a single glass for them to share. He got out flour, eggs, and milk and whisked them into a batter. "The last time I was here, your cousin was cooking breakfast for you." His tone was flat. "It was the shock of my life."

She stilled, drink halfway to her lips. "Is that why you took off?"

He paused. "The press tour was brutal. I was exhausted, distracted. Then I saw you at the market with him. The way you were together." He swallowed hard. "I've never experienced jealousy like that."

"Yoo-jin—"

He wiped the corner of one eye. The sizzle of batter hitting the pan filled the silence.

She ran her hand between his shoulder blades. "You could have asked me who he was."

"Would you have answered? We were barely speaking by then. I know it was irrational," he said, keeping his eyes on the stove. "But I couldn't help it. Then that thing with Min-ah went viral, and I realized how much it must've hurt you." His shoulders dropped. "I wanted to explain, but every time I tried —" His voice broke as he stacked the pancakes. "Your cousin—

he seems very close to you."

"Ian's my stepcousin," Hana said. "He's always been protective."

Yoo-jin set the plate between them. "He may be family—but he wants you. As a lover."

"Yes," she agreed. "I think he does." Nothing more could be said on the subject for now.

They ate with their fingers, passing the glass back and forth. Their conversation filled in the blanks of their time apart. He explained the publicity operation that spiraled out of his control. "Before I knew it, you were gone. Then I saw the pictures from London."

"I was so hurt," she admitted. Her words were jagged, too small for what she carried. "I had to get away. I was falling apart."

He folded her into his arms. "I'm so sorry, baby. Would you ever forgive me?"

"I'm here, aren't I?"

That night was the first time they both slept a dreamless sleep in months.

The looming question emerged the next morning over coffee. "What happens now?" he asked, eyes fixed on his mug.

Hana reached across the table, her smaller hand covering his. "We go slow."

He pulled her onto his lap. They held each other like survivors of a shipwreck, relieved to find safe harbor but conscious of how easy it was to be cast adrift.

They weren't whole yet. The hairline fractures in the relationship were still there. But at least they were no longer separate entities.

Steam curled from their mugs. They drank in silence, both knowing what had to come next. He would have to make sure this breakdown never happened again. She would have to explain her choice to Ian.

BORROWED TIME

It didn't happen all at once. Only a slow re-entry into each other's orbit, setting down new boundaries and avoiding old pitfalls.

Monday

Yoo-jin's toothbrush appeared again in Hana's bathroom. Blue handle against white porcelain, claiming territory. His gym bag sitting by her door, packed for the next day. They were silent declarations: he planned to return. Hana registered it but said nothing. *Don't get used to this yet. One night doesn't erase all those months apart.*

But when he slid into bed behind her, arm resting at her waist, her body answered before her mind could argue. This was what she knew—what she had missed.

"Is this okay?" he whispered, breath warm against her neck.

She nodded, not trusting her voice.

His mobile vibrated nearby. Then again. He ignored it. *His work calling.*

She could sense the moment balancing on a knife's edge. His career pulling one way, her presence another. Tonight, she was winning. But tomorrow?

Tuesday

"You're using my shampoo," Hana accused as Yoo-jin

stepped out of the steam, toweling his hair.

"Mine's empty. Objections?"

"You'll smell like jasmine all day."

"Good. Then everyone will know my girl likes jasmine." The words lingered between them, too loaded for day two. *My girl. She's my girl once again.*

His phone rang again while he dressed. Again, he silenced it.

"You can answer," she said, buttoning her blouse. "I know how managers get."

"Later. It's not important." *Two romantic comedies. A watch endorsement. A cooking show.* His agent's messages had listed all the opportunities in Seoul. Nothing like the career he had envisioned—but at least he could stay near Hana. *Don't fuck this up. Don't disappear on her again.*

Wednesday

Ian's gaze followed Hana across the conference room, noting the subtle changes. Her steps lighter. Hair loose around her shoulders. A calm he hadn't seen since London.

"The donor meeting went well," he said afterward, tone neutral and business-like. "I've prepared the follow-up materials."

"Thank you," she replied, equally measured.

"You look... rested." *You look like you're sleeping well again. With him.*

"I am," she said.

"Good." His fingers brushed hers as he handed over the folder. A touch that lingered a half-second too long.

She pulled away. *We'll need to talk about this. But not today.*

Later, when Yoo-jin asked about her day, she mentioned meetings, donor calls, grant applications. Not Ian. Not the tension crackling through the office. Some things couldn't bear scrutiny yet.

Thursday

Yoo-jin cooked while Hana showered. His phone rang twice—watch company, drama producer. He answered neither. *They'll wait. They always do.*

But that same strategic silence now threatened his relevance. Soon they'd find another handsome face. That thought should have made him panic. Instead, he wondered: *What if I chose this quiet life over call sheets? And then… what? Stay home as her househusband?*

His career defined his whole identity. Without it—

"Something smells amazing," she said, entering the kitchen in her robe, hair damp.

He turned to contemplate her. Domestic. Intimate. Possibly temporary. "Stir-fry," he said, voice rough. "Nothing special."

"Disagree." She stole a chunk of bell pepper from the cutting board. "Very special."

Her easy confidence always impressed him. Her work never caused her doubt—her path was clear, established. But his now appeared uncertain.

"My fan meeting tour is on the calendar."

"Ah, the ten-city parade of women proposing marriage to you," she teased, fingers tracing patterns on his forearm. "When?"

"Not for a couple of months." He kept his tone light. "I'm giving you a heads up before I'm mobbed by my future wives." *The very definition of hell.*

They let the subject drop. It was still distant enough to ignore.

Friday

Late night. Tangled sheets. Shared wine.

"Remember that fangirl who sent you underwear with your face printed on it?" Hana asked, head on his chest, leg draped over his.

Yoo-jin groaned. "Why would you remind me of that?"

"Because your horrified expression was priceless."

Laughter came easier tonight, after four days of rebuilding. Four days of careful navigation through emotional minefields. They had found this space where the old playfulness could emerge once again. *Don't rely on this. It's still new. Still breakable.*

But her body had already adapted to his presence. Her cells had rewritten themselves around his return, ignoring her brain's warnings.

Saturday

Morning light. Coffee. Fresh croissants. The weekend stretching before them.

Yoo-jin stepped onto the balcony to take a call. His agent's relief was palpable over the connection. "The watch company needs an answer by Monday. And both production companies are pressing for commitments."

"I'll look at the contracts," he conceded. *Romance dramas mean faking chemistry with other actresses. More Min-ah-type shit waiting to happen.*

"And the cooking show? They've called three times."

"Yes to that one. It films here in Seoul, right?"

"Yes, but—"

"That's my priority right now. Seoul-based work." Through the glass door, he could see Hana moving around the kitchen—a tableau he had missed, moments he wasn't willing to sacrifice again. But the alternative of turning down projects, becoming less visible, and watching his career fade was equally daunting.

There had to be a middle ground. A way to maintain relevance and nurture what he had with Hana. He just hadn't found it yet.

Sunday

Evening. One week back together. Hana's head was on Yoo-jin's lap, his fingers combing through her hair.

"I have to go to Busan on Wednesday," she said. "For meetings. Back Thursday night."

His hand stilled. "Okay."

One night apart. Their first since reuniting. A small test of this fragile peace. "I can come by Tuesday before you leave. And be here when you get back Thursday."

She heard what he wasn't saying: *I'll still be here. This won't break us.* She caught his hand and kissed it. *He's trying. We're both trying this time.*

They had navigated seven days of rebuilding, avoiding past landmines. It was tenuous progress. Nothing was solved, but nothing was broken either. For now, that had to be enough. But the ice beneath remained thin.

***

Ian's eyes burned reading the contract in front of him, its legal language blurring into meaningless patterns.

He adjusted his cuffs, a nervous habit. The actor's expression that night haunted him: hungry, desperate, determined. *Looking like a kicked puppy waiting to be let back in.* But what churned his stomach more was Hana stepping toward the man before his car had even turned the corner. *Seven days. That's all it took for her to forget months of her own misery.*

He glanced at his watch. A few minutes until his next meeting, not enough time to focus on work. Not enough time to banish the images flooding his mind: Hana's renewed appetite at lunch. The small smile when she answered the phone. The subtle lightness in her step. *She can't see history repeating itself.*

He straightened his jacket, studying his reflection in

the window—tailored suit, confident posture. A diametrical opposite to the actor's chaotic intensity. *Stability versus chaos. Why can't she see the obvious choice?*

A week isn't permanent. The ink isn't dry on their reconciliation. The thought steadied him. Seven days of makeup sex and emotional catharsis didn't erase the fundamental incompatibility in their relationship.

She owes me a conversation, at the very least. He would have to act before the new routine became ingrained. Before Hana convinced herself this time would be different.

***

"What are your plans, Hana?" Ian asked over dinner one evening.

She set down her chopsticks. "About?"

"You know very well." His voice remained even, but his knuckles whitened around his sake cup.

The sounds of the restaurant filled the background before she spoke.

"Yoo-jin and I are..." She paused, searching for words. "We're mending fences."

He had expected this answer. *Mending fences. Such a sanitized phrase for running headlong back to disaster.*

"And what's to prevent him from pulling the same stunt again when his next career crisis hits?" He leaned forward and watched his point strike its target.

Pain flickered across her face, brief but unmistakable.

"We're taking it slow," she said, voice soft but firm. "Working through things."

"And how does he fit into your life? The foundation, your philanthropy. Will he play a supportive role?" he pressed, keeping his tone concerned rather than confrontational. "Has he shown any interest in the work that drives you?"

She looked away, and that was answer enough. The actor

hadn't developed a sudden passion for education in rural communities. Hadn't lifted a finger to support her fundraising. Their worlds hadn't touched—and he doubted they ever would. *She sees it too. But she won't admit it yet.*

"Maybe he will now," she offered, but a note of uncertainty slipped into her voice.

"It's not the same sphere, Hana. His existence is public property. Your job requires trust, discretion, stability." He paused, allowing his words to settle. "Did you really think he could blend into your life as a true partner? Or will you always be adjusting to accommodate his reality?"

He saw the shadow in her eyes deepen. *One more push. Create a deadline.*

"Next weekend," he said, his tone softening, "I'm taking you motorcycle riding on Jeju. Get away from Seoul and get some perspective." He reached across the table, his fingers brushing hers. "We need a proper talk. It's high time."

After a moment, she relented. "Alright."

Relief washed over him. It was an opening. A chance to reset the board. *Remind her who was here when the actor wasn't. Who will be here after.*

***

Yoo-jin traced lazy patterns on Hana's bare shoulder. "Happy?"

"Hmm..."

"I meant customer satisfaction on a scale of one to ten?"

She laughed and swatted his arm.

These quiet moments had become his sanctuary. The world couldn't touch them here—no cameras, no schedules, no expectations. Only her warmth next to him, her scent on his skin.

"I'm going to Jeju next weekend," she said. "With Ian. Motorcycle riding." His finger stilled. The words stung like a sharp slap. *Of course, the bastard would make this move.*

"I see," he managed, voice even. But inside, jealousy clawed its way up his throat. He swallowed it back, conscious of their still-fragile peace. One possessive outburst could shatter everything they had worked to rebuild.

She turned to look at him. "He wants to talk."

It was obvious the Englishman would want to discuss him. Give Hana reasons why she should walk away. The man had been waiting, planning, positioning since London. "It's probably for the best," he said, surprising himself. "He's important to you. You need to sort things out with him."

The relief in her eyes was immediate. She nestled closer, her heartbeat steady against his ribs. Within minutes, her breathing deepened into sleep.

Yoo-jin remained awake, staring at shadows on the ceiling. His mind churned with unwelcome comparisons.

Ian Weston: Cambridge graduate, law firm partner, foundation board member, childhood confidant. He spoke her language of philanthropy and legacy-building. Family, technically, but that didn't prevent him from hovering like an emotional support husband.

And him? Designer watch and whisky campaigns. Variety shows that turned celebrities' inane chatter into entertainment. Romantic comedies with actresses who called him *'oppa'* even off-camera. Fan meets with scripted Q&As and choreographed smiles, while Hana sat in an empty apartment eating reheated leftovers and pretending it didn't bother her.

The lawyer gave speeches at economic forums. Yoo-jin gave interviews about how to keep his skin dewy during action scenes. *One of these things is not like the others.*

The rain intensified outside, drumming harder against the glass. *He'll remind her of all the ways I've failed. All the ways I'll likely fail again.*

His hand found the hollow of Hana's waist. She made a small sound, pressing closer. This—the physical connection, the undeniable chemistry—was something the cousin could never replicate. The way their bodies recognized each other, even in darkness, even in sleep. *But was it enough?*

First light crept into the room. He had to find a way to make this bond permanent. To bring it out of the shadows and into the open. To weave himself into the fabric of her complete life, not only these night-time hours.

The rain slowed to a gentle patter as dawn approached. Hana stirred against him. Yoo-jin held her closer, mind full of half-formed plans. *I can't stop her from going to Jeju. But I better make damn sure she comes back to me.*

ISLAND STRATEGY

Hana's arms tightened around Ian as he accelerated out of the curve, the BMW snapping to his touch. The coastal road unwound like a ribbon, sapphire ocean stretching to their right. He opened the throttle on a straight stretch and her delighted shriek made his chest expand.

Days of planning had gone into this weekend: the motorcycle brought from Seoul, a beachfront lodge that promised both adventure and comfort. Every choice was deliberate, designed for maximum effect.

But now, with Hana pressed against his back, strategy fell away. The moment was real. Unplanned. Flawless. *The actor can't give her this. The freedom to enjoy a normal life.*

They stopped at a scenic overlook where a handful of tourists were taking photos. "Hungry?" he asked, unstrapping their picnic from the bike's rear compartment.

"Starving." Her cheeks were flushed from the ride, eyes shining with excitement.

They settled on a stone wall, unwrapping gourmet *kimbap* and pouring hot tea from a thermos. A nearby couple smiled at them, the woman asking in broken English if he would take their photo. Ian obliged, then handed his own phone over, pulling Hana close for their picture. *No hiding. No looking over shoulders for paparazzi.*

She didn't stiffen or pull away as the shutter clicked. A

small victory.

"Having fun?" he asked as they remounted the bike.

Her arms circled his waist, chin resting on his back. "More than I expected."

***

After dinner at the lodge—fresh-caught fish, local *hallabong* wine—they wandered onto the dark beach. Ian had rehearsed this conversation a dozen ways. Now, watching Hana's face in the moonlight, the careful plans receded.

They settled side by side on the sand, close enough that their shoulders touched. Heavy unspoken words pressed against his ribs. Hana sensed it too—she leaned into him, her hand rubbing small circles between his shoulder blades.

"You know, Hana—this is how I've always imagined life with you."

"Yes, I know." Her quiet admission caught him off guard.

"We're good together, you know that." He stated it as a fact—not a question.

She laughed. "That's what you think. But it'll shock the hell out of my parents."

He turned to her, amused. "You'd be surprised. Last time I had dinner with your mother and Uncle Thomas—when they weren't lobbing daggers at each other—they both agreed I was the best thing for you."

"What?" She straightened. "When was this?"

"Last Christmas, when you didn't come home. Do you think they don't see it?"

The breeze picked up, carrying a sharp chill. He drew her close to keep her warm. *No more skirting around this.* "I love you, Hana." The words he'd kept locked away for years broke free. "Not as your cousin—as a man who wants to build a life with you."

Her body tensed, but she didn't pull away.

"I've loved you since you started university," he continued, voice steady. "When you moved to New York. Then Seoul. When you dated that flighty journalist. When you fell for the actor. All of it."

"But Yoo-jin—"

"Yoo-jin isn't like us. He belongs to a different world. His career will always come first—actresses, fans. Where does that leave you?" The sound of waves breaking was like an echo for every point he made.

"He and I have a special—" she started, her defense now sounding thin. "I can't explain it."

"Yes, for now. But what about for the future?" The question hung heavy, unanswerable. "I can give you long-term," he said, filling her silence. "You deserve to live a normal life. With a husband. With a family. Out in the open."

For an hour, he abandoned his lawyer's precision, laying himself bare like a man with nothing left to lose. When she shivered from the cooling night air, they rose, brushing sand from their clothes. He took her hand as they walked back to the lodge, her fingers cold against his palm.

Inside, he turned and rested his hands on her shoulders. "Think about it, Hana," he said, pressing a gentle kiss to her forehead.

She chewed her lip, catching his eyes. She leaned her head on his chest for a beat before raising her face to his. When she kissed him, Ian's control faltered, years of restrained feelings breaking through the surface.

She pulled back, conflict in her eyes. He released her without protest. "Let's sleep on this," she said, stepping back toward the hallway leading to her separate bedroom.

"Goodnight, Hana." His voice was gentle even as his heart hammered against his ribs.

He remained in the moonlit room, replaying the scene. He hadn't followed the prepared script. He had simply told her the truth.

And she didn't say no.

***

Moonlight cut silver stripes across the bed through bamboo blinds. Sleep wasn't coming. Hana pressed her fingers to her lips. *What is wrong with me?*

She'd started it. Thirty years of seeing Ian as family, undone in a second. Was it curiosity or weakness? The shock hadn't been the wrongness of it, but how natural it had been. How right. Which made her either honest or awful. Maybe both.

What kind of person kisses one man while planning to go home to another? *Answer: the kind lying to herself.*

Ian's words kept looping: *You deserve a normal life. A husband. A family. Out in the open.* Rational. Sensible. Everything Yoo-jin couldn't give, no matter how much they wanted it. Ian was the intelligent choice—stability, partnership, daylight.

But Yoo-jin. After two months apart, the relief in his eyes when she returned from London was devastating. Two weeks spent stitching themselves back together, swearing the promises would hold.

And here she was, thinking of another man. *Two weeks. You couldn't even make it past two weeks.*

Yoo-jin was fire and hunger, a bond so visceral it scared her. He pushed, frustrated, completed her in ways she couldn't articulate. With him, she felt alive but never settled—always braced for the next headline, the next camera, the next reminder that loving him meant living in the shadows.

Am I choosing safety over love? Or finally admitting what I really want, instead of what I think I should?

***

At breakfast, sunlight streamed past the lodge windows. The ocean sent a briny sharpness through the terrace doors.

Ian spread marmalade on his toast with the ease of a man who had slept well for the first time in weeks. "There's a hidden cove about twenty kilometers north," he said, scanning the map beside his cup. "Locals say it has the clearest water on the island."

Hana stirred her coffee and looked up at him with an absent smile.

He didn't crowd her. Last night's kiss had accomplished what years of careful positioning couldn't. Today wasn't for pressing advantages but for cementing new possibilities.

They spent the morning riding along the coast. Lunch at a weathered shack where old men played *Go* on overturned crates. He spoke Korean with the fishermen, negotiating for the freshest yellowtail as she looked on, amused.

Not once did he mention Yoo-jin or their future. Strategy had returned, but with patience. The groundwork was laid. Now the seeds needed to germinate.

On the small plane back to Seoul, Ian pretended to read the financial news, but his eyes kept straying to Hana's profile. When her voice broke the cabin's quiet, he was prepared for anything except her question.

"What would happen if I were to leave the foundation?"

He lowered the newspaper. This wasn't idle curiosity. This was Hana running scenarios, testing futures.

"We'd appoint another director. Preferably someone internal who knows the operations." His tone was neutral, professional, as though this were just another boardroom consideration.

Her next question pierced through that composure. "And if I stay in Seoul... would you move your law practice here?"

A jolt went through him. *She's mapping us. Actually*

considering us.

"I could," he replied, measuring each word. "My partners could look after the London clients, while I build a client base in Asia. It's feasible." He paused before adding the necessary truth: "But if you want a fresh start, it's best if you're not in Seoul."

Hope surged through him, though he showed nothing but calm. He squeezed her hand, feeling her pulse beneath his fingers. "But you have to want it, Hana. If you want it, we can make anything work."

A strategic retreat. He released her hand and returned to his newspaper, as if he had not just dropped a life-altering decision in her lap. *Let her come to the conclusion herself. Your fingerprints can't be anywhere.*

Later, as he pulled up to her apartment building, Ian switched off the car engine and turned to face Hana. "I'll see you tomorrow," he said, the simple phrase carrying layers of meaning.

Unease flickered in her eyes, as if she were standing at a precipice and considering the leap.

He refused to let her doubt to take root. He cupped her face, his thumb brushing her cheek. She didn't pull away. He lowered his head and kissed her—no force, no desperation. Only certainty. A kiss to remind her of what awaited on the other side.

When she kissed him back, he allowed himself a small smile. *Progress. Undeniable progress.*

***

Yoo-jin had been sitting in his car for an hour, an unlit cigarette turning between his fingers. After a sleepless night and growing dread, he needed visual confirmation Hana had returned. To him.

Until the lawyer's car pulled up.

Through the windshield, he witnessed the whole scene with excruciating clarity. The intimate conversation. The hands cupping Hana's face. Her lack of resistance. The kiss. Not forced. Not rejected. Reciprocated.

The cigarette snapped between his fingers. His reality shattered, sending a pain so sharp it made him clutch his chest.

She kissed him back. The simple act demolished every rationalization, every promise she had made before leaving. Every moment they had rebuilt after their separation. His hands gripped the steering wheel until his knuckles whitened, eyes fixed on Hana as she entered her building.

His mobile lit up seconds later: *Just got in. Really tired. See you tomorrow night?* The mundane message, as if nothing earth-shattering had occurred, twisted like a knife. He struggled to formulate an answer. Accusations? Questions? Pretend ignorance?

In the end, he typed the only words his devastated pride would allow: *Sure. Rest well.*

He started the engine, escaping before she might glimpse him from her window. Before she saw how that moment with the lawyer had wrecked him.

Once back at his penthouse, Yoo-jin stepped onto the balcony, staring into the darkness. City lights blurred as tears filled his eyes. *What did you expect? That she'd choose chaos with you over stability with him?*

BEHIND THE SCENES

When Yoo-jin walked through her door the next evening, Hana registered the dark circles around his eyes first. His white shirt was wrinkled at the elbows, hair unkempt, unusual for someone typically camera-ready.

He knows.

They crashed together without words. His arms squeezed her with none of their usual gentleness, grip too tight against her ribs. She pressed her face into his neck, buying time.

He tilted her chin up, eyes searching her face. "You're here."

She forced a smile. "Where else would I be?" *With Ian. That's what you're really asking.*

His thumb traced her jaw, the touch more clinical than loving. A shadow flickered behind his eyes. Not anger, but worse. Doubt.

"Rough day?" she deflected, hand working at the knot between his shoulders.

"Better now," he replied, his mouth covering hers in a fierce kiss. His fingers dug into her waist. This wasn't passion but verification.

They headed to the bedroom without speaking, discarding clothes along the way. When her legs hit the mattress, he paused, hands framing her face. "I missed you."

His gaze bore into hers. "Did you miss me?"

A beat.

"It was only two days—" She winced at her own defensiveness.

His face shuttered. "Two very long days," he corrected, easing her onto the bed. He observed her with unusual intensity, tracking each expression as if collecting evidence. His fingers moved with precision, mapping reactions.

He's comparing. Before and after. "What is it?" she asked when he stopped.

"Nothing," he lied. "Just looking at you."

His caresses lacked their usual softness. She hid her eyes, unable to bear his scrutiny. When it ended, he stayed close, still watching her. Then, anxious: "We're okay, aren't we, Hana?"

Her body tensed beneath his. She nestled closer, burying her face in his chest. The sound of rain tapping against the glass filled the silence.

"I saw you," he said, tone flat. "Last night."

Her blood cooled. She kept her face hidden.

"With him," he added when she didn't answer.

"I'm sorry," she said, words muffled against his skin.

His arms tightened around her. "I love you. I'm not going away."

She couldn't match his certainty. All she could do was hold him tighter, soothing him. "It's alright, baby."

***

Morning light hit Hana's face at an uncomfortable angle. She had forgotten to close the blinds. Beside her, Yoo-jin slept with unusual stillness, as if afraid any movement might wake her.

The tiny scar above his eyebrow stood out without its usual layer of concealer. A reminder that even his imperfections required management for public consumption. *Public. Somewhere we'll never be.*

She wasn't ready to let him go. Not yet. But she was projecting a different future for herself. Not a gaping void, but a different path. *I should be devastated. Why am I not?*

She must have drifted off, because when she woke again, his side of the bed was empty. A breakfast tray sat on the nightstand with coffee in a thermos, sliced fruit, buttered toast with the crusts removed. Beneath the cup was a note: *See you tonight. YJ.*

No grand declarations. No desperate pleas. Only a promise to return.

***

Ian surveyed documents spread across his desk. The panoramic view of Seoul provided appropriate perspective: he could see everything from here.

For three days since Jeju, he'd been reaching out to his network. Former clients, executives who owed favors, industry insiders.

The actor's life runs on paper trails. Follow the money, find the pressure points.

He picked up the phone and dialed Kim Jun-ho. Seven years ago, he had advised Kim on a merger that launched his career. Now head of brand partnerships at Star Entertainment, the agent remained a useful connection.

"Jun-ho, thanks for making time. How's life treating you?" He listened attentively—daughter's school acceptance, wife's new gallery, vacation home purchase.

"I've been seeing Yoo-jin Lee everywhere these days," Ian remarked after the appropriate small talk. "His Asian tour must be keeping you busy."

The agent laughed. "Nine countries in six weeks. The logistics are a nightmare, but the fan response justifies everything. Ticket sales broke records in Japan and China."

"And I hear he's expanding into fashion endorsements?"

Ian kept his tone casual, as if he were merely staying current with industry news.

"You have good sources. The luxury watch deal is finalized—they're shooting next week. The whisky brand is still in talks, but it looks promising. Premium products suit his image."

Ian made a note on his legal pad. "Speaking of image, I heard whispers about a non-celebrity he's close to?"

The long pause told Ian everything.

"There hasn't been any comment." The agent kept his voice neutral.

There it is. The pressure point. "Would that hurt his marketability?" Ian pressed while maintaining curious nonchalance. "If he were linked to someone?"

Kim sighed. "Look, you know how it is. For high profiles like Lee? His appeal depends on aspirational fantasy. The romance dramas, the luxury campaigns—they all sell better when delusional fans can imagine themselves dating him."

Ian's pen paused above paper. "So, the brands don't explicitly prohibit relationships, but—"

"They don't have to spell it out. His team knows the game. Female fan engagement can drop up to thirty percent when top actors go public with a partner. For someone like Lee Yoo-jin, that's significant."

Thirty percent. Quantifiable impact. "And the new American project? Still happening?"

"Filming starts in September in Los Angeles. Three months on location, at least." Pride resonated in the agent's voice—this was a major achievement for his firm.

After the goodbyes, Ian sat with fingers steepled under his chin. *The actor's cage is his own success.*

He pulled a document from his folder—a mock-up of an upcoming watch advertisement where the actor gazed from the page with manufactured intensity, a woman's manicured hand draped over his shoulder. Her face was not visible. *Exactly like Hana if she stays with him. Present but always cropped out of the frame.*

He opened the foundation's calendar on his laptop. The Henderson adoption program launch spanned multiple weeks with meetings, press events, and site visits. Diplomatic receptions and high-profile galas.

Hana's job needed her to be visible.

Yoo-jin Lee's career needed her to be erased.

Ian wouldn't have to explain to her why she and the actor would never work.

He only had to hold up a mirror.

SPOTLIGHTS AND SHADOWS

The annual Hope Bridge Gala that August was a short week away—Weston-Rhee's flagship fundraising event that would launch their new international child welfare program. The initiative was Hana's passion project, designed to streamline cross-border adoptions. Everything hinged on securing sufficient funding.

The day before, Ian dropped in as Hana reviewed the final preparations.

"Fendi's Executive Director will be at tomorrow's show. They're looking to partner with a foundation—a five-year commitment, minimum three hundred million ₩on annually, plus proceeds from a limited-edition handbag collection."

She frowned at her calendar. "I'm all booked until the gala. Can we schedule a proper meeting after?"

"No. They're only in Seoul for Fashion Week. We need to make an impression now." His voice was crisp, business-like. "Their people specifically mentioned the company's interest in children's causes."

"It's a good opportunity, but—"

"Hana," Ian interrupted, tone softening. "This partnership would fund the program for five years. Five years of guaranteed support, corporate legitimacy, and global visibility. We can't pass this up."

She relented, recognizing his logic. "Alright. I can move a few things around. But I've never been to a fashion show. I don't even know what to wear."

"Already handled. The dress will be delivered to your office by six. Nothing flashy. You'll look perfect." He snapped his notebook shut and turned to leave.

***

Seoul Fashion Week transformed the Dongdaemun Design Plaza into a hive of activity. Photographers lined the red carpet, cameras poised like weapons. Fans crowded behind velvet ropes, smartphones raised in anticipation.

Hana arrived early. She found a recessed spot near the entrance, angled enough to see the door without drawing attention. A skill she had honed in Yoo-jin's world—how to watch without being seen. She tilted her head at her reflection in the glass, examining the white Roland Mouret dress Ian had chosen. Crepe midi, sharp lines, classic but with an edge. *Who knew Ian had such an eye for styling?*

The first arrivals were fashion editors and minor celebrities. Soon, a black van with tinted windows pulled up. The crowd's energy shifted as the door slid open. Several models emerged in Fendi creations. Behind them, a familiar figure stepped onto the red carpet. Hana's breath caught.

Yoo-jin.

He moved with the confidence of someone inured to the spotlight, his smile calibrated for maximum impact. Two models flanked him, linking their arms through his as the trio walked toward the entrance.

"*Yoo-jin oppa! Yoo-jin oppa!*" Fans screamed over the arrivals area.

Camera flashes erupted in rapid bursts. He paused at intervals, offering different angles, flashing finger hearts to delighted squeals. The models draped themselves around him to showcase both their outfits and Yoo-jin's desirability.

He never mentioned this. Not even when we—The memory hit her like a splash of cold water. They had lingered in bed this morning, his fingers drifting in lazy circles over her skin, when he told her he would be busy all day.

On instinct, Hana shrank deeper into her corner as Yoo-jin's entourage approached. They passed within a few feet of her, close enough that she could smell the models' perfume, see the perfect line of his jaw as he laughed at their jokes. He walked past without glancing in her direction.

Annoyance prickled under Hana's skin. A little at Yoo-jin—and a lot at Ian. *Damn you, Ian. I'm sure you did this on purpose.*

As she turned to leave, bristling, a black Mercedes sedan pulled up. The door opened and an immaculate Ian stepped out. Hana stared, irritation forgotten.

He carried the confidence of a Forbes cover with the polish of GQ—Kiton suit, no tie, shirt open to a hint of bronzed skin. Curated stubble, slicked-back hair, and a hint of a smirk that knew its own effect. She blinked, caught off guard by her own reaction. *Christ. Since when did Ian look so*—

Photographers who had been resting raised their cameras, intrigued by this stylish newcomer.

Without slowing, he headed straight for Hana's hiding spot, greeting her with a kiss on the cheek. "Sorry I'm late," he said, voice low. "Traffic was a nightmare."

Before she could respond, he tucked her hand in the crook of his arm and drew her out onto the red carpet. "Smile for the cameras," he said.

She complied. Camera flashes lit up, capturing them together. *What is he doing? We're being photographed!*

He squeezed her hand as they strode inside, nodding and smiling to the press.

***

Inside the venue, Ian navigated with purpose through the glittering crowd. He kept Hana anchored to him, sensing her tension easing and giving way to natural poise. She still wasn't comfortable, but she was adapting. *She's a Weston. Of course, she would hold her head up high.*

"Oliver!" he called out, spotting his target near the champagne table.

The Fendi executive turned, face lighting with recognition. "Ian Weston! It's been ages!" They clasped hands, exchanging friendly banter. "Oliver, I'd like you to meet Hana Weston-Rhee, Director of the Weston-Rhee Foundation," Ian said, emphasizing her professional title. "Hana, this is Oliver Harrington, Executive Director for Fendi Asia-Pacific. We were at Eton together."

Harrington gave her a warm smile. "I've read about your work. Impressive."

Ian scanned the crowd. The actor stood surrounded by admirers, but his attention kept straying toward Hana. The two men's eyes met in silent challenge. *Let the first round begin.*

The lights dimmed, music thrummed to life, and Ian guided Hana to their seats for the show. Her step faltered as he led her to the front row. She hissed into his ear: "What are you doing?"

His face stayed neutral. "Getting clarity."

***

Yoo-jin's smile never wavered as he posed with the models, displaying a pleasant demeanor despite the chaos roiling inside him. He had spotted Hana the moment he stepped onto the red carpet—a flash of white in a corner, quickly hidden. He maintained his pace and kept his focus forward.

What is she doing here? Inside the venue, he moved

through the usual choreography—smiling, shaking hands, posing for cameras—while his eyes tracked Hana. She seemed cut from another world, her white dress all clean restraint amid the sequins and leather, a calm figure in a temple of excess.

When he saw the Englishman introduce her to the Fendi executive, the pieces clicked into place. These were people who operated at her level, who understood exactly who she was and what she represented. The lawyer wasn't just showing her off—he was demonstrating where she naturally fit in a world that would never ask her to hide.

As the lights dropped, his manager appeared at his elbow. "Front row, as usual," he said, pointing to the runway. "You're next to the Fendi brass."

It was only when he approached did Yoo-jin understand. Not the executives—Hana. With the lawyer on her other side. *Of course, he had arranged this too.*

He took his seat, acknowledging Hana with a small, polite nod—it was all he could offer with so many eyes watching and cameras recording. Only that morning, they had lain in bed, ignoring the clock while enjoying a quiet moment of closeness. Now, they sat rigid, facing forward like two strangers on a bus. Meanwhile, the "cousin" was relaxed, leaning close to comment in her ear. Casual. Unbothered.

At one point, their eyes met over Hana's shoulder. The lawyer's mouth curved in a faintest smile—not friendly, not even polite. Pure satisfaction. *Bastard's enjoying this.*

Music swelled as the lights dimmed further. The first model appeared on the runway, but Yoo-jin's attention was on Hana's profile, the careful distance she maintained, the slight tremble in her hand as she clapped. Yet he forced himself to focus, to smile at appropriate moments, to appear engaged with the show.

When the audience rose in a thunderous ovation, camera flashes blew up. Tomorrow, the headlines would carry a single image: Hana standing between two men—one who pretended he didn't know her, and one who claimed her in front of all.

***

The after-party buzzed with champagne and ambition. Ian kept one hand on Hana's back as they threaded through the crowd.

Across the room, the actor was already swallowed by his orbit of models, producers, and hangers. Ian caught Hana's gaze drifting in his direction more than once. Each time, he would trace small circles against her spine, drawing her focus back—on him, on their conversation, on the reality he was constructing for her benefit. The actor might command the center of the room, but Ian moved within the corridors of power.

"He's quite popular, your countryman," the Fendi executive remarked to Hana, following her glance. "Would you like to meet our brand ambassadors? I should introduce you."

Panic flashed across Hana's face.

Time for the final move. "Of course," Ian replied. "It's not every day we get to mingle with celebrities."

The trio crossed the room to where Yoo-jin held court with two models. The crowd parted with reluctance, creating enough space for introductions.

"Yoo-jin, Stella, Jiyon," Harrington said, "please meet Ian Weston and Hana Weston from the Weston-Rhee Foundation."

Ian extended his hand without correcting the assumption. "How do you do, ladies?" Then, turning to Yoo-jin: "Mr. Lee—what a pleasure to see you again."

Yoo-jin's tone was chilly as he clasped Ian's hand. "Likewise, Mr. Weston."

Hana managed a weak nod. "Hello."

Yoo-jin's eyes softened as he turned to her. "I know Miss Weston," he said. Then, catching himself, "From—from a fundraiser dinner last year."

Ian's mouth curled in a slight smirk at the slip. *Definitely play it down, movie star. How characteristic.*

"Did you enjoy the show?" Yoo-jin asked Hana, voice casual.

She found her composure, standing straighter. "The clothes are beautiful. I didn't know you were their brand ambassador."

"The campaign just started," he explained. "So I'm quite new."

Ian shifted closer to Hana to assert his presence. "It appears you will be the face of other luxury brands also—Breitling and Macallan, if I'm not mistaken?"

Surprise crossed Yoo-jin's face. "You're well informed, Mr. Weston."

Ian's smile was razor-sharp. "Your job must be exhilarating. Pushing romantic fantasies. And... selling dreams."

The subtle insult wasn't lost on Yoo-jin. His face tightened. "That's one way to look at it," he responded evenly.

Harrington, oblivious, chimed in with enthusiasm. "And Yoo-jin is very good at it! We expect Asian sales to skyrocket with him as the face of our brand."

"Well, good luck to you," Ian said, his tone balanced between sincere and dismissive. He turned to the Fendi executive: "Oliver, we should let these good people get back to their admirers. We'll be in touch about the sponsorship. Thanks for a great evening."

As they left, Ian could sense the actor's stare burning into his back. His hand rested at Hana's waist, guiding her deeper into the crowd.

Their eyes met for a brief second, and he let the message sink in: *See? Nothing difficult. Imagine being in public like this as your normal.*

***

They arrived at the restaurant late, but their corner table was waiting. After the chaos of the fashion show, this hushed atmosphere provided a welcome contrast.

"You said that was for clarity," Hana said once they were seated, fingers gliding over the embossed pattern on the leather menu. "It was more like a reality check."

Ian glanced up, assessing her emotional state. Her voice held more contemplation than anger. *She's processing, not defending. Progress.*

"It can be whatever you need it to be." He paused, letting the statement settle. "The Hanwoo ribeye looks good."

As the waiter departed, he leaned forward. "Did you see anything you liked at the show? You might want to place an order to have it for the gala." He saw conflict cross her face, followed by annoyance.

"You did this on purpose. You're acting like this was a shopping trip," she accused, dropping the pretense.

He sighed, setting down his wine with care. "I wanted you to see if you can really thrive in that world. It's superficial. It's ephemeral." He held her gaze, genuine concern in his eyes. "On top of that, it's a world where you'll never be acknowledged as his partner. Do you see yourself being a part of it?" *Attack the world he drags her into, not him. She'll fight for a man. She won't fight for a circus.*

She twirled the stem of her glass with irritation. "I'm hungry."

"I'm not surprised. Champagne and canapés can't sustain anybody."

Ian pivoted the conversation to their planned visit to an orphanage later that week. An occasion to present her with immediate, meaningful work to contrast with the artifice they had witnessed. *Two days to reframe what really matters. What you and I would accomplish together.*

***

The electronic beep of her security keypad startled Hana as she cinched her bathrobe tighter, fresh from her bath. Two o'clock in the morning was late, even for Yoo-jin.

The door swung open to reveal him, a disheveled shadow of the polished celebrity from earlier that evening. Hair mussed, jacket rumpled, tie missing. Cigarettes, whisky, and lingering perfumes clung to him like ghosts. His eyes struggled to focus.

"Hana," he said, the word slurring at the edges, a mirthless smile on his lips.

Her eyes adjusted to him in the semi-darkness. "How was the event?"

"Loud," he answered, fumbling with his buttons. "Then louder at the after-party. Then even louder at whatever came after that."

She didn't ask for details. He didn't need to tell her about the Gangnam club where models had crowded him, each drink blurring the memory of Ian and Hana entering the venue arm in arm. Her smile as she appeared under the spotlight at another man's side. And the lawyer's parting words: *Pushing romantic fantasies... and selling dreams.*

She poured a glass of water for him. He emptied it in several large gulps. "You and your cousin looked good together." *You and I never look like anything in public. Because we can't.*

"It was PR for the foundation."

"Must be nice," he said to the silence, "being someone's first choice."

When she reached up to wipe a small trickle from his chin, he backed away. "I should clean up," he said, voice rough with self-disgust. "I'm not fit to touch you."

The bathroom door clicked shut behind him, leaving Hana alone with her thoughts and the crush of his defeat.

Ten minutes later, she followed the sound of running water. Through fogged glass, his silhouette told her everything —one hand braced against the tile, head bowed, shoulders slumped, water sluicing over him. A man washing away more than the night's excesses. She let her robe slip to the floor and entered the shower.

He didn't turn, but his muscles tensed as she pressed herself to his back, arms circling his waist. Neither spoke as she worked the soap between her palms, lathering him in slow, gentle circles. Down his arms, across his shoulders, along his spine. His tension eased beneath her touch.

When her hands reached his chest, he turned. "I'm sorry."

"For what?"

"For not being him. For not being able to walk into a room with you on my arm." He pressed her hand to his heart. "And for needing this so much."

She rose on tiptoes to kiss him. He drew her to him as water continued to pour over them both.

Later in bed, as their heat ebbed into softness, Yoo-jin's desperate edge was replaced by a temporary quiet. His breathing slowed, eyes half-closed as Hana curled into him.

"I don't know anything about your work," she said. "I have no idea what you do."

He didn't speak for so long she thought he might have fallen asleep. "I got a couple of scripts. More romance."

She propped herself up to look at him.

"But I want to do something different—with real substance." He looked vulnerable in the dim light. "But I keep taking these roles. These endorsements."

"Why?"

"To stay in Seoul." His voice dropped. "Close to you."

She understood what he left unsaid. "You should have

told me."

"It's not very deep," he said, bitterness edging his words. "All I do is dress up and smile for the cameras. While you... you change lives with your work."

She caressed his cheek to soothe him.

"Seeing you there with him... and I can't even touch you." His voice caught. "What will you do about him, *Hana-ya?*" The question loomed over them like a malevolent breath.

"I have to go to Vietnam later this week. A site visit to an orphanage," she said instead. "I'll be away for a couple of days."

He lifted his head, alert. "With him?"

When she nodded, a soft sigh escaped him. He pulled her closer, as if afraid she might vanish. "Just tell me what I have to do," he whispered, voice cracking with desperation. "To keep us together."

His plea made her chest constrict. It didn't come from a celebrity basking in fame—but from a man drowning, looking to her for a lifeline. Instead of answering, she drew him to her and kissed him.

Afterward, Yoo-jin draped himself over her, leg and arm thrown across her body, clinging to her even in sleep.

Hana stayed awake, her mind shifting to darker territory. The question wasn't whether they could survive this—but what it would destroy along the way. Seeing him diminish himself, taking jobs beneath his talent to stay near her, surviving the constant insecurity that had driven him to her door tonight, drunk and desperate.

She had always thought she was sacrificing her needs for his career. But tonight revealed the opposite: he was sacrificing his ambitions for her.

That wasn't love. That was mutual limitation.

She closed her eyes. Perhaps what they needed wasn't compromise, but the courage to walk away—she to family and legacy, he to the spotlight that had always defined him.

PATERNAL INSTINCT

The August sun beat down on Ian's back as he sprinted across the makeshift soccer field, slowing his pace to let the children catch up. Sweat dampened his shirt, his jacket long discarded on a nearby bench. This wasn't the brilliant lawyer from corporate boardrooms. Here, dirt streaked his rolled-up sleeves, and laughter replaced his measured speech. *This. This is what it's all for.*

"Goal!" he shouted, throwing up his hands in mock defeat as a small boy in faded shorts kicked the ball past him. The players erupted in cheers, six little bodies piling onto him in celebration.

"That's five-three now," he called to Hana, who sat beneath an oak tree with toddlers gathered around her. "We're making a comeback!"

She smiled at him before returning to her story. Even from this distance, he could see the gentle way she adjusted her posture to accommodate the little girl leaning against her side. *She's a natural with them.*

A hand tugged at his shirt. "Again, Mr. Ian! Again!"

He turned his attention back to the game, dropping into a defensive stance that made the boys shriek with delight as they dribbled the ball around him. Their uninhibited joy pierced a deep longing he always kept guarded. *My own children someday. A son with Hana's eyes. A daughter with her smile.*

He was reviewing supply invoices when an agitated nurse hurried in, a small bundle in her arms. "Mr. Weston, I'm so sorry—there's been an emergency with one of our older kids. Could you perhaps—?" She gestured to the infant, torn between duties.

"Of course." Ian set aside the paperwork and took the baby from her. The tiny weight settled against his chest.

He sat on the infirmary steps, cradling the infant in one arm while preparing the milk with his free hand. A boy, judging by the blue blanket—regarded him with solemn dark eyes, tiny fingers grasping at air.

"Hello there," he murmured, testing the formula temperature on his wrist. "Hungry, are we?"

The infant latched onto the bottle, eyes never leaving Ian's face. This small human, dependent, looking at him as if he were the entire world. Without thinking, he hummed the same lullaby his mother had sung to him decades ago. The baby's hand found his pinky, gripping it with surprising strength.

At forty, Ian could sense the press of time. Not desperation, but awareness. His life was established. His career was secure. What remained was family—a home filled with the chaos and joy that only children could bring.

And he wanted it with Hana.

He was so absorbed in these thoughts and the feeding that he didn't notice her approach until she was standing before him with a group of older children. Her cheeks were flushed, her eyes glowing with exertion.

"The nurse had an emergency," he explained, his voice still hushed for the infant's benefit. "She left me with this little guy. We're managing, aren't we?" The last question was directed to the baby, who responded by releasing the empty bottle with a sigh.

He shifted the infant to his shoulder, one hand

supporting the head while the other patted rhythmically against the small back.

"You look like you've done this all your life," she observed, amused.

"Some things are instinctive. There's no need to learn."

Hana sent the children inside with gentle nudges. They thundered past, noisy and sweaty. "Wash hands first!" she called toward the low sinks. "No splashing," Ian added, too late. Water had already hit the floor. *Why do I bother? They hear 'splashing' and think it's a direct command.*

In the snack room, they tried to establish order. "Remember your magic words," she said, placing trays of *xôi*, bananas, and *bánh cam* on the table. *Please don't let anyone lick something and put it back.*

Then Duy snatched two pieces, Minh upended his juice, and someone yelled "I don't want sticky rice!" like a declaration of war.

Ian crouched to clean the puddle, the infant slung across his front like a sleepy marsupial. "No one panics!" *The floor needed mopping anyway. With my shirt.*

A loud wail erupted. Mai turned over her chair and then herself, landing dramatically on the mat. Hana scooped her up before the sob could reach full volume and kissed the tears away, murmuring, "Shhh, you're okay. Nothing's broken. Not even the chair." *We've got an Oscar nominee here. That fall was at least 90% performing art.*

Meanwhile, Ian used his calmest voice to settle a near-meltdown over a broken sesame cracker. "I'll trade you a whole one for that little half," he offered. The boy pressed his lips solemnly like it was a UN-level negotiation. *The fate of nations has been decided with less gravitas than this cracker exchange.*

All of a sudden, the baby grunted. Ian froze. Sniff test. *That's a launch of chemical warfare.* He gave Hana a meaningful look. She took one exaggerated step back. Then another.

"You've got this," she mouthed.

Mother of dragons. Father of nappies. He sighed with the air of a man who had seen things, and headed for the changing station like a soldier going over the top.

By the time he returned, the room had reached equilibrium. Children munched on bananas, mouths full and content. One napped on a beanbag. *The eye of the hurricane. Enjoy it while it lasts.*

"You're really good at this," she said as he settled the infant in a nearby bassinet.

He brushed sticky rice off his sleeve. "Children are a joy." *When they're asleep or somebody else's responsibility.* He looked around at the aftermath. "And a reward." *Said every exhausted parent clutching a glass of wine.*

He caught Hana observing him. Her gaze was different—quieter, more intense. Not curiosity. Closer to awareness. Like she was seeing a version of him she hadn't expected—but one that fit.

"I didn't know you liked kids this much," she said.

He glanced at the infant, now curled in sleep beside them, then back at her. A small smile tugged at his mouth. "I had to protect my image. But yeah—I love them."

"Have you thought about having your own?"

"Of course." He faced her. "And not one day—soon." He didn't say it to impress her—but because it was true. And perhaps now safe to say out loud. *And maybe, just maybe, we could share that one day.*

The baby began stirring and fussing. Ian lifted it from the bassinet and cradled it in his arms. When he looked up, Hana's eyes were on him, soft and luminous with contentment. For an instant, it was just the two of them—the chaos in the background faded.

FRAGILE ELECTRIC

The Grand Hyatt ballroom gleamed under crystal chandeliers. White orchids and blue hydrangeas adorned the tables, the foundation's colors transformed into living art. Hana checked the final details, nervous fingers worrying her mother's diamond pendant. The evening's goal was ten million dollars—enough to fund three new communities, to give hundreds of children a chance at stability. Tonight was more than a fundraiser; it was the continuation of her parents' legacy, carried forward through her hands. The responsibility pressed against her chest, familiar, but heavier than ever beneath Seoul's watchful eyes.

"Looks perfect," Ian's voice came from behind.

She turned to see him approaching in his tuxedo, bow tie not yet fastened, tablet in hand. Always prepared, always supportive. The foundation's backbone.

"The Minister of Health confirmed, and the CEO of Samsung Foundation moved his flight to attend." He studied her face with a perceptiveness that both comforted and unnerved her. "Are you alright?"

She nodded, still tugging at the necklace. "I'm fine."

He stepped closer, fingers untangling the gold chain. "He didn't have to come tonight." No need to specify who "he" was.

"It's a public event," she replied evenly. "And his presence will attract attention to our cause."

"That's not why he's coming." Ian's voice was gentle, but his eyes were steely. "This isn't his world, Hana. When the cameras start flashing, it becomes about him, not about the children."

"He's trying, Ian."

"I know. That's what worries me."

From the moment they received the RSVP, Ian clocked it for what it was: a power move. The actor was stepping onto his home turf, the enterprise he'd spent years building through legal counsel, connections, sacrifice. Everything bore his imprint. His rival had done none of that. But here he was, ready to bask in the attention. *This isn't charity. This is encroachment.*

As the first guests arrived, Ian joined Hana in the receiving line. She was radiant in a gold Marchesa gown, looking every inch the director and not just the woman who had wrangled a dozen preschoolers with him in Vietnam, both contemplating family and children.

They shook hands with politicians, diplomats, philanthropists—a parade of old money dressed in restraint and new money drowning in shine.

Moments later, a black Audi pulled up, its gleaming exterior catching each camera flash like a mirror. The door opened and Yoo-jin stepped out.

Impeccable tuxedo. Hair slicked back to look effortless. Not performing, but aware. He adjusted his cuffs, nonchalant, giving the cameras a nod and a half-smirk that landed somewhere between humility and command.

Yoo-jin approached and extended his hand—first to Ian, then to Hana.

"Thank you for coming," Ian said, the corners of his mouth lifting just enough.

"It's an honor to be here," Yoo-jin replied, cool and unflappable.

Ian glanced at Hana in time to catch that subtle shift

in her eyes, lingering a half-second on the actor after their handshake. A quiet pull. A private gravity. The kind that rewrote a room. *Brilliant. He's not yet inside, and she's already leaning in his direction.*

Ian drew a breath. It was going to be a long evening.

***

The cocktail reception buzzed with corporate power, political influence, and celebrity allure. Hana moved with purpose—introductions, donations, logistics. But tonight, the background static threw her off.

Yoo-jin was in the room, mingling among guests. *He came. Who would have thought?*

He hadn't attended one of these events since the Weston-Rhee fundraiser almost two years ago when he volunteered to be her escort. The night it all started between them. That detail sat at the back of her mind, surfacing in flashes—his unexpected ease in the room, the way he had looked at her as if he already knew her. How quickly things had evolved. How little she had expected any of it to last. *And yet—here we are. Still tangled up. Still impossible to define clearly.*

Her gaze drifted for a second. Yoo-jin stood by the central installation, speaking to another guest, looking calm. Polished. A little removed. This wasn't his scene, not really, but he wore it well enough. *He's making an effort for me.*

She wondered if anyone here had the faintest idea who he was to her. Most wouldn't guess. In his world, they existed in shadows. In her world, it was obvious they would too. *We're both hiding in plain sight. What kind of normal people live like this?*

She returned her attention to the conversation before her, thanking the guests with a polite nod. As if on cue, Yoo-jin passed behind her. His hand grazed hers—light as breath, deliberate, unhurried. A single line drawn across her skin. A small claim. A gentle reminder that he was there.

***

Throughout the evening, Ian tracked Hana and the actor while maintaining his duties. She was magnificent, a perfect diplomat and hostess commanding the room. With possessive pride, he imagined what it would be like to call her his wife. A real partner.

But then he would catch that sparkle in her eyes whenever they landed on the actor. A shift so subtle most would miss it, but to him, it was unmistakable. It was hunger, memory. A quiet pulse.

Jealousy knotted in his chest.

When the three of them found themselves in conversation again, Ian led the charge. "Mr. Lee. A pleasure to see you here. Philanthropy isn't your usual circuit. Must be a step down for you."

"Not at all. Celebrity galas tend to lack substance. Unlike what you do here."

Charming. Well-rehearsed. "Very good of you to make time to attend. I'm sure your schedule is jam-packed with photoshoots and fan meetings."

The actor didn't flinch. "It's only proper to recognize the foundation's work. And the people who dedicate themselves to make it happen." His eyes slid to Hana. Briefly. Deliberately. A public gesture laced with private meaning.

"Thank you for the kind words. We look forward to seeing you in your next film. Enjoy your evening." Ian guided Hana away with a light hand on her elbow. He waited until they were out of earshot before speaking. "Your friend cleans up well."

"He can do a lot of things when he puts his mind to it," she answered with a smile.

That stubborn loyalty again. "Perhaps. But it's a matter of consistency, isn't it?"

***

Yoo-jin had expected that glacial greeting from the lawyer.

Then Hana's hand was in his—cool, professional, brief. But in that short touch, he took in the light pressure of her fingers, saw that glint in her eyes. A private signal just for him. Even here, surrounded by people, there was a language that belonged only to them.

During the evening, Yoo-jin's gaze trailed Hana as she worked the room the way she did on their "first date." How long ago was it? She was in control—greeting donors, exchanging banter with foreign guests, checking in with her team. *This is her element. Like the movie set is mine.*

When she took to the stage for her speech, her voice carried across the room, confident and clear. She spoke with conviction, not flash. Only calm authority and a genuine belief in her cause.

Behind her, images played on a screen with children laughing, new facilities being built, volunteers distributing supplies. The silent documentary flowed with gentle transitions, showcasing the foundation's work.

Until a particular frame appeared, stopping Yoo-jin mid-sip of his champagne.

It was a photograph from their Vietnam site visit. The Englishman was holding a swaddled infant to his chest, gazing at Hana beside him. She wasn't looking at the baby—her eyes were on him. Her expression—soft, luminous, content—was one Yoo-jin had never seen before. Not even in their most private moments.

The image was breathtaking in its quiet implication. *Parents. They looked like new parents.*

A ripple moved through the audience, but Yoo-jin's heart had already gone still. He saw Hana turn to the screen, a small smile on her lips not meant for the room. It was a memory. She was remembering that moment, probably when she first saw the lawyer not as her colleague, not as family, but as someone closer. A man who could hold a child like that—a man who could father one.

His throat tightened. *I've been cast in hundreds of roles, but never as a father. I don't even know if I'd be any good at it.*

The champagne turned bitter on his tongue. He had memorized the lines of her body. Knew how she laughed, how she kissed, how she twisted her hair before bed. But he didn't know this.

He put down his glass, fingers suddenly clumsy. The crystal struck his plate with a sharp clink. *All this time, and I never asked what she wanted beyond us. Not once.*

When the crowd thinned and the band played a slow and nostalgic tune, he found Hana. "May I?"

She nodded. Their hands came together. The touch still fit. Still sparked.

They moved to the dance floor while the image of the infant still churned in his mind. "You look stunning," he murmured.

In a low voice and with a smile just for him, she answered, "And you look delicious."

His fingers settled against her back, finding the dip he knew by heart. "That sounds like a promise."

Her breath caught, a flush spreading across her chest. "It is," she whispered.

This is what we're good at. The in-between moments. The chemistry. But is it enough?

But the current between them had shifted. Yoo-jin could feel it beneath her skin. A hesitation she hadn't carried before. "You're amazing," he said.

She tilted her head. "I'm only doing my job."

"No." His thumb brushed her wrist. "You're more than that. You're the kind of person who improves people's lives."

Her gaze softened. "You always say the right things."

"Do I?" His voice dropped. "Then tell me something

honest."

She stiffened a fraction, but he sensed it.

"Do you ever think about... us? About our future?"

Her smile was vague, deflective. "I try not to—you never know what life has in store."

He nodded, but it didn't satisfy him. Her eyes met his—still affectionate, still full of warmth—but distant in a way that hadn't dawned on him until tonight. *She's calculated the odds. Already knows what's possible between us and what's not.*

"I think about you all the time," he said. "But maybe I haven't thought enough about... everything else." *And that's why you can't see a future with me.*

Hana smiled over his shoulder but didn't answer.

All of a sudden, their touch didn't seem electric anymore.

It seemed fragile.

Like an illusion that could shatter the moment we try to make it real.

FLEETING NORMAL

The early sunshine cast shy rays across the rumpled bedding. Yoo-jin's arm was draped over Hana's waist, his breathing deep and even against her neck. The previous night lingered in the pleasant ache of her muscles, the faint marks on her collarbone, his scent on her skin.

After their vigilant choreography at the gala, they had just made it through her door before the evening's restraint combusted, leaving them breathless and sated in a mess of sheets and pillows.

Hana studied his sleeping face. In repose, the sharp angles of his cheekbones softened, the perpetual alertness of his eyes veiled. Here was Yoo-jin without his careful masks, without the pressure of public scrutiny. Only the man.

His eyelids fluttered open, catching her watching him. A slow smile spread across his face.

"Breakfast?" she asked, caressing the outline of his lips.

He caught her hand, pressing a kiss to her palm. "Let's go out."

The suggestion caught her by surprise. Usually, they stayed home, away from prying eyes and camera lenses. But there was a newfound confidence in him this morning, as if driven by fresh resolutions.

"Are you sure?" she asked, searching his face.

"Absolutely. I want a normal day with you. Just once."

***

An hour later, they strolled through a quiet neighborhood far from trendy districts where celebrities were hunted. Yoo-jin wore his usual armor—baseball cap and glasses—while Hana walked beside him in jeans and oversized sweater. Coffee and pastries from a local bakery where the elderly owner was too busy with crosswords to notice who was buying her famous egg bread.

"Last night went well," he said. "I loved watching you."

"And you were impressive," she countered. "I've never seen you so... restrained at a public event."

He laughed. "I can blend in. Contrary to popular belief, I don't need to be the center of attention every minute."

"You were positively glowing. Even Ian commented on it. Said you cleaned up well."

He groaned. "Please don't quote your cousin to me. That man could insult me with a compliment and make it sound like a royal decree."

They slowed as they entered a small neighborhood park. No children played on the equipment yet. It was too early with dew still clinging to the grass. They found a secluded bench tucked behind a hedge.

City noise faded to the occasional passing car, the chatter of birds in the trees, the soft rustle of leaves. Steam curled from their paper cups, lifting the rich scent of coffee into the cool morning air.

Yoo-jin broke the silence. "Have you thought about having kids?"

The question sprang unexpected and weighty. Hana's fingers tightened around her cup, heat seeping through the cardboard. She searched his face for context, but his expression remained open, curious.

She took a careful sip before answering. "Yeah...

eventually." It was a safe answer, vague but truthful. She had never let herself imagine this scenario with him. Their relationship existed in stolen moments and shadows; there was no space in it for a future that real.

"Last night—that picture of you and your cousin with a baby in Vietnam. I've never seen you look like that."

"Like what?"

"Like you'd found something you'd been yearning for all your life." He paused. "I haven't thought about children before. But maybe I should have."

She deflected with a smirk. "Would you still love me with a swollen belly?"

He sat up straight, setting his drink aside. His palm slid under her sweater to rest against her stomach—not sexual but solemn, exploratory. "I'd love it even more," he said, voice dropping with a raw honesty that made her heart stutter.

"I want that with you," he whispered. "Not now—but someday. I want everything with you."

The sincerity on his face struck her as terrifying and exhilarating. For an instant, she pictured herself round with his child, his hands cradling her expanded body. She felt dizzy at the vision.

They stood to leave, the moment too significant to continue discussing outdoors. As they walked toward the park exit, he reached for her hand, twining their fingers. An instinctive gesture, a quiet declaration—so public, so unguarded—was more intimate than any sensual caress.

***

Neither noticed a young woman on a bench across the path, her phone raised as if checking messages. They didn't see her eyes widening in recognition, her finger tapping to capture what she was seeing. They didn't hear the soft click as the image was sent, accompanied by this message: *OMG is this Yoo-*

jin Lee?? With a woman??

By evening, their picture would be everywhere. Yoo-jin's face was unmistakable despite the cap and glasses. Hana's was in profile, not easily recognizable.

The hashtags *#YooJinGirlfriend* and *#YooJinDating* would trend within hours. Comments would flood gossip sites—some supportive, others vicious. Anonymous accounts would work to identify the mystery woman who had captured the heart of Korea's beloved star.

***

Hana and Yoo-jin, oblivious, continued walking through the park holding hands. "This is nice," she said.

He squeezed her hand. "It is."

As the morning progressed, the sunlight became brighter, occasionally dimmed by heavy clouds.

They spent the day in their private bubble. After lunch, they rode his Ducati through Seoul's main streets. Protected by tinted visors, they laughed at drivers stuck in traffic. Yoo-jin sped between cars, earning honks and stares for his recklessness. His mobile kept vibrating with unread notifications.

That evening, they dined with a group at Hwang's. The sommelier brought his favorite soju without asking. The chef prepared dishes not on the menu. Conversation flowed, both of them unaware of the awkward glances between their friends who already saw the photos spreading online.

Yoo-jin's hand squeezed Hana's under the table, as though the contact sealed a new, unspoken pact.

Back home, they made love with playful tenderness, neither noticing the intensifying rain against the window panes.

***

Across the city, Ian's phone screen blinked non-stop. Notification after notification interrupted his focus on work. The blue light cast harsh shadows across his face in the dimness of his hotel room.

The picture of Hana's hand in the actor's hit him like a kick to the solar plexus. His breath shortened as he scrolled through the comments:

So pretty!

I heard she's only a fling.

They make a beautiful couple.

Who the hell is she? Find out who it is now!

He reached for the glass on his desk. The Macallan vanished in a single swallow. He poured another, hands shaking and liquid sloshing over the rim.

Since he arrived in Seoul, his pursuit of Hana had been one step forward, two steps back. London. Jeju. Vietnam. Now this.

It was reckless. Public. Personal.

Fifteen years. Fifteen fucking years. Of patience. Of calculated moves. Of planning a life with her at its center. All upended by an actor who treated her like an afterthought.

His mobile chimed again—Thomas Weston. A mere three words: *Look after Hana.* His uncle never micromanaged, never got in the way. But he kept a close eye on everything—especially Hana. She was his only child, and he always counted on Ian to keep her safe.

Blood pounded in his ears. Even her stepfather expected him to fix this. To clean up their mess. To manage their fallout.

More notifications. More comments. More speculation.

"Enough!"

The shout tore from his throat. He hurled his whisky glass against the wall. The crash echoed through the room. Shards scattered across the carpet. Amber liquid streamed down the wallpaper.

He froze, stunned by his own outburst. In all his adult life, he had never lost control like this. Not when his mother died. Not when business deals collapsed. Not when he sat by as Hana dated other men.

The sight of his face reflected in the window startled him. The wild eyes of a stranger. Pupils dilated. A vein pulsed at his temple. His tie hung loose. His hair stood at odd angles where his fingers had raked through it.

The image remained on the screen. The actor's hand around Hana's smaller one. Their profiles turned toward each other in private communion.

He moved to the window and pressed his forehead to the cool glass. Seoul stretched out below, lights flickering in the darkness. Somewhere out there, Hana was with the actor while their reckless display was spreading online like wildfire.

Options spun through his mind. He could intervene. Use his connections to suppress the story. Shield her from whatever was coming.

Or step back. *Let her find out if the actor comes through for her when it gets ugly.*

The debris crunched under his shoes as he marched back to the desk. His hand hovered over the phone. Thomas was waiting for an answer.

He typed a response: *I'm handling it.* Three words that committed him to nothing specific.

He straightened his tie. First, create distance. Force Hana to navigate this crisis without him as a buffer. Have her discover firsthand whether the actor would prioritize her or his public image when the cameras came on.

It was cruel, perhaps. But necessary. Patience had gotten him nowhere. Maybe a few weeks of absence would accomplish what his presence couldn't.

CAUGHT ON CAMERA

When Hana arrived at the office the next morning, the place was quiet. Most staff wouldn't arrive for another hour. Her heels clicked against the hardwood, echoing through the empty corridor. A faint draft stirred the papers on the reception counter, the rustling sound disrupting the stillness.

She froze in the doorway, surprised to find Ian already at his desk—sleeves rolled up, a coffee cup half-drunk by his laptop. Dark circles rimmed his eyes and a stubble shadowed his jaw. His disheveled appearance suggested he hadn't slept.

He glanced up from his laptop. There were no good-mornings, no preliminaries. His voice was emotionless, like still water concealing undercurrents. "Tell me—do you enjoy appearing in public with Lee now?"

She frowned. "What?"

He turned his screen toward her with deliberate slowness.

A picture, grainy but discernible. Yoo-jin and Hana, fingers interlaced like teenage sweethearts, caught in a moment of unguarded intimacy now plastered online. Her face was turned in profile, but she was recognizable to those who knew her.

Her breath hitched, a cold sensation spreading from her chest all the way to her fingertips.

"You do realize that once the public finds you—people will be going through your garbage?" Ian's voice was quiet but sharp—disappointment, perhaps, or contained anger. "Camping outside your building? Following you to work? To the grocery store?" Each question landed like a stone thrown against glass.

"This wasn't planned." She stared at the picture, regretting how happy and carefree they'd looked.

"Do you have any plan at all?" he pressed.

She tugged at a loose thread on her sleeve. Apart from their conversation about children, there had been no talk, no roadmap, no tangible decision of what would come next. Her stomach tightened.

He sighed, dragging a hand over his face. "You have a public image to maintain, Hana. The foundation, your parents' legacy—it isn't something you improvise."

With that, he picked up his coffee cup, the ceramic scraping against the wood surface, and left the room. His footsteps in the hallway were heavier than usual, each one punctuating his disapproval.

***

The cold air blowing from the vents in the overlit conference room made Yoo-jin shift in his chair as he zoomed in on the photo on his manager's screen. The pixelated image of him and Hana was now shown back to him like incriminating evidence.

"They don't know who she is yet," Ji-hoon said, scrolling through the comments. "But it's a matter of time."

Yoo-jin's jaw clenched. Sweat beaded along his hairline despite the air conditioning. Twenty years of building his career. Millions invested in his image. And now this fallout may topple everything.

"With the fan tour starting, we have to get ahead of this," Ji-hoon continued, voice clinical. "No contact for a few days.

Until the worst blows over."

"No contact?" Yoo-jin's head snapped up. "I can't disappear on her."

Ji-hoon slammed the tablet closed. "You have to. We need you to be visible out there—alone. Dinner at Park's new restaurant tonight. The charity basketball game tomorrow. Distance yourself from the gossip."

"She's not gossip."

"To the public, that's exactly what she is right now." Ji-hoon drew a breath, softening. "It's temporary. Until we establish the narrative." He saw Yoo-jin reach for his mobile. "Call her now. Explain. Use the encrypted line."

Yoo-jin walked to a corner of the conference room when Hana picked up, seeking a modicum of privacy. Ji-hoon pretended to check emails but remained within earshot.

"You've seen it?" Yoo-jin asked, voice low.

"Yes." Hana sounded stressed. "Ian showed me."

He bowed his head, picturing her at her desk, the weight of the crisis collapsing on her shoulders. "I'm sorry. I shouldn't have suggested going out."

"I wanted to go too." A pause. "When will I see you?"

He glanced over at Ji-hoon, who was watching, expectant. "It depends on how things go. Late tonight, maybe."

"Maybe?"

He drew a sharp breath. "I have to make some appearances first. Put the brakes on the rumors." The word "rumors" slipped out before he could catch it.

A silence on the line.

"Hana?" He lowered his voice. "I'm sorry. I meant—"

"It's fine," she interrupted, sounding distant. "I understand."

She didn't. How could she? This image management that both sustained and imprisoned him. "I'll check in as soon as I'm done," he promised before hanging up. He stared at his phone, fighting the need to call back, to run to her, consequences be damned.

Ji-hoon stepped closer. "The car will pick you up at seven for dinner. Wear the navy Brioni suit. We've arranged for photographers."

Yoo-jin nodded, already dreading the performance ahead —plastic smiles, staged photo ops, damage control.

While Hana was left to weather the storm on her own.

***

Hana sat at her desk, staring at the darkened screen.

Rumors. That's what she had been reduced to. *What now? How do I handle this?*

She had no experience with public scrutiny. Yoo-jin lived in this world daily, navigated it expertly. She had hoped for guidance, for reassurance. Instead, she got "appearances" and "maybe later." She looked up at the sound of footsteps. Ian stood in the doorway, observing her.

"So? What did he say?"

"He's—managing the situation."

"Of course, he is. And where does that leave you?"

Her throat tightened. She had no answer.

He sighed, raking a hand through his already messy hair. "I have to be in London for a bit."

The words hit her like a slap. "What? Now? While this is happening?"

"Meetings that can't be postponed."

"When will you be back?"

"I don't know. I'll be in touch."

Panic flared in Hana's chest. "You're leaving? When I need —" She caught herself, but too late.

"When you need what? Support? Advice?" His voice

hardened. "Call your boyfriend. This is his world you've stepped into. Let him help you through it."

The door closed behind him with a click that somehow sounded more final than a slam. *Everyone's abandoning me. And it's only the beginning.*

Her phone filled with notifications. Friends, PR team, her mother Eun-ji demanding explanations: *Why am I seeing you with an actor on Twitter? What happened to the Seraphine heir? We can't have scandal.* A sharp laugh escaped her throat. Of course, her mother's first concern would be the foundation's image.

She thought of Seo Ji-hwan, who was everything a sensible woman should want—rich, kind, funny, mentally stable. Being with him was like settling into first-class—comfortable, smooth, safe. *I could be cruising in an Aston Martin instead of going off-road on an ATV without a seat belt.*

Her mobile showed nothing from Yoo-jin since their last call.

Work had always been her anchor, the one reality when everything else shifted. She reached for the folder of contracts, flipping it open, though the words blurred almost immediately.

But as she tried to focus—margins, clauses, signatures—her eyes drifted back to the silent device. The longer it stayed dark, the louder the question became.

When the world asked—would he say her name?

Or would he erase her with silence, as though she'd never been there?

She bent her head to the page, but a coldness spread low in her stomach, like the body already bracing for a blow it knew was coming.

SLOW ERASURE

London greeted Ian with a persistent drizzle, soaking into his overcoat until it dragged at his shoulders like penance. Black cabs hissed past, the Underground chimed, accents mingled in the air. *Better here,* he told himself. Away from the hard truths he'd left with Hana in Seoul.

He worked like a man possessed. Meetings filled his calendar from dawn to dusk. In the rare moments between appointments, his finger would hover over Hana's contact, but he would always redirect, checking news feeds for mentions of Yoo-jin Lee instead. *This is what restraint looks like. Not calling. Not texting. Just casual stalking of her boyfriend online.*

The actor was on a multi-city fan meeting tour. Eight events, extended to ten due to demand. Each venue sold out within minutes. *The movie star is out there performing while she sits home alone. Cosmic comedy.*

He sent Hana only work emails—terse, professional communication. Whenever her name appeared in his inbox, he would read her response twice, searching for signs of strain or unhappiness between the lines. But she was too skilled at maintaining appearances, even in writing.

On his fourth day in London, he met with Julian Hayes, a contact in a British press outlet with a strong Asian entertainment division. They sat in a dim corner of a Soho pub, the air thick with hops and wood polish, nursing pints while rain streaked the windows.

"So," Hayes said, wiping foam from his lip, "what brings you to my side of the world? Bit far from your charity circuit."

Ian's face stayed neutral. "Expanding our donor base. I've been following the news from Korea. Yoo-jin Lee's tour looks like it's a hit."

Hayes' eyebrows rose. "Didn't peg you for a K-drama fan."

"Professional interest," Ian replied. "His management team seems effective. They've added stops in spite of the recent... speculation." *Drop the bait gently.*

Hayes leaned forward, lowering his voice despite the pub's ambient noise. "Ah, the mystery girlfriend. Quite the hot topic. My editor's been pushing for some angle on that story."

"And?" Ian prompted, tone casual. "Is the rumor mill accurate?" *Asking as a curious bystander—with a Cambridge degree in manipulation.*

"Hard to say," Hayes shrugged. "Neither he nor his agency have confirmed anything. Standard deflection tactics."

Ian took a slow sip of his beer, the bitter liquid coating his tongue. "Perhaps someone should ask him point-blank. In public. Where he can't dodge."

Hayes looked up, intrigued. "That would certainly make for an interesting headline."

"It's a thought," Ian said, setting down his glass. *And the domino tips. Let's see where it falls.*

***

Three days later, at a fan meeting in Taipei, the press conference began with the usual softball topics. The room was overheated with flashing cameras creating a strobe-like effect that intensified the claustrophobic atmosphere. Despite the discomfort, Yoo-jin answered questions with easy charm and a genuine smile.

A journalist from an international outlet rose. "Mr. Lee, can you confirm or deny that you're dating someone special?

The leaked pictures aren't fake. Can you tell us more?"

A sudden hush fell over the room. Yoo-jin's features froze for a microsecond, a single bead of sweat forming at his temple. *Goddammit.*

He glanced toward his manager. Their eyes met for only a beat, but the message was clear: *You know what you have to do.*

His jaw clenched. He hated this. Detested how the truth became currency exchanged for silence, spin, control. *If I say yes, I lose everything. If I say no... I lose her.*

After a weighty moment, he blurted, "That individual is an acquaintance. I'm not in a relationship." His fingers tightened around his water bottle until the plastic crackled. "Next question, please." *There. I said it—a straight-up lie.*

But his poise had cracked. His subsequent answers grew shorter, his smile more strained. Twenty minutes later, his manager ended the session early due to scheduling constraints.

The denial was complete. Within hours, speculation exploded across social media. Fan sites dissected his response, his body language, the tightness around his eyes. He drifted through events on autopilot, smile rigid, eyes hollow. *It's done. I've shoved her off a cliff.*

Fans were delighted. Their precious boy was still available, still *theirs*—what a relief. Comments poured in celebrating his "focus" and "professionalism," with women playfully declaring they were back in the running and dismissing the mystery girlfriend as if she'd been nothing more than an annoying fly that got swatted away. *Glad you're all pleased. Meanwhile, I can't even look at myself in the mirror.*

***

In his London office, Ian watched Yoo-jin's press conference on his tablet, whisky glass in hand. The warmth from each sip matched the satisfaction unfurling in his stomach. The actor's disavowal of Hana wasn't only about privacy—it was about preserving the shine of his brand. And once again, he sensed the tide turning in his favor.

He could almost picture it: Hana watching herself being erased in real time. If he knew her—and he did, better than anyone—she'd be hurt but never say a word. She'd never demand a place at his side. She'd take the silence, absorb it, rationalize that it was the cost of dating a celebrity like Yoo-jin Lee.

But that evening would temper any gratification he felt.

The dining room of the Weston family home in Hampstead had not changed in a hundred and twenty years. The same Edwardian furniture. The portrait of Ian's great-grandfather looking down sternly from above the fireplace. The heavy silver cutlery that required excessive polishing.

Ian sat across from his father Henry and his uncle Thomas, the table between them set like a mahogany battleground. The three men wore suits despite the private setting. Thomas had loosened his tie a quarter inch, the Weston equivalent of casual attire.

"The Jinqiao acquisition looks promising," Henry Weston said, slicing into his roast lamb with meticulous care. "Their East Asian routes would complement our North Atlantic operations."

Ian nodded, twirling the stem of his wine glass before responding. "Their fleet is aging. Five of their vessels will need dry-dock refits within eighteen months."

"Which we've accounted for in our valuation," Thomas clarified. His voice was measured, but his gaze would not meet Ian's. "The synergies outweigh the capital expenditure requirements."

The conversation proceeded with the emotional temperature of a board meeting. Shipping routes. Integration timelines. Tax implications. All discussed in polite, clipped sentences that covered the tension humming beneath. *They blame me for not being in Seoul. For not being with Hana.*

Ian maintained his composure, contributing appropriate insights while navigating the undercurrent of disapproval. His uncle hadn't mentioned Hana once. The omission spoke volumes. *Say it. Just say what's on your mind.*

When the meal ended, Thomas broke his reserve. "I must say I'm surprised to see you in town," he said, stirring his coffee.

The statement hung heavy in the air. Classic Weston—a gut punch disguised as small talk.

"Some urgent matters needed my attention."

Henry Weston looked up from his coffee, fixing his son with the look Ian had dreaded since childhood—disappointment couched in stoic restraint. "I'm sure Hana is doing her best holding the fort alone," he said in a mild voice.

There it is. The tribal elders closing ranks. Ian's molars clenched, his knuckles whitening around the coffee cup handle. The need to defend himself rose like bile in his throat—*It's for her own damn good!*

But he swallowed back the outburst. "Hana will be alright," he said, setting his cup down with all the calm he could muster. "We have to trust her. She'll get it right."

The fleeting glance between his father and uncle said it all: abandoning Hana wasn't a strategy—it was a weakness, a failure of character.

I'm showing her what life with the actor truly means. Even if it has to hurt.

***

"Ma'am? Vietnamese official, line two." Jin-ah hovered at the doorway, hair fraying like her sanity. *Ma'am? She always calls me Boss. She must be losing it too.*

"Give me five minutes."

Another buzz—a text from Yoo-jin. *Hope your day's going*

well. Landing in Hong Kong now. Second city of the tour.

No mention of the photos. No lifeline. Just cheerful updates, as if she were one of a million fans. Her reply was just as thin: *Thanks. Busy day. Good luck with the fan meet.*

The intercom again. "Compliance needs signatures by noon."

By midmorning, Jin-ah staggered in with the Henderson contract and a teetering stack of folders. "Samsung called again. If we don't respond today, they'll redirect funding."

The hours collapsed into calls, memos, decisions. By lunch, she was reassuring Samsung about brand security. By afternoon, Jin-ah placed the latest PR report on Hana's desk, avoiding her eyes. It was the transcript from the press conference, Yoo-jin's voice in stark black and white: "The individual in the photo is an acquaintance. I'm not in a relationship."

An acquaintance. Why not? What did I expect him to say—lover, soulmate, future mother of his children?

"Ma'am? Are you alright?"

"Fine. Just tired."

Jin-ah fidgeted. "Everyone's relieved. It would've been worse if—"

Yes. Much worse if he'd said the 'individual' was his girlfriend—and she worked here. Hana dropped her head into her hands.

By nine, the office was empty. Her inbox was brimming. Her eyes burned. Her lover had erased her in public.

But she was still upright. Just.

***

While Hana struggled in Seoul, Yoo-jin was paraded across Asia like a prize-winning poodle. Smile here, pose there, croon the same recycled love songs, field the same sugar-dipped questions. He hated all of it. The pageantry. The infantilization. Dancing like a circus seal so strangers could clap and squeal before forgetting his name on the flight home. But the cameras were rolling, the fans were shrieking, and the brand had to stay intact.

Taipei

"What was your favorite scene in *Starlight Romance*?"

Yoo-jin smiled on cue. "The rain scene... when they kissed." *I've said this in five interviews this month.*

Screams erupted. Fifteen hundred women in matching pink headbands, sobbing over a drama he hadn't thought about in ages.

Next question: "What's your ideal girlfriend type?"

"Someone kind. With her own dreams and passions." *Someone I can stand next to in front of the damn cameras.*

Then came the paper bag. "Time for 'Guess the Food'!" Blindfolded, Yoo-jin reached inside and grabbed something slimy. The audience counted down. *Ten. Nine. Eight.*

More squeals as he pulled out a soaked piece of *tteokbokki.* It flopped in his hand like a severed alien finger.

"Awww! Yoo-jin *oppa* is sooo cute!"

Cute? I'm a grown man. Not a fucking golden retriever.

Hong Kong

New country, same circus.

Yoo-jin decked out in bunny ears, angel wings, daisy sunglasses. The crowd *lost it.*

"*Aegyo* time!" the host shouted.

He made finger hearts. Puffed out his cheeks. *Forty years old and still doing this shit like it was 2012.*

Through his ridiculous heart pose, he spotted someone filming. In two hours, it would be online.

Would Hana laugh? Cringe? Wonder how she ever let this grown-ass man dressed like a toddler at Halloween become her life?

Manila

"Marry Me!" A name was drawn from a bag—Carmelita from Davao.

Yoo-jin playing househusband for a lucky fangirl. Purple bathrobe. An apron. A floral headscarf.

Fake cooking. Fake dishwashing. Real shrieks. *Method actor cosplaying as an ajumma from a 90s sitcom. Career-defining moment.*

He blew kisses to the audience.

And died a little inside.

Singapore

"*Yoo-jin-ssi*, wear this for the princess game!"

He glared at a plastic crown encrusted with fake gems. "I'm a forty-year-old man, not a pookie."

The coordinator blinked. "But the fans—"

Fuck it. He put on the crown. Screams. Flashes. Social media clips.

In the dressing room later, he gazed at his reflection —crown askew, eyes hollow. He tapped a message to Hana: *Everything ok?*

Her reply came during his third outfit change: *Handling it.*

Those two words said it all. She was handling it. Alone.

And him? He was on stage, wearing a glittery crown, playing "Choose Your Princess" in front of five thousand fans like it was a completely normal job for an adult man.

I'm failing her. I know I'm failing her.

***

Nine PM. Hana entered her apartment, shut the door behind her, and slid down against it until she hit the cold tile. *Made it home. Achievement unlocked.*

Thirteen days since Yoo-jin left for his tour. Two weeks

since Ian disappeared to London. Two weeks of pure hell at the office.

Her phone chimed. *Yoo-jin: Finished in Manila. Heading to Singapore tomorrow. Miss you.*

She should respond, when lifting her thumbs didn't seem like climbing Everest. After ten minutes on the floor—was it ten? Time had gotten slippery—Hana dragged herself to the kitchen. Opened the fridge. Stared inside. *What was I looking for? Food? Wine? The will to live?*

She grabbed a bottle of Chablis.

Her curiosity pulled her to Instagram. Yoo-jin's feed bloomed with tour photos—perfect hair, perfect smile, perfect life. Thousands of likes. The show rolled on without a care. *Nice to see someone having fun.*

She clicked on Ian's profile. *Yeah, check on the other deserter. Let's see if he's enjoying himself.*

Recent posts: none. Classic Ian—all work, minimal personality.

Older posts. England: sharing an umbrella outside the British Museum. Jeju: on his motorcycle, her hair wild in the wind. Vietnam: the baby in his arms and her leaning close. Her eyes lingered on his face longer than she would admit. The deep blue of his eyes. That almost-smirk. *I should be furious. Why do I miss him?*

Before logic intervened, her fingers typed: *I miss you* and hit 'send.' Her eyes widened in shock. *Shit. What the hell did I just do?*

Hana dropped the device like it burned her. *Wine—need wine right now.* She rummaged through a drawer for a corkscrew, finding instead a small plastic case—her pill dispenser. *Why is this here? When did I...?* She counted the remaining pills. *Tuesday's still there? Or was that Wednesday's? What day was it anyway?*

She set it on the countertop and opened the wine. *One task completed. Gold star.*

In the living room, she looked at the framed selfie taken at the market with Yoo-jin. Both smiling. Both pretending to be strangers in public. She recalled asking him at the time: *Can't we act like a couple at all?* And his reply: *It's complicated... But the short answer is no.*

Her phone vibrated—Min-ji. *Hey, scatterbrain! We're waiting for you at Blue Lagoon. Jae-won's promotion. I texted you yesterday.*

Shit. She typed back: *Sorry, I forgot.*

Min-ji: *Yeah, like you forgot Sora's birthday last week? She's still pouting. And our weekly brunch. Twice.*

She replied: *I'll be right there. Tell S I'm buying an extra round.*

She downed her wine, grabbed her keys, and tossed the pill dispenser back into the drawer. *I'll figure it out tomorrow. When I'm a functional human again.*

***

Yoo-jin returned to Seoul on a Thursday evening, four weeks after he left. He came straight to Hana's apartment, exhaustion in the shadows under his eyes and the slight slump in his posture.

He pulled her into a hug, cupping her face, eyes searching hers. "How have you been?"

Like hell. I've been in hell. She forced a smile. "Fine. I've been fine."

He kissed her as if to erase the weeks apart. She kissed him back, but the eagerness wasn't there.

As they lay together, she let him pull her closer, her hands resting at his shoulders instead of clinging. He moved with determination; she moved with care, almost caution. They knew the rhythm of each other's bodies, but this time there was a subtle disconnect—small pauses, glances not met, words swallowed.

Afterward, he held her tight. She settled into his grip, eyes open in the semi-darkness. Her palm smoothed his hair once, then fell still at her side. He propped himself on one elbow, studying her face in the dim light. “You look tired,” he said. “Has it been difficult?”

She looked over his shoulder at the poster on the wall. The truth sat heavy on her tongue: *Yes, watching you deny me to the world was difficult. Feeling like your dirty secret was difficult. Missing Ian was difficult.* Instead, she said, “Busy with the office. The foundation doesn’t run itself.”

“Has your cousin been checking in from London?” His voice carried a forced casualness.

“Work emails,” she replied, not mentioning the unanswered text she had sent. “Nothing more.”

Relief washed over his face. “Good. I mean—I’m glad you’ve had space.” Then, quietly: “I was really worried. But you handled everything so well. Thank you.”

Hana turned to look at the ceiling, breaking eye contact. The plaster had a tiny crack she had never noticed before, a small imperfection in the otherwise pristine surface.

***

Days passed, settling into a strange new pattern. Yoo-jin became more relaxed knowing Ian remained in London. The threat diminished, his confidence grew. Meanwhile, Hana found herself more detached, observing their relationship as if from afar.

They stayed behind closed doors, cooking elaborate meals at his home or hers. The domesticity, once a comfort, had become suffocating.

There was no discussion about his agency’s official statement denying the dating rumors, though it hung between them like smoke. The memory of that morning when they walked hand-in-hand through the park, dreaming aloud about children, now floated in the distance like a moment from someone else's life.

One evening, as Hana chopped vegetables for dinner, Yoo-jin burst into the kitchen, phone in hand, face alight with excitement.

"I got it," he announced. "The Kim Jae-wook project. My agent just called—they want me for the lead. Lee Dong-wook dropped out at the last minute."

"That's wonderful," she said, happy for him. At last, a serious dramatic role to break him out of the romantic typecast.

"Filming starts in a month. Mostly location shoots—Jeju, Gangwon Province, and other places I've never even heard of."

"How long?" she asked, knife pausing mid-chop.

"Four months, give or take."

He was beside himself with excitement. "This is great! With the American project on hold, the timing couldn't be better!"

She glanced down at the cutting board.

His smile dimmed. He held her face between his hands. "But I'll be back every break I get. You know that, right?"

"I'm happy for you," she repeated, but there was a shift inside her, like a final piece sliding out of alignment. *Secrecy. Absence. Endless.*

Later that night, as Yoo-jin slept beside her, Hana lay awake, listening to his breathing. The moonlight filtered through the curtains, casting his beautiful face in silver. She memorized the curve of his lips, the fan of his eyelashes against his cheeks, the line of his jaw. *I love you. But I'm so tired of being tucked away, alone.*

Her phone glowed on the nightstand. A new email. From Ian, of course—who else would send work correspondence at 3 AM?

But when she opened it, there was no business to discuss. Only two short sentences that made her breath catch: *I miss you too. Returning to Seoul.*

ALPHA COLLISION

It was a mild September evening when Yoo-jin pushed open the door to Hana's apartment, the familiar scent of her jasmine diffuser greeting him like a welcome hug. He had texted that he would be late, but managed to wrap his meetings early—a surprise he was sure would make her happy.

The sound of laughter stopped him cold. A deep, masculine chuckle mingled with Hana's lighter tones. His hand froze on the doorknob as the living room came into view.

There was the cousin, sprawled on the sofa like he belonged there, one arm stretched along the back cushions. His tie was loosened, top button undone, amber whisky catching the light as he gestured with his glass.

Beside him—too close—Hana sat with her legs tucked beneath her, holding a drink. Her cheeks were flushed pink, eyes wide with an animation Yoo-jin hadn't seen in weeks. *Great. She's glowing now. All it took was a posh accent and a lifetime of inside jokes.*

"Yoo-jin!" she startled, almost tipping her glass. The surprise in her voice was genuine—and telling.

Wasn't expecting me. But he was. Look at him—feet up like he pays the fucking rent.

The lawyer, however, didn't flinch. He rose with languid confidence and extended his hand. "The man of the hour," he said, his English accent more pronounced than usual. "Back from conquering hearts across Asia."

Oh good. He rehearsed that one.

Yoo-jin stepped into the apartment, letting the door close with a decisive click behind him. He accepted the other man's handshake, noting the firm, almost challenging grip.

"I heard your tour went well." The lawyer tilted his glass in a mock toast. "Ten sold-out venues, wasn't it? Impressive." The compliment somehow sounded like anything but.

"Thank you." Yoo-jin approached Hana and planted a kiss on her lips. He poured himself a drink from the bar cart. The crystal decanter clinked sharply against the tumbler. "Are you visiting Seoul for a few days and leaving again?" *Don't get too comfortable on that sofa, mister.*

Yoo-jin settled into the armchair opposite them, noticing how the Englishman reclaimed his spot next to Hana. The three of them formed a triangle, uneven and tense.

"Actually, I'm staying for a bit," the lawyer replied, his casual tone at odds with the direct challenge in his eyes. "There's a lot of work to do, and Hana could use the support." He glanced at her with pointed concern. "Some things require a consistent presence."

The barb landed as intended. Yoo-jin's jaw tightened, but he remained calm, drawing on his acting experience. The ice in his glass cracked as he swirled his drink. *Right. So I'm the flaky one. Not the guy who ghosted for half a decade and now thinks he's her anchor.*

"How convenient," he said, a touch of steel in his voice. "I'll be on location soon for a new film. Four months of shooting." He placed subtle emphasis on the length of time, watching the other man's face for a reaction. "Kim Jae-wook's project."

"I read about that. Quite a departure from your usual romance dramas. Though I suppose at some point, one needs to diversify." The condescension was unmistakable, reducing

Yoo-jin's entire career to lightweight entertainment.

Yoo-jin leaned forward. "Art moves millions. Unlike... mergers and acquisitions."

Hana shifted, awkward, the leather sofa creaking beneath her. "Ian got back yesterday. He's been helping me with our children's healthcare initiative."

"I didn't realize you needed help with that." *Of course, you don't think I'm capable of anything besides fan service and finger hearts.*

"These investments need significant legal oversight. It's my area of expertise." The lawyer took a leisurely sip of whisky. "Don't worry. I'll look after things while you're... busy."

Before the tension could thicken further, Hana placed her glass down with a decisive clink. "We were going to have dinner at Hwang's." She looked between them like a diplomat navigating hostile territories. "Why don't you come with us, Yoo-jin?"

The Englishman seized on his hesitation. "Oh, don't worry about rumors," he said, voice dripping with false sympathy. "We can pretend she's with me." He reached over, his hand brushing Hana's shoulder in a friendly gesture but lingered too long. "Wouldn't be the first time."

Yoo-jin's fingers tightened around his tumbler, the crystal edge pressing into his palm. The muscle in his jaw jumped with tension. *Get your damn paw off her.* He looked at Hana, whose eyes pleaded for peace. Then back at the lawyer—*smug bastard*—already savoring his win.

He studied the ice cubes in his drink, weighing his options. *I'd rather choke on foie gras than let him sit across from her all night with that smug grin on his face.* He exhaled, forcing his shoulders to relax. "Why not?" he said at last, draining the whisky. "I'd love to."

"Brilliant," the lawyer said, rising to his feet and offering his hand to Hana. "Shall we?"

***

At the restaurant, Chef Hwang, a close friend of Yoo-jin's, escorted the party to their corner table. "The usual for you, *Hana-ssi?*" the chef asked, his weathered face creasing into a smile.

Before Hana could respond, Ian stepped in. "Perhaps the tasting menu tonight, Chef? I missed good cooking so terribly in London." *Establish dominance early.*

The chef beamed. "Of course, sir. And the wine pairing?"

"Please," Ian confirmed, not bothering to consult either of his companions. *Let's see how our golden boy likes being sidelined. Three... two... one...*

Right on cue, Yoo-jin's eyes narrowed. He pressed in, elbows on the table. "Actually, Hana's been wanting to try the new sea bass dish. Isn't that right?" He turned to her, eyes softening.

Ian suppressed a smirk. *So predictable. Can't help playing the attentive boyfriend when it's safe away from prying eyes.*

Hana looked conflicted. "The tasting menu sounds wonderful," she said with tact, "and perhaps the fish could be included?"

The chef nodded. "A special customization. Excellent."

Ian approved her choice. *She's trying to keep the peace. Always the diplomat, our Hana. Too nice for her own good.*

As the chef retreated, a strained silence settled over the table. Yoo-jin took a slow sip of water, his eyes never leaving Ian over the rim of his glass. Ian held his gaze, allowing himself a faint smile. *Amateur intimidation tactics. Save that scowl for when you have to play a North Korean dictator.*

"So," Ian said, turning to Hana, "tell Yoo-jin about our new adoption initiative. I'm sure he'd be fascinated."

She brightened, professional passion overriding awkwardness. "We've developed a pilot program to streamline the process for families with limited resources." She gesticulated with excitement. "And provide pro bono work. Ian's connections at his London firm were very helpful," she added, a note of warmth creeping into her voice.

Ian swirled his wine glass. *That's right. While you were playing dress-up for your fans, I was helping her build something that matters.* He could see Yoo-jin absorb this information, noting a slight tightening around his mouth. The first appetizer arrived—a delicate construction of raw fish and micro-greens—and Ian savored both the dish and the moment.

"How long have you been working on it?" Yoo-jin asked, his tone casual.

"About two months," Hana replied. "We hashed out the final details when Ian was in London."

"Hana's brilliant with the psychological assessment protocols. She understands, on an intuitive level, what makes a good parent." He glanced up at Yoo-jin. "The desire to create a family, to build something lasting." *What you'll never give her. Not when it interferes with your precious career.*

The sommelier appeared, pouring a crisp white wine that Yoo-jin barely tasted. His attention was fixed on Hana as she explained the program, her zeal obvious in every gesture, every inflection. "You should see these couples. Their desperation, their longing... They'd do anything for a child."

Ian observed Yoo-jin's throat tighten as realization dawned in his eyes. *She wants children. Look at her face when she talks about it. Another dream you're silently crushing.* "Some things can't wait forever," he remarked, his hand covering Hana's. "Biological clocks and all that." *Low blow, perhaps—but necessary. Someone has to remind him what he's asking her to sacrifice.*

"Ian—" Hana warned.

"Just an observation," he replied, turning to Yoo-jin. "But I'm being rude. Tell us about your new film project. Something quite different from your usual fare, I understand?" *Let the actor monologue about his "craft." They do love to hear themselves talk.*

"A noir action thriller," Yoo-jin confirmed, grateful for the change of subject. "No romantic subplot." His tone carried a slight defensiveness that Ian found amusing.

The main course arrived—seared sea bass for Hana, succulent short ribs for the men. The tension at the table had taken away everyone's appetite, though Ian made a show of enjoying his meal. "I've always admired actors," he continued, taking a small bite. "The ability to become someone else. To shed identities like clothes." He met Yoo-jin's gaze. "But I imagine it must be exhausting, always playing different roles. Hard to know who you really are after a while."

Yoo-jin's knife scraped against his plate, the sound jarring.

"Some professions require more authenticity than others. Lawyers, for instance, are paid to argue positions they don't necessarily believe in."

"True," Ian conceded with a thin smile. "But at the end of the day, I'm still Ian Weston. I don't need to negate who I am or who I'm with to protect my career." *Direct hit. How does it feel to be the one hiding in plain sight, superstar?*

"That rumor you had to deny at your press conference," Ian mused, changing subjects. He tapped a finger against his water glass. "Good call addressing it head-on, one way or another. Deflecting would have looked... weak." *Remind her how fast he disavowed any connection to her in public.*

Ian saw Hana stiffen and the actor glance at her with silent anxiety. The man's hand remained clenched in his lap, not daring to reach for hers though they were seated side by side.

"It was an executive decision," Yoo-jin said carefully. "My agency has protocols."

Protocols. Listen to him. Like she's some security breach to be managed. "Of course." Ian's tone conveyed understanding while his eyes stayed cold. "Image management. Essential in your line of work."

He leaned back, relaxing his posture and draping his arm over the back of Hana's chair, letting his fingertips brush her shoulder. "You have to admit it's difficult for those caught in the crossfire. Collateral damage, as it were."

Before Yoo-jin could respond, Ian shifted his attention to Hana, examining her face with genuine concern. "Have you been eating properly? You look thin." He softened his voice. "Those shadows under your eyes—"

Ian saw worry on Yoo-jin's face as he turned to look at Hana—maybe for the first time in weeks. The hollowness in her cheeks, the pallor beneath her makeup, the fatigue around her eyes. Everything he had catalogued upon his return.

"I've been busy," she said, uncomfortable with the scrutiny. "The foundation—"

"—needs you healthy," Ian finished. His hand moved from the chair back to her shoulder, a brief, supportive squeeze. "Perhaps an early night is in order." *I know what's best for her. And I'm not afraid to show I care, no matter who's watching.*

Dessert arrived—an artful construction of dark chocolate and berries—but no one was interested. The evening had served its purpose. Ian had taken measure of his rival—a man trapped by his image, unwilling to risk it even for Hana.

The ride back to her apartment was largely silent. Yoo-jin stared out the window at Seoul's passing skyline, tension radiating in the confined space. As he pulled up to the building, Ian glanced at them in the rearview. "I can drop you off here," he offered. "Is the front door okay—or should I use the back entrance?" His eyes met Yoo-jin's in the mirror. "For privacy." *Your move, actor.*

"The front is fine," Yoo-jin said coolly, though Ian caught

the slight tension in his jaw, the way his hands stayed clenched in his lap.

"Perfect." Ian turned off the engine and let the silence settle. In the rearview mirror, he watched Hana's fingers find Yoo-jin's—a gesture of support that the actor couldn't even acknowledge properly.

When Ian's eyes met hers in the reflection, an understanding passed between them. Recognition of what she deserved versus what she was getting. *Eventually, she'll stop pretending it was enough.*

Ian stepped out to open her door, already planning his next move. The actor had shown his hand tonight—all defiance, no solutions.

Now it was Ian's turn to show Hana what being someone's priority really looked like.

SHIFTING LOYALTY

The elevator hummed upward, too bright, too slow. Yoo-jin stared fixedly on the glowing numbers, each one a small verdict against him. His reflection in the steel doors showed a man slumped, defeated. He ground his teeth until his jaw hurt, bracing for a conversation he was sure to lose again.

Hana reached out and rubbed his back. "Ian was just being Ian."

Being Ian. Perfect, reliable, legitimate Ian. "He was being honest."

Inside the apartment, Yoo-jin headed straight for the balcony. He needed air, space, perspective. The city sprawled below, millions of lives unfolding in orderly patterns while his own spiraled into chaos. He lit a cigarette. *Back to old habits. How fitting.*

Behind him, the door slid open again. Hana slipped her arms around his waist, her cheek pressing between his shoulder blades. He pulled her to his side, tucking her under his arm. The warmth of her body should have anchored him.

"Your cousin has it all figured out," he said, voice flat. "The good, decent lawyer offering you a respectable life."

"Stop," she said, but without conviction.

Can't stop. Can't pretend. Not tonight. "You know what he said? That you deserved consistency, not chaos. Someone you can introduce to your parents without a PR team on call."

"He had no right—"

"He's not wrong, Hana." *That's the worst part. The man's fucking right about everything.*

"Come to bed," she said, taking his hand.

His fingers twined with hers, muscle memory overriding the disconnect. The simple gesture that used to be electric was now robotic, a performance of intimacy rather than the real thing.

In the bedroom, Hana reached for him. His hands moved on instinct, tracing the curves he knew by heart. This had always been their sanctuary, their most reliable form of communication.

The need was there. But the more he tried to capture it, the more distant it became. His frustration mounted, until he had to admit defeat. He rolled away, covering his eyes with his forearm. Humiliation burned through him. "I'm sorry," he whispered.

"It's fine," she said. "You're tired. It's been a long day."

"It's not that." He couldn't say more. Couldn't confess that the Englishman's calculated words had found every insecurity, every doubt, every fear he had harbored since the beginning.

They lay together for a long moment without speaking.

Hana drew him to her, his head finding the hollow of her shoulder, his arm across her waist. Her fingers threaded his hair, a gesture of comfort that only deepened his shame. "We're okay," she said, but the reassurance sounded empty to him.

Yoo-jin said nothing. *We're not okay. We haven't been for a while.* His arms tightened around her, the physical closeness compensating for the emotional distance. She continued caressing him, but he could sense her attention drifting, her mind elsewhere.

Sleep came in jagged segments, consciousness fading in

and out like a badly tuned radio. In the early morning hours, he reached across the bed to find only emptiness, sheets cool to the touch. Hana had left without him noticing. That stung more than it should have.

He lay still in the half-light, listening to her quiet movements in the kitchen.

***

When the alarm sounded, Yoo-jin was half-buried under the sheets, mind foggy from the restless night. Weariness settled on his chest like a dull weight. From the bed, he watched an indecisive Hana at her closet, trying on different outfits. She finally selected a charcoal shirt dress—sleek, polished. Not her usual rushed choice to get out the door. She lingered, adjusting, reconsidering. *Primping for the lawyer.*

The thought burned beneath his ribs. He rose and headed to the kitchen, going through the motions of making breakfast. Juice. Toast. Ordinary tasks to mask his inner despair.

The toaster popped as Hana entered. Her perfume, stronger than normal, reached him before she did. “Busy day?” he asked, watching her add a splash of milk into her coffee. The question sounded hollow, a placeholder for what he really wanted to say.

“The usual,” she replied, dodging his eyes. “Meetings with Ian to fill him in.” Then, like an afterthought: “What about you?”

He chewed his toast, crumbs scattering on the table like his chaotic emotions. “Preproduction prep work.” A childish impulse prodded him to add, “I might be late tonight.” *Testing if she cares. How pathetic.*

Hana downed her coffee, leaving a perfect lipstick crescent on the rim. “It’s fine,” she said, checking her watch. She leaned in for a kiss—brief, mechanical, cold. The kind given to a relative, not a lover. She moved toward the door, heels clicking against hardwood.

That wasn't a kiss. That was a formality. Yoo-jin stood frozen, listening to the diminishing sound of her departure. The elevator chimed like punctuation—period, end of story.

The apartment seemed suddenly too big, too quiet. He touched his lips where she'd kissed him, finding nothing but a ghost contact. *She's already gone.*

Not physically. That would come later. But emotionally, the distance was growing by the minute. He picked up his phone to send her a text—anything—to bridge the gap. *But to say what? Have a good day? Miss you already? I saw you mentally leave me this morning?*

He put the device down, screen dark. *Maybe the lawyer was right. She deserves better.*

The thought should have spurred him into action, to fight harder. Instead, he was torn in opposite directions. He couldn't give Hana what the cousin offered. Not unless he sacrificed the career that took decades to build. The identity that defined and shaped him.

He stared at his reflection in the kitchen window—no longer the polished celebrity, but a man watching his relationship disintegrate one small moment at a time, unable to take a decisive step forward.

How many more mornings like this before she doesn't come back at all?

***

Hana arrived at the office humming—actually *humming*—which she hadn't done since her twenties. She glimpsed herself in the elevator mirror—grinning like a fool who'd just hit the jackpot, when all it was, really, was Ian.

She stacked the morning's proposals with unusual enthusiasm, fired off emails while checking the corridor every few minutes. Two hours in, his office remained dark.

When Ian's footsteps finally echoed down the hall, she dove for her laptop, pretending deep fascination with quarterly budget reports. "You're late," she said without looking up, fighting a smile.

He appeared in her doorway, navy suit impeccable, hair still slightly damp from the shower. Not movie-star handsome like Yoo-jin, but he had a way of filling a doorframe that made her forget what she'd been typing. "Had to take care of a few things." He shot her a conspiratorial wink before disappearing into his office.

Two hours late and I'm beaming like he brought me ice cream and teddy bears. By noon, she'd invented three unnecessary reasons to go to his desk. She'd linger near his door, laughing too hard at a joke that was only mildly funny.

"You're in a good mood," he observed, leaning back in his chair.

"Am I?" She tried for casual and landed somewhere near giddy. "Must be the coffee."

During their afternoon strategy meeting, she found herself watching his hands as he sketched out project timelines. The same hands that had held hers—in London, in Jeju—steady and warm.

When he looked up and caught her staring, she felt heat climb up her neck. "Earth to Hana," he teased. His grin suggested he knew exactly where her mind had wandered.

At five-thirty, when the office had mostly emptied, Ian stretched and closed his laptop. "Drinks? The legal team's celebrating something—"

Hana fidgeted in her seat. Yoo-jin had looked so defeated over coffee that morning, like he already knew he was losing her. The responsible thing would be to go home, call him, try to salvage whatever they had left.

Instead, she heard herself say, "Sure, why not?"

***

The bar buzzed with after-work energy. Hana squeezed into the booth beside Ian, their thighs touching, his arm draped casually along the back of her chair. Around them, lawyers and consultants unwound from their day, nobody caring who was sitting with whom. *This is what normal feels like.*

"You look pensive," he said, sliding her wine closer.

"Just thinking how nice this is. Being out without..." She gestured vaguely.

"Without worrying someone's taking photos?"

"Exactly." She took a sip, savoring both the drink and the freedom. "No strategic seating. No checking exits. Just... people having fun."

Ian's fingers found the back of her neck, a gentle touch that sent electricity down her spine. "What a refreshing concept."

When they left an hour later, he took her hand like it was the most natural thing in the world. Not a calculated move or a stolen moment—just two people walking together in broad daylight. *Ten points to Ian for the public hand-holding,* she thought, stealing a glance at him. *Minus fifty for Yoo-jin, who's probably wearing sunglasses indoors right now.*

As her building came into view, her steps slowed. Yoo-jin might be upstairs, pacing her living room with that careful expression he wore when he was trying not to appear worried. Or he might not show up at all—also as likely these days.

"You okay?" he asked, noticing her hesitation.

She nodded, though her stomach tightened.

He squeezed her hand before letting go. "See you tomorrow."

She watched his taxi disappear into traffic, part of her wanting to chase after it. Inside her apartment, she checked her mobile: no message from Yoo-jin. The silence that used to worry her now felt like relief. *When did seeing him become something I have to brace myself for?*

***

Three Weeks Later

Ian didn't hover—credit where it was due. He maintained his usual rhythm: donor calls, site visits, budget meetings. Professional distance during work hours, casual warmth after. But he noticed everything.

The way Hana's posture changed when he entered a room—shoulders back, chin lifting slightly, like she was presenting herself for inspection. How her eyes followed him around, then darted away when he looked back. Her laughter now came in layers: a cool one for work, a warm one for him. *Fifteen years of patience, and she's finally seeing what's been right in front of her.*

One late evening in the office, reviewing documents over Chinese takeout, she offered him a taste of her *kung pao* chicken—holding out her chopsticks, a gesture she'd made a thousand times before. "Try this, it's perfect."

He accepted the bite, his hand steadying hers and lingering for a moment. Her breath caught, color rising in her cheeks. "Good?" she asked, a little breathless.

"Very," he said, holding her gaze.

She looked away first, flustered.

A ghost of a smile flickered at his lips. *She doesn't even realize she's doing it. That's how I know it's real.*

When her mobile buzzed with a text—probably the actor wondering where she was, why she wasn't at home waiting—she only glanced at it before turning back to their conversation.

Let the movie star have his headlines and red carpets. I'll take what truly matters.

MIDNIGHT RAIN

Hana still spent her nights with Yoo-jin, but that was beginning to change.

What had once been intense, almost frantic, had settled into routine—familiar rhythm more than craving. She often found herself lying beside him in silence, waiting for his breathing to slow before sliding to the other side of the bed. In that liminal space between sleep and wakefulness, it wasn't Yoo-jin she saw, but Ian. Not the cousin from her childhood, but the man who was fast becoming essential to her.

What she didn't realize was that Yoo-jin only feigned sleep, his eyes closed but his consciousness painfully alert, registering every inch of growing distance separating them. Her withdrawal cut him like a physical pain, a slow-bleeding wound that no amount of pretending could heal.

One night, as rain tapped against the windows, they lay side by side, both awake though neither acknowledged it. The soft blue glow of the digital clock cast their profiles in ghostly light. Sleep remained far off.

"It was a mistake," he said at last, voice cutting through the darkness, "to have denied the rumor."

Hana turned her head, studying the sharp angle of his cheekbone, the shadow beneath his eye. "It's fine," she said. "It's over."

He continued to stare at the ceiling. "At the time, I

didn't want people to dig into your life, to expose you to that ugliness." His throat worked as he swallowed. "But now, I see that it made our relationship seem... shameful."

An uneasiness crept up. For weeks, she'd been drifting toward a different path. Now, Yoo-jin was tugging her back. "It's okay," she repeated, the words coming out flat. "It's done."

"But I hurt you." His voice cracked on the admission. "I couldn't deal with it during the tour. The constant questions, the speculation." The silence stretched, weighted with regret. "I thought we could fix everything afterward. Then I realized there was no good time to do it. So I stuck my head in the sand like a coward."

She sat up abruptly, tugging the sheet around herself. "I said it's okay. You can't go back and change what happened."

"Can't I?" Yoo-jin rolled onto his side, facing her, his expression raw in the half-light. "Because I see you pulling away from me. I can feel it, *Hana-ya.*" The old endearment, so rare now, fell between them like a stone in still water. "And I know it's because I wasn't brave enough when it mattered."

Her eyes pricked with sudden tears. "What do you want me to say? That we should break up?" The words came out harsher than she intended, defensive.

"Just tell me the truth." His voice was barely above a whisper. "Do you think about him when you're with me?"

The directness of it hit her like a slap. She covered her face, shoulders shaking. "Don't."

"That's what I thought." His quiet acceptance made it worse—she could have fought anger, defended herself against accusations. But this resignation left her nowhere to hide.

She rose quickly from the bed, pulling on her robe with jerky movements. In the kitchen, she poured wine with trembling hands, the deep red liquid sloshing close to the rim. The first sip burned her throat—too large, too fast.

She heard him moving around the bedroom. Soft rustle

of clothing. The harsh rasp of a backpack zipper. He appeared in the doorway, fully dressed, keys already in his hand.

"You're leaving." It wasn't a question.

"I'm going on location early tomorrow." He moved toward her slowly, as if afraid she might bolt. His arms wrapped her from behind, his chin resting on her shoulder. "Let's take a break. Think it over."

She spun to face him, wine glass clutched like a weapon. "Just like that? You say when we go public, you decide if we break up—"

"No." His hands found her face, thumbs brushing away tears she hadn't realized were falling. "But this pretending—it's killing me."

Before she could respond, he leaned down and pressed a kiss to her temple. Brief. Tender. Final.

He released her and headed for the door, not looking back.

The soft click of the latch echoed in the sudden silence of the apartment. She stood frozen, the wine glass trembling in her grip, her chest heaving as reality began to sink in.

***

A chill ran through Hana.

This was what she had been working toward—this clean break. So why did it feel like oxygen had been sucked from the room?

Without conscious thought, she set down the glass and hurried to the door, her bare feet padding on the hardwood. Her hand lingered on the knob for a heartbeat before twisting it hard.

The hallway was empty, but she could hear the soft hum of the elevator. She ran, her robe billowing behind her, reaching it just as the doors began to close. Through the narrowing gap, she caught a glimpse of Yoo-jin, head bowed, shoulders slumped.

"Wait!" she called, voice breaking. She jabbed at the call button, frantic.

The doors reversed, opening to reveal Yoo-jin looking up, disbelief written across his face.

She flung herself forward on instinct, colliding into him, gripping him with desperation as if snatching at a lifeline. "Don't go," she whispered into his neck. "Please don't go."

For a moment, he stood frozen, arms at his sides, as if unable to process this reversal after he'd begun the work of letting go. With a sound that was half sigh, half sob, he pulled her against him. They clung to each other in the harsh fluorescent light, two people who had glimpsed the edge and stepped back.

"I thought—" he began, voice rough.

"I know," she cut him off. "I know what I've been doing."

He cupped her face, thumb wiping her wet cheeks. "I couldn't do it anymore. Going through the motions—"

"I'm here now," she said, hands clutching his shirt.

The elevator doors tried to close, bumping against his backpack before reversing. He picked it up, and she took his other hand, leading him back to the apartment.

They came together in the half-dark of her bedroom, streetlights casting slivers through the curtains. Hana reached for him first, closing the distance she had created.

Their first kiss was awkward—her robe belt snagged, their noses bumped—but then his mouth found hers again, steady this time. She clung to him, fingers pressing hard into his shoulders—their kisses urgent, as if making up for the weeks of doubt and silence. She tugged him closer, nails grazing his back, while his hands slid up her sides, grounding himself in her presence.

When he moved inside her, they both stilled, anchored to each other. Breaths held. Hands clasped. She sensed the fear in her chest loosen, the panic dissolve; his jaw unclenched against her shoulder, insecurity slipping away.

Their rhythm was unhurried, less about desire than about holding on. As the pressure built and released, their eyes stayed locked, unblinking, reminding each other, *We're still here. We're still us.*

Afterward, he rested his head on her shoulder, her fingers drifting through his hair. His weight was solid, a tether she hadn't realized she missed.

But even as she held him, an uncomfortable thought surfaced. *What about Ian? What about—?* She batted it away.

"Nothing's fixed," she said quietly.

"I know."

"But I couldn't bear for you to leave."

"Me neither." He traced the freckle on her collarbone, the one he always said looked like Jeju Island. "We'll figure it out."

But they both knew it wouldn't be that simple.

When Hana's breathing deepened, Yoo-jin stayed awake, listening to the rain drumming against the window. Tomorrow would come with all its complications. The lawyer would still be there, offering her what he couldn't. Their fundamental problems remained intact.

But tonight, they had chosen each other again.

Maybe not forever. Maybe not even for long. Only for now.

Yet he knew—very soon, he would have to make a decision.

INTO THE OPEN

Bright October light shone through the windows. The night's storm had passed, leaving behind a crystalline fall day, deceptive in its perfection—much like the fragile peace between Hana and Yoo-jin.

No celebratory triumph, no passionate declarations. Their core issues still pulsed beneath the surface like a wound with a temporary bandage.

Yoo-jin sat at the kitchen table, buttering Hana's toast. His breath caught when she appeared in the doorway, fresh from her shower. He reached for her when she approached, pulling her onto his knee. He nuzzled her throat. "I love your smell," he murmured, breathing her in like oxygen.

She traced the contours of his face—the angle of his cheekbone, his lower lip, the faint shadow beneath his eyes. His beauty still moved her after all this time. But it was the tenderness in his gaze that touched her. She leaned down, pressing her lips to his. She slid from his lap to sit opposite him.

He pushed the plate toward her, the toast still warm, butter melting over the clean edges. "Do you have to go to work today?" he asked, tone casual, though his fingers drummed a nervous rhythm against the tabletop.

She glanced up with a smirk. "Why? Do you want to stay in bed all day?"

He sat forward, resting his forearms on the table. "Come with me on the filming location."

Her eyes didn't mask her surprise.

"I want to show you where the shoot will be for the next couple of weeks. There's hardly anyone there yet—only the technical crew setting up." He paused, adding, "The countryside is really pretty this time of year."

She set down her toast. Yoo-jin had never invited her to a set before. His work had always been a separate realm. "Are you sure?" she asked, searching his face for any hint of doubt.

She ran through her day's agenda—nothing that couldn't wait, except... Ian. She pushed away the thought. This moment mattered. This was Yoo-jin inviting her into his sphere. "Okay," she said, softening. "Let's do it."

He exhaled, relieved. "It's only a couple of hours south," he said, reaching across the table to brush a crumb from her lip. "We can take the car or the motorcycle. Which do you prefer?"

Her face lit up. "Motorcycle."

While he showered, Hana paced the living room, phone pressed to her ear, her thumbnail between her teeth. "I'm taking the day off," she told Ian, voice light. "I'll be back tomorrow."

A beat of silence on the line, then his measured response: "You know what you're doing." It was a small statement loaded with disappointment.

***

An hour later, the city receded behind them as the Ducati carved through the greening countryside. The engine's vibration thrummed through Hana's body, her arms wrapped around Yoo-jin's waist, forming an intimate cocoon. The wind tugged at her hair, carrying the scent of earth and wildflowers. Each passing mile loosened the knot in her chest.

When they reached the filming location, the late morning

sun had burned away the lingering mist, revealing rolling hills dotted with clusters of trees and the occasional traditional *hanok* house in the distance.

The site bustled with purpose. Workers unloading equipment, carpenters hammering at half-constructed set pieces, production assistants consulting clipboards as they moved between the newly delivered trailers.

Yoo-jin guided Hana through the organized chaos with his hand on her back, pausing to introduce her to crew members. To her surprise, he didn't attempt to disguise or diminish their relationship. "This is Hana," he would say, his voice carrying a note of pride that was new and startling.

He showed her the technical aspects, gesticulating as he explained camera positions and lighting. "The director wants to capture the sunrise through those trees," he said, pointing toward a distant grove. "We'll shoot at four in the morning for the exact light quality."

At lunch, they sat at a long folding table with the crew, paper plates filled with a simple but hearty stew and rice from the catering tent. No one commented on their relationship, but people exchanged knowing glances and small smiles.

"First time on a film set?" asked a veteran cameraman, passing Hana a bottle of water.

"First time," she replied, glancing at Yoo-jin, who was deep in conversation with the art director.

The older man chuckled. "About time. Been shooting his pretty face for five years now. Never seen him bring anyone before."

After lunch, they mounted the Ducati again to explore the countryside. They found a meadow overlooking a valley, grass still damp from the night's rain. He spread his jacket on the ground, the leather warm from the sun.

Their silence shifted into introspection.

"Are you worried about the rumor mill starting up

again?" Hana asked, plucking a wildflower and twirling it between her fingers.

He shook his head. "People on sets don't gossip to the press. Among themselves, yes—we're probably a hot topic over there right now." He nodded toward the distant film site. "But not to the outside. There's a code."

"That's good to hear. Do you think they caught on to us?"

He reached for her hand. His palm was warm, his grip firm and certain. "Anybody with eyes can see how much you mean to me." He said it with conviction, as if stating a natural law.

Hana squeezed his hand, even as an unbidden image of Ian flashed through her mind. She blinked, turning her focus back on Yoo-jin.

He took a deep breath. "I want us to be like this everywhere," he said. "No more sneaking around. Or pretending we're strangers when we pass each other in public."

"Are you sure?" she searched his face. "You know I'd never ask this of you. Your image, your career—"

"I know," he interrupted. "And I love you for it. But it's hurting us." His eyes held hers, unflinching. "It's hurting you."

The truth was undeniable. The constant vigilance, the careful choreography of their daily life, the way she existed like a secret he kept rather than a woman he loved.

"What happens when they find out?" she asked, her practical mind already spinning through scenarios. "Your agency will have opinions. Your fans—"

"We won't confirm or deny," he replied, tone firm. "We live our lives. The public has to accept that it's our personal life, not entertainment for their consumption."

Hope blossomed in her chest, fragile yet persistent, like the first green shoots after winter. But doubt crept into her just as quickly. "The press won't leave me alone just because I'm not famous. You know that."

"In theory, they can't harass a private citizen without consequences."

She saw his determination, but also a fear he was holding in check. "You've thought this through."

"It kept me up all night. I feel like I've been given a second chance. I want us to be like a normal couple. I don't want to overthink it."

He paused, vulnerability flickering on his face. "What do you say?" *Please. Say yes.*

The weight of this choice wasn't lost on Hana. She was standing at a crossroads—one path leading toward an nebulous chapter with Yoo-jin, another toward a well-defined future with Ian.

But the comfort of Yoo-jin's presence, the history between them, the depth of her feelings for him—all drew her to him like gravity. She leaned into him, her head finding the familiar hollow of his shoulder. "Alright," she whispered against his neck.

On the ride back to Seoul, with the sky bleeding red and gold, their bodies moved in rhythm but their thoughts traveled different routes.

Relief washed over Yoo-jin—no more hiding, no more secrecy. For once, he was choosing real life over image. And he was choosing her.

Behind him, Hana's mind spun in more complicated directions. *How will I tell Ian?* The question made her stomach clench.

As the city lights appeared on the horizon, he felt her arms tense around his waist. He covered one of her hands with his own, a brief touch of reassurance before returning to the handlebar.

Whatever comes next, we'll face it together.

Neither of them could have imagined the cost of that promise.

FALSE DAWN

Ian saw the change the moment Hana walked in.

She arrived at the office fifteen minutes late, her steps lighter, radiating a subtle energy that had not been there the day before. He kept his eyes on his screen, fingers typing nonsense he would delete later, tracking her every move as she settled into her morning routine.

So that's how it is.

He had known something was different from her text last night. The brief "made it home safe" with no follow-up. After weeks of gradual closeness, the sudden detachment was like a door closing.

"Conference call with Tokyo at eleven," he said when she appeared in his doorway, voice neutral, professional.

She nodded, her smile distracted. She dodged his eyes.

Ian returned to his work. Throughout the day, he caught peripheral glimpses of her through his open door—smiling at her phone, tapping her pen with a faraway look. Each time, a coldness settled heavier in his chest.

At the coffee machine, she hummed under her breath, unaware of his approach.

"Good mood today," he commented, reaching past her for a mug.

"Oh, you know." Her cheeks colored, a guilty tell from childhood.

"Lunch? Go over the Daejeon proposal."

"I'll grab something later," she deflected. "Lots of stuff to catch up on."

Avoiding me now. He leaned against the doorframe. They had stood like this last week, planning a visit to an art gallery. Her eyes had danced with anticipation. Now, she couldn't even look at him.

"You and Lee—something's changed, hasn't it?" The startle in her eyes confirmed his suspicion.

"Ian, I—"

"You don't owe me an explanation," he said, though neither believed it. Not after the weeks they had spent growing closer, redefining their dynamic. Not after she had let him believe there might be more.

"We had a good talk yesterday. He and I. Things are different now."

He gave her a brief nod, turning to leave. *Yes, I bet they are.*

***

Over the following week, Hana and Yoo-jin began their careful foray into public spaces. No grand announcements. Just the two of them, stepping out together.

~~~

"Is this seat taken?"

Hana glanced up from her gallery program to find Yoo-jin beside her—no cap, no sunglasses. Just him, in plain sight. "It's all yours," she said, steadier than she felt.

He sat down next to her, shoulders brushing. The artist droned on about composition and light. She heard nothing, aware only of his proximity and the absence of whispers or camera clicks.

His fingers found hers between their seats. When she didn't pull away, he let their hands rest together.

She waited for gasps, points, flashes.
~~~

Nothing happened.

~~~

"That's Lee Yoo-jin," one waiter whispered to another as they approached.

Hana tensed. Yoo-jin's hand settled on her back. "Breathe," he murmured.

The hostess led them to a corner table where their friends were already seated—just another table in a restaurant full of Seoul's beautiful people, all too self-absorbed to care.

Sang-min perused the menu. "The veggie burger is amazing here."

Sora rolled her eyes. "You say that about every restaurant."

Their easy banter swept away Hana's nerves. Beneath the table, Yoo-jin's knee pressed against hers. At the end of the meal, he signed his name clearly on the check. No subterfuge.

The waiter bowed politely and walked away.

~~~

In the elevator to her apartment, Hana breathed with relief. "That wasn't so bad."

"No. It wasn't."

"Nobody batted an eye," she said, wonder in her voice.

"I told you. We're not that interesting."

***

The night before Yoo-jin left to go on location, they lay together talking in bed, moonlight streaking across the rumpled sheets. He propped himself up on one elbow to study Hana's face. Her eyes, half-lidded and content, met his with lazy affection.

"What?" she murmured, smiling at his intensity.

"Nothing," he replied, tracing her cheek with his fingertip. His mind flashed back to that first Sunday on his motorcycle almost two years earlier: *I want her close to me.* "Just thinking about how it could be for us—coming home every day together, waking up together, grocery shopping together."

She caught his hand, pressing a kiss to his palm. "You make it sound so simple."

"It should be." His voice held new softness. "After I'm done filming, we could look for a new place together. Or you could move in here until the—"

"Until the what?"

A grin tugged at his lips. "Wedding?"

"Ha!" She pushed herself up against the headboard. "You'd have to get down on one knee first, Mr. Celebrity."

"Don't worry—you'll get the cheesiest proposal imaginable. And the gaudiest ring," he promised.

She stilled, holding up a finger. "Wait. Did you hear that?"

He glanced around, confused. "What?"

"A cascade. Rushing water." Her eyes danced with mischief. "The sound of your female fans weeping all over the world."

"Is that so?" In one swift motion, he pinned her hands above her head, making her squeal. He tickled her ribs mercilessly while raining tiny kisses down her neck.

"Stop!" she gasped, squirming. "I give up!"

He relented, both breathless from laughter. Their playfulness faded to contemplation. He traced a light finger over her navel. "And maybe... a baby after?"

"Twins!" she countered, without missing a beat. "Two for one special."

"Boy and girl. Very efficient."

Silence settled between them, comfortable and warm. She caressed the outline of his mouth. "I want them to have your beautiful lips."

"Anything else? I should write down your order."

"Your eyes," she continued, tracing his eyebrows. "My punctuality."

After a moment, she whispered, "We're really doing this, aren't we?"

He nodded, eyes never leaving hers. "Yes, we are." He pulled her to him, catching her lips in a kiss as she wrapped her legs around him.

With these nascent hopes, happiness seemed not only possible but inevitable.

***

November.

A week after Yoo-jin left Seoul to film his new movie, a photo appeared online.

Someone at the gallery opening had captured them in an unguarded instant—Yoo-jin leaning down, his expression attentive as Hana spoke, their physical proximity conveying unmistakable intimacy.

Within hours, the hashtags *#leeyoojingirlfriend* and *#leeyoojindating* trended on social media. Fan accounts dissected the image in obsessive detail—the location, the date, their looks and their body language.

This time, the leak didn't blindside Hana. She had been bracing for it since they decided to stop hiding. Still, seeing their private moment displayed in the media made her nauseous.

At dinner that evening, Ian set down his glass and regarded Hana steadily across the table. "So," he said, swirling his wine with forced casualness, "I see you're in the news."

She kept a neutral face, focused on twirling pasta around her fork. "I'm not. Yoo-jin is."

He wasn't amused. His eyes, usually warm with affection for her, were now sharp. "I assume you two have a plan this time? Unlike the previous... incident."

"We're not going to confirm or deny. The public will have to get used to it."

She changed the subject, but he would not move on.

"This is reckless, Hana." His eyes fixed on hers as he drummed nervous fingers on the tablecloth. "I don't have a good feeling about this."

"It's fine, Ian. Please don't worry."

***

On his movie set, Yoo-jin squinted at the phone in the gloom of his trailer. Makeup artists would complain about the circles under his eyes the next day. It was the third night in a row he'd stayed up past two.

"Another gossip blog picked it up," Hana told him through his earbuds. "Still only speculation—*Who is Lee Yoo-jin's mystery woman?*"

"What are they saying?"

"The usual. That I'm an actress or model." She chuckled. "I must have missed my true calling."

"I'm sorry," he said, the words sounding inadequate.

"We knew this might happen." Her voice carried forced lightness that pained him.

***

The next day, Hana's mobile buzzed on her desk. Another notification. She flipped it face down without looking.

"You should see this," Jin-ah said from the doorway, tablet in hand, expression grim.

It was a fan forum with another photo of her and Yoo-jin leaving a jazz club, his hand on her back. The image had been edited to show monstrous, dark shadows extending from her fingers toward Yoo-jin's heart. *The witch who stole him*, the caption read.

"There are more comments," her assistant swiped to

another page.

Let's boycott his new movie!

He belongs to his fans, not some random woman.

He could have ANYONE. Let's make #LeaveYoojinAlone trend.

Hana pushed the tablet away. "I have a site report to finish."

Jin-ah fidgeted nervously. "Shouldn't his agency do something?"

"Why would they acknowledge the rumors if they can ignore them?"

***

On location, Yoo-jin paced the length of his hotel room, phone pressed to his ear.

"It's manageable," Hana said.

"Don't lie to me." He stopped at the window, staring at nothing. "I've seen what they're posting about you."

An uncomfortable pause. "It's just internet noise—it'll pass."

"I'm coming back."

"You can't. You have three more weeks of shooting."

"I don't care."

"I do." Her voice strengthened with determination. "I'm fine."

What she didn't tell him was how she checked her surroundings before getting in her car, or how she now took different routes home each night.

***

As the online hate continued unabated, Ian reviewed the security footage from the office's front door. Two young women had been loitering across the street for the third day in a row, phones raised whenever people exited.

He contacted their security firm. "I need more personnel. Two at the main entrance, one in the lobby, and a close detail to escort Ms. Rhee to and from her vehicle."

"Understood, sir."

"And I want coverage at her residence. Discreetly."

He ended the call and opened his browser. A new headline had appeared on an entertainment blog: *Internet Sleuths Identify Lee Yoo-jin's Mystery Woman: Weston-Rhee Foundation Director*

Below it, Hana's professional headshot beside a candid photo taken with telephoto lens of her entering her apartment building, unaware she was being photographed.

Ian swore under his breath. *Fuck. It's started.*

***

Between two meetings, Hana nipped into a nearby coffee shop. The door chimed as she entered. Conversations paused. Heads turned. Phones rose.

She kept her gaze forward. The barista's eyes widened with recognition. "It's you," he murmured, excited.

"A double espresso, please," sliding her card across the counter. She ignored the stares but heard the whispers: "That's her." "What does he see in her?" "Poor *oppa*."

Someone brushed against her, jostling her arm. Hot liquid sloshed over her hand, burning her skin. She hissed through her teeth at the sting.

"Sorry," said the young woman, voice sweet as syrup, sneering eyes behind oversized round glasses. She didn't look sorry at all. She looked satisfied.

Hana blinked. Wiping her hands with a napkin, she stared back at the woman. "No," she said with quiet steel. "You're not."

They glared at each other—one challenging, the other daring. A full beat passed. Hana didn't flinch.

A suited man appeared in the corner of her vision, striding toward her. He placed himself between the two women, touching Hana's arm and speaking into her ear. "Let's keep moving," he said, voice low and firm. "Don't engage."

But Hana's eyes stayed locked on the woman's for a second longer. *You don't rattle me.*

Only then did she let herself be guided away, pulse quick but spine straight.

"Ms. Rhee, I'm your security detail. There's a car waiting."

"I didn't call—"

"Mr. Weston's orders." He gestured to a black sedan. "Let's get you back to the office."

***

At lunchtime, Hana hurried along the sidewalk, head down. Kim, the security man, maintained pace beside her.

"Bitch!" The word cut through the street noise.

She flinched but kept walking. A small group of young women tailed them with jeers. "Does he know you're just using him for fame?"

Kim advanced, speaking into his wrist mic. "We need the car at the corner."

"Whore!" Another voice, closer. Her cheeks burned.

Business people turned to stare. A couple stepped aside, watching the scene with uncomfortable fascination.

***

"Is this the life you really want?" Ian asked that evening as they worked late.

Hana looked up, startled by the sudden question after hours of companionable silence.

"Scrutinized. Judged. Hated by strangers who don't even know you," he continued, insistent. "Having your work—your parents' legacy—tainted by association with celebrity gossip."

Her fingers stilled over her keyboard. She took a deep breath. Doubt crept in, cold and insidious. Was this sustainable? Was it worth risking the foundation's reputation for a relationship that had proven fragile once before?

"I don't know," she replied, voice cracking. "I only know that I want to be with him."

***

"Cut!" The director's shout broke through the fog in Yoo-jin's mind.

Mud caked his boots. Rain—artificial, but cold nonetheless—had soaked through his jacket. He had been running for hours, chasing a killer who existed only in script pages.

"Again," the director called. "More desperation this time."

Yoo-jin closed his eyes. He recalled Hana's face that day in the countryside. Remembered his emotional response following their near-breakup: *Let's live like a normal couple. No more sneaking around.* At the time, it had seemed like the right decision—the only way forward for them.

"Places!"

He moved to his mark, feeling the weight of the prop gun against his hip. His character was hunting a killer. But back in Seoul, he had inadvertently put a target on Hana's back.

"Action!"

Yoo-jin ran through the mud, the desperation on his face now entirely real.

***

That evening, Hana pushed through the main revolving door, barely noticing the cool night air as she stepped into the street. Kim and another security detail trailed fifteen feet behind, still emerging from the building. Tomorrow's donor pitch cycled through her head. Numbers. Phrases. Details—

"There she is!"

A group of women materialized from the side a parked van, fanning out on the sidewalk. In a lightning flash, hot liquid hit her chest. Coffee soaked through silk, the shock stopping her mid-step.

"Skank!" Another splash in quick succession into her face and eyes, blinding her. "You're ruining his career!"

She froze, speechless.

"Slut!" More hot liquid hit the side of her head before she could catch her breath. Coffee ran down her neck, under her collar, down her back. Someone's phone was raised, recording. Passersby stopped and stared at the commotion.

Kim reached her in two strides, shielding her body with his. A second detail materialized, shoving between the women as they tried to advance again.

"Move, move, move!" Kim's voice, urgent in her ear as he propelled her back toward the door. Twenty seconds from exit to re-entry. Maybe less.

In the lobby, she stood frozen. Coffee dripped onto marble. Plip. Plip. Her blouse clung to her skin. Kim spoke into his wrist mic. Words she couldn't process. Security phrases. Threats. Protocols.

In the bathroom mirror, Hana saw a stranger with mascara tracks, coffee-stained skin, and wide, dazed eyes. She fumbled with paper towels, hands shaking violently.

The door opened and Ian appeared, face like thunder. "I'm okay," she said. But her voice sounded wrong—high, thin.

"This ends now," he snarled through clenched teeth.

She was trembling, unable to say anything else. Twenty seconds had changed everything. *Everyone saw. Everyone will see.*

Because the footage was already uploading. Already spreading. The Weston-Rhee Foundation director, dripping coffee, humiliated on a public sidewalk.

Later, towel-dried but still shivering, she watched Ian coordinating security personnel and legal teams. All moving with urgent purpose.

"You're staying with me tonight," he said, guiding her toward the parking garage. It was not a request.

Those twenty seconds had propelled her into a new reality. *Is this what being with Yoo-jin really means?*

***

As soon as they arrived at his hotel, Ian sent an assistant to collect Hana's things from her apartment. Thirty minutes later, the woman called back, voice panicky. "Sir, she's been doxxed. Her name and address are everywhere online. The building's mobbed."

Ian's face darkened. "What about security?"

"The building management is pushing back and threatening to charge people for trespassing. But it's chaos. She can't come back here."

"Understood." He hung up, and turned to Hana who was sitting at the foot of the bed and rubbing her arms as if trying to stay warm. She had showered, washed the coffee from her hair and skin, but the humiliation remained. He knelt in front of her, voice softer now. "Why don't you eat something?"

She shook her head. "I'm not hungry."

"You have to." He placed a bowl of soup on the side table. "A few bites. Then you can rest."

Too drained to argue, she forced several spoonfuls past her lips. When she finished, Ian pressed a small pill into her palm. "Xanax," he explained. "Doctor's orders."

She swallowed the medication and curled beneath the covers, exhaustion dragging her under.

***

Two hours south of Seoul, Yoo-jin was focused on a crucial

scene that had run well into the evening. He was unaware of the day's events and it wasn't until midnight that he saw the missed calls, the urgent messages, and the video that had gone viral.

His hands shook as he dialed Hana's number. One ring, two rings, three...

The line connected. The lawyer's voice, cold and cutting as a blade. "Hana can't talk right now."

"Where is she?" Yoo-jin demanded, panic rising in his throat.

"She's asleep," Ian replied, each word clipped and final. "And safe now. No thanks to you."

"What happened?"

At this question, Ian's self-control snapped. "What happened was you didn't think through the consequences of going public! Did you really think your goddamn fans were going to let Hana live her life? Are you naïve or stupid?"

"I didn't think it would come to this," Yoo-jin said, defensive even as he blamed himself.

"That's right!" Ian thundered. "You didn't think! And now she's a target for every fucking lunatic walking the street!"

Silence stretched between them, heavy with accusation and guilt.

"Look, I'm sorry," Yoo-jin said, struggling to keep his voice steady. "I'll figure out how to stop this."

"Yes. You do that," Ian replied, cold fury in each syllable. "In the meantime, don't come near Hana. You'll only make things worse."

"Wait—" Yoo-jin's voice rose, urgent. "I need to talk—"

The line went dead. He stood alone in his trailer, the phone still clutched to his ear, absorbing the consequences of an emotional decision that had plunged the woman he loved into a waking nightmare.

***

That night, Ian didn't move from his chair near Hana's bed.

Every few minutes, he glanced over at her, wrapped in the hotel's thick duvet. She stirred fitfully, whimpering, her face creased with distress. When he heard a faint, broken sob, he went to her. "Hana," he murmured, shaking her shoulder.

Her lashes fluttered, lost somewhere between sleep and the effects of the Xanax. "No," she mumbled, voice thin and frightened. "Please… stop."

He swore under his breath and slipped into bed beside her, pulling her into his arms. Her body was tense, but as he stroked her hair, she exhaled, her breathing deepening again. He pressed his lips to her temple and whispered, "It's okay, baby. Sleep. I'm here."

He had waited for this moment—for Hana to see the dark side that shadowed Yoo-jin Lee's fame—but he had never imagined this kind of attack and humiliation. Coffee on her coat today, whispers and stares every day after. She looked so small, curled in his arms. He would protect her, bring her to reason.

What he didn't know was how much darker it was about to become.

SCORCHED BOUNDARIES

Morning light sliced through the curtains, disorienting Hana. The luxurious bedding had an alien feel against her skin. The hotel room smelled faintly of expensive flowers but scrubbed clean of life. It was not home. Never home again.

Ian's voice cut through the silence, low and urgent on his phone. When he saw she was awake, he ended the call and brought her coffee.

The porcelain cup shook between her fingers. "How bad is it out there?"

He didn't look up. "If online hate were the only problem." He drew a deep breath and faced her. "The cybersecurity team had flagged some dark web activity overnight."

She went cold, blood draining from her face. "What do you mean?"

"They've identified two accounts making credible threats. Discussions about your routine, your whereabouts. These aren't internet trolls anymore."

She gawped at him, pulse thundering in her ears. This was beyond fan hysteria, beyond outrage. This was real. Instinctively, she scooted near him, sliding under his arm. Ian pulled her close, pressing a firm kiss to her head. "It's okay," he murmured. "I'll deal with this. Why don't you work from here today? You're safe in the hotel. I've got some business in town.

I'll check in later."

As he reached for his coat, another buzz sounded. He glanced at the screen, face darkening.

"What is it?"

He let out a heavy sigh, rubbing his temple. "It's your building management. There was an incident in the parking garage. Your car was set on fire. Someone disabled the CCTV."

She sank into the nearest seat. "What?"

His tone was grim. "That means they know which unit you live in." He sat down beside her, taking her hand in his. "This isn't simple harassment anymore. They knew exactly where to go. When to do it."

He rubbed small circles over her knuckles. "They've crossed into your real life, Hana. Not headlines. Not gossip. You."

He let that settle before continuing. "This world... Yoo-jin's world. The cameras, the adoration, the obsession—there's a cost. And the people around it, people like you, end up paying it too."

His next words came slower, more deliberate. "You don't have to make this your life. You don't owe it your safety and peace of mind."

He leaned toward her. "And we don't know how much worse this will get. But I do know this—you don't have to stay and let it collapse on you."

His eyes held hers, steady and unyielding. "Think about it."

***

Over the following three days, Hana existed in limbo. The hotel suite became both sanctuary and prison—plush carpets absorbing her restless pacing, Egyptian cotton wrapping her in fitful sleep. Beyond the window, Seoul kept its relentless beat; inside, her life was put on pause.

She worked, absent-minded, fingers moving over the keyboard as her thoughts drifted. The foundation's PR team sent hourly reports. The situation online seemed to stabilize with newer scandals pulling attention elsewhere. Even the rabid fan forums had quieted.

What surprised her most was the countercurrent that emerged after the coffee attack video went viral. For every hateful comment, ten supportive ones appeared. Fans with genuine love for Yoo-jin started hashtag campaigns: *#RespectYoojinsChoices* and *#TrueFansSupportHappiness*. One popular fan site posted: *Don't listen to the minority. We want you to be happy.*

The foundation received flowers, dozens of bouquets with cards signed "From Lee Yoo-jin's real fans" and "We apologize for the behavior of a few."

Jin-ah showed her an entertainment blog: "Look at this part. His fandom is organizing charity donations in your name."

Hana managed a small smile, but couldn't bring herself to read the details. The support was touching, but the attention itself, positive or negative, disturbed her on a deep level. It was a different kind of violation—complete strangers disregarding boundaries and discussing her relationship with Yoo-jin as if they knew them intimately.

After a while, Hana asked her assistant to share only the necessary reports. She didn't turn on her TV and canceled her news alerts. "It's better not to know what they're saying," she told Ian. "Even the encouraging comments. It's… intrusive."

***

Eight days later, Hana stood at the hotel room window, watching the city awaken. Sunlight glinted off distant buildings like fragments of hope.

"I'm going home," she announced when Ian returned from his morning run.

"You think that's wise?"

"I can't hide here forever."

Concern flickered across his face before he agreed. "I'll arrange it."

Hana's phone rang as she packed her belongings. Her building manager's name illuminated the screen.

"Ms. Rhee." His voice was stiff and anxious. "There's been an incident."

Ice spread through her veins. "What kind of incident?"

"A break-in. Quite severe. Police are here now." A pause. "Somehow, the security system was overridden and the CCTV disabled."

The device slipped from her nerveless fingers. Ian was beside her in one quick stride, retrieving it.

"We'll be there in twenty minutes," he said into the receiver before turning to her. "Breathe, Hana."

The drive was interminable. Each traffic light, each pedestrian crossing became an obstacle between her and the truth waiting in her apartment.

When they reached her floor, yellow police tape marked her door like a wound. Two officers looked up as she approached, recognition in their eyes.

"Ms. Rhee," one officer greeted her. "We've documented everything."

When she stepped inside, the smell hit her first—spray paint and spilled wine, overlaid with an acrid and chemical odor. Her curated sanctuary had been transformed into a canvas of hatred.

Blood-red letters screamed from her living room wall: "WHORE."

Across her kitchen backsplash: "DIE BITCH."

Over her parents' photograph: "GOLD DIGGER."

Her books—first editions collected over years—lay

eviscerated, pages scattered like wounded birds. Plants had been ripped from their pots, soil ground into rugs her mother had brought from Turkey. In the bedroom, her mattress gaped open, cotton innards spilling onto the floor.

On her vanity mirror, written in her own lipstick: "SLUT."

Bile rose in her throat. These weren't mere strangers—they were violators who had touched her things, judged her life, and left their hatred embedded in every surface. Their message couldn't be clearer: *We know where you live, we can reach you anytime, and nowhere is safe.*

She staggered backward, the air too thick to breathe. Ian caught her elbow, steering her into the hallway. His phone was at his ear. "Detective Park. It's worse than reported—" His voice sounded distant, underwater.

The last thing she saw as he led her away was her Marchesa gown from the gala hanging from her bedroom door—slashed to shreds like a sad, murdered ghost.

***

Back at the hotel, Ian pressed a glass into Hana's hands. She took a large sip, the brandy burning her throat.

"You can't go back." His voice cut through her spiral.

She nodded, numb. "Where will I go?"

"I'm looking into a safe house. Private access, top security." He sighed, glancing at his tablet. "There's more." He swiped to a document. "Our cybersecurity found chats on dark web forums—specific threats against you."

The room swirled around her. "What kind of threats?"

"Death threats."

The crystal tumbler slipped from her fingers, shattering on the marble floor. Fragments scattered like her future—broken, irretrievable. Her life, threatened by strangers whose only grievance was her relationship with Yoo-jin.

Her voice cracked. "How did this happen? How did falling

in love with someone become a death sentence?"

The dam broke. He pulled her into his arms as sobs tore through her body, his shirt growing damp beneath her cheek.

"It's not love that's the problem," he murmured into her hair. "It's who you fell in love with."

She clung to him like a drowning woman, grief pouring out of her—not only for her violated apartment, but for the life she had lost, her future shrouded in fear.

When her tears had subsided to hitching breaths, Ian tilted her face up to his. "I'll do whatever it takes to keep you safe," he said, calm and unshakable. "But you have to decide if this is the life you want—always looking over your shoulder, moving between safe houses, living behind security."

Fresh tears spilled down her cheeks. She couldn't find the words to answer him.

***

That night, after Hana had fallen into exhausted sleep, Ian sat in the armchair beside her bed, watching the steady rise and fall of her chest. The strong sedative the doctor prescribed had finally dragged her into a deep, unbroken sleep she hadn't managed in days.

Her face was pale, dark circles rimming her eyes. Over a week since the coffee attack. Her car set on fire. The break-in. And now, death threats.

This wasn't what I wanted. He pinched the bridge of his nose, fighting both fatigue and a gnawing guilt that had kept him awake night after night. Yes, he had wanted Hana to see the incompatibility with the actor's world. Yes, he had maneuvered to make that point clear. But he had underestimated how far a few deranged fans would go.

For god's sake, boy, do something. Thomas Weston's uncharacteristic message had haunted him all day. Her stepfather, who never flinched, never panicked, had sounded the alarm. Things had gone too far, even by his standards.

Ian had tried to convince her to leave the country. Go to London. Or Surrey. Or Cornwall. Anywhere away from Seoul and the actor's more unstable fans. But she had refused, citing the adoption program launch scheduled for the following week. "I'm not abandoning those children because some people can't separate fantasy from reality," she had said with that mulish set to her jaw he both loved and found maddening.

She stirred in her sleep, a small sound of distress escaping her lips. He leaned close, ready to wake her if the nightmare took hold, but she settled again. *So vulnerable. So goddamn stubborn.*

His mobile vibrated with another text from her stepfather: *Update?*

Ian answered: *Sleeping. Safe. Security in place.*

The curt reply came within seconds: *Insufficient. Get her home now.*

What could he say? That he agreed? That he was more powerless than he had ever been? That for all his planning and maneuvering, he had no solution for this crisis?

He let the screen dim in his hand. Events were outrunning him. And he feared they might be gaining speed. For now, all he could do was press harder, convince Hana to choose safety over the actor.

But what if she refuses?

STRUCTURAL DAMAGE

After almost two weeks at the hotel, the walls of the suite appeared to inch closer each morning.

Hana stood at the window, forehead pressed against the cool glass, watching people twenty-three floors below. A businessman crossing the street. A woman buying treats from a snack cart. A runner cutting through the park. Two friends laughing over coffee.

Her laptop chimed with another email. Work was her last grip on normalcy. She buried herself in proposals and reports, letting spreadsheets and grant applications drown out the chaos.

The phone rang—a jarring intrusion in the quiet room. No one called the hotel line except Ian.

"Ma'am?" Her assistant Jin-ah's voice, cracking. "I—I need to tell you something."

Ice formed in Hana's stomach. "What's happened?"

"Your car. In the office parking. It was vandalized."

The words didn't make sense at first. Her Mini Cooper was set on fire in her building garage over a week ago.

"No, your company car," Jin-ah clarified. "The black Hyundai."

Vandalized. In the secure underground carpark at the foundation headquarters—a facility with security guards and key-card access and CCTV.

"How?" The question came out hollow.

"Still unclear." Jin-ah's voice dropped to a whisper. "The guard stepped away. Only for a minute. That's when it happened."

A strangled sound escaped Hana. Not only her home. Now her workplace, the last safe territory, the final frontier of her previous life.

"The police are here. Mr. Weston is on his way back from a meeting. He told me to call you."

"Is anyone hurt?"

"No, but—" Jin-ah cleared her throat. "People are taking pictures. Other tenants. It's already online."

Of course, it was. Everything was public now. Every violation, every loss, consumed by hungry strangers with smartphones and hashtags.

"I'll get back to you," Hana managed, setting down the phone with unnatural care, and stumbled to the bathroom.

She made it just in time to the toilet before emptying her stomach. Her body heaved long after there was nothing left, cold sweat beading on her forehead, tears mingling with saliva. When the spasms subsided, she curled on the marble tiles, the cool surface against her hot cheek the only reality in a world dissolving around her.

***

That was where Ian found her an hour later. Without a word, he scooped her up from the floor and carried her to the bed as if she weighed nothing. Hana didn't resist, didn't speak. What words could describe the systematic destruction of her life?

He disappeared into the bathroom, returning with a wet cloth that he pressed to her forehead. He handed her a glass. "Small sips."

She drank. The water had a metallic, foreign taste.

"I'm handling the car situation," he said, voice calm. "New

security protocols at the office. The police are treating it as a targeted attack."

She looked at him with vacant eyes. "Targeted. Yes."

"The safe house will be ready tomorrow." His hand covered hers, warm over her icy skin. "This will pass, Hana."

"When?" The question hung without answers. When would she be able to walk in the open again? When would strangers stop hating her for being with someone? When would her life resume?

Ian looked away. "There's something else." His voice was more careful now. Professional. The tone he used when delivering difficult news to the board.

She looked up at him, numb.

"Three major donors have withdrawn their support." His thumb traced circles on the back of her hand. "The Mirage Group, Kim Holdings, and the Jang Foundation. They've cited... concerns about recent publicity."

The words struck her like physical blows. The Mirage Group funded their children's healthcare costs. Kim Holdings backed their rural education programs. And the Jang Foundation...

"The adoption program," she whispered.

He nodded. "On hold. For now."

A stillness settled over the room. That was her passion project, the initiative she had poured her heart into for months. Children waiting for homes. Families waiting for children. All of it was suspended because she had dared to love a man with a public face.

"This isn't fair." Her voice was small, devastated.

"No," he agreed. "It isn't."

She looked past him at the city lights against the early evening shadows. "They're destroying everything. My home. My safety. Now my work." Her fingers curled into the bedspread. "What's left?"

Ian's mobile buzzed—Yoo-jin's name illuminated the screen. Four missed calls already. He silenced it without comment.

"Your work isn't destroyed. The foundation continues. We'll find new donors." His tone softened as he went to sit beside her. "This isn't your fault."

"Isn't it? I chose this. I chose him."

"You chose to love someone. Not this—" he gestured at the world beyond the window, "—this insanity."

She turned away, curling into herself. He remained seated on the bed, silent and watchful, as darkness claimed the room.

***

Later, when Hana's breathing had deepened into sleep, Ian returned Yoo-jin's call.

"What? Another attack?" Yoo-jin demanded, forgoing greeting.

"Yes." Ian moved to the suite's living area, voice low. "And the donors are withdrawing."

A sharp intake of breath. "How is she holding up?"

"As you would expect with her entire life collapsing around her." The words came out harsher than Ian intended.

"I'm coming back," Yoo-jin said, desperation edging his tone. "The film be damned."

"And what would that accomplish? More attention? More targets painted on her back?"

"I can't sit by while she suffers!" His voice cracked. "This is my fault. All of it."

Ian moved to the window, the same spot where Hana had stood that morning. "For once, we agree."

A silence followed, heavy with shared guilt—Ian's calculated maneuverings, Yoo-jin's impulsive decision— both men's love for Hana, now broken by their choices.

"My agency's lawyers are pursuing every avenue.

Restraining orders, criminal charges, civil suits against the fan sites promoting violence."

"Too little, too late." Ian's reflection stared back at him from the darkened glass, hard-eyed and resolute. "Too much damage has been done."

"I'll make it right," Yoo-jin insisted. "Somehow."

"Will you?" Ian's voice dropped low. "Can you return what she's lost? Her peace? Her freedom? The children who won't find homes because the adoption program is suspended?"

A wounded silence.

"Let me talk to her," Yoo-jin said. "Please."

"She's sleeping. For the first time in days. I won't wake her for your absolution."

"Then tell her I—"

"Love her?" Ian finished. "That fixes nothing."

"Tell her I understand if she has to... leave." Yoo-jin forced out each word like shards in his throat. "Tell her I won't fight it if she— if she wants to be free of this... Of me."

Ian straightened, surprise displacing hostility. "You'll accept to end it?"

"If that's what it takes."

"Alright, I'll tell her."

The call ended. Ian remained by the window, phone still against his ear though the line had gone dead. Seoul's nightscape glittered beyond the glass, indifferent to the conversation that had altered the pieces of his meticulous plans.

Lee Yoo-jin offering to break up with Hana. Unexpected.

He lowered the device, replaying the actor's words. His resignation had sounded genuine—no dramatic flair, no martyrdom, only quiet acceptance of what had to be done. For her safety.

Damn you. Don't make me respect you now.

A soft sound from the bedroom interrupted his thoughts. He turned, watching a restless Hana shift beneath the covers, her brow furrowed in sedated sleep.

He moved to her bedside. Her hair had fallen across her face, tangled and damp with sweat. With careful fingers, he brushed it back.

"Shhh," he murmured, though she wasn't fully conscious. "You're safe."

Her breathing steadied at his touch, her features relaxing. He pulled the duvet higher around her shoulders and stepped back after she quieted again.

His mind looped back to Yoo-jin's proposition. *If the actor removes himself from the equation, the threat drops. No more tabloid speculation. No more stalkers.*

Tomorrow, the safe house would be ready. He would have new protocols in place. Recruit donors, restart programs. Rebuild Hana's professional life, brick by careful brick. *It could work.*

He went back to the window, bracing one arm against the frame as he stared out at the city. *I'll give him this—it's the most selfless thing he's offered to do since this nightmare began.*

His reflection looked back at him from the darkened glass, questioning. *But could he really walk away forever? And stay gone?* Ian wasn't certain the actor would be capable of that final sacrifice.

Or if Hana would let him make it.

***

The phone rang shortly after nine. Hana had been staring out the window for over an hour, trying to summon the will to start her day.

Yoo-jin.

"Hi," she answered, putting him on speaker as she sat up against the headboard.

"Hana." His voice filled the quiet room.

She pulled her knees to her chest. "How's the set?"

"Cold. Wet." He drew a sharp breath. "That's not why I called."

"I know."

The pause lingered. She could hear him sigh, imagining him sitting alone in his trailer, exhausted.

"I should be with you," he said.

"You're where you need to be." Her tone was steadier than her conviction.

"How are you? Really."

She blinked back tears. "I'm... managing."

"Your cousin sent me updates about... everything that happened. I'm so sorry."

Neither mentioned what "everything" was. What would be the point?

More silence.

"Hana, I've been thinking—about us."

The shift in his tone made her tense up. "What about us?"

"All of this— it was because I decided to go public."

"That was our decision. We made it together."

"I know. But.. maybe I should put out a statement."

"To say what?"

"That we've broken up. That you're moving on. I'll take full responsibility." His words were careful, measured. "It might be enough to make them stop."

She waited a moment to make sure he had finished. "You want to negotiate with terrorists?"

"I want you safe."

"And you think they'd believe some press release? They broke into my apartment, Yoo-jin. They're not going to be satisfied with a statement."

"It just has to be convincing."

"No." Her tone was quiet but firm.

"Hana—"

"No," she repeated. "You promised me a proposal, remember? A gaudy ring. A wedding. Twin babies. Your exact words."

A small, sad laugh escaped him. "I did say that, didn't I?"

"You can't walk out on me now."

"All I care about is keeping you safe." The lightness faded. "That's all that matters to me."

"And all I care about is our future." She uncurled from her protective position, shoulders straightening. "If we give in to them, nothing will ever change."

"I just—" He exhaled slowly. "I feel so helpless. I'm here, you're there, and I can't do anything."

"You can finish your project. Maybe your agency can do something." A pause. The sting of tears hit, quick and sharp. "But I want you. Don't leave me."

"Oh, baby." Relief, love, and worry mingled in his voice.

A drawn-out silence as both struggled not to break.

"Hana—"

"Yes?"

"I wonder if you shouldn't—" He took a steadying breath. "Get out of the country. Go somewhere safe."

"No. I'm staying here with you."

He sighed. His resignation shifted into reluctant determination. "Alright. We'll get through this."

***

After they disconnected, Hana sat in the quiet room, feeling small in the big bed. Her hand still clutched the phone, knuckles white, as if it were a lifeline to Yoo-jin rather than mere cooling metal and glass.

The door opened with a soft push. Ian stood in the

doorway, his expression neutral. Too neutral. The kind of blankness that took effort to maintain.

She wiped her eyes. *He heard. He must have heard.*

"Breakfast?" He held up a paper bag and a cup of coffee, voice light. "I got you a chocolate croissant from that fancy French bakery you like. The one with the rude owner who thinks selling pastries is a form of charity."

The normalcy of the gesture—so at odds with what they were going through—made her throat tighten. She managed a weak smile. "Thanks."

Ian laid the pastry and cup on the bedside table. His gestures were smooth, betraying nothing of what he was thinking. He moved to the window, adjusting the blinds to let in enough morning light without creating glare.

Gratitude and mild annoyance warred inside Hana. *Always fixing things. Always managing the environment.*

"Jin-ah will stop by later with the Henderson briefs," he said, his back to her as he fussed with a latch. "I need to make some calls about the safe house."

A slight flattening of tone in his voice told her everything his demeanor was trying to hide.

"Ian—"

"Eat it while it's warm," he cut her off. Before she could answer, he was gone, pulling the door shut behind him.

In the hallway, Ian stood motionless, one hand still on the doorknob, the other pressed flat against the wall for support. He drew a measured breath, then another, forcing his heart rate to slow by sheer will.

Hana's declarations to the actor replayed in his mind, clear as if she were standing beside him: *Don't leave me. I'm staying with you.* Not *I love you*, but more visceral. More primal. *I want you.*

Her words settled in his chest like stones. It was obvious now. She would not leave Korea. Would not leave Yoo-jin Lee.

Not after a break-in, not after a physical attack, not after the damage to her career and reputation.

He pushed away from the door, straightening his shoulders. His options were fast narrowing to a single focus without any broader strategy. *Just get her to the safe house—and quickly.*

It wasn't a solution. It wasn't even a plan.

But it was all he had left—if he had any hope of containing the danger.

CRIMSON CROSSING

Two hours south of Seoul, the sun sank behind distant hills, casting the film set in amber twilight. The crew worked around Yoo-jin, adjusting lights for the next scene, checking camera angles, testing sound levels. To them, he was focused, immersed in his character as a brooding detective who failed to stop a killer's rampage.

None saw his trembling hands as he read the latest text message from his manager: *Legal team pursuing maximum social media censorship. Drafting a statement distancing you from alleged personal associations.*

In a rage, he flung the phone against the trailer wall. It shattered, plastic and glass exploding. Not enough. A folding chair followed. A coffee mug. A stack of script revisions. His foot sent a small table crashing onto its side.

The tight space couldn't contain his fury. He burst outside, ignoring startled crew members as he stalked behind the line of trailers where no camera would capture his breakdown.

"Fucking useless!" he snarled, driving his fist into the metal siding of an equipment truck. Pain shot through his knuckles—good, real, immediate. He struck it again. And again. Blood smeared the polished surface, bright crimson against silver.

His agency wasn't protecting Hana. They were defending

their investment, their star, their revenue stream. While Hana's life disintegrated, they drafted press releases about his "alleged personal associations" and consulted marketing experts about brand damage control.

Meanwhile, the lawyer—his archrival—was the one standing beside her, guarding her, comforting her.

His knees hit the dirt, bloody fists pressing against his eyes. The parallel stung—he had completed a similar shot that morning with his detective character, once again too late, raging over another dead body in frustrated defeat. The director had praised his authenticity, his emotional rawness. If only they knew.

"*Yoo-jin-ssi*?" A hesitant production assistant stood a few feet away. "They're ready for the next scene."

He lowered his hands, not bothering to hide the tears or the blood. "Tell them I need five minutes."

The woman nodded and retreated. Yoo-jin glared at his damaged knuckles, at the blood already congealing in the cool evening air. Physical pain—controllable, definable—unlike the helpless anguish consuming him from within.

He pulled himself upright, drawing deep breaths. In ten minutes, he would be Detective Park again, channeling this same rage into his performance. It made him laugh—his finest acting, born from his greatest failure.

As he turned back toward the set, his battered phone in the trailer buzzed with a call he wouldn't receive for hours.

***

Ian paced the penthouse suite, checking his watch for the third time in five minutes. 8:47 AM. Kim, his head of security, was late.

Of course he's late. God forbid something should go according to plan this week.

Exhausted and weary from sleeplessness, he scrolled

through the cybersecurity report that had arrived overnight. The highlighted sections made his jaw clench: *Elevated threat level... coordinated targeting... recommend immediate relocation...*

Very helpful. As if we're lounging around here by choice.

A muted buzz caught his attention. Thomas Weston—again: *Latest on situation?*

So Thomas. Three words where two would do. "Fix this" is what he really means.

Ian could picture it perfectly: his uncle, impeccable in Savile Row, sitting in his London office with one eye on financial reports and the other on news updates about his stepdaughter. Waiting with that particular brand of upper-class stoic patience that was more like a blade hovering over your neck than actual forbearance.

The suite phone rang. He snatched it up before it could wake Hana in the adjoining room. "Yes?"

The concierge: "Mrs. Rhee Eun-ji for you, sir."

He exhaled, resigned. "Put her through."

Perfect. The morning wouldn't be complete without both halves of divorced parenthood weighing in.

"Ian." Eun-ji's voice was sharp, dispensing with pleasantries. "This can't continue. Thomas and I both agree. You must make Hana understand—"

"Eun-ji, she's an adult. I can't make her do anything."

"You have influence. Use it."

Yes, tremendous influence. That's why she's ignoring my advice and still planning to reunite with the human lightning rod.

"I'm trying," he said, keeping his voice low. "The safe house will be ready today. She's agreed to relocate this afternoon."

"Not a safe house. London. She needs to be in London. Away from this madness. Away from... from that man."

How? Drug her and put her on a plane? Fascinating how

both parents now want the same thing after fifteen years of not agreeing on the time of day.

Ian pinched the bridge of his nose. “I’ve suggested that. Multiple times.”

“Not strongly enough, clearly.” The accusation hung heavy. “Thomas says—”

“Thomas and I are in regular contact.” A diplomatic lie. “We’re handling this.”

By “handling this” I mean we’re both watching helplessly as she stubbornly clings to a relationship that’s destroying her life. But sure, we’re “handling” it.

“Are you? Because from where I stand, my daughter is still in danger while you accommodate her infatuation with—”

A knock at the door saved him from the rest. “My head of security is here. I have to go.” He hung up before she could protest, took a steadying breath, and opened the door.

Kim stood in the hallway, tablet in hand. “Sir. Everything’s nearly ready.”

“Nearly,” Ian repeated, the word sounding like gravel. “We discussed ‘ready’ two days ago.”

“The specifications were... extensive.” Kim’s face remained impassive. “CCTV in every room took more time than expected.”

Ian stepped out, closing the door behind him. “Walk me through it.”

Kim pulled up schematics on his device. “Three-layer security perimeter. Biometric access at all entry points. Cameras covering every approach. Panic buttons in each bathroom as specified. A 24/7 monitoring station. Bulletproof glass on all windows.”

“Communications?”

“Secured line, satellite backup. No cell signals in or out without going through our encrypted relay.”

Which means she’ll hate it. No direct contact with the actor unless we allow it. That conversation will be delightful.

Ian nodded, scanning the layout. "And the staff?"

"Vetted. Triple-checked. All former military or intelligence."

"The transfer plan?"

Kim swiped to another screen. "Two identical vehicles, different routes. Decoy team deployed thirty minutes ahead. Your vehicle will have four-person security detail."

This is what it's come to. Moving her like a high-value target through hostile territory. All because she fell in love with a celebrity actor.

Another nervous glance at his watch. "When will it be actually ready? Not 'nearly' ready."

"We need to do a final walkthrough this morning. Then we can move her in by 2 PM."

"I want to see it."

"Already arranged. Car's waiting downstairs."

Ian nodded, glancing behind him. Hana was still sleeping, exhausted from days of tension and restless nights. She had agreed to a safer location, but still refused London. Still refused to put distance between herself and the actor.

One battle at a time. If Thomas and Eun-ji expect me to stuff her into a diplomatic pouch and ship her to London, they'll be disappointed. Though I'm starting to see the appeal.

"Give me a minute." He slipped back into the suite. Hana's door was still closed. He knocked and opened it when there was no answer.

She was awake, sitting up in bed, scrolling through her phone.

Checking for messages from him, no doubt. Heaven forbid she miss a text from her knight in shining armor, heroically filming a movie two hours away.

"Morning," he said. "Kim's here. The safe house will be ready today. We need to do a final check."

She looked up, her face pale with fatigue despite the night's sleep. "Both of us?"

"Just me for now. I'll be back in about an hour. We'll have lunch here before transferring you over."

The resignation in her eyes made his chest twist with pain. This wasn't how things were supposed to go. Not for her. Not for them.

"It's temporary," he said, moving to her bedside. "Until we get this under control." *Another lie. As if any of this is "controllable" as long as she insists on staying with him.*

The look she gave him said she didn't believe that anymore than he did.

On instinct, he leaned down and dropped a kiss onto her hair. "Try to rest. Everything will be alright." *The biggest lie yet. But what else can I say?*

In the hallway, Kim waited with professional patience. "Sir, our cybersecurity people sent another update—"

"I saw the report." Ian's voice hardened. "Let's go. I want every detail perfect before she sets foot inside that house."

They left the suite when the next security team arrived for their shift. A soft buzz came from his pocket—another text from Thomas Weston: *Update?*

He silenced the phone. Let Thomas wait. Let Eun-ji fume. The elevator doors closed. Ian caught his reflection in the polished steel—the tension lines around his eyes, the tight set of his jaw. *She'll be safe. That's all that matters for now.*

Everything else—Yoo-jin, her parents' demands, his own complicated feelings for her—all of it had to be secondary.

As they descended, Ian squared his shoulders, breaking down each problem into manageable pieces.

He would handle it all with utmost care—measured, precise, flawless.

Because he couldn't risk anything less.

***

After Ian left, Hana rose, showered, and dressed. She chose a slim pencil skirt and burgundy silk blouse—professional attire despite having nowhere to go. A small rebellion against her circumstances.

She had converted the dining table into a desk where she spread out project proposals, budget revisions, meeting minutes. She highlighted sections of the Henderson proposal as she sipped her third cup of coffee. If they secured this funding, the administrative framework of the adoption program could remain intact until the media storm passed.

She looked at the clock—10:00 AM. Ian would be back soon. He had left this morning looking worn. Deep shadows under his eyes, immaculate appearance showing strain: askew tie, same cufflinks two days in a row.

"Get some rest," she had told him last night. "I'm not going anywhere."

He had given her a tight smile, not finding humor in her attempted joke about her virtual house arrest.

She understood his worry. The persistent calls from her mother, the terse messages from her stepfather—all wore on him. They wanted her out of Korea yesterday, preferably on the company jet back to London. He had spent hours trying to convince her, his usual composure fraying at the edges.

"At least consider it," he had said. "Temporarily."

But her call with Yoo-jin had strengthened her resolve. They would weather this crisis together. His voice had been steady, determined: *We'll get through this.*

A soft knock interrupted her thoughts. "Room service."

Hana checked her watch—right on schedule. Ian had arranged for breakfast delivery at the same time each morning, a small attempt at normalcy.

"Coming," she called, standing and stretching. She

crossed the room, mind still on the paperwork she wanted to complete before Ian returned.

She opened the door to find a young woman in the hotel's crisp black and white uniform, pushing a catering cart in front of her.

"Good morning." Hana stepped back to allow entry. "You can set it by the window."

She went back to the dining table, gathering documents to clear space. "You can leave the bill. I'll sign it."

But when she heard a sharp click of the lock on the suite door, a sudden tension prickled at the base of her skull—animal instinct, primal warning. She turned.

The hotel employee stood ten feet away, cap discarded, eyes burning with a hatred so raw it distorted her features. In her hand gleamed a long fillet knife.

"Hey princess—you think you're special?" the woman hissed. "You slut."

The words triggered a memory, a déjà vu. Time compressed. Hana registered small details with unnatural clarity—the woman's youth, her imposing build, the hotel ID dangling from her neck.

Her eyes darted around the room. Bedroom door to her right. Main exit behind the intruder. Panic button in the bathroom—too far. The distance between them was shrinking with each heartbeat.

With a sharp jerk, Hana yanked the white cloth off the breakfast cart, sending dishes and cutlery crashing to the floor. Porcelain exploded against marble. The woman flinched as shards scattered across her feet. Hana whipped the tablecloth forward to wrap it around the knife and wrench it from the assailant's grip. But the fabric billowed through the air, useless, and the woman jerked back, slashing wildly. The blade caught the edge of the cloth, tearing through it.

Hana kicked the cart hard, its weight slamming into

the attacker's hip before shattering against the wall. But she recovered quickly, the knife never wavering.

In a panic, Hana scrambled sideways toward the mini bar on the near side of the room. She grabbed a bottle of Grey Goose and smashed it against a console behind her. It exploded in a shower of glass and vodka, leaving jagged edges in her grip.

The assailant screeched with incoherent rage and charged at her.

They collided in the center of the room, the attacker driving Hana backward. She swung the bottle, aiming for the eyes, but only managed to slash a cheek, enraging her attacker. The woman snarled obscenities, catching her wrist mid-swing with a crushing hold that threatened to snap bones. With a half scream, half grunt—she twisted Hana's arm outward until the bottle fell from her numb fingers, clattering to the floor.

"Bitch!" the woman shrieked through gritted teeth, her face inches away from Hana's, breath hot and sour. "He's mine! You hear me? Mine!"

Hana wrenched herself free and stumbled a few steps away. The attacker lunged again, wild and fast. Hana ducked under her arm—but her heel caught the edge of the coffee table and she went down.

She hit the floor hard, shoulder slamming against marble, breath torn from her lungs. Stars exploded across her vision. But adrenaline overrode the pain—she twisted onto her back as the woman closed in, boots pounding like hammers.

The knife gleamed overhead.

Hana kicked out with both legs, catching the woman's shin with brutal force. The attacker stumbled—a grunt of pain, knees buckling—but recovered with inhuman speed. She raised the blade again, eyes wild and unseeing.

This time, there was nowhere to run.

With a shriek of pure rage, the woman hurled herself forward, pinning her victim to the floor.

Hana screamed—loud, terrified. Her arms flailed to push off the attacker, but the woman's weight bore down, clamping her in place. She straddled Hana's torso, knees digging into her ribs like vises.

"Die, you fucking bitch!" the woman spat, voice cracked and raw, all humanity gone from her eyes.

The knife rose overhead, metal catching light.

Hana threw up her hand in desperate defense.

Steel punched through her right palm with sickening force, the blade tearing through flesh and tendon like paper. The shock was instant and blinding—white-hot agony that knocked the air out of her.

The knife kept going—straight into her chest, burying the metal tip in the soft space between her ribs.

A sharp, searing pain exploded through her body. She couldn't breathe. Couldn't think. Heard only the wet sound of her heartbeat, thick and slowing.

Her peripheral vision blurred.

Somewhere—distant, muffled, came a shout. A crash. Heavy boots pounding across the floor.

Someone yelled her name. Maybe. It could have been in her head.

The crippling weight was yanked off her body. A loud, animal-like shriek.

Her world narrowed, edges dimming—she saw Yoo-jin's face, laughing in the sunlight. Heard Ian calling her name. Caught a whiff of her mother's Shalimar. Felt Thomas' steadying hand on her bicycle seat. The sharp images retreated quickly like waves pulling back from shore.

Hana blinked up at the ceiling and for a moment found herself observing the scene as if from above. Everything seemed to slip far away.

More voices. Shouting. Radio static.

A hand on her cheek—gentle, shaking.

"Ms. Rhee—ma'am! Look at me!"

She tried to focus—couldn't.

The light overhead blurred, tilting. Warm liquid oozed over her skin.

Then—nothing. No more pain. No more fear.

***

Moments before, outside the suite, Park and Choi had been exchanging banter, relaxed after waving through the room service delivery. Both men towered over six feet, built like linebackers—a stark contrast to the lean, somber security personnel that usually patrolled the VIP corridors.

"So I told her," Park said, continuing his story, "the next time her cat gets stuck in a tree, to call the fire department."

Choi's belly laugh echoed down the hallway. "Your sister-in-law is something else."

Park's mobile buzzed. He checked the screen and grinned. "Speaking of trouble." He put it on speaker. "Honey, you—"

A sudden crash from inside the suite. Something heavy hitting a wall. Glass breaking.

Both men straightened instantly.

"Gotta go," Park snapped, pocketing his device.

Another smash. Louder.

Choi reached for the door handle. Locked.

"Ma'am?" he called out with sharp raps on the door.

No answer. Another heavy thud.

"Shit." Park pressed his shoulder against the door, pushing hard. The solid wood didn't budge.

From inside, a muffled voice shouted incoherent words.

Then—a scream. High-pitched. Panicked.

"Move!" Choi shoved Park aside. He took two steps back, raised his right leg, and slammed his boot into the door beside the lock. The wood splintered but held.

Again. Harder.

A third kick cracked the frame.

The fourth blasted it open, wood splintering.

They surged inside.

The scene hit them in fragments—overturned furniture, broken glass, blood smeared over marble tiles.

A woman straddled a body on the floor, a knife already buried in her chest. As they rushed in, she yanked it out, raising it high for another strike.

Park lunged across the room, covering the distance in three strides. He grabbed the woman's wrist mid-stab, twisting until bones cracked. The weapon clattered to the ground.

She shrieked—an animal sound—and clawed at his face with her free hand.

Choi seized her around the waist, hauling her off Hana. The woman kicked wildly, connecting with his shin, his groin. Spitting profanities. Fighting like a creature possessed. "You can't have him!" she screamed. "I'll kill you all!"

Park swung his fist and caught her square in the jaw. Her head snapped back, eyes rolling up. She went limp in Choi's arms.

He dropped to his knees beside Hana.

Blood. So much blood. It pulsed from her chest with each weakening heartbeat, soaking through her burgundy silk blouse, pooling beneath her.

"Ms. Rhee—ma'am! Look at me!" He pressed his hands over her wound, the warm wetness seeping between his fingers.

Her eyes fluttered, unfocused.

Choi tapped his wrist mic, voice sharp with urgency. "Emergency in the penthouse suite! VIP with multiple stab wounds. Get me an ambulance! She's bleeding out!"

***

Ian sat in the back of the sedan, watching Seoul slide past the tinted windows. Kim remained silent beside him, scrolling through his tablet. 10:30 AM. They'd be back at the hotel in fifteen minutes.

The safe house was perfect—secure, comfortable, isolated. Everything he had specified. The staff was competent. The security systems were state-of-the-art.

And yet.

For a man who made his living predicting market trends five years out, Ian found himself unable to project the immediate future. How long would Hana remain there? A week? A month? Until Lee Yoo-jin finished his damn movie? Until the rabid fans latched on to another obsession?

She'll be a prisoner. The thought soured his mouth. A well-appointed prison was still a prison.

The car slowed for a red light. Ian checked his watch again. He had promised Hana to be back for lunch, then they'd move her to—

Sirens pierced the noise of the morning traffic. Two fire trucks blasted past their sedan, lights flashing.

Roused from his thoughts, he looked up to see them disappear around the intersection toward their hotel. A cold dread settled in his stomach.

"Follow them," he ordered.

The driver accelerated through the now-green light. As they turned the corner, his suspicion crystallized into fear. The emergency vehicles were already stopped in front of the hotel's circular drive and responders were rushing through the main entrance.

"Faster," he barked, already reaching for the door handle though they were still moving.

Kim was on his phone immediately. "Park. Report." His expression darkened as he listened. "We're approaching now."

The car had barely stopped when Ian flung open the door,

taking the hotel steps two at a time. Kim followed close behind, mobile still glued to his ear.

The hotel manager intercepted them in the lobby, face ashen. "Mr. Weston! I've been trying to reach—"

"Where is she?" Ian demanded.

The hotelier grabbed his arm, steering him toward a service elevator held open by staff. "The paramedics just arrived. This way."

They ascended with excruciating slowness. Ian's heart hammered against his ribs, each beat thundering in his ears. He could feel sweat beading at his temples, his collar suddenly too tight.

"What the fuck, Kim?" he managed through gritted teeth.

Kim held up one hand, motioning for him to wait. After what seemed like years, he hung up. "An incident—with Ms. Rhee."

"No shit," Ian snapped. "What the fuck happened?"

The elevator doors slid open before Kim could answer, revealing controlled chaos. Hotel security, police, and medical personnel crowded the hallway outside the penthouse suite. Voices overlapped, radios crackled, orders shouted.

Ian shouldered through them all, not registering their presence.

Then he was inside.

Time slowed.

The room he had left mere hours ago was transformed. Furniture overturned. Glass shattered. And blood—so much blood—spreading onto the cream tiles in a widening circle.

At its center, Hana lay motionless, eyes closed, skin ashen. Two paramedics worked over her—one applied pressure to her chest while another prepared an IV line.

Ian approached as if in a daze, falling to his knees beside her. He reached out to touch her shoulder. His hand came away slick with blood.

"Sir! Step back!" The medic's voice sounded distant. "Give us room!"

"Hana," he tried to say, but his throat choked on her name. His second attempt came out as a ragged whisper: "Hana!"

Hands pulled at him—Kim, maybe, or security—trying to move him back. He resisted, reaching for her hand. It was wet, limp, and horribly misshapen, a jagged wound piercing straight through her palm.

Only when they lifted her onto a stretcher did he relent, sitting back on his heels. Blood roared in his ears. Unblinking, he stared in shocked silence as they attached her, placed an oxygen mask over her face, checked her IV.

"Pulse is weak," one paramedic called out. "But she's alive."

"Airway secured."

"IV's in."

"Let's move."

They wheeled her past him, her face obscured by the oxygen mask, her burgundy blouse now black with blood.

Kim's hand gripped his shoulder. "Mr. Weston! Let's follow them to the hospital."

Ian nodded shakily, using the wall to push himself to his feet. His legs were unsteady, his hands numb. He looked down at them, red and wet with Hana's blood.

Movement in a corner caught his eye. A young woman sat on the floor, handcuffed, surrounded by police. Her face was contorted with fury, accentuating a deep, bloody gash on her cheek and a large purple bruise across her jaw. Her eyes locked on him, blazing with a hatred so raw it made his stomach churn. She spat a torrent of foreign words at him, full of rage and venom.

The madness of it all struck him like lightning—intense, blinding. This wasn't random violence—this was the price Hana paid for loving someone like Yoo-jin Lee. The toxic fan culture that turned ordinary people into monsters, that sentenced Hana to die for the crime of existing in his world.

Ian's vision tunneled, edges closing in. It was only when Kim shook him that he remembered to breathe.

BY A THREAD

The hospital corridor stretched before Ian like a sterile purgatory, antiseptic scent burning his nostrils as he paced its length for the hundredth time. Seven hours since they had wheeled Hana through those double doors, blood soaking crimson through hastily applied pressure bandages. Seven hours of not knowing if she would live or die.

Eight steps to the water fountain. Turn. Twelve steps to the nurse's station. Turn. The rhythm of his footfalls blended with his silent mantra: *Live, Hana. Please live.*

The detective—Park or Kang, he couldn't remember—stepped into his path again, notepad in hand. His voice was calm as he rattled off details Ian hardly registered.

"—an employee accepted a bribe… fake ID to bypass the guards… security team wasn't adequately briefed—"

The words were muffled, distant—like sounds underwater. He could see the man's mouth moving, but nothing penetrated the haze. Nothing mattered except what was happening behind the closed double doors.

"We'll need a formal statement later," the detective finished, tone softening. After a pause, he gave Ian's shoulder a brief, awkward pat.

Ian nodded a stiff goodbye and resumed pacing. The overhead lights buzzed—a constant, maddening hum like the static in his brain.

Guilt came crashing down on him. He had failed her. He had left her alone. He had not protected her. The thought looped, an unrelenting accusation with each breath: *Your fault. Your fault. Your fault.*

When the surgeon emerged, Ian shot to his feet. The woman's face was emotionless, offering no clue. "Mr. Weston?"

"Yes." The word scraped his raw throat. "How is she?"

"Ms. Rhee made it through surgery. She's in critical but stable condition. The knife missed her heart by centimeters, but punctured her right lung and lacerated the subclavian artery. We've repaired the artery and reinflated the lung. Her right hand sustained severe trauma—the blade severed tendons and fractured two metacarpal bones."

Ian struggled to process the information, clinging to the only words that mattered: *She made it.*

"She's lost a substantial amount of blood. We've placed her in a medically-induced coma to reduce oxygen demands and give her body time to stabilize. The next 48 hours will be critical."

"But she'll live?" Ian's voice cracked.

"Barring complications, yes. She's young and otherwise healthy. That's in her favor."

Ian's legs threatened to buckle as he tried to focus on details about recovery timelines and potential concerns. As the surgeon prepared to leave, she paused. "There's something else."

Ian's stomach went cold. "Yes?"

Her neutral mask softened, a trace of empathy breaking through. "Ms. Rhee was pregnant. Her bloodwork confirmed it —early, no more than six or eight weeks. The trauma and blood loss caused a miscarriage."

Ian reeled backward as if struck. The hospital corridor blurred and shifted. "She was—?" His voice failed him.

"I'm sorry. At this early stage, the body expels the

pregnancy on its own. We'll monitor her hormone levels. Physically, she should recover."

Physically.

Ian managed a nod. The woman gave him a sympathetic look before walking away, leaving him rooted in place.

Alone, he stumbled back to the molded plastic chair, his mind struggling to process what he'd heard. His hands gripped his knees as he forced himself to breathe.

Hana was pregnant.

She lost her baby.

Another scar, another burden for her to carry.

But she will live.

His breath came in ragged bursts. Then he shattered—silent, wrenching sobs that folded him in half. Seven hours of terror and guilt erupted at once, his body convulsing with grief he'd held like a poison in his chest. His hands—rock-steady through blood and crisis—trembled like leaves.

When it ended, a steely determination set in. Cold, clarifying rage. He straightened, dragged his sleeve across his face, and began to plan.

Fire the entire security team. Hire specialists with military backgrounds.

Take Hana out of the country the moment she was stable. London, perhaps, or somewhere more remote. Switzerland. The lake house in Geneva.

His mobile buzzed—Hana's parents, donor concerns, press inquiries. He fired off quick and efficient replies, a man transformed by purpose. By the time a nurse approached to inform him he could see Hana, his face had settled into a mask of control, with only the redness around his eyes betraying his earlier breakdown.

***

"Cut! Perfect. That's exactly the devastation I wanted."

The director's shout hardly registered as Yoo-jin remained kneeling beside the prop body, the scene's emotional toll lingering after the cameras stopped. He had channeled every ounce of his helplessness and anxiety about Hana into the detective's discovery of another victim.

"Let's reset for the partner's reaction shot," the director called.

A hesitant production assistant approached him. "*Yoo-jin-ssi*—" He held out his phone. "I think you should see this."

The headline punched the air from his lungs: *BREAKING: Actor Lee Yoo-jin's Girlfriend in Critical Condition After Knife Attack.*

The world tilted. The set around him—the crew, the cameras, the lights— dissolved into white noise. His eyes scanned the brief article with frantic speed.

...attacked in her hotel room... assailant believed to be an obsessive fan... currently in surgery... condition critical...

He was moving before conscious thought kicked in, stumbling toward his trailer like a man struck blind. The assistant director's voice followed him—schedule, scenes, costume changes—but he heard none of it.

Fifteen minutes later, helmet secured, he gunned the Ducati's engine. The two-hour drive to Seoul stretched in front him, an eternity of asphalt and fear. He took a turn too fast, tires skidding before catching.

His mind conjured devastating images—Hana bleeding out on the marble floor. Hana on the operating table, surgeons elbow-deep in her wounds. Hana dying, alone, while he shot meaningless scenes for a film that now seemed absurd.

The highway unspooled beneath his wheels as he wove between vehicles, pushing the motorcycle to its limits. Wind tore at his clothes. The engine's scream matched the silent howl in his chest.

When the Seoul skyline appeared, he navigated straight

to Sevrance Hospital, where the article said she had been taken. The media presence outside the entrance confirmed he was in the right place. A cluster of reporters and photographers sprawled across the sidewalk like vultures.

The instant he took off his headgear, they swarmed.

"*Yoo-jin-ssi!* Is it true the attacker was your fan?" "Do you blame yourself?" "What is your relationship with Ms. Rhee?" "Has her condition stabilized?"

Microphones were thrust into his face. Camera flashes blinded him. He pushed through without a word, face set in stone, helmet clutched like a shield. Security intervened, fraying a narrow path for him through the frenzy.

Inside, he barked Hana's name at the information desk and received directions to the ICU. The elevator ride was endless; his reflection from the mirrored doors was haunted, filled with fear.

***

The ICU waiting area was empty except for Ian, standing near the glass partition and speaking on the phone. When he looked up and saw Yoo-jin, naked hatred flashed across his face. He ended his call midsentence.

"You've got a nerve showing up here," he snarled, crossing the space between them in three quick strides. His hands connected with Yoo-jin's chest, shoving him backward. "This is on you! All of it!"

Yoo-jin absorbed the blow without resistance, the impact rippling through his body. He staggered, shoes squeaking against the polished floor. He didn't look at Ian—his eyes were already on Hana lying beyond the glass wall separating the waiting area from the ICU pod. The sight struck him harder than Ian's fists ever could.

Hana lay motionless, tubes and wires hooking her to machines that beeped and hummed with mechanical indifference. An oxygen mask covered half her face. Her skin had the waxy pallor of near-death, dark hair plastered to her scalp. Her right hand, heavily bandaged and immobilized, rested on a pillow—the same hand that had caressed his face, now maimed.

He moved past Ian as if in a trance toward the glass barrier. His palms pressed against its cool surface, as if attempting to breach the distance between them. His forehead followed, resting on the panel as tears ran down his cheeks. His breath fogged the partition in rhythmic clouds, obscuring and revealing her with each exhale.

"The handiwork of your fans," Ian's voice came from behind him, fury in each syllable. "She almost died. The knife missed her heart by centimeters. Severed tendons in her hand. She may never have full use of it again."

Each word came at him like a gut punch, but Yoo-jin didn't turn, didn't tear his eyes away from Hana. The monitor beside her bed pulsed with each heartbeat—steady but weak, so different from how it had raced under his touch when they lay together.

After a long moment, he asked, voice almost inaudible, "What happens now?"

"The second she's stable enough to travel, I'm taking her out of this country." Ian's tone left no room for debate. "Away from this insanity. Away from your toxic world and its crackpots!"

Yoo-jin pressed his palms harder against the glass, as if through sheer will he could reach through and touch her. "Can I go in? For a minute?"

"No. You've done enough." Flat. Final.

A silence settled over them, filled only by the muffled beeping of machines.

At last he turned away, every detail of Hana committed to memory. He passed Ian without a word. As he headed back toward the elevator, he heard the lawyer calling out to him.

"Yoo-jin."

Ian shifted his weight as if debating whether to speak. "Hana was pregnant." The words hung in the sterile air. "Six weeks. She miscarried."

Yoo-jin felt the ground lurch beneath his feet. His heart went still.

A baby. Their baby. Gone. He searched Ian's face for any sign of lies or heartlessness, but found only exhaustion and a reluctant empathy.

In two strides, he was inside the ICU pod. The mechanical hum of equipment surrounded him as he approached Hana's bed. His hand shook as he reached out to stroke her hair.

His face twisted with guilt. His chest heaved with silent sobs. He leaned down, whispering, "I'm sorry. I'm so sorry, Hana."

He didn't know how long he had been standing there, tears streaming down his face. He held her uninjured hand between both of his, planting desperate kisses on her knuckles, willing her to wake up, to hear him, to forgive him.

As the minutes passed, a terrible truth dawned. The attack had been carefully planned and carried out—the assailant was an obsessed fan who couldn't accept that Yoo-jin loved Hana in real life, and would kill to eliminate the woman who had "stolen" her fantasy from her.

This was the consequence of his fame. His choices. His presence in her life.

"Sir," a nurse approached at last, voice gentle but firm. "You'll have to leave now."

With a shuddering breath, he straightened. His fingers traced the line of her face one more time, memorizing the feel of her skin. He bent down for a final kiss, his lips lingering on her forehead.

"Goodbye, Hana," he whispered, eyes stinging. "I have to let you go. I don't want to hurt you anymore." The decision was formed with sudden clarity. He would disappear from her life. It was the only thing left that he could do to keep her safe.

When he stepped out of the room, Ian was standing guard at the door like a faithful sentinel.

"Thank you," Yoo-jin said, voice raw. "For telling me about the baby."

"You had a right to know."

The admission surprised them both, an unexpected honesty cutting through their long-standing animosity. For the first time, they saw each other clearly: two men who loved Hana deeply and would do anything to protect her.

Yoo-jin turned his head away. "I won't be coming back," he said, wiping his face with the back of his hand.

"You're walking away?" Ian's gaze doubted his sincerity. But the self-serving actor he had always considered Yoo-jin to be wasn't there. Standing before him was a defeated, broken man.

"She deserves better." Yoo-jin's voice cracked on the final word. "A life without cameras and stalkers and knives."

Ian exhaled. A grudging respect flicked over his face. He straightened and extended his hand to the actor.

Yoo-jin regarded the offered hand for a moment before taking it. Their handshake was brief but firm, an unspoken truce forged in mutual grief.

"Thank you for everything. Please keep her safe.Make her happy."

Ian nodded.

Yoo-jin turned to leave, each step down the corridor heavier than the last. Behind him lay a piece of himself. Ahead, nothing but the empty shell of celebrity.

***

The moment he was outside, the press surged again. He ignored them, pulling on his helmet and mounting his motorcycle.

As the engine's roar drowned out the cacophony of voices, a single thought circled: *loving Hana had killed their child and almost killed her—staying in her life would only finish the job.*

He twisted the throttle, accelerating away from the hospital—away from Hana, away from the life they had once dreamed for themselves. The wind bit through his jacket, cold and merciless against his skin—so different from their first motorcycle ride together, when possibility had seemed as limitless as the open road.

With painful clarity, he remembered when that yearning first surfaced: *I want to be her safe place.*

Now, this memory taunted him like a cruel joke. A sharp, bitter laugh escaped him. The thing he had wanted most—to protect her, to shield her—was the one thing he could never do for her. The glare of his fame had found her, marked her, nearly destroyed her.

As the hospital shrank in his rearview mirror, he could feel her phantom warmth against his back, the ghost of her laughter in his ear as they had leaned into curves together, her trust in him absolute. He had slowed the bike back then, reluctant to reach their destination, just to prolong each second of having her close.

Now, he pushed the motorcycle faster. To keep his promise, in the only way he knew—by becoming the absence that might finally keep her safe.

***

When tears blurred his vision beyond safety, Yoo-jin veered onto a small access road, cutting the engine at a grassy overlook. He had driven without direction, without thought, until his body gave out. The silence rushed in, oppressive and accusing. He yanked off his helmet and stumbled to a sloping knoll, legs buckling halfway up.

The view devastated him—golden fields stretching

toward distant hills, the late afternoon sun casting everything in soft light. With a sharp pang, he recalled bringing Hana to a similar spot a month ago. How they had sat together, her head on his shoulder, deciding to face the world together as a couple.

That decision, made in a flash of optimism, had led to this moment. To Hana lying critically injured in a hospital bed. To the loss of their baby.

The solitude now enveloped him. He let himself cry—broken, heaving sobs pulled from somewhere deep in his gut.

Time stretched until the distant sound of a vehicle penetrated his grief. A black Range Rover parked alongside his abandoned motorcycle. Two figures emerged—his manager and his best friend, the only two people who could have tracked him here.

They approached without hurry, settling on either side of him.

"Hey, buddy," Sang-min said, squeezing his shoulder.

Ji-hoon said nothing, patting Yoo-jin's knee as he lowered himself to the ground. The three men sat in silence.

Sang-min reached into his jacket and produced a silver flask. He unscrewed the cap and handed it to Yoo-jin, who took it with trembling fingers. The whisky burned a fiery path down his throat, momentarily eclipsing his pain.

"We had it all planned out, Hana and I. No more hiding. I wanted to show her that I was proud of us... that she wasn't some shameful secret." His voice caught on the last words.

Sang-min took the flask and sipped before passing it back. "You couldn't have known what would happen. Those obsessed fans—that's not on you."

"With respect," Ji-hoon cut in, his tone measured and analytical, "there was relative safety in discretion. The data supports this. Celebrities with private relationships statistically face fewer—"

"Data?" Yoo-jin laughed, bitter. "Is that what Hana is? A statistic?"

Ji-hoon adjusted his glasses. "I see a woman in a hospital bed because we miscalculated the risk factors." He sighed. "This is Korea—fans don't only follow you, they claim you. We've seen what happens when idols date or step outside the mold. Careers ruined. People driven to the edge. It's not new."

"But I couldn't ask her to live like that," Yoo-jin raked a hand through his disheveled hair. "What kind of life is that? Me pretending to fall in love with female co-stars on screen while she waits in obscurity? Never acknowledged, never—" He broke off, throat tight.

"Some women accept that arrangement," Ji-hoon stated. "It's a professional necessity for people in your position."

"Hana isn't 'some woman,'" Sang-min reminded him gently. "She had her own life, doing her own meaningful work."

Yoo-jin took another long swallow of whisky. "What should I have done? Tell me."

Sang-min drew circles in the dirt with a stick. "You didn't have any good options, brother. You couldn't keep her hidden away, but bringing her into the open was a risk." He shook his head. "Some of your fans can't acccpt rcality."

"My fucking life," Yoo-jin spat, kicking a stone roughly with the heel of his boot.

A contemplative quiet settled over them as the sun dipped further into the horizon.

"What now?" he asked, voice hollow. "What do I do now?"

Sang-min opened his mouth, but closed it again, lost for words.

Ji-hoon shifted, stealing a glance at his watch. "The production can't wait long," He put a comforting hand on Yoo-jin's shoulder. "We've moved scenes around for two days, but there are limits. I know the timing is... inappropriate. But there are fifty crew members whose rent depends on this film's completion."

"Always the practical one," Yoo-jin murmured, but there was no anger now. Only resignation.

The mention of the film—*Nameless*—sounded surreal, as if it belonged to another lifetime. Yesterday, he had been worried about delivering an emotional scene. Today, the idea of faking despair while actually unraveling was unbearable.

"You have two choices," Ji-hoon said, voice mild. "You can walk away from everything—the movie, your career, all of it. Or you can find a way to keep going—not because it's easy, but because sometimes work is the only thing that keeps us from spiraling."

Darkness had claimed the countryside now, stars emerging in the sky. A chill crept into the air as Yoo-jin considered the older man's words.

"I don't know..."

"You don't have to know," Sang-min replied. "You only have to try. One scene. One day. One foot in front of the other."

Ji-hoon stood, brushing grass from his pants. He held out a hand to help Yoo-jin up. "Come on—I'll drive you back. You're in no condition to ride."

As they headed to the vehicles, Yoo-jin glanced at the Ducati. The machine had carried him and Hana through fleeting moments of bliss, but was never built for a long journey. Now, it would return to Seoul without him, as she would soon leave Korea without him.

"Sang-min can take the bike," Ji-hoon said, guiding him toward the Range Rover. "We've pushed tomorrow's call time to noon. That gives you fourteen hours to pull yourself together."

As his friend mounted the motorcycle, Yoo-jin felt a strange detachment in watching someone else take control of what had once been his.

Like Hana. Like his future. Like the path ahead, whatever it might be.

Tomorrow, he would return to the set. He would speak lines written by someone else. He would pretend to be someone he wasn't.

And perhaps, in pretending, he might find a way forward without her.

DISTANCE BETWEEN

One week later.

The ceiling kept changing. Sometimes tiles, sometimes swirls. Sometimes darkness.

Hana blinked, trying to anchor herself. Pain bloomed somewhere distant, like thunder on the horizon. The medication held it there—threatening but contained.

Where am I?

Hospital. The thought floated up through murky waters. She had been here... how long? Days blurred together, marked by the soft beep of machines and the sting of needles.

She remembered fragments. Glass breaking. A face twisted with rage. Then nothing.

Her uninjured hand moved to her chest and touched the thick padding of bandages. Something had happened. Something bad. The details skittered away when she reached for them.

She closed her eyes, summoned his face—*Yoo-jin*. The name brought comfort but no clear image. The mirth in his eyes whenever he smiled at her. His nose, straight and perfect. The curve of his lips. But when she tried to assemble his features into a whole, they blurred and shifted, refusing to come together.

Why can't I see him?

It was like trying to hold water—the harder she grasped,

the faster it slipped away. The drugs made everything soft-edged, distant. *Even him.* Exhaustion forced her to release him back into the haze.

"...stable now, but we're watching for infection."

Voices drifted in and out. Doctors, nurses. Words that should have had meaning: *punctured lung, nerve damage, reconstructive surgery.* She let them wash over her, too tired to make any sense of them.

Often, she would feel a lingering kiss on her forehead. But when she opened her eyes, the room was empty. A dream. A ghost touch.

"My darling girl."

Her eyes fluttered open at the familiar voice.

Thomas Weston stood beside her bed, wire-rimmed glasses catching the fluorescent light. His lips were pressed tight, holding back a rush of unspoken, unconditional love.

"Daddy—" The word scraped her dry throat.

He held her good hand, his touch gentle as if afraid she might shatter.

Behind him, her mother, with the fragrant notes of Shalimar preceding her. Her lips were pressed tight, holding back a litany of reproofs. *I told you so. I warned you. Why didn't you listen?*

"*Hana-ya.*" Eun-ji's voice wavered, the only audible sign of her distress.

Hana tried to keep her eyes open, to speak, but the medication pulled her again into visions filled with broken glass and screaming.

When she woke next, sudden panic gripped her.

Ian?

Her eyes darted around the dim room, heart racing, setting off monitors. Where was he? He should be here. He was always here.

A nurse appeared to check readings and adjust her IV.

"Ian," Hana managed, the word thick on her tongue.

"Mr. Weston stepped out for a moment," the woman reassured her. "He'll be right back."

The fear subsided only when the door opened and Ian entered, coffee in hand, exhaustion etched into every line of his face. He set the cup down and moved to her side when he saw she was awake.

Relief flooded Hana, so intense it brought tears. Her good hand reached for him, fingers curling around his sleeve.

"You're here," she whispered, her words slurring.

"Always." His voice was steady, comforting.

She drifted again.

When lucidity returned, so did shame—this helplessness wasn't hers. She had never been dependent, never clingy. Not even with Yoo-jin.

Now, she couldn't bear for Ian to leave her sight. "Please don't go," she blurted once, when he mentioned getting fresh clothes from the hotel.

His eyes softened. "I'll be back before you know I'm gone."

"Were you here the whole time? When I was..." She couldn't remember the word. *Unconscious. Dying.*

"Every minute," he said.

She cried then, unable to stop the tears though she tried to blink them away. "I'm sorry. I don't know why I'm—"

"Shhh." He stroked her hair. "You don't need to explain."

At night, when pain broke through the medication and sleep wouldn't come, she took comfort in seeing him dozing in the chair beside her. She would touch his arm to anchor herself to him in case the nightmares returned.

At other times, in the liminal space between waking and dreaming, she thought of Yoo-jin. Where was he? Had he called? Visited? She couldn't remember. She wanted to ask Ian, but stopped—fearing the answer, or perhaps the look that might cross his face.

Once, she thought she heard Yoo-jin's voice in the corridor outside her room. She tried to call out, but no sound came. By the time the door opened, it was someone else.

"Ian," she whispered later, when the room ceased spinning. "Has—?" She couldn't finish the question.

A disquiet flicked over his face—too quick to read in her medicated state. "Don't worry about anything right now. Just focus on healing."

She nodded, too tired to press further. She let herself drift again, the painkillers dragging her under.

In this strange half-life of recovery, only Ian remained constant. He was there every time she opened her eyes, steady when everything else shifted and blurred.

She clung to him, knowing somewhere in her foggy state that it wasn't fair to him. His whole life was now reduced to caring for her. But she still reached for his hand when the pain surfaced, still called his name when the trauma returned.

And he never left. Never showed impatience. Only sat beside her bed and waited as her mind slowly cleared, one confusing day at a time.

***

December, four weeks after the attack.

The jet gleamed on the tarmac, pristine white against the morning sky. Ian looked at his watch—8:35 AM. Everything was on schedule.

The medical team was getting Hana ready for transport. The hand specialist in Geneva was waiting. Thomas and Eun-ji had prepared the lake house for her recovery. He had arranged it all—every detail accounted for, every contingency planned.

Except one.

"Yoo-jin," Hana blurted, the name both a question and a plea. She clutched Ian's sleeve as the medics moved to lift her stretcher. Her eyes, glassy with tears and pre-flight sedatives, locked onto his. Her voice was thin but clear.

It was the first time she had spoken his name since waking up in the hospital. For days after she regained consciousness, he had often seen her staring into the distance, searching.

"He's on location." Ian's pained expression shifted to tenderness. He squeezed her hand. "Filming in Gangwon Province."

She kept her anxious gaze on him, concentrating on his words.

"I told him we were leaving. He won't be coming."

Won't be coming. The sedatives pulled at her consciousness, but not before she registered the finality of what she heard.

Ian saw hope drain from her eyes. His thumb brushed away the tears that trickled down her temples into her hair.

His mind flashed back to the ICU waiting room right after Hana's surgery. Yoo-jin Lee had stood before him, hollow-eyed: *I won't be coming back. She deserves better. A life without cameras and stalkers and knives.*

Ian had respected him for his decision, even as he questioned whether the actor could stay away. But days passed with no visits, no calls. Only flowers with a card signed "YJ."

He had given Yoo-jin the details of their flight. A simple text: *Private airfield. 9 AM tomorrow. If you want to say goodbye.* The small mercy cost him more than she knew. He had sent it against his better judgment, against his instinct to sever all connections between Hana and the man whose fan had almost killed her.

He had done it for her. To give them a chance to end things properly.

But the airfield remained empty. No car, no motorcycle. No last-minute arrival to delay their departure.

Now, watching her fingers twitch in his grip as if reaching

for something already gone, Ian had an unexpected twinge of regret. Not for Yoo-jin's absence—that was the right choice, the only choice—but for Hana's pain. For the closure she would not get. Not today. Not ever.

The medical team was waiting for his signal. "Sir? We have to board now."

He nodded, rising from his crouch. He didn't need to scan the airfield. The actor would not come. He had made his decision in that sterile hospital corridor—and whatever his flaws, the man had meant what he said.

As he followed the stretcher up the airstairs, Ian considered the path ahead. He would care for Hana. See her through surgeries, rehabilitation, and recovery. Marry her, when the time was right. Build the life they should have had all along, before Yoo-jin Lee ever entered the picture.

But he also knew that a part of her would always be sealed off, where she kept her memories of Yoo-jin Lee.

Could he live with that?

He settled into the seat beside her, watching her face relax in sedated sleep. Peaceful now, removed from pain. He found her uninjured hand and held it.

Yes. He could. He would.

Because living with a partial Hana was better than without her. Even serving as her caretaker, her support, her safety was enough, if it meant keeping her in his life.

The cabin door sealed shut. The engines hummed to life.

Ian closed his eyes, settling in for the long journey ahead.

***

From the shadow of a distant hangar, Yoo-jin watched Hana's departure unfold in silence.

He had driven through the night from the filming location in Gangwon Province, arriving before dawn. The security guard, a fan of his latest drama, had been persuaded to let him access the grounds with an autograph and a selfie.

Now, he stood motionless as medics loaded her onto the waiting plane. Even at this distance, he could make out her small form beneath the blankets, dark hair a stark contrast against the white pillows.

Cruel memories of happier times ambushed him.

Their first duet.

Their first kiss at the nightclub.

The first time they made love, clumsy and playful.

The brief weeks when they shared a tiny life, unknown to him until it was gone.

Now, after two years of complicated happiness, she was no more than a damaged figure being wheeled out of his reach. A pain tore through him, sharp and unforgiving.

Medical personnel boarded after her. Followed by Ian Weston, his stride faltering for a second before mounting the steps and disappearing into the aircraft.

The door closed with a thud.

Yoo-jin stepped out of the shadows, moving to the edge of the tarmac as the plane began to taxi. His hands hung at his sides, useless—unable to wave, unable to reach out, unable to do anything except witness this ending.

The engines roared as the plane gathered speed and lifted into the morning sky. He stood still, watching it climb, becoming smaller and smaller against the vast blue, a glint of metal catching light.

Until there was nothing left.

Only then did he move, sinking to his knees on the hard concrete. Tears blurred his vision but didn't fall. He had cried himself empty in the days since the attack.

This pain was different—not the sharp agony of immediate loss but the hollow ache of finality. Of knowing he had made the right choice—the only choice that could protect her.

Now, the real distance between them lay not in miles, but in the emptiness carved into them both.

As the morning sun climbed higher, Yoo-jin rose to his feet.

He had a film to finish. A life to rebuild.

A path to walk that would never again cross with hers.

PATHS DIVERGED

May, eighteen months later

Spring cast the Surrey countryside in watercolor hues of green and gold.

The 19th century manor stood calm in the late afternoon light, ivy curling over stone, its gardens like an image lifted from an English fairy tale. Two Labrador retrievers raced across the expansive lawn, barking with joy in the soft spring air.

On the terrace, Hana sat with a cup of tea, watching the dogs play. At thirty-five, she carried a new serenity—one born of suffering and healing, of losing and finding oneself again.

Her right hand, though bearing the scars of multiple reconstructive surgeries, now moved with almost the same fluidity as before. Only certain complex gestures remained out of reach, a permanent reminder of that terrible day a year and a half ago.

The sound of tires on gravel announced Ian's return from London. Moments later, he rounded the corner of the house, briefcase forgotten in the car, jacket discarded, sleeves rolled up from the unseasonable warmth.

"There's my lovely wife," he called, crossing the terrace to join her.

Wife. The word still sounded new, though they had been married for close to four months now. The ceremony had been intimate—only family and closest friends at a small country church. No photographers, no announcements, no security. Quiet vows exchanged under stained glass light.

"How was your meeting?" Hana asked as he bent to kiss her.

"The usual chess game. The Kensington merger will go through." He settled beside her, loosening his tie. "More important—how was your call with the adoption agency?"

A smile bloomed across her face. Genuine, unguarded joy that had become more frequent with each passing month. "Two more families matched this week. The Seoul coordinator says our new screening protocols are working perfectly."

The foundation's projects had been reborn, phoenix-like, from the ashes of that terrible time. With operations now spanning London, Geneva, and Seoul, the adoption program Hana had once feared lost forever now helped more families than ever before. Her trauma had transformed into purpose, her healing intertwined with the children she placed in loving homes.

As the sun lowered in the horizon, Hana's expression dimmed. Her eyes clouded over, turning inward to some distant memory. Her breathing quickened. She tugged her sleeve over the scars on her right hand.

Ian recognized it at once, as he always did. He reached over, covering her hand with his in a gentle squeeze. "I'm here," he said. The gesture anchored her, drawing her back from the precipice of remembered trauma.

She nodded, returning to herself. These episodes had become less frequent over the months, but he suspected they would never disappear. One had to learn to live alongside them.

He knew where her mind went in these moments. Whose face appeared in her memory. He had made his peace with it. Respected that parts of her would always belong to someone else.

She looked down at the scars on her hand again. “My period came today.”

He sighed, understanding her disappointment. His thumb traced patient circles over her knuckles. “It’s alright. Maybe it’s too soon to try. We don’t have to rush—we’ll get there. I promise.” Standing, he held out his hand. “Come on, let’s take the dogs for a walk before dinner.”

Their fingers remained intertwined as they moved across the lawn, calling to the exuberant Labradors. His strength supporting her, her presence completing him.

On impulse, she wrapped her arms around his waist, a sudden emotion catching in her throat. “I love you,” she murmured, burying her face in his neck.

“I love you too,” he replied with the same steady devotion that had carried them through their bleakest moments.

It wasn’t perfect. Hana would always carry the traces, visible and invisible. The tremors might never subside. Certain sounds would always make her heart race. And a part of her would always wonder about a different life, a different love, cut short by circumstances no one could control.

But here, in this tranquil corner of England, they knew their future would be alright.

***

November, two years later

The applause was deafening, a wall of sound crashing over Yoo-jin Lee as he approached the podium. Camera flashes created a strobe effect around him, each burst of light capturing his composed expression from every angle.

He was dapper in a tuxedo, but his demeanor had changed since his last public appearance. Still handsome, his features now carried a new depth. The fine lines at the corner of his eyes had deepened, and strands of silver threaded his temples

—not enough to diminish his appeal, but to suggest a man who had aged not by years but by loss. His eyes, once described by a film critic as "magnetic," now appeared tight at the edges, haunted somehow, as if searching for someone no longer there.

Nameless, the psychological thriller that had consumed him during the lowest point of his life, had swept the Grand Bell Awards, earning him Best Actor for his portrayal of Park Do-yoon, a police detective tormented by his failure to protect a woman he loved.

The symmetry was brutal and precise. While filming scenes of a man spiraling into despair, Hana had been fighting for her life in a hospital bed. Art and reality were bleeding together until he couldn't tell which pain belonged to his character and which was his own.

"Thank you," he said into the microphone after clearing his throat, his voice reflecting the trained modulation of two decades in the spotlight. "This honor belongs to Director Kim Jae-wook and our incredible crew who brought this story to life."

He looked out at the sea of faces—industry peers, critics, reporters capturing every micro-expression. All waiting for the expected platitudes, the humble acknowledgments, the scripted gratitude.

Instead, Yoo-jin set the gold statuette on the podium.

"Two years ago, while filming *Nameless*, someone I love deeply was attacked by a person claiming to be my fan." His voice caught on the word *love*, the present tense a revelation in itself. The audience held a collective breath. "She almost died because I had mistakenly believed our union could exist in the public eye."

He paused, aware of his manager's panicked gestures from the wings and the live broadcast capturing every unscripted word.

"We in the entertainment world cultivate fantasies. We sell the illusion of intimacy, of availability. And sometimes..." he faltered for a second before continuing, "that fantasy turns dangerous. I lost the most important person in my life because I naïvely thought I could have both—her and this career."

The silence in the hall was now absolute but for the whir of cameras documenting a moment no publicist would have approved.

"I'm profoundly grateful to the fans who have supported me with respect and kindness through the years. But tonight, as I accept this honor, I'm also announcing my withdrawal from the film industry."

Gasps rippled through the audience, quickly hushed as he continued.

"This movie," he gestured toward the award, "captured the essence of pain and regret. The cost of obsession. I didn't have to act in these scenes—I was living them daily when I returned to an empty house at night."

His knuckles whitened against the podium's edge.

"At the end of the day, I'm just a man," he concluded, voice dropping to almost a whisper. "Capable of love and loss like everyone else. It's time for me to remember that."

He bowed deeply—a final gesture of respect to the industry that gave him everything but took away what counted most—before walking off the stage without looking back.

Later, after declining interviews and ignoring the media frenzy from his announcement, Yoo-jin emerged from the venue alone. His bow tie hung undone around his collar, award tucked under one arm as if he had already forgotten its significance. A cigarette—a habit he had quit and resumed countless times—dangled from his fingertips, its ember glowing in the night like a tiny, fading star.

A soft rain had begun to fall, turning the pavement into

mirrors under the street lamps, reflecting his solitary figure in fractured light.

His face gave nothing away but his eyes were distant, chasing the thread of a faraway tune. How easily everything had come together back then—the piano, Hana's fingers on the keys, the melody of their duet. How quickly it had all unraveled.

He paused at the bottom of the steps, oblivious to photographers—his face tilted upward to let the rain wash over him, a man shedding one life before stepping into another.

One photograph, rendered in stark black and white by the *Hankyoreh* newspaper, would accompany articles about his retirement worldwide. The image captured the moment when Yoo-jin Lee, the celebrity actor, cast off his final role. Critics would later note how the statuette hung loosely from his grasp, as if fame itself was a burden he could no longer bear.

In the semi-darkness of his penthouse that night, Yoo-jin walked stiffly through the cold rooms that ceased to feel like home. Moving boxes lined the walls, half-filled with remnants of the life he was leaving behind. The piano that they used to play—her laughter filling the room whenever he missed a note—stood shrouded in protective covering.

From the safe, he removed a small velvet box containing a ring he had bought for Hana before everything fell apart. Simple, elegant—but she never got to wear it.

Beside it lay a Polaroid photograph, edges worn from handling, of Hana wrapped in his shirt, standing on the balcony at dawn and silhouetted against the first light, smiling over her shoulder at him. He had taken it on their last morning together, when they had believed their future could be as bright and joyful as her smile.

On his desk, a one-way ticket to Busan waited alongside a passport and a leather journal. He would visit his parents, then go... somewhere. Anywhere. Places without cameras, without recognition. Places where he might eventually learn to live with the hollow space she had left behind.

He stretched out on the couch, arm draped over his eyes. The bed seemed impossible these days—too large, too quiet, too full of her absence.

He imagined she would hear about his retirement. He hoped she would understand the message in his decision. That he had come to see, too late, what truly mattered. That some things cost more than they were worth. That he would abandon it all—the empire of image he'd spent decades building—for one chance to choose her first.

And finally, that he would always put her safety and happiness over his own.

Even if that happiness no longer included him.

***

Hana was replying to emails when a notification chimed from her Korean news feed.

The headline caught her eye: *Actor Yoo-jin Lee Announces Shocking Retirement After Sweeping Grand Bell Awards*. Her hand stilled over the keyboard. A sharp intake of breath.

Yoo-jin had only resurfaced in the media after the release of his latest film. As she waited for the article to load, her fingers moved subconsciously to her chest, tracing the slight indentation of her scar beneath her blouse. The phantom pain, less frequent now but never gone, sliced across her skin.

The image appeared: Yoo-jin walking alone down rain-slicked steps, holding a statuette carelessly like an afterthought. But it was his eyes that held her—familiar eyes, shadowed with a sadness she sometimes saw in her own.

She had not seen or heard from him since that day two years ago when he left Seoul to film *Nameless*. They had spent their last night making love and forming plans—wedding, children—when the sun peeked over the horizon and they dashed out to the balcony to snap pictures. It was their sunrise —a new day, a fresh beginning.

They had not said goodbye when she left Korea. Since then, she had rebuilt her life with Ian and focused on her recovery. He had told her about the miscarriage when she was strong enough and left her alone to grieve. That loss was like a tiny mark—invisible, but always present.

She read Yoo-jin's speech, his voice coming back to her with startling clarity—the same deep timbre when they sang together, the same gentle drop when he said her name.

The public would see a principled stand against toxic fan culture.

She saw a man renouncing the spotlight that would not make room for her beside him. *"I lost the most important person in my life because I naïvely believed I could have both—her and this career."*

Hana's throat tightened. Even now, Yoo-jin's words could reach across continents, pressing on a chord that had remained stubbornly alive.

Her phone chimed with a text from Ian: *Meeting wrapped early. Dinner at Riverside? That table by the window you like is available.* His thoughtfulness, through small and consistent kindnesses, brought a smile to her face. She replied: *Perfect. See you at 7.*

She returned to the photograph. With her fingertip, she traced the outline of Yoo-jin's face on the screen, lingering over his lips, which she had once loved obsessively.

The media would analyze his retirement as a professional move, perhaps a short hiatus. Only she understood the magnitude of his sacrifice—turning his back on the career that had forged his identity.

"I understand," she whispered to the image, as if he might still hear her—certain he knew his absence was the part of him she would always carry.

She closed the article and sat in her office until dusk settled, fingers caressing her wedding band—a gentle reminder of the life she had chosen, the happiness found in the aftermath of tragedy. Ian had been there through her recovery, patient and steady, never pushing but never retreating. Their transition from stepcousins to lovers to spouses had been as natural as the changing seasons. Different from Yoo-jin's wildfire intensity, but no less real.

***

At dinner that evening, Ian observed Hana with quiet solicitude. "I saw the news," he said. "About Lee."

She met his gaze, appreciating his directness, his refusal to pretend. "Yes, I did too."

He reached across the table for her hand, thumb brushing over her wedding ring. "Are you alright?"

Was she alright with the path she had chosen?

Was she alright knowing what Yoo-jin had given up?

Was she alright shouldering both her past and her present?

"I am," she said, squeezing his hand. It wasn't a simple answer, but it was true.

Ian didn't press. Hana's history with Yoo-jin Lee was a chapter written in permanent ink. His consolation came from knowing he didn't have to compete with a man who had chosen to remove himself from her life.

"He did the right thing," he said after a moment, surprising her. "Walking away. It was brave."

"Yes," she agreed, filled with a complicated gratitude. "It was."

***

Later, as they walked home along the Thames, Hana leaned into Ian's solid presence. This was her reality now—this good man, this peaceful life, this city of rain and muted colors. At the same time, Yoo-jin stepped back from Seoul's bright lights and lenses for the last time.

Ian drew Hana closer to him as they continued on their shared path, while across the world, Yoo-jin embarked on a solitary one.

Three lives scorched by fame. Their stories had no true endings—only beginnings, written in the ashes of what came before.

AUTHOR'S NOTE

Have you ever wondered why Korea's most eligible bachelors seem perpetually, mysteriously single? Walk through any airport and you'll see them: devastatingly handsome men in their thirties and forties, flanked by security, waving to screaming fans, hair perfect, love lives invisible. They've mastered every profession on screen—surgeon, CEO, time-traveling prince, zombie-fighting prosecutor—yet somehow never achieved something as basic as public dating.

If parts of **Spotlights and Shadows** felt unhinged, that's because fandom sometimes is. Psychologists call it a *parasocial relationship*—that weird one-sided bond where you feel like you know someone who has never met you. Social media supercharged this illusion, creating curated intimacy at scale. Fans respond as if they're in a very committed, very exclusive relationship—one the celebrity never agreed to. Most of the time it's harmless. But sometimes admiration curdles into entitlement: *I've given you my loyalty, my money, my time—so you owe me.* That's not romance. That's possession.

Researchers even have a term for the darker edge: **Celebrity Worship Syndrome**. Mild cases look like posters on the wall. Severe ones look like tracking flight schedules, sending death threats to girlfriends, or sneaking into apartments. In Korea, these extreme fans are known as *sasaengs*—infamous for bugging hotel rooms or showing up at family homes. It's devotion turned invasive.

Lee Yoo-jin, my leading man, is a fictional composite of these charming, talented, perpetually single actors. No one person inspired him—he's a stand-in for the universal dilemma of Korean celebrities navigating a world where privacy is a luxury, love is a liability, and fans believe they own their hearts. His story asks what happens when the carefully maintained fantasy collides with inconvenient reality: real human feelings. After all, we've all dreamed of these men through our screens. This is what happens when one dares to dream back.

The characters and events in this story are fictional and heightened for drama. Any resemblance to real persons—living, deceased, or perpetually unattached—is coincidental, though it may reflect the universal quirks of entertainment culture.

If You're Curious

Though **Spotlights and Shadows** is fiction, it leaned on scholarship about fame, fandom, and the Korean Wave. Three books in particular shaped the backdrop:

• *Celebrity* by Chris Rojek — a reminder that stardom is less about talent and more about the machinery of image-making.

• *Fans: The Mirror of Consumption* by Cornel Sandvoss — an unsettling look at how devotion can tip into obsession, and why some fans feel they own pieces of their idols.

• *Hallyu 2.0: The Korean Wave in the Age of Social Media* by Sung-Ae Lee & Anthony Nornes — essential for understanding how Korean pop culture went global and why fan behavior feels both intimate and unhinged at scale.

THROUGH THE GLASS DARKLY SERIES

Through the Glass Darkly delves into the perilous collision of fame, obsession, and the digital age.

Spotlights and Shadows (2025) follows an established superstar who lives under the constant glare of the public eye, where every photo, every post, every public appearance is magnified, dissected, and shared. For some, admiration blurs into fixation—parasocial relationships fueled by social media turn curiosity into intrusion, and desire into danger.

Into the Light (2026) examines the other side of the coin: the hidden watcher who becomes dangerously entwined in the celebrity's life, crossing the line from obsession to violence, proving that the cost of exposure is more than just lost privacy—it can be life-changing.

These intertwined stories reveal how perception distorts reality, and how even the most controlled public image cannot protect against the darkness lurking just beyond the lens.

Through the Glass Darkly is a darkly luminous, gripping series about the perils of visibility, the fragility of safety, and the deadly consequences when adoration turns toxic.

Printed in Dunstable, United Kingdom

74504041R00215